TELL ME A SECRET

TELL
ME
A
SECRET

SECRETS #1

ANAÏS VENTURA

Escolástica
Press

For more information or to book an event, contact Escolástica Press at contact@escolasticapress.com.

Book Cover by Miblart

First Escolástica Press edition, 2025

10 9 8 7 6 5 4 3 2 1

Publisher's Cataloging-in-Publication Data
provided by Five Rainbows Cataloging Services

Names: Ventura, Anaïs, author.
Title: Tell me a secret / Anaïs Ventura.
Description: Tempe, AZ : Escolástica Press, 2025. | Series: Secrets, bk. 1.
Identifiers: LCCN 2022921361 (print) | ISBN 979-8-9872198-1-2 (paperback) | ISBN 979-8-9872198-3-6 (hardcover) | ISBN 979-8-9872198-2-9 (hardcover w/ dust jacket) | ISBN 979-8-9872198-0-5 (ebook)
Subjects: LCSH: Arranged marriage--Fiction. | Billionaires--Fiction. | New York (N.Y.)--Fiction. | California--Fiction. | Romance fiction. | Illustrated works. | BISAC: FICTION / Romance / Contemporary. | FICTION / Romance / Billionaires. | GSAFD: Love stories.
Classification: LCC PS3622.E58 T45 2025 (print) | LCC PS3622.E58 (ebook) | DDC 813/.6--dc23.

In memory of the sweetest grandma, for always believing in me and showing me the meaning of true love. I love you, Mamá.

This book contains mature content, including references to alcohol and drug use, sexual themes, abuse, assault, blood, torture, and death.

TELL ME A SECRET

PLAYLIST

Spotify:
Profile: Authoranais
Playlist: Tell Me A Secret

Youtube:
Username: @authoranais
Playlist: Tell Me A Secret

PRICE FAMILY RULES

Family Motto: No One Is Above a Price.

1.) The reputation of one is the reputation of all.

2.) A Price must never succumb to addiction.

3.) Ties of matrimony do not alter a Price's identity.

4.) The Price heir must maintain integrity.

5.) The head of the family makes the final decision.

LAST HOPE

Felicity

I ripped the paper from my sketchbook, crumpled it, and dropped it on the table. That was probably the most hideous skirt I had ever designed. The black-and-white checkered pattern was too plain, the skirt too asymmetric, making it look more like someone had wrapped themselves in a curtain and called it a day. The ruffles at the bottom were definitely the worst part. I leaned my head on the white leather seat of my private jet and looked out the window. There were no clouds in the sky, and thankfully, the sun was on the other side. The sound of the plane engines created a soft hum that I had always liked since it reminded me of a pink noise machine.

I had an Airbus A350. The interior design was exquisite, and my initials were on the seats. Two bedrooms, a conference room, a dining room, and a living room with gorgeous leather seats adorned the plane. The front had first-class seats with flat beds for my employees. I loved that piece of metal.

"For the past week, all you've done is throw away anything you draw. What is wrong?" Milton's deep and rough voice sounded scary to most people, but to me, it brought comfort. "Is it because we're going back home?"

I sighed before I could stop myself. Not showing what I was feeling was the way I'd been taught to survive, but the older I got, the harder it was to keep it all bottled up.

New York was home. A home I loved and at the same time hated. For the past two years, I had been in Hanover, New Hampshire, getting my master's in business. Although I was home almost every weekend, I still had a break from my family during the week.

"Sighing is not a response," Milton said. My eyes immediately met his dark brown ones. His tone was stern, but his eyes were soft.

Milton was fifty-nine, and he had been my main bodyguard since I was four years old. He had a bald head by choice and a nicely trimmed goatee. He was six feet five, with a medium build and deep brown skin. Sometimes I wished he was my father, but that would mean the universe didn't hate me.

"I'm sorry," I said. "I like that I'm going home. I've missed my house, the city, the food, the people, but Father hasn't told me what he wants from me. Does he want me to go work at his company full-time? Am I still going to be the family's cleaner? It's been silent for the past month, and I don't know what to make of that."

I ran my thumb over my soft-pink-painted nails as the uncertainty crept in. I had always known what was expected of me. I followed the rules; I did what I was told, and I was good at it. Now that I was done with the degree Father wanted me to get, I hadn't received new instructions.

Milton rubbed his chin between his index and middle finger before saying, "Instead of being worried about the future, just enjoy the freedom until it's gone."

"That's easier said than done," I sighed.

The devil never slept. I knew that not just because he was my father but because the phone was ringing and his name was flashing on the screen like he could hear us talking about him.

"Good afternoon, Father," I answered.

Alexander Price had never been one for small talk, so I wasn't surprised that he immediately started barking orders at me. "When you land, you need to deal with your cousin Phillip. Simon has decided that he is no longer welcome in the family. Make sure you clean up the PR mess he created too. I sent Milton the images someone posted about this online."

"Yes, Father," I said. My voice trembled slightly.

"Is there going to be a problem?" he asked.

"No, Father," I replied. It wasn't like I could ever disobey him.

I heard a man in the background calling for my father, letting him know it was his turn. That was most likely the Chief Justice of the US Supreme Court since they golfed together regularly.

"And, Felicity . . ." Father paused briefly before he continued, "I don't need to remind you of the importance of following the family's rules, do I?"

"No, the rules are what keep us in power," I said. Out of everyone in the family, I was the only one who lived by those rules no matter what.

The first rule reminded us that one mistake could cause harm to the entire family. It wasn't about us as individuals; we were all part of a single cell.

Rule number two ensured that we always kept a clean mind so that none of our businesses would ever be affected.

The third rule meant that no matter what family we married into, our family was still more important, so we weren't allowed to change our last name, and our offspring needed to have our last name as well. It was part of the contract our spouses had to sign before marrying into the family.

The fourth rule was in place to make sure the heir never had an issue when it was time to take over the family business.

The last rule gave the power to the head of the family to make decisions for our family. The head was our leader, and we followed them no matter what. The head could only be removed if the family council found that they were unfit for the position and could cause harm to the family's reputation.

"Don't be like Phillip." With the amount of disdain in his voice, you would think he never broke a rule, but he did. "As the cleaner, we're counting on you to take care of the family. If you can't do that, you know the consequences."

He could just say "you would be terminated or murdered"— why beat around the bush? "Yes, Father."

He hung up, and I looked at Milton, who already had the images of Phillip pulled up on the tablet. "What are our orders?" Milton asked. My other five bodyguards, Levi, Omar, Daniel, David and Butch, had been seated away from us, but now that there was work to do, they all joined us at the table.

"Exile," I said. They all nodded and got to work.

By the time we landed, we had researched everything the media had on my cousin. It wasn't the first time I'd had to clean one of my family's mistakes, but dealing with outsiders was easy compared to internal conflict. I didn't have to see an outsider at family meetings and dinners.

"Did we get a response from all the TV networks and newspapers?" I asked.

"Yes. They already knew not to publish anything," Milton responded. I was sure they did, just like I was sure they would send me a hefty bill.

This was the first time that I had arrived at my aunt's house and instead of feeling contempt, my entire body felt tight, knowing I was about to destroy her son's life. I dismissed her personnel and waited until only my team, my aunt, and my cousin were left in the house.

"Felicity, please, have mercy!" my aunt begged. She was kneeling in her living room while Phillip sobbed next to her. Why did they always have to cry?

"We cannot ignore the rules, Aunt Nora," I said. She had tried to plead for my cousin, but he'd broken a rule. "I will remove him from the family tree, and he will renounce the Price name. If I find anyone in the family guilty of aiding him, they will suffer the same fate."

She reached for me, but I took a step back. Her hand dropped to her side, and her eyes landed on the Serpenti bracelet she had given me for my birthday. As if transfixed by the emerald eyes of the snake, she stayed kneeling without moving.

I stared at my thirty-one-year-old cousin, wondering where it had all gone wrong. Phillip had icy blue eyes like most of the members of our family, but what he didn't get was our drive. Our family owned the biggest holding company in the world, Price Investments. We all started learning how to invest and do business before we could walk, so it wasn't that he was incapable; he was just lazy. He leaned back on the black leather couch, letting his head fall back as he stared at the chandelier above him. He hadn't said a word since I'd gotten there.

My aunt's minimalistic yet elegant house was by far my favorite in the family, right behind mine. My love for fashion and good taste all came from her. I never really got to spend much alone time with her, but she was a passionate interior designer. It wasn't a job that most in my family would consider up to their standards, but she'd shut everyone up when she'd created a multimillion-dollar company out of it. She was more of an inspiration to me than my mother could ever be. She was the reason I'd become a fashion designer.

After my father threw me into a mental asylum when I was eighteen to keep me under his control, I had nothing but time. I spent almost a year in a room, learning everything I could. When I wasn't studying, I was sketching. By the time I was released, I had designed four different collections and a full business strategy. I launched my company the same year, and it became the brand all the teenagers wanted to wear.

Milton forced a tablet in front of Phillip so he could sign the documents to transfer his shares in our company to my aunt. As I turned around, my aunt woke up from her daze and threw herself at me, but one of my guards was there before she could touch me. "Please, he's my only son." The look of desperation on her face should have been enough to make me feel sympathetic, but I didn't. None of them had the right to complain or ask for mercy when I made their lives easy. I fixed everything for them. No matter what mistakes they made, I cleaned them and made sure it was as if they'd never happened. All they needed to do was fake it for the public and follow the rules. I was a babysitter for my rich and spoiled family.

I rolled my eyes at her because we both knew that was not how it worked. "Your *son* should have known better. He's a disgrace to this family. The only thing he knows how to do is snort coke and bring shame to the Price name."

She flinched, and her bottom lip quivered. "I'll take the punishment for him. He made a mistake; it was only one time," she implored.

"Mom!" my cousin called out from behind me. She rushed to her mother's side, holding her close while she practically pushed her brother out of the way. "Felicity, why are you here?" April asked.

I pointed to the pictures on the floor. Her eyes widened upon seeing her brother passed out next to a table covered with drugs; another photo showed him seemingly forcing himself on a woman. Launching herself at her brother, she screamed, "You selfish bastard! How many times did we tell you to stop?" I lifted an eyebrow at my aunt, who quickly realized April's mistake.

Aunt Nora tried to pull her kids apart as tears streamed down her face. Milton looked at me expectantly, but I was enjoying this little circus act. He scowled at me, which made me grin. Aunt Nora lost her step and fell on her back. "Stop! Now!" I exclaimed before she could go back in and get hurt. My cousins stopped fighting and slowly looked at me. My aunt's midlength disheveled blond hair and runny mascara had me bringing my finger up and twirling it around in a circle. My guards immediately turned away from her. I couldn't imagine what it would feel like to have people stare at me while I was in such a vulnerable state.

"I'll overlook the fact that you all knew and didn't come to me. Thank you for giving me more to clean up," I said. The pictures of Phillip doing drugs were everywhere. That and the news of his abuse towards women were all over social media. I expected more women to speak up against him in the next couple of days. My team had to scrape the internet trying to do damage control, but it was too late. The family's image had taken a hit. Even if I wanted to help him, Simon already considered him a financial loss since his contributions to the family's success were minimal, if not nonexistent.

April took a step towards me, and Milton came to stand between us. "We were helping him. Why would we ever come to Miss Perfect knowing that you would do exactly what you're doing now?" she shouted.

"And you're lucky you're not going with him," I quipped, pushing my long strawberry-blond hair back. "I could have helped him if I'd known. Now everyone knows, and there's nothing I can do for him. You did this to him, not me." He had always been useless; he was never able to earn any money for the family, and in my family, if you couldn't earn money, you were nothing. "The rules are in place to make sure we're always at the top. We have three hundred years of legacy. I won't let anyone ruin that."

"It's easy for you to separate families because no one has ever cared about you," April sneered.

Aunt Nora gasped and pulled her daughter back. I wasn't going to hurt her for being honest. I only cared about the rules. Whatever opinion they had about me didn't matter. There was nothing they could say to hurt me. I knew who I was. What they always failed to see was that I was only following my orders to enforce the rules. Did they think I wanted to be running around babysitting everyone in the family and making sure they behaved so our reputation wasn't ruined?

No, I didn't.

I hadn't asked to be the family's cleaner; I wasn't even given a choice. The head of the family decided everyone's fate. Though I would admit that I believed in what I did because I believed in the rules. Without them, our family wouldn't be as powerful as it was.

I walked out, not willing to spend a second more of my time with someone who didn't understand sacrifice. Milton opened the passenger door of the SUV for me, and I hopped in, ready to go home and work on my sketches. The car always smelled like cinnamon and leather, just like Milton.

"Are you happy to be back in New York City?" Milton asked. The sarcasm in his tone had me rolling my eyes.

"Ecstatic," I replied with the same amount of sarcasm. "There's nothing better than getting off a plane and immediately having to deal with family drama."

Although working for my family was exhausting, I only had to do cleanup work every couple of months. It was rare that someone stepped out of line. Most of my time was spent on my fashion design company, attending socialite events, and helping my father run his companies.

I leaned my head back and closed my eyes, my fingers tapping absently against the car door.

"What's on your mind?" Milton asked, interrupting my sigh.

"Being in school gave me an excuse to be away and a false sense of freedom. Getting a master's is just another thing that's expected from a Price. It may not be written in the rules, but it might as well be. Academic achievements are just another bragging point for my family. Anything that shows the world that we're better than them. We're the wealthiest, the smartest, the most respected, famous, and attractive." For my family, life was a contest and we won. "That's why Phillip's behavior confuses me. He's had everything since he was a child. He had not only money but parents that loved him and supported him. Out of everyone in our family, Aunt Nora is the only one that openly shows the love she has for her kids. Did my father even bother to show up to my graduation?" I didn't let him answer as I waved my hand in the air in frustration. "No! All I got was a press release that talked about how proud Alexander Price is that his only daughter graduated from Tuck at the top of her class. I didn't even get a call. Because why would my father ever congratulate me on something I'm supposed to do?" I let out a shaky breath as the words stopped rushing out of my mouth. I'd said more than I should have.

"We're here," Milton announced. I was thankful that he didn't make it awkward. He knew I just needed to vent; I didn't need a response.

I opened my eyes to see the peach blossoms that lined my driveway. The flowers had already started to fall, and the fruit would start to grow soon.

"We can disappear." My head shot up as I stared at Milton. *What did he just say?* "We can disappear," he said again like one time wasn't enough. "You can start a new life and be free. Don't you want to know what it's like to be happy?"

My tone was harsh with many people, but never with Milton; today was an exception. "Never suggest that again," I hissed.

He gave me an unconvincing nod before looking away.

Everyone had to make sacrifices for their families, and I wasn't the exception. No matter how much I complained, I wouldn't leave our legacy behind.

2

IDK YOU YET

Felicity

My muscles were sore after training with Milton this morning. Typically, we trained every day, but this week had been a cheat week. I wanted to go back to bed instead of having this meeting, but unfortunately, work came first. I took a sip of ginger tea as Daniel, one of my bodyguards, dropped a file on the table in front of me.

My house had four floors, not counting the basement. The left wing of the second floor was used as office space. There were ten offices and one conference room. When there was important business we needed to discuss, like today, we huddled in the conference room. I liked bright, clean spaces, so the white chairs paired with the black table made the room feel relaxing. The gold window frame helped by giving it an elegant touch.

David whistled as he read the document Daniel had just given him. Levi, David, Daniel, and Omar were brothers from Israel. When I'd first met them, it was hard to tell them apart, but after a couple of days, I'd started to notice how their physical differences matched their personalities. Daniel was leaner than his brothers, but that didn't mean he was less deadly. His buzz cut and unfriendly dark eyes made anyone want to put some distance between him and them. He was our technology specialist and liked to spend most of his days plastered to a computer screen reviewing the security cameras.

Daniel cleared his throat before speaking. "We received this file last night regarding a contract signed with a Mafia member. It came directly from Simon Price." Everyone turned to look at me, before I could hide that my nails were digging into my palms and my lips were pressed tightly together. I tapped the table once and Daniel continued. I had only been back for two days, and Simon was already torturing me. "Matthew Kavanagh, thirty-two, raised by a single mother in Dublin before they moved to New York when he was twelve. He was recently connected to the Irish mob, where he's trying to rise through the ranks. He's been involved with human trafficking and prostitution."

I closed my eyes and took a deep breath. How had we gotten involved with the Mafia? We stayed away from them. It was better for business that way, since no one wanted to work with a company that was connected to the mob.

"I know what you're thinking, and you won't like the answer," Daniel said.

"Benjamin," I murmured as my gaze met Milton's concerned one.

I didn't need his confirmation, but Daniel gave it to me anyway. "Yes, but Kavanagh's involvement with the Mafia is recent; when Benjamin signed a contract with him, there would have been no record of this."

If Benjamin wasn't in my life, I wouldn't believe one person could have so much bad luck. He was the only member of my family who cared about me and the most important person in my life. Which was contradictory considering how much I wanted his father, Simon, dead.

"I'm texting Butch to bring Benjamin," Milton said.

Butch and David were the muscle of the group. Butch was huge, and I mean huge, as in he had to enter some doors sideways. I had no idea where Butch came from; all we knew when Father hired them was that he was a package deal with the Israelis. David wasn't as big or tall, but he was still built like a heavily tattooed John Cena. David was Daniel's twin and the second youngest of the brothers.

I read the contract that my dear cousin had signed and everyone waited until I was done. Weed? Really, Benjamin? Out of all the companies he could have chosen, he'd invested in a saturated market. Between the taxes and supply issues, it wasn't even worth it for us. "Contact the firm and have them put a block on Benjamin's account. From now on, any transactions over ten thousand have to be approved by me." I didn't bother to look up as I gave the order. I knew it would get done.

I didn't know how long it had been since I'd started analyzing the contract, but as Benjamin and Butch arrived, the sun had already started to set. "Amira," Benjamin said as he kissed the top of my head. "How is my favorite cousin?" He was the only one in the family that called me by my middle name. He'd once told me he couldn't say Felicity without thinking of an eighty-year-old woman.

Unlike Benjamin's sister, who had light brown hair and the family's signature icy blue eyes, I might as well have been Benjamin's twin. Same strawberry-blond hair, chocolate-brown eyes, oval face, and pale ivory skin. His high cheekbones and snub nose gave him a regal appearance that was hard to miss. He was twenty-four and just a couple of months older than me. At six feet tall, he was two inches taller than me. I wanted to stay mad at him, but as I looked up at his innocent face, the corners of my lips tipped up. I hated how soft I was with him.

"I would be better if you stayed out of trouble. Sit," I demanded. He obediently took a seat next to me. I passed him the contract he'd signed as everyone else left the room. "That's a nice contract you drafted; it's ironclad." He immediately grinned at me as his eyes shined. I sighed, remembering that he never understood when I was being sarcastic.

"I know. I was very proud of it," he said while nodding his head.

"No, you dummy. You're supposed to leave a loophole for yourself and make it impossible to break for the other party. Remember, you're a Price. We don't play fair." We should have been able to break the contract with little effort, but thanks to him, we couldn't.

He scrunched his nose as he looked at me, confused. "I know, but he's my friend."

"We don't have friends in business," I argued.

He leaned close to me and covered my hand with his. "Stop. I hate when you tap your fingers." I did too. I never noticed when I was doing it. "Look, I know you're annoyed with me. I promise I won't do it again. If you have this file, it means that something is going on, so what is it?"

"Your father wants me to terminate the contract. Tell me everything you know about Kavanagh. Leave nothing out, no matter how insignificant you think it is, okay?" As the heir of the Price family, Benjamin's reputation needed to be protected. If anyone found out that he was linked to the mob, it would damage his image, and that was not something we could afford.

The hierarchy was in place to protect the family. There were four main positions: the head, the hand, the heir, and the cleaner. Simon was the head of the family, which meant he was in charge of the family and our company. Father was the hand; he gave counsel to Simon and helped him run the company. Benjamin was the heir, and he was being trained on everything that had to do with the company so he could one day take over. I was the cleaner, and my main job was to enforce the family rules so that our reputation was always protected.

I called everyone back to the conference room so Benjamin

could give us all the details on our target. The faster I was done with this, the better.

It was barely seven a.m., and I was already being summoned to my father's house. "Father," I said, greeting him. He was sitting behind his massive bubinga wood desk.

"Sit." I would rather stand, but I did as I was told, like always. "I heard you're going to Los Angeles and Whitlock to deal with Kavanagh and for Amber's birthday," he said. His brows were pulled together tightly, making his small features look even smaller. There were bags under his blue eyes, and his hair was losing all its color faster than I expected. He was thin—way too thin for it to be healthy. I bit my tongue to stop myself from asking him if his monthly checkup had come out fine. He would only reprimand me for caring.

Father always asked me questions like he didn't already know the answer to them. "Yes, I was on my way to the airport. Whitlock is less than two hours away from LA, so I'll stay there since I promised Amber I'd go to her birthday party. Kavanagh is currently at his LA vacation home. I don't know when he's coming back to New York, so it's better if I just go to him," I responded.

"Good, this is very important, so you can't make any mistakes. Do you understand?" I barely had a chance to nod before he was asking the next question. "What do you know about the Whitlock family?"

"I don't know anything about them," I said. I'd stopped keeping track of the new families after social media kids were considered important.

"The city became incorporated around sixty years ago. The name was changed to Whitlock to honor the brothers that helped with the urbanization. They're a very wealthy and influential family, and most people expect them to become one of the most powerful families in the country due to their political ties. We've tried to do business with them, but they've refused, so you'll marry the eldest son of the family and move to Whitlock after the wedding," he stated.

"What?" I shouted as my body pushed forward. How did you go from a boring history lesson to a marriage agreement in less than twenty seconds? His eyes cut to the door to my left and then to me, making a tingle of fear run up my spine. At the threat of what was behind that door, I forced myself to sit back and used a lower tone. "I thought after everything I've done, I could pick my husband." After all the sacrifices I had made for my family, I wanted to make my own choices. I wanted to feel something. I wanted more.

I didn't want to be ungrateful, because I was born into a family that gave me many opportunities. I was proud to be a Price, no matter how vile that made me. I was a weapon that they molded exactly how they wanted. Still, that didn't mean I couldn't want more, right?

"You shouldn't be wasting your time thinking about trivial matters. I've already decided. Besides, who's going to want you if I don't intervene? You're not wife material, unlike your cousins. Men like women that are gentle and kind. I didn't raise you to be either of those things," he said.

You didn't raise me at all! I wanted to shout, but I knew better. I gave him a sweet smile as I said, "Father, I've proven my worth time and time again. Since I took your place and became the family's cleaner, I made sure that our image was always intact in the eyes of the public. Is Simon not pleased with my performance? Is this about Phillip? Because I already took care of that." I tried to keep my emotions in check, but my heart was beating frantically. This ruined all my plans. I didn't want to be tied to some man that I didn't choose. I wanted to pick someone I could make happy. This was the only thing I thought I could control. "Is this because you want me to marry before Clara? Because you're trying to prove you're superior to Simon?"

The chair crashed to the floor as he got up. Instead of running, my body stayed paralyzed as I watched his chest rise and fall in anger. The lines in his face became more prominent, and his nostrils flared.

"Watch how you speak to me," he exclaimed. "You're just worthless trash, nothing more."

I nodded while biting the inside of my cheek. I shouldn't have said that. I knew he hated talking about Simon. I hated talking about Simon. I hated everything about Simon.

Straightening his tie, he picked up his chair and sat down. Although Father was the older brother, Simon had inherited the company. The firstborn always inherited it all, but Father had ruined it for our family by breaking rule number two. He was an alcoholic who couldn't control his impulses, and although he had since stopped drinking, it was already too late. Father didn't take losing his position well. To him, being second and having to serve his brother was the worst punishment my grandfather could have given him. I didn't take this well because I had been trained under my grandfather and father since I was a baby to be the next heir of the company; now that Simon had the company, I was left with nothing.

Unless Simon made a mistake, I had no chance of being the heir again. I had spent two years trying to find something on him that would force the family council to vote him out as our leader, but there was nothing. He was too meticulous, and even if I didn't want to give him credit, he was managing the company well. If it came to a family vote and Simon was removed as the head of the family, Benjamin and I were the only viable candidates. Benjamin had no chance to win against me. I was more prepared to run the company, and everyone knew that.

"You'll meet your fiancé two Saturdays from now. I'll send you the details. You may leave," Father declared.

I knew better than to argue with him when he was upset. "Is it okay if I take a couple of days off? I can get to know Whitlock and make sure I'm prepared." His eyes narrowed at me, but I kept my gaze steady. If I had to spend the rest of my life with some random man who wasn't my Westley, then I sure as heck was going to live my life for the next couple of days. "Just Milton and me," I added.

He stared at me for a couple of seconds. "Very well, but the Kavanagh case is priority."

"Thank you. Goodbye, Father," I said as I walked away. Of course, he didn't bother to respond.

"Miss Price," the maids and butlers said as they bowed while I passed them by. I would normally acknowledge their response, but today my mind was elsewhere. So this was it? The instruction I was waiting for from my father? Why didn't I think of it? Of course this would be the next step. I wasn't opposed to marriage; I knew having a family was an important part of someone's image. What I didn't like was that I had no say in the matter.

As soon as my bodyguards saw me walk outside, they entered the SUVs. Like always, I got in the one with Milton and David. The moment we got to my plane, I locked myself in my room. I couldn't think while I was sleeping, and right now the last thing I needed was a pity party, so I forced myself to sleep, and thankfully, I rested for the next five hours.

Whitlock was greener than I expected. There were trees everywhere, and the city looked tiny from the plane. Milton opened the door to the rented beach house and dropped our bags in the small foyer. It was only him and me since my other guards had gone to LA to do surveillance on Kavanagh.

All the walls were different pastel colors, from yellow to aqua, pink, and purple. I loved it; color was exactly what I needed right now. "I'm giving you a room on the second floor, the last door on the corridor. There's a tree you can jump to if anything happens," Milton said.

I nodded while staring at the painting of a couple walking down a street, illuminated only by the streetlights. What did it feel like to make someone so happy that they loved you?

"Princess?" Milton's arm came around my shoulders, and I leaned into his embrace. "What's wrong?"

"I always thought there was somebody out there for me, someone who would be happy when they saw me, but I'm never going to be enough for anyone." The soft words carried across the house, and I could feel them echo in a desolate tune. Father was right; I wasn't wife material.

"You are nothing." Mom's words rang in my head, and I wished I could turn them off. I stared at the painting harder, trying to focus on the streetlights and not my thoughts. Mom didn't like being in the same room as me, let alone acknowledge my existence, so why was I still affected by her words?

"Get that out of your head right now," Milton demanded. "I know what you're thinking about, and that woman doesn't know anything about you. If that Whitlock boy doesn't value you, then he's just plain old stupid. You're the best thing that's going to happen to him."

I rolled my eyes at him. "Who knew old age would make you sentimental?"

He stared at me with eyes as hard as steel. Milton was a no-nonsense type of man, but with me, he was as soft as cotton candy, so when he looked at me like I was being unreasonable, I tended to listen. This time, I didn't know how to believe him.

"Wait . . ." His words repeated in my head: *that Whitlock boy.* "How did you know?" I asked.

"There was a press release saying you were engaged to a mystery man, and your father sent the file a couple of hours ago. You were in the room, so you clearly didn't want to talk about it. We did some research. The Whitlocks seem to be a good family, very respected. But Elias never finished college and he likes to party." So that was his name, Elias.

"Any big scandals, rumors, addictions, girlfriends?" I asked. I didn't want to make it real, and thinking about him would do that, but I was a little curious.

"The entire family is very clean. His parents are still together, and he has two younger brothers." He handed me the tablet with Elias's file and took a seat on the couch. I sat on the chair across from him. "He parties all weekend and drinks a lot, but when we hacked into his social media, all his messages were about music. We think he's trying to be a music producer. There are many pictures in the tabloids of him with women, but he never responds to any of their messages. During the week, he doesn't seem to be doing much. Most days he stays at home, others he goes to the Whitlock Children's Home to play with the kids. He's still living with his parents."

I scrolled to the next page, and there he was. Elias Kane Whitlock, tanned skin, dirty-blond hair, vibrant green eyes that smiled at you, and a smug expression. He was handsome, but there was nothing special about him. He looked like every other blond-haired, green-eyed man I'd ever seen.

"Next page," Milton said, and I swiped to the next page. "He was arrested four months ago for beating up a guy at a bar. Turns out the guy was trying to take advantage of a girl, and he stepped in. His brothers—"

I interrupted him before he could continue. "That's enough. He has no ambition, is a drunk, sleeps around, and doesn't bother to at least respond to the women he sleeps with. Is my father trying to humiliate me?" My voice rose a couple of octaves as I said the last part. I got up and paced around the room, needing to shake the emotions off. "Do I look like a babysitter?" This had to be a joke. "I do not want to be responsible for a man-child."

Milton's lips were pursed as he followed me with his eyes.

"My life is already hectic, and I want something normal. I want to come home to a husband who only has eyes for me and will cuddle me on the sofa while I watch clichéd romantic movies. They don't even need to come from money because I can pay for my own things." Of course, I would never say that to my father. "Father said they didn't want to do business with us, but they're accepting a marriage agreement? What kind of logic is that? Unless they think they can get money out of us just because my family is allowing their son to marry me." I chuckled at the thought; it wouldn't have been the first time a family had tried that. Their son would belong to me. Rule number three meant I couldn't change my last name, and he could forget about passing his name to our children. He wouldn't get a penny of my family's money or mine, and he needed to follow the Price rules. "I know I have no right to complain, but I'm also tired of just existing. I want to live, even if it's just for a day, you know?"

I rubbed my fingers against my temples, feeling the start of a headache. "Let's just focus on Kavanagh and getting through the week."

Before Milton could say anything and my tears started to fall, I rushed up the stairs. I took my clothes off and jumped in the shower, where the water could hide how I was losing control over my emotions and I could pretend I wasn't crying.

3

HAVE WE MET BEFORE?

Felicity

A shower turned out to be exactly what I needed to bury all my feelings in the bottom of the black hole I had opened just for them. I sketched for a couple of hours and then connected with my friend Amber, who invited me to a Whitlock party. Amber had moved to Whitlock last year to chase the party scene. We hadn't seen each other since—not for lack of trying, but between school and work, there was never time.

My team reported that Kavanagh was having a party tomorrow, so there was nothing for me to do until then.

I finished putting on a modest high-waisted bikini. It was black with a gold pattern on the edges of the top and bottom. It looked good on the model, but on my slim figure, it seemed plain, like everything else. The top made my full B cups look smaller, but at least the bikini bottoms did me a favor by accentuating my ass. My hair fell in waves down my back, and I was happy with how it turned out. Putting on clear lip gloss and mascara, I couldn't help but smile. I had only been in Whitlock for a couple of hours, and I already felt different.

My phone beeped with an incoming message from Amber, telling me she was already here. Letting out a nervous breath, I put on a white crochet cover-up and ran down the stairs.

"Milton, Amber's here!" I yelled. He was already waiting for me at the door.

I rushed outside, where night had already fallen, and immediately got pulled into a hug by Amber. I had known her since we were babies. She was wearing a stunning red bikini that left little to the imagination under an open-front bikini cardigan. Her rich brown skin was practically glowing.

Amber was petite but had an hourglass figure that people would pay big money for. She had added caramel highlights to her curly brown hair, making it look vibrant.

"I'm so happy to see you!" she said with tears in her eyes.

"Me too!" I exclaimed, excited to see her, excited for anything that made me feel something.

She gave Milton the address before we turned to each other again. "So, tell me . . ."

Oh no, I know where this is going. I shouldn't have told her.

"You're getting married to one of the hottest guys in Whitlock! I've seen him a couple of times, and he is drool-worthy. A total player, but at least he has a perfect smile, and have you seen those eyes?"

I didn't bother to answer her question before asking, "Are you sure he won't be there?"

She rolled her eyes at me like I had no reason to be worried. "I've told you like six times, we don't run in the same crowds. Elias only hangs out with the elite crowd, so he will definitely not be there tonight."

I nodded, relieved that I didn't have to run into him.

The party was in full swing by the time we arrived. People were drinking and dancing everywhere. I begged Milton to stay outside so that I could enjoy the night. He didn't like it, but he agreed.

Every person there looked suntanned, like all they did was spend time at the beach. I loved the beach, but only at night, when I didn't have to worry about sun damage.

I followed Amber as she pulled me to a corner where her friends were.

"Hey, guys, this is Felicity. She's like a sister to me," Amber said with a big smile on her face.

"Hi, everyone," I said with an awkward wave. Where did that wave come from? Completely out of my element, I felt my walls trying to come back up, but I pushed them down again. *You got this. Just be friendly; it's not that hard.*

A stunning blond pulled me to her and hugged me before passing me along the group like I was a potato. I wasn't used to people touching me, but I didn't want to be impolite, so I tried not to grimace or throat-punch them.

"Here. Drink up." Amber handed me a shot, and I took it. It wasn't bad for cheap vodka.

Everyone went to dance, but I stayed back, not wanting any compromising pictures to be taken. The only awful pictures of me I wanted out there were those taken by my team, which I carefully vetted before they were released.

I could feel people's eyes on me, even though I was plastered to the wall. Something bumped softly into my shoulder, and I turned around quickly to see the culprit. A tall guy with light brown eyes winked at me as soon as our eyes met. I tried to take a step back, but the wall was right there. "Are you passing by or staying?" He extended his tattooed arm, offering me a red Solo cup as he waited for my answer. If his jawline was more defined, it could have cut diamonds. He had short, dark auburn hair, high cheekbones, and dimples.

"I don't understand what you're trying to ask me," I said, ignoring the cup.

He pulled his hand back as he leaned on the wall and relaxed his shoulders. "Most people come to Whitlock only for the party months. I'd never seen you here before, so I know you're new."

I moved my body closer to him and batted my eyelashes; he seemed interesting enough. "Maybe you just never noticed me before," I purred.

"Trust me, I would have remembered." His gruff voice became lower as his eyes briefly stared at my lips. "Also, my sister is kind of obsessed with you. She forced me to watch a red carpet with her just because you would be in it. You were on the screen for ten seconds, and I thought she would melt. How does it feel to be so famous?" And just like that, my interest died. I knew people would know who I was. I just didn't want it to be the only reason they wanted to talk to me.

"Ryan!" a girl yelled, and the guy in front of me turned to look. "I need a beer pong partner." He turned back to me and then to her. As he stepped closer to me, I knew what his answer was going to be, so I stopped him before he responded to the girl.

"Go. You're not what I'm looking for."

He tilted his head and looked at me for a couple of seconds before a grin appeared. "You should consider taking a walk on the beach if you get bored here," he said, giving me a two-finger salute before walking away.

Since almost everyone was in the pool area or inside the house, I had a good view from where I was standing, and it didn't look promising. A rowdy crowd suddenly entered, making the already small space feel suffocating. I hated rowdy crowds. I had thought it would be a more mature crowd, but instead, I was stuck with high schoolers. One guy who could barely stand rushed past me to lift his friend. For some reason, everyone around them laughed and didn't stop him. After a couple of seconds of trying to juggle his friend, the drunk guy lost his step, and they both came falling towards me. I quickly stepped out of the way, deciding I'd had enough, and rushed past an open door that led to the back patio. I breathed a sigh of relief as soon as the gentle ocean breeze captured me.

I left my sandals next to the stairs and made my way down. The sand felt so good beneath my feet. There were no lights or moon, but the stars shined fiercely. We were in the middle of May, so it was still a little cold at night, but this was the perfect weather for me. I jumped back as I felt the wet sand and started walking along the coastline, admiring how the ocean danced.

"Careful," a voice to my right warned. I looked down and saw a cooler in my path.

"Thank you," I said, turning to look at my savior.

"No problem," he replied. I could barely see him, but his outline suggested that he was tall with broad shoulders. "Not enjoying the party?" he asked.

"Not my scene. You?" I took a step toward him.

His voice was sweet and rough, almost intoxicating. "I'm recovering."

My curiosity got the best of me. It was a weakness. "From?"

"A heartbreak," he said.

Tell me more, I internally pleaded. I wanted to hear more about how his heart had been broken. "And your idea of recovery is being in the dark on your own?"

He grinned at me, and I took a step closer because I felt like I needed to see him. He had a square jaw and wide lips. His short hair looked either dark blond or light brown.

"Beer?" he asked with a carefree smile.

I loved his smile.

"Sure, you need a new one?" I hoped his answer was yes because I wanted to stay right here. *Serial killers are also charming, Felicity.* Shut up, brain.

"If you don't mind."

I grabbed two beer bottles, and he scooted over to give me more space on the towel he was sitting on. I sat down without questioning what I was doing and left my phone on the sand behind me.

He opened our beers, and I took the opportunity to ask more questions. "How long have you been recovering?"

"Two years," he said.

I laughed because, what the hell, two years? I looked at him, and he was watching me with a big smile. I couldn't tell if he was serious or joking. "Seriously? Two years? She must have been perfect."

"I'm joking, I'm not heartbroken, at least not anymore. I don't believe in perfection. I liked her when I was thirteen. She left on the day of my twenty-third birthday with no goodbye."

"Why didn't you go after her?" I didn't like to meddle in people's lives because I didn't want anyone asking about mine. Still, there was something about this man that had me very intrigued.

"I called."

He said it like that should have been enough. "For someone who was in love for ten years, I feel like a call wouldn't be enough to confess all your feelings." I gave him a pointed look.

"Do you always say what's on your mind?"

I finished my beer before answering. "Not really." I felt like his eyes were burning into mine. I couldn't tell what color they were yet.

"The conversations were awkward, as if we didn't know each other anymore. So, I stopped calling and dated other girls," he confessed.

"Another?" I asked, waving my empty beer bottle.

"Yes, but I'll get it this time," he said while getting up.

"Why is the cooler so far away? It doesn't seem like you need the exercise."

He smirked. I smiled at him with teeth and everything. It felt natural to smile at him.

"The further away it is, the less I drink. The hassle of getting up becomes too much after a while." He handed me another beer, and I took a sip. "Are you saying that you think I look good?"

Unable to hold my cough, I gasped for air as the beer tried to go down the wrong way. He patted my back, not bothering to hide his grin at my pain and embarrassment.

"Calm down, tiger. All I'm saying is you look fit. I can barely see your face, so I don't know what the rest of you looks like."

He laughed again, which sent a shiver through my body.

I liked it.

I wanted to make him laugh more. He walked behind me and pulled something from a bag. The next thing I knew, he was wrapping me in a blanket. *He saw you shivering and brought you a blanket!* His hand brushed my shoulder, and I swore electricity ran through my body. I didn't know if he felt it too, but we both turned to look at each other the moment it happened. His eyes were intense, like they could see everything. He cleared his throat and sat next to me again.

"Thank you," I whispered.

"NP," he responded. I burst out laughing, and he followed. Our laughter echoed throughout the empty beach.

"I've never heard someone actually say the abbreviation." I shook my head, and he just continued laughing.

He told me all about the girl he used to love. Platinum blond with ocean-blue eyes. Their families were close, and she was his and his brother's best friend. She was two years younger than him and had a big heart and a gentle smile. She left to go to New York to finish her degree in English literature and stayed after she got a major publishing deal.

I wished I was the love of someone's life.

"What about you?" he asked.

"No heartbreaks," I said with a shrug.

"You've never had a heartbreak? Not even a tiny one?" His voice sounded confused, like that should be impossible.

"Nope, I would need a boyfriend for that, or a crush." I probably should have kept that to myself, but there was something comforting about talking to him, maybe because he was a stranger.

His eyebrows rose in shock before he asked, "How's that even possible?"

"My father is very protective." What I didn't say was that I could only date whoever my family wanted, because that sounded pathetic.

The backyard lights suddenly turned on, providing a little more visibility. The stubble covering his face looked attractive on him, and his wide-set eyes were looking at me almost tenderly as they scanned my face. His curved, rosy lips were round and smooth, and I wished he would close the distance between us right now. There were some Hispanic features that enhanced his masculine face. He had the perfect mix of strong and soft features.

He leaned closer to me, letting his eyes search my face before asking, "Why did you really leave the party?"

Was this going to be a reveal-your-deepest-and-darkest-secrets session? "I felt suffocated and needed fresh air," I said, not afraid to answer that question. "If you don't want her back, why are you still moping?"

His body became tense as soon as I finished the question. I waited patiently, looking directly into his eyes, hoping he would answer instead of avoiding it. After what felt like two minutes of silence, he finally answered.

"I rarely think about her, and the feelings are no longer there, but my mother brought up marriage today and she insisted on looking for someone for me to date." He sighed as he passed a hand through his hair. The way the muscles in his arms contracted had me biting my lip. "I'm married to my job. I've never put effort into trying to have a relationship with anyone because it's not a priority for me. Sometimes I wonder if maybe things would be different if she'd stayed. We already knew each other, so I wouldn't have to work on building a relationship."

So he was only thinking of her because it would be easier to date her since he wouldn't need to take time off work? I wasn't expecting that answer. I didn't know what I was expecting, but it wasn't that.

"Do you think that makes me an asshole?" he asked, taking my silence negatively. The truth was, I was no one to judge.

"No, I'm not a relationship expert, but it sounds like you might be confused about what love is." A lopsided grin pulled at his face.

"What's your name?" he asked.

I hesitated before telling him because I didn't want him to treat me differently. He'd find out eventually, but for today, I wanted to be just another girl. "You can call me Fee. Yours?"

"Are you trying to be secretive?" he asked with a smirk.

"A little," I said, looking at him seductively.

His eyes landed on my lips briefly before saying, "Leo."

"Well, Leo, nice to meet you," I said formally, extending my hand to him.

"Pleasure to make your acquaintance, Fee," he said while shaking my hand, and another current of electricity shot through my body. I was starting to understand why sleeping with a stranger was exciting. I didn't want to let go of his hand, but I didn't want it to be awkward. His hand came down with mine. Our fingers interlaced in the sand, and I bit my cheek to hide my smile. It might have been the beer talking, but I could definitely feel a connection.

"It's your turn to tell me a secret," he said.

"Um . . ." I couldn't think of any secrets that I could tell him. Everything that I could say was already published somewhere. He was patiently waiting, just looking at me with the permanent smile he had on his face. "I hate beer." He looked at the five empty beer bottles next to me and burst out laughing. "What? I didn't want to be rude, and you have nothing else," I said, laughing with him. His thumb was rubbing mine, so it was hard to concentrate on anything else but him.

"I have to pee," I told him. I didn't want to leave, but I couldn't hold it any longer. I felt like I wouldn't ever see him again if I left. He smirked and turned to the ocean.

"You have an entire ocean," he said while waving his hand.

"Ew." I scrunched my nose, and before I could register what was happening, he leaned in and gave it a quick kiss. My heart skipped a beat.

"Come, fishes pee in here all the time." He pulled me up and walked towards the ocean. I was still shocked about the nose kiss, but my feet decided to follow him while I had a mental breakdown.

I yelped as soon as I touched the cold water. Leo gave me a sideways grin, and I stared at his lips for longer than I should have.

"One moment," I told him before running away from the wet sand and taking off my cover-up. I ran back to him sluggishly, feeling the weight of the alcohol. I didn't stop in time and collided with his body. My hand fell on his stomach, and even through the T-shirt, I could feel his abs. Warm hands held my waist as he steadied me.

"Ready?" Green. His eyes were definitely green.

"Let's go," I said before I chickened out. He took his shirt off and threw it as far away as possible.

Hand in hand, we ran towards the ocean. As soon as I tried to power through the water like a bulldozer, I fell and took him down with me. Oh my God, it was freezing. "Eeeeep!" I shrieked as the ice-cold water enveloped us.

Leo roared in laughter, and I joined him. This was precisely what I needed—just some fun with a random guy. It was how I imagined spring break would be.

The waves crashed into us, making it hard to get up. Leo

stood up first, then pulled me to him. The warmth of his body helped me feel better about being in the ice-cold water. He held my hand again, but this time we walked the rest of the way until my shoulders were barely above the water.

The water felt less cold once we were fully submerged.

"You done?" Leo asked.

I could feel my whole body blush with embarrassment. He winked at me, making me laugh again.

I was done, but I wouldn't admit it. "That's embarrassing. Don't ask me that." I had never laughed this much in my entire life. I didn't even know what was so funny.

I felt alive. There was a warmth that I had never felt before.

"Why not? Everyone needs to pee. In fact, I just finished." I scrunched my nose at him and moved the surrounding water. He leaned in and kissed my nose again. I looked up at him and got lost in his eyes. This was it. It was now or never. I closed the distance between us and gave him a peck on the lips. His lips didn't respond, and I felt my stomach dip. This was stupid. Of course it wasn't like in the movies.

As I was about to step back, his hands came to my waist, pushing me against him. My hands landed on his shoulders, looking for something to steady me after his sudden movement. His eyes roamed my face until they landed on my lips. He leaned forward, and my breath caught in my throat when his lips landed on mine. I had been kissed before, but it hadn't felt like this. Never like this.

There was no hesitation as he guided my lips with his. His fingers dug deeper into my flesh when my tongue touched his. Our tongues explored each other's mouths; it was almost magical. I wrapped my arms tighter around his shoulders, getting as close as possible. Something in my body was begging me to get closer to him.

I didn't know how long we stayed there kissing, but my lips felt swollen.

The cold water ruined the moment when I shivered, and he broke the kiss. No, no, no! Why?

Our lips were still touching as he whispered. "Let's go back and get you warmed up."

My voice was barely audible as I said, "Okay." My heart was thundering in my chest. I wished it would calm down, but as Leo pulled me to him, my brain no longer wanted to help me. I was sure he could hear it too.

We returned to the towel, picking up our clothes along the way. His shirt was back on, and I tied my cover-up, but it did nothing to help with the cold. He lay down on the towel and motioned me to sit on top of him. I put one knee on each side, and he pulled the blanket over us.

"Do you hear that?" I thought he meant my heart—it was pounding so loud I was sure he could. My cheeks burned, and I was grateful for the dark.

He took my hand and placed it above his heart. It beat just as hard as mine. There was no way he was feeling this connection as much as I was. I took his hand and showed him how mine felt. He smiled at me, and I laid my head on his chest. His arms came around me, hugging me tight against him. I fell asleep to the beat of our hearts.

4

———

BROKEN

Leo

Fee's face disappeared into the crook of my neck, and her body was wrapped tightly against mine. Her breathing evened out before two minutes had even passed. I wrapped my arms tighter around her to protect her from the cold and because, damn it, she felt like she belonged right where she was.

What the heck was wrong with me? Where was this feeling coming from? I had slept with many women over the years. Women I met at galas or business events that understood there were no feelings attached, it was just a night for both of us to relieve our stress. When we were both done, I never wanted anything from them. I didn't care about their names, what they liked or if I would ever see them again. But with Fee I cared about all those things and more. I wanted to get to know her.

I moved her hair away from her face and stared at her full lips. It wasn't like I could see much, but I could imagine them.

Yes, I was aware that I sounded like a creep.

I'd never seen anyone with lips as full as hers or as soft. I could have kissed her until I froze to death, but she was shivering, and I knew it was time to end it. I could feel her heart thundering the moment she was against my chest. I had to put her hand on my heart so she wouldn't feel embarrassed or nervous; I wasn't sure what she was feeling.

Was she really tired, or was she so comfortable with me that she fell asleep before I could even count to sixty? I was hoping it was the latter of those two options. I ran my fingers against her smooth hair as I stared at the sky. Peace like I'd never felt before surrounded me. I couldn't remember the last time someone had made me laugh as much as she did or made me want to spend more time with them.

My heart finally decided to calm down, and as it did, I felt Fee's heartbeat match mine. It was a soft melody, like they were singing to each other.

My phone vibrated next to me, and I couldn't help but sigh. I positioned my face away from her as I whispered, "Hello."

"Son, how are you doing?" Dad's voice was deep and cheerful, which might seem like a jarring contrast, but it went well with his warm and supportive nature.

I turned to look at the girl in my arms. "Couldn't be better. You?"

"That's good. I know you're going to Florida next week, and I wanted to see how the marketing proposal for the new chip is going. Do you want to meet before or after you go to Florida?"

For a moment, I had forgotten all about the issues at work. It had been a long day, and being dragged to this party by my business partner and friend, Ryan, had not improved my mood. Dad had been on edge for the past couple of months, and I had no idea what the problem was, but it was driving me crazy.

"We can discuss it when I get back," I responded. The marketing team was still trying to find a launch strategy that was different from our competitors. Our sales had skyrocketed after our newest microchip launch, and now we were one of the leading electronic companies in the country, which meant more work and more responsibilities. The company I'd founded was also growing faster than I expected, and having to juggle that and my father's company at the same time had proven to be challenging.

"That works for me. Goodnight, Polo," Dad said before hanging up.

"Leo," Fee mumbled.

I liked the way she said my name—tentatively, almost like she was trying to figure me out with just three letters. No one had ever called me that; most people just called me Polo, but since she was being secretive about her name, I played along with her. I didn't expect how much I would like the way she said it.

She was different from anyone I'd ever met, yet familiar. It was refreshing that she didn't mind asking hard questions that people would normally not ask. She didn't seem interested in my last name or my family. I couldn't remember the last time I'd had a conversation with someone who hadn't asked me for a favor or wanted to pitch me a new business idea. In Whitlock, having your business endorsed by a Whitlock was the best marketing tool.

I looked up at a sky that seemed to be darker than before. Fee's sweet peach scent mixed with the ocean breeze was my new favorite smell. Had the ocean always been this peaceful, or was it all her?

A realization settled in my chest that I'd have to let her go when she woke up, and my peace went with it. I wanted to know who was hiding behind those fearless but lonely eyes. It already felt like she was mine. I didn't know how that was possible, but how else could I explain how perfectly we fit together? She didn't feel like someone I'd just met. I didn't want to let her go, but I also didn't want to scare her away. What if she didn't want to go out on a date with me? Agh, this was going to drive me crazy.

"Is this what you meant, Grandpa, when you said I would know when I found the one?" I whispered.

A shooting star fell right above us as if it was the answer to my question.

I didn't know why I did it, but as the star fell and she stirred on top of me, I made a wish.

5

I WAS MADE FOR LOVING YOU

Felicity

So warm. So comfortable. I heard my phone ringing, but I didn't want to get up. Leo shifted beneath me, but I refused to move. One of his arms was still around me, so I snuggled deeper into his chest. I heard him chuckle, which made me smile. Someone cleared their throat, and I finally opened my eyes. Amber was standing a couple of feet away with a shocked look on her face. Her friends were behind her, and I could see other people I didn't recognize. Why would she come with all these people?

"Are you drunk?" Her voice came out in a lofty tone. She was wasted.

I sighed. A drunk Amber was never a good thing; she was emotional and unpredictable.

"No, why?" I could feel everyone's eyes on me.

"You're half-naked and on top of a stranger." She looked at me like I'd gone crazy. I'd been there for many of her one-night stands. What was the difference if I did it?

"It's nothing." I could feel Leo stiffen. Crap, that wasn't what I meant. "Just because I've never found someone worthy of my attention doesn't mean there aren't any good ones out there," I quickly added before he got the wrong idea. His hand caressed my thigh, and dear Lord, that did things to me. Things I wanted to explore and learn how they felt.

"Sorry for the freakout," Amber said. "I've never seen you with anyone; it's shocking. Especially now that . . ." She didn't finish, and I was so grateful for that. Although the news of my arranged marriage had come out today, I didn't need the reminder to ruin this moment.

"I know. It's all good," I assured her. Everyone kept staring at us, and I rolled my eyes in annoyance. "Oh, quit judging," I snapped. I watched their eyes widen as if they expected me to welcome them with open arms. "Everyone can go now." They began to leave, but a flash went off, and Amber turned around, pissed.

"Who was that? Who took that picture?" Amber yelled. Some people turned around, but most just hurried away. Whoever it was, it didn't matter. It wasn't like I didn't release countless pictures of my fake dating life.

I felt Leo move beneath me, and I put my hand on his chest to prevent him from getting up. "Let it go," I told them.

Amber turned to look at Leo, leaning closer to him. She looked at me with wide eyes before looking back at him. "You're . . ."

"Nope, I don't care," I said, stopping her. I'd spent my entire life around the same people. People that I judged by their profession and the name attached to them.

I didn't want to do that with him. I wanted something new and fresh, not tainted by the outside world. To find out everything about him on my own. Knowing his name would make me Google him. Even if I tried not to, I knew I would.

"But . . . why don't you want to know?" she asked.

I turned to look at Leo before answering her. "He's Leo, and that's good enough for me."

She nodded and wiped the remaining tears away. "We have to go. It's almost three a.m., and Milton will be worried." Damn it, I forgot about Milton.

"Wait for me in the car. I'll be right there." She left without another word.

I met Leo's passionate eyes. "Have I scared you yet?" He shook his head. "Are you a serial killer, drug dealer, or have any STIs?" He laughed and pulled me down against his chest for a hug. "Hey, serious questions," I said, but I couldn't help it; I laughed with him.

"No, no, and I'm clean," he finally responded with that smile that had me wanting to trace his lips with my tongue. I leaned in and did just that. His fingers dug into my thighs, and his eyes closed; other than that, he stayed incredibly still.

When the following words came out, they sounded breathless. "That works for me. It's three nos from me too." There was something about him that made me want more. Were these my crazed teenage hormones finally making an entrance? Licking someone's lips shouldn't feel erotic.

"Are you okay? I can ask around to see who took the picture." That was sweet of him, but completely unnecessary. What was Elias going to do? Get upset? I didn't care what he thought.

"That's fine. Amber is just overprotective." She'd been like this for the past couple of years, and I really wished she would calm down and stop overreacting to every little thing.

"What do you mean by a night of freedom?" he asked.

I decided to tell him the truth, not wanting to start whatever this was with lies since there was more about him I wanted to know. I watched him nervously as I told him what I expected would make him run for the hills. "I was told yesterday that I'm engaged and will meet my fiancé next week." There was a shift in his eyes. I held my breath, waiting for his rejection.

"Do you want to get married?" My fingers tightened involuntarily around his bicep, and I quickly let go. "Don't shy away from me now," he said, grabbing my hand midair and interlacing our fingers.

"I want to get married, just . . ." I trailed off as my throat closed up. This wasn't the time to be vulnerable, so I swallowed my emotions back down.

"Not like this," he finished for me. I shook my head slowly.

"Not like this," I agreed. "I'm hoping once the guy realizes how incompatible we are, he'll cancel the engagement." I didn't believe Elias would cancel it, and even if he tried there was no way my father would allow it, but I also didn't want Leo to think I wasn't available. Even if it was just until next week, I wanted to talk to him more.

"Can I take you to breakfast tomorrow?" he asked.

Wait, what? He wanted to take me out! I tried to hold my smile, but I couldn't. This was the first time in years that someone I was intrigued by had asked me out. I supposed breakfast wouldn't interfere with my evening plans, and I could spend more time getting to know Leo. Keeping it together as best I could, I answered. "Yes, but I want something very normal. A local's place." He sat up and gave me a peck on the lips.

"I can do that." We stared at each other, just smiling. My hand came to his jaw, and I traced it with the tip of my finger. "I'll walk you out."

He pulled his cooler with one hand and held my hand with the other. We silently made our way to the backyard and exited through the patio door. I felt an incredible amount of peace. Like he could absolve all my sins.

As soon as we made it to the sidewalk in front of the house, I saw Milton turn the car on and make his way toward us. His eyes were on the man beside me. Leo brought my attention back to him as his arms came around me, and he placed a kiss on my neck. I turned in his arms, laying my ear against his strong chest.

"Give me your phone, okay?" His warm breath against my neck sent chills down my spine.

We exchanged numbers, and I hopped in the car. I looked into his eyes while the car left him behind. My stomach felt like I'd just gotten off the Drop of Doom—not that I would know how it felt, but I'd seen videos.

Where would he take me? What would I wear?

"I heard he's a good guy," Amber said softly.

I nodded, still staring out the window, even though he wasn't there anymore.

She squeezed my hand and exchanged a look with Milton. "You're important to me, Felicity." I shifted closer to the door, uncomfortable with her words. "I know you don't believe me, and I know I messed up when we were kids. But you are. I've seen the bruises you tried to hide and the hard exterior you never want anyone to penetrate. I've known you all twenty-four years that we've both been in this world, and I've never seen you look at anyone like you looked at him. Let him in. Maybe it'll all work out in the end."

Her comment caught me off guard. There was no way my father would break this marriage deal. It wasn't something I wanted either. If my family needed me to get married, I would get married. This was only going to be a fun weekend, nothing more. I didn't know what he did for work, but I knew he was too good for my family. My job involved reading people and getting everything I wanted out of them. I could tell right away when someone walked on the other side of the line from where I stood.

I was the queen of my world, not because I was the most sadistic, but because I didn't care who got hurt in the process.

LEO CALLED early to make sure I was ready for breakfast. I jumped out of bed to get ready the moment he hung up.

My heart started pounding when I heard the doorbell. I had my hair up in a messy bun, with very light makeup and natural pink lipstick that accentuated my reddish lips. I was wearing an oversized white tee with black Manolo combat boots.

Grabbing my Re-Nylon mini backpack, I hurried down the stairs. Leo was already there, talking to Milton. He was wearing a navy shirt and jeans. When he heard me run down the stairs, he turned around and barely had time to catch me before I slammed into him. His arms came around me, and we both started laughing.

"Hey," I said against his chest. God, he smelled good. Like a delicious concoction of amber and wood.

"Hey back." He placed a kiss on my forehead and asked, "Ready?"

As I stared into his eyes, I realized that I'd missed the full effect last night. They were clear, with no malice or hidden agendas; I didn't know what to make of that. "Yeah," I whispered before turning to a frowning Milton. "Can we go on our own?" I asked in a pleading tone.

Milton looked at me apologetically. "Princess, you know I have to be with you at all times."

"But—" I started to speak, but Leo pulled me to his chest and interrupted me.

"You can trust me, sir. We'll be in contact throughout the day. You have all my information and my address." I saw a business card between Milton's fingers. He always pulled background checks, so he would know almost everything about Leo the moment we walked out.

Milton nodded, and I was in shock.

Pure shock.

My mouth was wide open, and I just kept looking between them. Leo's smile was so big that I thought his face would be permanently fixed with that smile.

"Who are you?" I asked in disbelief. Before he could respond, I brought my hands up and shook my head. "Forget it. I don't want to know. Let's just go. I'm starving."

Right now, it was enough to know that I was safe. There was no point in filling myself with the false hope that he was someone my father would approve of. My mind would start making plans to alter the situation so I could get my way.

He opened the door to his white BMW, buckled me in, and gave me a quick peck on the lips before he closed the door.

The city was magnificent. Everything looked immaculate—nothing like New York. I'd always love my home state. It was impossible not to get lost in the rich history each building represented. New York wasn't just land. It had its own personality and character. My family was part of that, and so was I. I wondered if Elias felt as proud of what his family built as I did.

"What are you thinking about?" He grabbed my hand and intertwined our fingers.

"How clean this city is. It's small, but everything is so well designed that it looks massive." He brought my hand to his lips and kissed it. "Although it's almost a little too clean. It makes it boring."

He chuckled, and I decided his laugh was my favorite sound in the world. "So you would like it more if it was dirty?"

"Not necessarily dirty, just less perfect-dystopian-looking," I said.

"I think the Whitlocks would disagree." He winked at me before looking back at the road.

"Maybe," I mumbled. That was the last family I wanted to discuss.

We pulled up at an IHOP, and the place looked packed.

"IHOP!"

"Yeah, we don't really have a lot of casual places here. Everything is kind of extravagant, so I thought this might be the most chill place."

By the cautious way he said it, he believed this was bad. I

unbuckled my seat belt and did some weird contortions until I was on his lap.

His lips twitched as he looked at me.

I kissed him hard. He opened his mouth for me, and our tongues danced with each other. After several minutes, we were both panting, and I could feel his erection on my ass.

"What was that for?" he said, still breathing hard.

"I've always wanted to come to IHOP, thanks." I beamed at him. Freaking beamed. I didn't know I could do that. He frowned, but it quickly turned into a grin.

"Let's make this a special breakfast." I opened the door to his car and hopped out. He grabbed my forgotten backpack, and I skipped to the door just because I'd always wanted to do it.

When we got to the door, I grabbed my phone so we could take a picture. Leo kissed my temple and hugged me from behind. I vowed to myself that I'd never release this picture to the press. It was mine to keep.

"Stay close," he whispered against my ear. "People in Whitlock are nosy."

As soon as we walked in, the hostess waved at him. I kept my face down so no one would recognize me.

"Your table is ready. Your server will be here soon to show you the way," the hostess said. I didn't turn to look at her since she was young and would most likely know who I was. "Thank you," we said at the same time. Leo kissed my hand and brought me close to him.

"I asked them to put their most private table on hold, so no one bothers you," he murmured. Leo must have been at least six feet four, so I had to stand on my tiptoes to give him a quick kiss. Should I have been more careful when I was in the middle of a busy restaurant? Yes. Did I care about anything else other than this man right now? No. He was thoughtful, and that meant something to me.

"Hi, I'm Alice. I'll take you to your table."

I turned to our server, but her eyes were on Leo. He was definitely one of the city's eligible bachelors. We followed her to a booth in the far corner of the restaurant. There was nothing next to it.

It was perfect.

I slid into the booth, giving my back to the restaurant so no one could see me. Leo slid right next to me. His arm came around my shoulder, and he pulled me closer to him. I placed my hand on his lap and looked at him. He was staring right at me. We were so comfortable with each other that it felt like we'd done this a million times. The server told us about the menu and the restaurant's limited items. After she was done, Leo squeezed my shoulder, and I noticed he wanted me to respond.

"No, thanks. That'll be all for now," I told her with a soft smile. She glanced at Leo one more time before she left, but he was still looking at me.

"Rude," I muttered.

He kissed me softly, but his whole body shook with laughter.

"Are you always laughing?" I asked against his lips.

"No, just with you." My stomach grumbled, and I remembered we were here to eat.

"I don't know if I want the original, blueberry, or chocolate chip." I stared at the menu, but there were too many options, and I wanted to try them all. "Okay, I've decided!" I announced. "Original short stack with bacon, sausage links, and hash browns."

The server returned to take our order, and Leo ordered a short stack of every pancake flavor and French toast. When I asked why he ordered so much food, he shrugged and said, "I want to know which ones are your favorite."

When the food finally arrived, it looked and smelled delicious. I spread the butter, poured the syrup until it was swimming, and took a huge bite. "Mmmm," I moaned. It was so sweet. My mouth was having a party. I looked at Leo, since I noticed he hadn't moved. His gaze was so heated that I felt like it could burn me. He leaned in and licked the syrup from the corner of my mouth.

"Do you like it?" he whispered, still close to my mouth. At that moment, my heart decided it wanted to be the reincarnation of John Bonham.

"I love it." He leaned back, smiled, and started eating his food.

Leo wasn't a talker, but he was big on PDA. His fingers were constantly caressing me as he asked me questions. I talked about my time in college and how I'd graduated early, which was basically by slaving away since my teenage years. He was impressed that I had a bachelor's in fashion design aside from my master's. My heart skipped a beat when he looked at me with admiration.

"So, what's the verdict?" he asked.

I was so full, I didn't think I could eat again until tomorrow. "Tres leches and original were my favorites. You?" I asked. Tres leches was incredibly sweet and tasty. I wouldn't be eating pancakes every day, but I could enjoy them once a year.

"Original and chocolate chip." Our server brought the bill, and I grabbed my backpack, but Leo didn't let me pay. "When you're with me, everything is on me." I tried to say that wasn't fair, but he didn't let me. "Nothing you say will make me change my mind." Then he kissed me with so much passion that I forgot entirely what I was trying to object to.

We walked out of the restaurant hand in hand, smiling at each other. He made me happy; he didn't look at me with pity. I wanted to make him happy too.

"Ready to leave?" he asked.

He leaned on his car and pulled me into his arms, holding me tightly against his chest. We were waiting for Milton to pick me up since I should already be on my way to LA. I still needed to study the blueprints for Kavanagh's house. "I guess," I mumbled.

His eyes smiled at me as he said, "You sound so convincing."

"It's not my fault you didn't make this date suck." He couldn't blame a girl for wanting to stay with him a little longer.

"It's not my fault you're busy this afternoon or else I would keep you to myself all day," he fired back.

Milton parked right beside us, and before I could step out of Leo's hold, he hugged me tighter before letting go. "I'll text you," I said.

He nodded as he folded his arms around his chest.

For the second time that day, I watched him until he disappeared from my sight.

6

IN YOUR UNIVERSE

Leo

Fee had a childlike innocence. It was as if she was experiencing the world for the first time. I could easily get lost in her smile and the light in her eyes when she got excited.

"What do you think, Mr. Whitlock?"

"Huh?" I asked, confused.

Seven sets of eyes were staring at me with their eyebrows pulled up. After Fee had left, I'd come back to work since I had to catch up on the meetings I'd canceled to go out with her. I would be sitting in this conference room for the next eight hours with no breaks, but it was well worth it. I focused on the presentation displayed on the screen in front of me and tried to forget the woman that plagued my thoughts. The colorful graph had big numbers displayed on it, but none of them explained anything.

"Four times faster than what?" I asked the marketing team.

"Our competitors, sir."

"Which ones? And why are we putting that our microchip is *seven times* more reliable? Based on what?"

They looked between each other before someone gave me an answer. "Well, this is how the companies under Price Investments are presenting their new products. Everyone is doing it now. It's impactful. It looks good and sounds better. No one is really going to ask those questions. We took most of these metrics from studies that were done on our old product and the operating systems of other competitors."

It took everything in me not to grunt at the mention of Price Investments. Just because all other companies followed whatever trend they set didn't mean we had to do it too. Or did they expect me to run a scheming, unscrupulous company too?

"I understand that it's how other companies do it, but we need to be clearer. We're not going to do things because someone else does it. We've always been clear and transparent, and I would like for it to stay that way. Let's reschedule this meeting for next week and you can present another proposal. How does that sound?"

I dismissed the meeting after getting their affirmation.

"Mr. Whitlock," my assistant, Grant, called from the door as the HR team was making their way inside for our meeting. "Your mom would like to talk to you. She says it will only be a couple of minutes."

"Where's my brother? He should be here to lead this meeting," I asked, looking at my watch. The meeting was scheduled to start in five minutes.

"He texted to tell me he would be here on time. What should I tell your mother?"

I grabbed his phone and walked to my office. I could spare Mom a couple of minutes. "Hey, Mom, what's going on?"

Mom's sweet voice came out in a hushed tone, so I knew she was in public. "Thanks for picking up. I know you're busy, but I'm here with the matchmaker and wanted to know if we should add you to the dating list. Have you thought about what I said? Did you talk to Riley? Her mom is really hoping you guys get together, but we don't want to intrude in your relationship." Was this really what she was calling me for?

"Yeah, I thought about Riley. It just won't work out for me, sorry, Mom. I don't want to do this matchmaking thing either. I'll let you know when I'm ready." I was entertaining the idea for less than a minute when Fee popped up in my peripheral and stole all my focus as she walked down the beach and straight to me.

"The company will eat you alive if you just focus on that. Your life will pass you by and it will be too late when you realize you forgot to live it and you're all alone." Mom sighed.

"I know you're worried, Mom, but I will make time for that. I have a meeting to get to and your eldest son isn't here yet, so we both can't be late." I understood family was important, but I still had time to think about it.

"He told me he had something to do this morning," she said. My assistant stood at the door to my office, and I waved him in, grabbing the papers he was offering. I started flipping through them, analyzing the company's quarterly metrics. Everything looked better than last quarter. Mom continued to talk, but I was no longer paying attention. "Don't be too hard on him. He has a lot on his mind right now with the wedding and all. I think he's really excited and nervous, but he's trying to act cool."

"I can imagine," I answered automatically because that sounded like an appropriate response to whatever she was saying. "Sorry, Mom, I have to go. I'll talk to you later."

"Love you."

"Love you too," I said before hanging up and taking care of the meeting of the only department my lazy brother, Elias, was in charge of managing.

By the time Elias arrived, the meeting was already over. "I'm sorry I'm late," he said as he entered the room while the staff was leaving. His white shirt was half tucked into his black pants and his suit jacket looked like it had never seen an iron. How did he manage to get it so wrinkled? The day he wore a tie, I would be impressed.

I sighed and looked at my watch. My next meeting was about to start. "I don't have time to go over everything with you. Meet with the HR manager—and fix your shirt and hair. It looks like it hasn't seen a comb in ages."

Elias chuckled, running his hand over his dark blond hair. He walked behind the chair I was sitting on and wrapped his arm around my neck, swaying from side to side. "It's nice to see you. Feels like I never do anymore."

"Come to work and you'll see me every day," I grumbled, pulling his arm away.

"I already have some plans this week, but I'll be around next month," he said.

"By plans, you mean you have parties to go to?" I asked.

He sighed as if he thought I was about to give him a lecture. "I'm only enjoying myself for now. Once I have kids, I need to be the best parent."

"Kids? I thought you weren't thinking about that anymore. You barely do your own stuff; do you know how much responsibility you require to have a child?" He was a child himself. Why was he even thinking about kids?

"I'm more responsible than you guys give me credit for. Anyway, I'll go talk to the manager and then I'm going to take some toys to the kids at the children's home. Do you want to go with me?" he asked.

I shook my head. "I can't, I have meetings all day."

"Okay, let me know if you want to go to the party. I'll send you the location." He winked at me and walked out the door.

"Don't call me when you wake up drunk with no ride home!" I called after him. He was hopeless.

The managers started walking in and I got ready for my next meeting.

7

LOVE ME ANYWAY

Felicity

The moment I walked through the doors of Kavanagh's house, drugs were offered to me on a silver platter. Benjamin had wanted to come, but there was no way I was letting him near a party like this. Most of the lights were dimmed, and with the loud music, I felt like it was enough to drive me insane. I made my way to the bar—where Levi had already clocked Kavanagh—making sure that my hips and firm steps were enough incentive to get everyone I passed by to notice me.

Women strolled around in bikinis and barely-there dresses—and I fit right in. My rose-gold minidress exposed most of my cleavage and was only held up by a string behind my neck. It was completely backless and so low-cut that it barely covered my ass. According to Benjamin, that was Kavanagh's weakness.

I twirled my hair around my finger while I leaned forward and chuckled at something the bartender said. I was in Kavanagh's line of sight. Although he was surrounded by at least ten women, he'd never taken his eyes off me since I'd sat at the bar ten minutes ago. I had been pretending not to see him, but I was aware of his every move.

Levi was sitting on the other side of the bar since Milton had refused to let me come alone. Levi was my second-in-command and the youngest of all the Israelis. He was a tactical genius, according to Milton. He had short brown hair and penetrating light brown eyes. It didn't help that he had muscles of steel that just made his features sharper. He wasn't much older than me, but his brothers respected him as their leader, and that said a lot.

"Mr. Kavanagh says you'll like this better," the bartender said, leaving a shot in front of me.

I eyed the shot suspiciously. "Where is Mr. Kavanagh?" The bartender pointed at the man in question, who already had his hungry eyes analyzing me. I picked up the drink and winked at him before downing the shot. Kamikaze—my favorite; at least he had good taste. I turned away from him, knowing that would get his attention. He was probably hoping I would go to him, but I had other plans.

Grabbing my clutch, I made my way to the back of the house, where the second staircase was located. Thanks to the blueprints Daniel had given me, I knew every inch of the house. There were guards positioned in the hallways, but as I passed the first set without any issues, I knew they had received a message to back off. I made my way up the stairs and stood in front of the window wall. It didn't take long before I heard someone come up the stairs. A hand landed on my naked back, and I did my best to suppress the shudder. I hated being touched by strangers. Maybe that wasn't accurate anymore, because I didn't mind being touched by Leo at all.

"Did you like the shot?" Kavanagh asked against my ear, interrupting my thoughts.

I shrugged, turning towards him. "I've had better."

His dark eyes searched my face before giving me a grin. I understood his appeal and why women were all around him. He had a defined jaw that I could tell was freshly shaven. The rest of his features were rounder, giving him a baby face. It was odd that his features didn't mask the aura of danger that surrounded him. "I recognized you the moment you walked in." He grabbed my hips as he stood behind me and pushed me against his erection. "Tell me, little Price, to what do I owe this visit?" Moving my hair to the side, he kissed my neck. "Is it business or pleasure?"

It took everything in me not to smash the back of my head against his nose. "A little bit of both," I whispered, pushing deeper into his lean chest.

"Follow me, then." He grabbed my hand and pulled me in the direction of his room. After he unlocked the door, he tried to grab me and push me against it, but I ducked underneath his arm to escape. I made my way to the red couch in front of his bed without giving him a second glance. I didn't fear men like him. Their egos were so inflated that they never expected a woman to know how to defend herself. "What's your choice of drink?" Kavanagh poured himself some whiskey as he looked at me expectantly.

I looked down at his toned body while slowly licking my cherry-red lips. "You." A slow smile appeared on his face at my words.

His almost-black eyes and raven hair promised a night of temptations. Too bad I wasn't into the slimy type. More importantly, I'd never even been with a man. I opened my clutch slowly, hiding it between the couch and my body, and took out a small round patch.

He left his drink on the table in front of us while he practically sat on top of me. "Benjamin said you didn't come to these types of parties. He never wanted to share you with me." His breath fanned my cheek, and his finger followed the trail of the dress from my neck to the valley of my breasts. The way he swallowed while staring at my body made my stomach roil. A thought that hadn't occurred to me earlier but should have came to mind now. Was I expected to be intimate with my future husband? Surely Father didn't expect that... right?

Sex wasn't the only problem. The logical next step after marriage would be kids.

"What is it?" Kavanagh's voice brought me back to reality, and I realized I still had the drug patch between my fingers. I brought my arm around his neck, which he took as an invitation. His lips made their way down my clavicle, and I placed a soft kiss on his neck before I sucked and licked along his spine. I placed the drug patch on the base of his neck, and he was so focused on me that he didn't even notice. The patch adhered to liquid, which broke the thin film that covered it.

His hand cupped my breast, and I leaned my head back, letting out a soft moan. Taking into consideration that he'd been drinking, it should take around seven minutes for the drug to take effect. I had seven minutes of pretending, seven minutes with my thoughts, and seven minutes of my brain going crazy at the realization that my first time would be taken away from me by a fake marriage. Kavanagh's fingers touched my thong, making me jump at his sudden intrusion. He grumbled at me as his hand tried to go back.

"I have to freshen up," I said, pushing against his chest and getting on top of him. Leaning into his ear, I whispered, "When I come back, I want you to fuck me so hard your name is the only one that ever falls from my lips." I jumped out of his lap before he had a chance to grab me.

The bathroom door was open right next to the couch, so I didn't even have to pretend like I didn't know where it was. I closed the door quickly and brought the toilet seat down so I could sit. I pulled my phone from my clutch and dialed the only person I could talk to about this. Jane took her sweet time picking up. "Felicity?" she said in a sleepy voice.

"I have to get married, and married people have sex. I don't know what to do because I don't want to have sex. Well, I do. I really, really want to know what it feels like, but not like this." I did my best to whisper, but as I felt the panic rise, my voice went with it. I didn't even want to think about kids.

"Married? To who? Start from the beginning!" my best friend demanded. She definitely sounded more awake now. I told her the short version of what had happened as fast as I could. "Where are you? Why are you whispering?"

"I'm working, and I have to go back now." Kavanagh hadn't made a sound, so I was hoping he was already zombified. I'd given him just enough of a modified devil's breath to control him but not enough that he wouldn't remember what happened.

"As soon as you get home, come directly to me so we can talk, got it?"

I nodded before realizing she couldn't see me. "I won't be home this week, but I'll call you when I'm done with the job or tomorrow if you're asleep." I hung up on my best friend and personal assistant, feeling better about the situation. There was no need to panic; I always got the job done.

I texted Levi an update before unrolling the contract I had in my clutch and leaving the bathroom. The contract outlined the termination of the partnership between Kavanagh and Benjamin. All I needed was their signatures.

Kavanagh was staring at his hands as he twirled them around, and that was the only indication I needed to know that he was ready. I only used devil's breath when I had to seduce a man. They never took me to court because they remembered signing the contract. The key was making sure they believed they were so blinded by lust that they signed just to have me; none of his friends would remember him being drunk since he'd barely had anything to drink. In reality, the drug made him susceptible to all my commands.

He was my puppet.

I left the agreement on the table before straddling him. He

blinked rapidly as he saw me, like he forgot I was still there. "Do you remember what you promised me?"

He nodded as he opened his mouth, but no words came out. His tongue would be heavy from the drugs, which was a nice side effect, but he'd remember all of his thoughts, thinking he'd actually spoken the words. I responded to all of his grunts like I knew exactly what he was telling me.

"You can do whatever you want to me." I untied the knot behind my neck, letting the dress fall, exposing my breasts. His eyes zeroed in on my nipples, and his mouth immediately searched for them. I let him take me in his mouth while running my hand against his neck. I found the drug patch and took it off. We wouldn't be needing that anymore.

His hands were rough against my waist, but I let him use me a little longer since it would help trick his brain into believing everything he was thinking about really had happened. I stared at the white ceiling, focusing on the blades of the fan. The air from the fan refreshed my skin, and that was all I felt as a stranger's mouth and hands were on me. I felt nothing as his tongue circled my nipple before sucking on it. Maybe this was how sex would be. I could block it out like I did with everything else. How hard could it be? Something told me it would be different with Leo. I shook my head, trying to clear my mind and focus on the job. All that mattered right now was to make sure Benjamin wasn't linked to the mafia, ensuring his reputation was safe.

I hated this part of my job, but Kavanagh would never agree to terminate the contract. I could threaten him, but that would bring more problems, and I needed it to be a clean transaction with no messes to clean up afterward. I never left loose ends, especially when it had to do with Benjamin.

"Baby," I whispered, "will you do something for me?" I pulled on his hair until his unfocused eyes met mine. I sat next to him and discreetly put the drug patch in my clutch before taking out a pen. "Sign this, and you can be with me all night." He stared at the pen but didn't take it. I leaned in and whispered in his ear. "It's a termination of your contract with Benjamin. I promise there's nothing else. After you sign it, I'll take you in my mouth and let you come on my face." I put the pen in his hand and pointed to where he needed to sign. I ran my lips down his shoulders as he signed the termination agreement. "Thank you. Now you can do everything you were thinking about." I let my words settle in his mind, creating another smokescreen for his brain.

I guided him to his bed and took his white polo shirt off. "Take off the rest," I instructed, pulling the covers back while he got naked. When he was done, I pushed him onto the bed until he fell and turned off the lights. "You feel so good. Keep touching me right there," I said, almost laughing at his grunt. I guided his hand to his erection and let him work on himself. "You're the best I've ever had." I waited until his grunts stopped to tell him to sleep. After his breathing evened out, I ruffled the bed and rubbed my lips against the pillows. Then I poured a good amount of the whiskey down the drain. I was happy this was over; doing this type of job was always uncomfortable. I'd rather torture someone until they gave me what I wanted.

I sat on the couch for another thirty minutes in case Kavanagh woke up. The shadows from the lights outside danced against the curtain, creating the monsters I was afraid of as a child. Monsters that Father would always help me slay.

So what if I had to have sex with my future husband? I had a week to find someone I could use on my own terms. If I had to sleep with someone, it would be because I chose them. I wanted my first time to be special, memorable, perfect. I wouldn't let my father or Simon take that away from me. They'd already taken my soul. I wouldn't let them take anything else.

Daniel and David would stay in LA for a couple of days to monitor Kavanagh. The rest of my bodyguards were going back to New York since a couple of pictures of Benjamin going out partying were released. I didn't trust Benjamin to stay clean when he was out with his friends. I sent Benjamin a text reminding him to behave and that I would be home soon. If I had to move to Whitlock and leave Benjamin alone, I would need to hire someone to help him get sober. I'd tried it before, but it had never worked since he always left rehab. This time I would have to leave him no choice.

Milton was waiting for me in the SUV. The moment I got in, I texted Leo.

> Want to go out tomorrow afternoon?

It was already two a.m., so I doubted Leo was awake, but I hadn't been able to stop thinking about him. I wanted to call Jane, but that would have to wait until I slept. My phone vibrated, and I couldn't answer fast enough.

"Hey," I whispered.

"I have a couple of meetings until ten, but I can be available after. What time should I pick you up?" Leo mumbled the words, and his voice sounded groggy.

"I'm sorry, I didn't mean to wake you up," I said. I should have waited to send that message.

"Typically, I wouldn't wake up for a message, but I've been thinking about you all day," he replied. I bit my lip, trying to hold my smile.

I didn't want to keep him on the phone for any longer, so I answered quickly. "Pick me up at noon."

"I'll be there at noon. Sweet dreams, Fee."

"Goodnight, Leo." I hung up and held my phone to my chest. I couldn't wait to see where he took me tomorrow.

8

IT'S YOU

Leo

"The zoo!" Fee exclaimed, jumping out of the car, her eyes shining with joy.

The wind softly blew against her red summer dress, the weather perfect for being outside. I smiled as I watched her look up at the sky. The sun bathed her fair skin, making her radiant like an angel.

"Hurry, hurry. I hear the animals hide."

I quickly texted Milton our location before grabbing her hand and running to the entrance. Dad had had this zoo built five years earlier, and it was well kept. I'd texted the park manager this morning to make sure no one called me by my name or bothered her. Seeing how people reacted to her at the party, I knew she had to be famous. She looked familiar, but I didn't know where I had seen her. Part of me was happy that she didn't want to know my name. Although nothing made me prouder than to be a Whitlock, I wanted to be more than my last name. So I understood why she wanted to keep her identity a secret for now.

The line wasn't long; it only took us ten minutes to get inside and to the first exhibit. I noticed the employees kept their heads down when we passed them. Fee stopped at every exhibit, where she talked to the animals, and I swear they all looked at her like they followed her every word. Some of them even got closer the moment she was near the glass or fence.

"Look!" she told the king cobra, pointing to her snake earrings. I had my arms wrapped around her waist, with my chin resting on the top of her head. The snake nodded in acknowledgment, or at least that was how it looked to me. "Did you see that?" she asked, looking up at me. Her eyes were shining with joy, and I nodded because I did see it. I saw my future in her eyes.

"Do you think she's lonely?" Her eyes lost their light for a fraction of a second before turning hard. It was like she didn't like being sad and completely turned off all of her emotions. It wasn't the first time she'd done it today. I frowned, wanting her joy from earlier to return. Her fingers caressed my frown lines, and I grabbed her hand to give it a kiss; immediately, her eyes lit up again. *What happened to you, Fee?*

I didn't know if it was for my benefit or hers, but I turned her around and crushed her to my chest. "I don't know, but she looks happy to see you," I whispered against her hair.

"You think so? You think I made her happy?" *You're like a ball of fucking sunshine. How could she not be happy?*

Two little boys ran up to the snake, and Fee stepped aside to let them pass. We left the reptile room, and the moment we walked out into the heat, she looked at the sun with tight lips. She followed the path covered by trees without noticing how the men that we walked by were staring at her. One of my male employees licked his lips while staring at her legs. Instinctively, my lip curled up, followed by a low growl. His eyes came up to mine before quickly turning away. Fee's laughter had me looking at her. She pulled her bottom lip between her teeth, trying to hide her smile. I shouldn't have been that possessive, especially knowing she had a fiancé.

Did it count when it was an arranged marriage? She hadn't even met him, and I was going to take advantage of that because I couldn't stop thinking about her all night. I would have been lying to myself if I didn't admit that my hope for today was to confirm that she was meant for me.

Maybe she had decided she didn't want to go through with the wedding. Why else would she give me a chance unless she had doubts? I could have asked her, but that would have been taking it too fast. I used my thumb to pull her bottom lip away from her teeth, then leaned down to suck on it gently. She stopped breathing as soon as my lips touched hers. She tasted as sweet as honey. I grabbed the back of her head with both of my hands and leaned my forehead against hers, staring directly into her siren eyes. They called to me like nothing ever had. I could see the danger lying beneath them, but I wanted to follow her call anyway.

"You're intoxicating."

She took a big breath before saying, "You're very quiet."

I grinned at her random comment. "Does that bother you?"

"No, sorry. I sometimes blurt things out when I'm uncomfortable. Not that you make me uncomfortable. You make me feel incredibly safe. I only talk like this with my friend Jane, so I don't know why I can't stop talking right now. Maybe it's because it's hard to organize my thoughts when I'm around you."

My thumbs gently caressed her pink cheeks, and her arms wrapped around my middle. "Don't be embarrassed. I find you refreshing, and I like hearing you speak. This is the first time I've had a real chance to relax in years, and it's all because of you."

"Why can't you relax?" she asked.

"I'm managing my dad's business until one of my brothers decides to step up. Mom wants him to retire so they can spend more time together. She says she wants to travel around the world before she can't walk anymore."

Concern laced her soft features. "Is she sick?"

"No, she's just overly dramatic." She chuckled, and I pulled her towards a gift shop. "Let's go this way."

I looked around the shop until I found what I was looking for. *Bingo.* She threw her arms around me the moment we stood in front of the hat shelf. "Thank you," she whispered, burying her head in my chest. "No one's ever done anything like this for me. How did you know?" Fuck, I wished she hadn't said that. I took her chin between my thumb and index finger until she met my eyes. There was a smile on her face, but no emotion in her chocolate eyes.

She was hiding . . . again.

"You looked at the sun like you wanted it to freeze. Now go and get whatever you want." Her eyes lit up as if I had told her she'd won a million dollars, not cheap trinkets and clothing. She tried on every single hat, making a pile of the ones she liked and discarding the ones that didn't pass her test. Then she tried on her "like" pile again and repeated the process until she declared she'd found the perfect one. I thought she was done, but then she glided to the other side of the store and repeated the process with scarves.

When she swayed her hips, it wasn't just a walk; it was like she was floating. Which made no sense because she walked with purpose, but it didn't make it less graceful. Everyone in the shop stopped and stared at her, enthralled. That was when it hit me—this was another part of her I hadn't seen yet.

Confident, passionate, determined. She was in her element, and it showed. She laid the final two scarves on the counter and tapped her middle and ring fingers on the wood. When she found the scarf she wanted, she wrapped it around the beige safari hat, ripped away the adjustable string from the hat, and stuck the ends of the scarf inside the grommets.

She put the hat on and tied the ends of the scarf around her neck. "What do you think?" she asked. I thought she was the most beautiful woman I had ever seen, so that was exactly what I said.

"You're the most beautiful woman I've ever seen." There were several grunts and murmurs of agreement behind me. I knew she had a fashion degree, but I'd never thought of fashion as something more than fabric sewn together. But watching how lost she was to the world around her while she worked was mesmerizing.

She chewed on her lip as she stared at me from underneath her eyelashes. I grabbed her hand and pulled her to the cash register because if I didn't, I was going to push her against the wall and kiss her until we were both senseless. Since there were kids around, that didn't seem like a smart choice.

"Can I please have a hat just like hers?" a little girl asked, pointing at Fee's creation while we walked out. The mom shook her head, telling her they couldn't afford it.

"Do you mind if I give it to her?" Fee asked, looking at me with pleading eyes.

Of course I didn't mind, but that didn't seem fair after she'd spent so much time working on it. "Would you prefer if you made one for her? That way, you get to keep yours." She threw her arms around me before going to talk to the little girl's mom. This was a win-win situation; she got to keep her hat, and I got to watch her do everything all over again.

We found a bench hidden in a corner in front of the chimpanzees. Her arm immediately wrapped around me, and I loved how comfortable she seemed to be with me. "Are you close to your family?" I asked. I analyzed every part of our conversations so far. From the little things she said and the way her friend had been scared for her the other night, I already knew her family wasn't good to her.

"When we were kids, we were closer, but after my grandfather died, my father and uncle fought all the time. We didn't see each other much after that. I only saw them at family events where we pretended we were the perfect family." My arms tightened involuntarily. "Amber was always there. She would come over often since she lived next door. We grew up like sisters. Except she had the freedom that I always envied."

So, she was trapped, and now they were forcing her to marry? What kind of family did that? Why was she still with them?

"In college, I was just the boring unapproachable girl with tons of security guards wherever I went. At first, people would invite me places, but after a while, they stopped asking. I don't like people. I can only be sociable for a couple of hours at a time. After that, I stayed in my circle—celebrity friends and other heiresses."

"Have you tried taking back some of that freedom?" I played with her hair to calm myself down. My body was starting to feel tight, and although I understood the feeling, it wasn't something I felt often.

"It's not that easy. My family is . . . complicated," she finally said. I could tell it was hard for her to share this by the way her nails dug painfully into my hip. I didn't think she'd noticed, and I wasn't going to point it out. If this was what she needed, she could draw blood for all I cared. "I'm proud of my family's legacy because it's taken great sacrifice to get us where we are. It's a lot of work and not as easy as people make it seem. Most people think if you give them a million dollars, they could be as good as us, so we're all just nepotism babies, but they miss the point. Anyone in my family could turn a dollar into something. It's not about the money. We're the most powerful family for a reason. Knowledge is the real power. However, I dislike some of our traditions and how cynical they've made us. The pressure that my last name holds is a lot for some to bear. No one wants to fail."

She talked about her family like they were more powerful than the president. I only knew one family that held that much power, and they were all thieves masquerading as investors. I hadn't known her for long, but I knew she couldn't be a Price. My grandma would have reprimanded me for being judgmental toward someone I didn't know, but there were so many rumors about them that it was impossible to ignore. I would never do business with a Price.

"What about your family?" she asked.

"My family is very relaxed, but I've always felt the responsibility of taking care of my brothers and our company. Sometimes I just want to worry about myself and not try to set an example. I feel like if I'm not always perfect, I'll let everyone down," I shared because I wanted her to know that I trusted her too. Her fingers slowly released my hip as she relaxed.

"Do you regret carrying all that weight on your shoulders?" she asked.

"No. It's part of who I am. I don't mind taking care of my family." I wanted her to let me take care of her too. "Did you ever rebel?" I asked. I wanted to know more about her. I wanted to take her pain away to a place where it could never touch her again.

"I sneaked out once with a guy. Guys would ask me on dates, but my father always rejected them, and I could never go out. He would say those boys weren't worthy to date a Price. I got tired one day and snuck out of the house in the back of our maid's car. She didn't notice I was there. I called a taxi and met the guy at a movie theater. When I came back home . . ." She shuddered at the memory, and my body went cold. I could feel her fear. "Let's just say I never tried to date again."

Wait.

Did she say Price?

That was impossible. I couldn't have heard her correctly.

I pulled her chin up and saw the unshed tears.

Fuck!

She looked so innocent.

An entire family couldn't be evil; of course, there had to be some good people around. Did it matter if she was a Price? I needed to decide that right now because if it did, I had to walk away. There was no way I wanted to be involved with Alexander or Simon Price, and if she wasn't the daughter of one of them, she was still related in some way, shape, or form. Was I really about to judge her based on who her father was?

As far as I knew, Alexander Price, who was nicknamed the devil because of his cutthroat way of doing business, had a daughter that rumors said was just as bad as, if not worse than, him. What if Fee was that daughter?

"Did he hurt you?" I tried to keep my tone neutral, but she'd just thrown a fucking bomb at me. My brain and heart were divided. I hated that she was a Price, but I hated even more that I could feel her fear as she shuddered from the memory.

"No," she proclaimed.

"Lie. I can tell when you lie." I wanted to find whoever had touched her and break their arm while they begged her for forgiveness. Fuck! Why was I thinking like this? My chest rose as I took a deep breath. I'd never felt an urge to protect someone like this.

She leaned back and looked into my eyes. "We just met. How could you possibly tell?" *Because I feel like I've known you forever, because you were made for me, and now I don't know what the fuck to do, but I don't want to walk away.*

"Does it feel like we just met?" *I can answer that for you because I know you feel it too. It's a no.*

"No," she whispered.

"Me either," I responded to her unspoken question. Her eyes widened in shock, but I knew what she was thinking. I'd never felt this way before. I felt whole, but now I was also confused. Business and personal life weren't the same thing. I just needed to separate the two.

"What, now you read minds too?" she joked.

I smirked. "Not everyone's, just yours. It's your eyes. They're so expressive and hypnotizing, like they hold the key to all my secrets."

"Would you give me the key to all your secrets?" she asked.

"Yes," I replied with no hesitation. I'd made up my mind. I didn't care if she was a Price. From the way she talked about her family, it seemed like she didn't want to be a part of it. Maybe I was looking at it all wrong. My parents were supportive, but what if they weren't? What if I had grown up in a family like hers that only cared about money? Would I still be the same person? Or would I be fighting every day to find my place among the chaos? The fact that she'd been able to survive in a family like hers and still be as sweet as she was meant that she was a fighter.

"I can't give you false hope," she said.

And there it was—what I liked the most about her. Honesty.

I hated the idea of her marrying someone else, someone who wouldn't give her the freedom she deserved. I was going to save her from her family, no matter the cost.

"I'm sorry, we're supposed to be having fun. I'm not ready to let you go just yet. Do you want to go to my apartment? It's a bit small." The light returned to her eyes, and she nodded in response. "I would take you to my house, but by the time we make it through the door, my housekeeper would have already called Mom to let her know I brought a girl home."

"The apartment is perfect," she agreed with a soft smile playing on her lips.

Our fingers were interlaced as we made our way to the car. I didn't know if I should ask her, because what if it made me feel differently about her? But fuck it, I needed to know. "Which Price are you the daughter of?" I kept walking casually, like the answer didn't matter. Her head snapped toward me, and she almost tripped. I knew the answer before she even said the name.

"Alexander," she murmured.

I nodded while keeping my gaze locked toward the exit.

Well, fuck, she was the devil's daughter.

I waited for my need to be close to her to disappear, but the feeling didn't come. I guess the answer didn't matter after all. I wanted her just as much as when I first saw her.

She was mine.

Before I got in the car, my drunk brother called, asking for help. I turned to look at Fee and sighed. Between spending more time with Fee and my brother, I knew who I wanted to be with, but since I couldn't leave him stranded, I took Fee home, cutting our date way too short. I really wanted to punch him.

9

LLYLM

Felicity

My phone dinged with a message from Leo, and I jumped slightly at the unexpected sound. I had barely gotten any sleep, instead dealing with Benjamin's indiscretion, so my body was tired. I was seriously considering locking him up underground so he could never go to another party.

LEO

Sorry about yesterday, I just finished helping my brother.

I had a great time. Do you want to hang out this afternoon? Let's have a do-over as if our time never ended.

I had a good time too. Today works, but are you okay with something more relaxed? I'm not in a sociable mood, but I want to spend time with you.

Glad you said it, 'cause I feel the same way. I'll pick you up at 2 p.m. and we can stay at my apartment, deal?

Deal!

He picked me up right on time. The moment I walked down the stairs, he held me to his chest and took a deep breath against my hair. It was as if he needed to hug me, so I held on to him just as hard. When a couple of seconds had passed, he whispered, "You ready?"

I nodded against his chest although I wasn't ready to let go.

Leo's apartment was in a modest neighborhood. It looked like a bachelor pad with only the essentials. From what I could see, he had two bedrooms, one bathroom, a kitchen, and a dining/living room area. It felt cozy, like a home. I could tell he had money, so I was surprised that he didn't live in an extravagant house. New money families tended to be flashy, which, in my eyes, was just tacky. The only thing on the wall was a frame with a Cubs T-shirt. As part owner of the best team in New York, I would have liked to object to that.

"Water?" he offered.

"Yes, please." His apartment smelled delicious, and the table was set for two. "Did you cook this, or did you order it?"

"If I'm inviting you to my place, I'm cooking. I hope you like it. This is Grandma's recipe." He pointed to the kitchen island and said, "Take a seat. You get to watch me cook. I didn't want it to be soggy."

I practically jumped on the kitchen island chair and leaned my chin on my hands as I watched him expertly fill circles of dough with the meat he must have prepared before he'd picked me up. Then he wetted the edges and folded the dough into a half-moon shape. He finished by pressing the dough together with a fork and throwing me a wink. Clearly he knew his way around the kitchen, because the moment those turnovers entered the piping-hot oil, I would have run away screaming. He stayed calm while he smiled at me and talked about learning how to cook from his mom and grandma. The way his eyes lit up and his body vibrated in excitement made me feel like I was right next to him, experiencing exactly what he did.

"Do you need help with anything?" I asked, since all I had been doing was sitting there while he did the cooking and the talking. Somehow he knew I didn't want to talk, so he did it for me, and I knew from the past two days we had been together that he didn't talk much.

He nodded. "Can you please take out the sauces and salad from the fridge? It's the three bowls right next to the sour cream. I made passion fruit juice if you want to take that out as well. There's ice in the freezer. These are done, so I hope you're ready to eat."

"With how good everything smells, I'm dying to eat!"

The empanadas were a beautiful golden brown, and the salad was a great addition to not make me feel bad for eating something fried. He should definitely bottle the chimichurri and pink sauce. Even the passion fruit juice was perfectly tart while still having a bit of sweetness to help refresh the palate.

"You should have been a professional chef," I said as I moaned before taking another bite of the fried goodness. This recipe reminded me of my nanny Ana; his family was probably Hispanic, which would make sense since he did have Hispanic features.

"Happy you liked it." His lips twitched, and I really liked that. Not many people had a genuine smile when they saw me.

"Is this where you bring all your conquests?" I asked with a smirk.

We were done eating, and I was helping him set up the dishwasher.

"No." He grinned. "This apartment has been mine since my

grandparents died a couple of years ago, but aside from my family, you're the only other person I've ever brought here."

"Why?"

"Privacy. It's my favorite place, and I don't want anyone to know about it," he said. I had one more of his secrets that I got to keep. "It's a reminder of where we came from and how far we've come. I never want to forget the lessons Grandpa taught me." Pulling me to the couch, he sat down but deposited me on his lap instead of letting me sit next to him. Wrapping my arms around his shoulders, I enjoyed the proximity.

This felt right.

"Would you tell me more about your family?" I requested gently, hoping it wasn't a boundary I shouldn't cross.

"My grandfather was the eldest of three brothers. They were very close, like my brothers and me. After they lost their parents to a warehouse fire when they were young, my grandpa took over caring for the family. He was barely seventeen but had been working for years. He begged for jobs everywhere. He was dedicated, and because of that, he started doing housework for prominent families. That's how he caught Grandma's eye."

The way he looked so deeply into my eyes made me forget how to breathe for a good minute; it was soft and tender.

"You remind me of her," he said.

I didn't know what to say, so I didn't say anything.

"She was strong-willed and fierce. Made him work harder just to push him, but he never complained. He quickly got promoted to oversee the entire estate, and when he did, he went for my grandma." Leo took my lips in a slow kiss before continuing. I brought my hand to his neck, enjoying the feel of his skin against my fingers.

"He told her she had two choices: live a life with him where she would have love but nothing more, or marry someone where she might get everything but not all the love he could give her.

She already knew what she wanted before he asked. She was just waiting for him to choose her too."

I snuggled into his neck and placed a soft kiss there as I whispered, "What happened next?"

"Her father loved Grandpa, so he didn't object. They got married shortly after. Ultimately, they got more than they had ever dreamed of. Although Nana always said all she wanted was him."

There was love and admiration in his voice.

"They seem like a great love story." I wondered what it felt like to come from a family with so much love. Maybe that was why he was so gentle.

"They were. My parents love each other, but what my grandparents had was different. It was a love that was so pure that it was almost tangible. Growing up watching them made me wonder if I could ever have what they had."

Maybe we could. Where did that come from? Pushing that thought to the back of my head and needing space from him, I got up. "Show me your bedroom."

"Is that an offer?" He wiggled his eyebrows. I laughed, but I didn't respond.

He grabbed my hand and guided me to his bedroom. He had a queen-sized bed in the middle, a nightstand on the right, and a dresser at the foot of the bed. There was a small walk-in closet and another bathroom. It looked clean, and there weren't a lot of products. Shaving cream, deodorant, and lotion. That was it. I left the bathroom and saw Leo sitting on his bed. I walked towards him, and he opened his legs to make room for me. He wrapped his arm around me, and I leaned into him. There was something that made him so addicting, like this was exactly where I should be.

I took a step back, and I didn't know what possessed me to be so bold, but I pulled off his shirt and threw it on the dresser. His eyes were so aware of my every move that they took my breath away. I had never been one to feel remorse for my sins, so I wouldn't start now.

"Hazel." He looked at me, waiting for me to clarify. "Your eyes. I thought they were green, but they're hazel."

I moved my hands to his belt, and thank God they weren't shaking. The heat from his eyes ignited something within me as I unbuckled it. He reached for me, but before he could touch me, he lowered his hands and turned them into fists. I unbuttoned his jeans and pulled the zipper down. He hissed, and I stopped to look at him, thinking I'd hurt him.

He shook his head.

I knelt on the floor and took off his boots next. I put my hands on his jeans in a silent request. He lifted himself up slightly, allowing me to take them off.

He was gorgeous. I was toned, but he was chiseled, and was that an eight-pack? You could see how much work he put into those arms and shoulders, which were definitely my favorite part of his body. His skin was a dark bronze with faint tan lines. His jaw was currently held so tight that I feared it would snap. I wondered where his family was from. He looked like he was of Mexican descent. Maybe South America, but he didn't look Caribbean. I wanted to ask, but I pushed my curiosity away. This wasn't about his family but about getting to know him as a person.

Elias, my future husband, was part Puerto Rican on his mother's side, which was one of the good things about him. I was familiar with the culture since my nanny was also from the island.

Leo's hands took me away from my thoughts when they touched the hem of my shirt. I lifted my arms up so he could pull it off. He looked at me with appreciation, and I couldn't help but blush. Training with Milton every day since I was young had its benefits. He kissed my stomach softly, making my skin tingle, before he took off my sneakers. He grabbed the hem of my jean shorts and looked at me as if asking for permission.

I nodded, although a feeling of uncertainty swept in. What if I wasn't ready for this? Was this pushing it too far?

He waited a couple of seconds before slowly peeling them off. I was standing before him with only a peach thong and a matching bralette, while he was in his boxer briefs.

Grabbing me and putting me right in the middle of the bed, he came toward me like a lion toward its prey. I should have felt vulnerable, but I didn't. I felt powerful. I'd always wanted to know what this felt like, and I finally got to experience it with someone I chose, not a man I was forced to marry or another Kavanagh.

His body was on top of mine, but he was careful to keep his full weight off me. "Are you sure this is okay?"

"Yes," I whispered. This was what I needed.

He kissed my forehead, nose, jaw, and then my lips. I gasped at the sensation running through my body and opened up for him. It had never felt like this before. Even if I wanted to block the feeling of his touch, I wouldn't be able to. His tongue was demanding, asking for all I had. My nails ran up his arms until I got to his shoulders. His hand found my hard nipple, and I moaned into his mouth.

Yes, I wanted more.

He kissed me harder, exploring my mouth and letting me explore him. I opened my legs and wrapped them around him, feeling the pressure build between my thighs. He ended the kiss but immediately found my nipple. Oh my God, I didn't know it could feel this good. He alternated between them, making my entire body tight. Reaching behind me, he unclasped the bralette, throwing it somewhere before his mouth was back on me. My body was in tune with every touch and every kiss he pressed on my skin. I didn't let the noises I was making embarrass me. I couldn't hold them in.

The next thing I knew, his lips were traveling down my stomach, and he stopped right on top of my most intimate area. His lustful eyes fell into mine, and I nodded. My nails dug into the palms of my hands as he kissed my thighs tenderly. I didn't know what to do. What if I sucked? I'd watched porn, but I'd read that it wasn't the same as the real thing.

He took my thong off but never took his eyes off mine; my chest was rising and falling rapidly, watching his hungry eyes. "Trust me," he whispered right before his tongue came out and started licking me. He growled and held my legs, pulling me closer to his face.

"Oh, God." My legs were already shaking, and I could feel my orgasm right at the tip of my fingers. "Leo, that feels so good. Don't stop," I whimpered.

"Fuck, you taste so fucking good," he said before continuing his assault.

"I'm going to come." I chanted his name, begging for something—I didn't know what. I just knew I needed to beg. I never wanted this to end.

He kept licking and sucking on my clit until I yelled in ecstasy. My legs were trying to close, but he held me down and kept eating me until I stopped shaking. I blindly reached for him, and he was there. He kissed me, and I deepened the kiss, tasting myself in his mouth. My hands were trying to find his underwear, and once I finally found his erection, he groaned in my mouth.

"Teach me," I whispered.

"This is going to be fast." Grabbing my hand, he showed me what he liked. He kept kissing me while we worked on his length. After a couple of minutes, his body tensed, and I looked down to see the white cream falling on his abs. I wanted to lean down and taste him, but I didn't want him to think I was weird. Leo stared into my eyes and gave me one last kiss.

"That was . . . wow." I didn't know what else to say. I hoped he liked it as much as I did.

"You're the sweetest fruit I've ever tasted."

Before I could answer, he got up and carried me to the bathroom, bridal style. My nerves were gone as we showered together. His hands roamed my body gently as he scrubbed my skin, leaving kisses behind every so often. Once he was done, I did the same for him. We lay on his bed, and I waited for him to send a text message before settling into his chest and closing my eyes.

Would it feel like this with Elias? Would he make goose bumps form everywhere he touched?

If this was what being with someone should always feel like, no wonder everyone loved it so much.

I yawned softly, tired from my sleepless night.

"Sleep," Leo told me. "I set the alarm for nine." He turned off the lights, and I did just that.

10

LOVE YOU IN MY MIND

Felicity

*L*eo's best friend called to remind him about the party he had promised to attend tonight. I didn't want to accept the invitation, but I wasn't ready to go home. I was nervous because these were his friends. I'd never been a people person, but I knew how to win them over if I wanted to. This was different. I had made a persona for him. I didn't know how to fake my way through a situation like this while I wasn't myself.

I got lost in Leo's soothing touch as he caressed my hand. My body relaxed when I focused only on him.

I looked at the dashboard, and it was a little past eight.

"Milton!" I gasped. I'd completely forgotten about updating him. I quickly dialed his number and got an answer on the first ring.

"Princess," he said.

"Milton, I'm sorry I forgot to call you. We left Leo's apartment, and we're going to an arcade now." I was twenty-four and financially independent, yet I still had to report my whereabouts as if I were thirteen.

"I forgot to tell you, but Leo texts me every time you guys are leaving a place and again when you arrive."

I looked at him. His face was only lit up by the streetlights. That was why he was texting every time we got somewhere. He was making sure I was safe. I squeezed his hand in a silent thank-you, and he squeezed it back.

"Are you still there?" Milton asked.

I blinked rapidly and took my eyes off Leo. "Yeah, sorry, I got distracted."

"Remember what I taught you and stay safe. Call me right away if you need anything." He sounded tired. I made a mental note to get home early so he could get some sleep.

"I'll make sure to be there by twelve," I said.

"Don't worry about me," Milton said gently. "Just focus on having fun."

I disconnected the call just as Leo pulled up in the arcade parking lot. Leo grabbed my hand as we walked toward the entrance.

"Wait," I said, stopping abruptly just before he opened the door. "What are the names of the people that are attending?" I should have asked this question before I'd accepted. I'd been so focused on myself this week that I'd completely forgotten about Elias.

Leo gave me a confused look, but he answered anyway. "Mike, Ryan, Myriam . . ."

Once he was done naming everyone he could remember, I sighed in relief.

"The place is closed tonight, so it'll only be a small group. They'll love you," he said, whispering the last part before opening the door. I nodded, happy that he believed that but not confident that it would actually be like that.

As soon as I passed the door, Leo slapped my ass. I turned around, shocked, and hit his hand away. I burst out laughing when I saw his grin. "You seemed nervous." He pulled me to him and kissed me, which made it sloppy because we were both laughing.

"Holy shit," someone behind us said.

At least twenty pairs of eyes were on us. Some were looking at Leo, others at me. Most of them had their mouths wide open.

"Felicity Fucking Price!" Michael Wright, a guy who was in my class, yelled. We did our master's program together, and he was the only one I would seek out for any team projects since he never pushed me to talk about personal stuff. Leo's hand came to my waist possessively. "Well, don't just stand there. Come over and say hi," Michael said. Leo pulled me with him, and I grabbed his hand way too tight, but he didn't complain.

Leo and Michael hugged with big grins as they greeted each other. People went back to bowling or playing other arcade games, but I could feel their eyes on me. The space was intimate, decorated with bright neon lights and dark carpets. There were eight bowling lanes, but only some of them were occupied. Leo was correct; there were a maximum of thirty people in here.

Leo brought me closer to him, but before he spoke, Michael talked again. "I never thought I would see the devil's daughter laughing." He had a big grin on his face. My body tensed as he used the name people had given me. I looked at Leo from the corner of my eye, but he didn't seem to recognize the name. Maybe his lack of reaction at the zoo meant that he already knew who I was, but why hadn't he told me? Did he not care? His thumb caressed my hand, and I realized he'd probably noticed my change. I forced myself to relax and ignore the need to leave.

"I guess miracles do happen," I murmured.

Michael pulled me to him and gave me a big hug. While I was surrounded by a six-feet-one man built like a lineman, I tightened my death grip on Leo.

"I heard you were engaged to a mystery man. I'm happy you found someone like Polo. You guys will be good for each other." I was about to tell him that Leo wasn't the man I was engaged to but stopped myself before I could say something. How exactly was I going to explain that I was with someone who wasn't my fiancé? "I'm surprised Polo actually came without his laptop, which is most likely thanks to you, so thank you." I nodded, a little confused by his words since I hadn't seen Leo work at all today.

Mike introduced me to his friends, and although the girls looked nervous, they practically threw themselves at me, barely able to contain their excitement. The men kept their hugs to themselves as Leo towered over me with both hands on my waist.

I breathed a sigh of relief when Michael, aka Mike, pulled us towards his bowling lane and motioned us to sit. I could still feel everyone's eyes on us without having to look around. Leaning into Leo's ear, I whispered, "I'll be right back. I need to go to the ladies' room." He nodded and pointed toward the direction of the bathrooms.

The bathrooms were on the left side of the hall, but instead of going in, I made my way to the exit door at the end of the hall. I didn't see an alarm on the door, so I opened it and welcomed the fresh air. I turned the doorknob and made sure I could get back in before closing it. The dark alley smelled terrible since the garbage had clearly been sitting there for the last couple of days, but the silence was welcome.

Leo already knew who I was. I knew that was why he didn't turn to look at me. Did that mean he didn't care or that he'd never heard rumors about me? Hopefully, it was the first one because out of everyone, I didn't want him to think less of me. I cleaned my clammy hands on my shirt; there was nothing to be worried about. If he had a problem with me, I was sure he would have already ditched me. We were just getting to know each other, nothing serious.

I took a step forward when I heard the door open behind me, but before I could turn around to see who was joining me, I was slammed against the wall face first while a man's body kept me in place. A jolt of electricity rushed through my body in excitement. "The devil's daughter," he whispered against my cheek. I could smell the alcohol on his breath and stayed still.

"Do I know you?" I asked.

"Do you know me?" He chuckled dryly as he brought his hand around my neck. "You ruined my family, you fucking bitch!" His scream echoed against my ear, making it ring.

I let out a small laugh. Did he know how many families hated me? He needed to be more specific than that. He gave himself enough space to turn me around and smash my back against the wall. He squeezed my throat as he growled in anger. I smiled at him, watching his bared teeth and big, dark eyes. There was enough light to make out some of his features, but I didn't recognize him. I leaned my head back, trying to get more air.

"It's not so funny now, is it?" His other hand painfully squeezed my waist as he leaned close to me, making the alcohol smell more pungent. "Do you remember John Martin? He's my father. You took everything away from him. Now he's in prison."

I knew exactly who he was talking about. I remembered all the jobs I'd done, and I failed to see how this was my fault. John Martin was an entrepreneur from Nevada who had gone to Simon asking for money. He'd promised he would pay within five years, but Simon never saw a penny of that money. I was called in to collect it, but he refused, leaving me no choice. I took every penny he had and forced his company out of business. I didn't know what he did to land in jail, but that had nothing to do with me. Don't borrow money you can't pay back.

Typically, these little run-ins made my life more exciting, but I didn't have time to play this game. "Let me go, and I won't break your hand," I rasped. It was getting harder to breathe, and I didn't want Leo to come looking for me. He squeezed harder, and I'd had enough of this. Grabbing his arm with both of my hands, I twisted my body away from him, which caused him to loosen his hold. Before he could react, I brought my elbow up and slammed it underneath his jaw. He fell back and tripped, banging his head hard on the asphalt. Just then, a group of loud guys opened the door and looked around when they noticed us.

"Is everything okay?" one of them asked.

"Yes," I responded. "I think he's drunk. He was slurring his words and fell. He was complaining about something, but I couldn't understand him." My attacker groaned and mumbled something incoherent.

"Shit, we'll get him home," the guy said.

I thanked him and made my way inside. As soon as the door closed, I leaned against the wall and took a deep breath. That was close. I didn't need Leo's friends looking at me like I was a victim. I checked myself in the bathroom before going back to Leo. The moment his eyes landed on me, a smile broke across his face, and I couldn't help but mirror it. Whatever happened in the back alley was over, and he didn't need to know.

There was plenty of seating space, but Leo pulled me to his lap, and I didn't object. I put one arm around his neck and rested my head on his shoulder. The guys talked about sports and we did some bowling before leaving at midnight.

Leo opened the car door for me as we got to my house. I quietly got out of the car. *Would it be dangerous if I invited him to stay the night?*

"I had a great day today. Thank you," I said, leaning on the car and stretching my hand, gesturing for him to come closer. He stood in front of me but didn't touch me.

"I feel like if I touch you, I won't be able to take my hands off you," he murmured.

I felt the same way.

"I can't remember the last time I had this much fun," he said, looking so deeply into my eyes that I swore he could see directly into my soul. Against my better judgment, I raised my hand to his jaw, feeling his five o'clock shadow before moving it to the back of his neck and pulling him to me.

He placed his palms on the car but made sure that the rest of his body wasn't touching me. Our lips touched, and I saw the sparks. He lost whatever internal battle he was having and forcefully grabbed my hair in one hand and wrapped his other arm around my waist. I let my fingers disappear into his soft hair and pulled him closer to me. He sucked my tongue into his mouth, making me moan. When he let it go, I gently pulled his bottom lip between my teeth. The moment I released it, his lips were back on mine. There was no space between us, and I didn't want there to be any. I wanted to stay right there forever. I felt the way my blood was flowing through my veins, and my ears could only hear the thump of my heart and our ragged breathing. Something I had never felt before touched every corner of my body; it was warm and tingly and magical. I didn't know if he felt it too, but we both slowed down and opened our eyes.

"Leo," I whispered against his lips.

"Yeah?" His soft voice made me want to hold him close and never let him go.

"Is it crazy—what I'm feeling?" My words came out shaky. I didn't think it was normal to feel this much in just a couple of days.

"I don't know, but I'm right there with you." He kissed me softly and took a step back.

That small step felt like a mile.

I wished he hadn't taken that step.

I wished this day would never end because when it did, I had to go back to my reality, and there were so many things I still wanted to try. I couldn't hold on to him. He was too good for me, and it wasn't fair that I was using him, even if he was the perfect man to be my first. He deserved someone who could commit to him and cherish his kindness.

"I know you have other commitments, but text me or call if you want to talk, 'kay? By that, I mean text me and call me."

"Leo . . ."

"Fee . . ."

"I can't go against my father. Besides, we just met. Let's just stay friends, okay?" Something about that statement made my heart clench. *You just like him because he's a choice you made.* Somehow, I knew that wasn't true. There was something different about him. He was calm but firm. He carried himself with confidence, but not arrogance. Behind those beautiful eyes, there was a hint of his dominant side that sometimes came out, but I could tell he was trying to keep it hidden. I wondered if he knew that was his weakness—being too good.

"Is that what you want?" His eyes were so intense, they almost looked gold.

"No. But I don't have another choice," I breathed out.

"I could talk to your father about us and see where it goes."

I almost laughed in his face like a maniac. If he only knew the consequences of that, he would have never suggested it. The least he would have done to me for disobeying was a couple of days of torture, and that was if I got lucky.

I didn't know if it was because I had to get married and I'd never really given it much thought before, but I wanted him. If I had to marry someone, I wanted it to be him. He made me feel things I'd never thought I could, and what was worse was that I was letting him. He passed through my walls like there was a door that was left open just for him.

I was sure it wasn't love, but it was the sweet promise of it.

You weighed all your options when deciding to go into a business transaction. I could be the wife he needed. I understood the sacrifices. The chemistry was there. I wouldn't be just a trophy wife. I brought a lot to the table. He was attractive. I was attractive, so we would be considered a good couple in the eyes of society. I could make him so much money that he wouldn't want to get rid of me. He could learn to love someone like me.

To follow the rules.

Before I could stop myself, the words rushed out. "If maybe

you could wait for me a couple of years until I get divorced and, and—" And what? How did I even finish that sentence?

Leo took another step back as his mouth fell open. "Are you really asking me to wait for you until you get a divorce?"

"I know it sounds bad, but I like you. I don't want to let you go. I just need a couple of years to get out of my family's claws." To find a way to reclaim my position as the heir. Once that happened, I could choose whoever I wanted.

"Felicity, I'm not going to be waiting for a married woman. Do you realize how insane that sounds?"

Of course I knew how insane it sounded. I had nothing on Simon. Becoming the heir was next to impossible, but I didn't want to let Leo go. There had to be something I could do. I just needed time to figure it out.

"If you do get married, I hope you're both happy and there's never a need for a divorce. Now if you decide that you want to give us a chance and not get married, I'm only a call away," he said as he closed the distance between us, and his hands caressed my arms.

I averted my gaze to the ground, not wanting to see if the way he looked at me was different. I liked that he always seemed happy to be with me; I didn't want to see his disappointment.

"Okay," I whispered. "Drive safely."

I rushed inside the house to avoid any more of this conversation. He called out for me, but I ignored him. I leaned against the doors and slowly fell to the floor. What was I thinking when I asked him that? He just made me feel so alive that letting him go felt almost impossible.

I needed to remember who I was.

In a couple of days, I would be meeting my future husband. Just the thought made me want to throw up. *Get it together, Felicity.* "The reputation of one is the reputation of all," I chanted.

You get the job done, always.

11

I HEAR A SYMPHONY

Leo

There was a knock on my office door. I looked up to find Dad walking in with takeout bags. I was surprised to see him since I had felt like he was avoiding me. I don't know why. It was just an irrational feeling. He was barely at the office these days since he was working from home. "Grant said you hadn't eaten, so I stopped by your favorite restaurant and got us some pupusas," he said with a soft smile. I was a carbon copy of Dad. The same hazel eyes, light brown hair and strong jaw. The only thing I got from my mother was a tad more melanin and some Hispanic facial features.

"Thanks, Dad, you can start eating," I said as I looked back at the email I was typing. Dad put the food on the rectangular table to my left and started taking it out.

"Come eat before it gets cold. Work can wait."

"I still have two emails to send and—" I stopped talking when Dad suddenly grabbed my chair and rolled me to the table. I laughed at him, but what was I going to do? "Fine, I'll eat. Not that I have another choice."

He sat down next to me and motioned for me to start eating. I grabbed the pupusa and took a big bite. The cheese and shrimp combination was delicious. "Listen to your dad, you need to take breaks. You mom is already on me, saying I'm killing you with so much work. What will she say if she knows you're also not eating?"

I nodded since my mouth was full.

"How's your company doing?" he asked.

"Busy. We had to turn down some business until we hire more staff. I'm scared that we're growing too fast, so I decided not to take on any new clients. I have a major bank that we had already discussed a partnership with, but we haven't met yet. If we work with them, it will be a great opportunity." I took a sip of lemonade before I ate another pupusa. Dad looked at me with smiling eyes. "What?"

"Nothing, I'm just proud of you," he said. There was nothing better than hearing those words from Dad. He had always been the most supportive person in my corner no matter what I decided to do. I had the best parents. "I heard the marketing team didn't like that you had them change their entire proposal."

Did they really have to go and complain to Dad about it? "Yeah, they thought it was okay to say our chip was I don't know how many times faster than an old irrelevant model from years ago," I said.

"Don't be too hard on them. They need to follow the new marketing trends too."

"Yes, but they also need to be clear with our customers," I pointed out.

"I know, just don't be too stubborn. You need to learn when to let certain things go," he said.

"I do know, don't worry." Dad gave me a look but didn't say anything. "I'll give you an update when I get back from Florida like I promised." I didn't think that was being stubborn. Things needed to be done correctly. "Everything okay with you?"

There was a slight tension in his eyes at my question, but he immediately hid it. "Everything is great," he said with a grin. I could tell he was lying, but I knew he would tell me when he was ready, so I let it go. See? I could let certain things go. "You're still going to Florida this week, right?"

"Yes, I have some meetings I can't miss."

"Good," he said absently.

We finished eating and I threw the trash away. Dad went back to his office and without anything to distract me, my mind wandered to Fee. I had done a good job of trying not to think about her by keeping myself buried in work. I tried to reach out this morning via text but after her "I'll be busy" response, I got the hint that she didn't want to speak with me. I didn't want to admit that I'd been thinking about waiting for a married woman. I understood that it wasn't morally acceptable to be rooting for a marriage to fail, but I was falling for Felicity Price. I hated the lucky bastard who was going to marry her. Why did she have to be in an arranged marriage? What evil and archaic people decided this? I hated the Prices and her fiancé's family.

When it came to who she'd marry, I'd already put two and two together. Karl Rothschild was the only person in Whitlock able to match a Price. I'd met him once during a charity event that he'd organized, and he'd spent all night bragging about the donation he made to the children's home. I didn't see how he and Fee would work. She needed someone who let her be herself; she wasn't another trophy for him to display as his newest toy. She was independent and full of life; all she needed was someone to help her spread her wings and let her fly.

Maybe I should tell her I'd made a mistake, and I would wait for her. What was a couple of years? I could wait a couple of years. But what if she fell in love with him and I was waiting like an idiot? Why was this so complicated? I just wanted to make her happy, but she wasn't mine to make happy.

COULD YOU LOVE ME WHILE I HATE MYSELF?

Felicity

"Hold!" Amber yelled at me while doing a victory dance. She threw her tennis racket and caught it while wiggling her ass. "Damn, you're sucking today."

I had woken up yesterday to a good morning text from Leo, but I had just replied back with *I'll be busy*. I didn't know how to address him. I'd been trying to figure out what to say. It's not like I could say "Just kidding!" Telling him I was busy wasn't a lie; I had sketched all day. It was rare that I got a chance to lose myself in my designs.

I was scared of what I felt when I was with Leo. It wasn't normal to trust someone like I trusted him. The way I'd talked to him about my family and feelings wasn't right. I shouldn't feel comfortable telling him about those things. I shouldn't feel comforted when he held me in his arms like he was trying to protect me from the world. I didn't need protection, but it felt good to be wrapped around him, especially while I slept.

"Let's go for brunch," I called out.

I cleaned my sweaty palms on my purple-printed skirt. I had

paired it with a lilac sports bra. Amber was wearing a white dress with a mesh back.

"How are you holding up?" she murmured. She linked her arm with mine while we walked toward the bathroom to wash our hands.

The answer to that was . . . confused. "I don't know. I miss him, but my future is planned. It's just stupid to get my hopes up. I'll probably talk to him tonight and see how he feels."

"Maybe something will change." I knew she was trying to be a good friend, but I couldn't allow myself to believe in lies. Father was hell-bent on unifying forces with the Whitlocks. My family controlled most of the politicians in the east and south of the country; now they wanted to form ties with the Whitlocks to gain more allies on the West Coast. Father would never walk away from that kind of power, even if it cost the happiness of his only daughter. Although I felt like there was something else he wasn't telling me.

"Maybe," I responded. Maybe Elias would refuse to get married.

We entered the restaurant, and the hostess took us to a table close to the windows. I looked at the menu but didn't have an appetite for anything. Amber talked about her birthday party on Friday. Apparently, she had invited all the heiresses and models she could find because there would be over two hundred and fifty guests.

"Who are the prominent families in the city?" I asked. Her eyes went wide as she played with the collar of her dress. "I was cross-referencing the people that do business in Florida and Whitlock. I haven't worked with any families here, so they haven't been on my radar, but I should know his family." Amber continued to stare at me with tight lips. "One of the Bass grand-children recently entered the Florida market. Is he a Bass?"

"You said you didn't want to know who he was. Are you sure you want me to tell you?" she mumbled.

"Tell me the names of the families."

"We have the Whitlocks." I didn't want to be reminded of them. "Medicis, Johnsons—the cleaning Johnsons, not the textile ones. Mountbattens, Pritzkers, Rothschilds, and the up-and-coming Ortiz family. No one knows much about them."

"You have an actual Rothschild living here? What do they do?" I felt like a rookie. I should have done my research before coming here. Leo couldn't be a Rothschild; he had no German features. All the important Johnsons were married, and he had to be from a Hispanic family. His family was new to wealth, so he must be an Ortiz since, except for the Whitlocks, the other families had been around for several generations.

Suddenly, a laugh cut through the dining room, and my eyes immediately searched for it.

I knew that laugh.

I had been dreaming about it for two days.

The hostess was walking him and a girl who'd just nudged his shoulder to a table. The girl had wavy auburn locks and fair skin. She was wearing no makeup, and she still looked stunning. She had on a basic white tennis skirt outfit and was laughing with him with stars in her eyes. Because why would she not? He was gorgeous and sweet.

Leo's eyes met mine, and he stopped walking. The hostess asked him something, but he didn't respond. He was just staring at me. The girl beside him frowned and looked at him. He turned to the hostess and motioned to our table.

Oh, hell no, was he already on a date? He better not come here, especially not with that woman in his arms. I felt red-hot jealousy flowing through my veins. She wasn't technically in his arms, but that was how my mind was looking at it. Amber stopped talking, turning around to see what grabbed my attention. They made it to our table, but he was just staring at me, not saying a word.

"Hi." The girl next to him spoke first. I didn't respond. I

would win this staring contest. I heard Amber mutter a hello. He crouched and was suddenly right in my face. My heart stopped, and my breath caught, but I tried hard not to let him notice.

"Can we sit here?" he asked.

Ha! I win. I wasn't sure why I made this into a contest, but it was helping me not lose it right now.

"There are no seats available," I said slowly, my words laced with venom. Hopefully, he caught it. The bastard just smirked at me.

"Are you still trying to hide from me?" he asked with the smirk firmly in place.

"I'm not hiding," I deadpanned. He looked at my ponytail and frowned. Leaning forward, he took the tie out of my hair and passed a hand through it. As soon as his scent hit me, warmth filled my body, making me squeeze my legs together.

"Much better," he whispered.

Before I could protest, his lips landed on mine, and my treacherous body responded. I grabbed the back of his head and pulled him to me. The fresh taste of his mouth was more addicting than I remembered. Amber murmured something under her breath, which reminded me we weren't alone. I broke the kiss, and dear Lord, I couldn't be near this man.

"We're in public," I told him with a shaky breath.

"And?" He gave me a sweet peck on the lips before talking to the hostess. "Please join another table with this one and make sure you let everyone know that they should not address me by my name." He winked at me, and if I was an ice cube, I would have melted right there.

"Of course, right away, sir." The hostess waved a hand at some servers, and they connected another table to ours. Leo sat next to me and grabbed my hand. The girl sat next to Amber.

"Why are you here?" I asked him.

"Because I'm hungry."

I rolled my eyes at him. "You know what I mean. Why are you sitting here?"

"I walk in and see my girl staring daggers at me and Cassandra, who's my cousin, by the way." He motioned to the girl, and she waved at me. Her hand shook as if she was trying to contain her emotions; she was probably a fan. Being the face of the family and being involved with major fashion brands gave me more recognition than I wanted sometimes. It was always weird to see someone look at you in awe. I gave her a soft smile. "So, I came over before you get the wrong idea. Meanwhile, I'm thanking all the stars that you're here because you've been ignoring me, which has been driving me crazy." His girl?

"I wasn't ignoring you. I was just taking a slight break to clear my head." I didn't owe him an explanation, so why was I giving him one?

"And how did that go? Am I out of your system yet? 'Cause that kiss says otherwise." He was grinning from ear to ear.

"You know, I never noticed how infuriating you could be." I couldn't deny that I was thrilled to see him. Now that I was looking at him, I felt like I missed him more than I thought. He grabbed the other side of my chair and turned me toward him, effectively caging me in. His nose caressed me from my neck to my shoulder.

"Missed you, Fee." He kissed the spot below my ear that drove me crazy, knowing precisely what he was doing to me. "Did you miss me?"

"No," I responded breathlessly. I closed my eyes and enjoyed how his skin felt against mine.

"How much, love?" he asked against my ear, completely ignoring my response.

There was no point in denying it, so I told him the truth. "I thought about you all day." He liked that answer because he rewarded me by licking the spot that made my body tighten. God, I was weak.

"Then why didn't you call?" The way his breath fell on my skin like a warm blanket had me leaning toward him.

"I didn't want to hear your disappointment in me." I couldn't blame him if he was disappointed. I had no shame. Aside from cheating, there was little I wouldn't do. Asking him to wait for me to get a divorce was stupid.

Thankfully, the server came to take our orders, and Leo returned some of my personal space. I didn't want to have this conversation here.

Apparently, Cassandra and Amber had met before at the club. Amber promptly invited her to her birthday party. My appetite returned with full force. I guess all I needed was Leo next to me. He and I ate silently while watching the girls talk about absolutely nothing important. Sometimes I wondered why Amber still talked to me. Aside from barely responding to her when she texted me, I only talked about fashion with her. Even then, she wasn't that interested in the history of the pieces.

I finished my omelet and then eyed his pancake. There was only one bite left. Before I could steal it, he grabbed the syrup and bathed the pancake. Just how I liked them. He pushed the plate closer to me, and I squealed in excitement. I took the syrupy goodness and moaned happily. Leo smiled at me, and Amber gasped.

"You're eating that?" Amber asked, shocked.

"Yeah, it's so good." I took a sip of my orange juice and leaned into Leo's embrace without thinking. He pulled me tighter into his body. Amber grinned. I could see that she was happy for me.

"So, Leo," Amber began, eyeing me curiously. "Do you have any plans for Friday? We're all going to my birthday party. It'll be fun."

"I leave today, and I won't be back until Sunday. I have a couple of last-minute business meetings in Florida," he replied.

What? He's gone? Today!

The waitress came by to pick up the plates. Leo told her to put everything on his account.

We headed over to the golf course. It was only ten a.m., so the weather wasn't bad. The girls happily chatted about the clothes they were wearing to the party. I watched them talk excitedly as Leo and I walked behind them.

"So, this is it. You're gone today, and I won't see you again?" I didn't want this to end. My voice sounded bitter even to my own ears.

"I wasn't disappointed," he said, answering my statement from earlier. He pulled me to a stop and turned me to face him. "I did feel a bit disrespected, but I can see where you're coming from. What I said that night about being a call away is true. I plan on pursuing you until you tell me to stop or you get married, which-ever comes first."

"But what if I don't choose you in the end?" I asked.

"Then I guess I wasn't convincing enough, but I've never been one to lose, so I'm not worried." He smirked at me, and I really wanted to smack him in the arm. He said it like it was so easy.

He grabbed my hand and started walking again. We spent the next hour playing golf. By that, I mean the girls talked about things going on in Whitlock while I watched Leo swing like a pro. His ass looked fantastic. The way the muscles on his back flexed all the way to his arms had Amber and me looking at each other.

Our afternoon was interrupted by Leo getting a call from his assistant. The girls were a couple of steps ahead of us when his phone rang. When he was done with the call, he grabbed my hand and stopped me. "My assistant called to let me know my driver is waiting for me, so I have to go. Promise you'll call if you need anything. I know you're meeting your fiancé, but I think there's something here. Don't you?" he asked. His jaw was closed tightly. I leaned in and kissed it, feeling it relax against my lips.

Yes, I felt it too. "I'll call," I promised.

"I'll be waiting."

I hugged him tight and nodded into his chest. There was a knot in my stomach. I needed it to go away.

After giving me a lingering kiss on the lips and another below my ear, he left.

Amber hugged me and whispered that everything would be all right. I didn't need soothing, but I didn't tell her that because I knew it would be rude. I was just confused. Not recognizing the emptiness in the pit of my stomach, I tried to regain my composure when I remembered Cassandra was still here. She looked at me with pity before saying, "Come on, girly, I have the perfect cure for this." Did she have the perfect cure for poison? Because that was what I was. We spent the afternoon at Cassandra's house, where we discovered Ryan was her brother—of course Amber invited him to her party, so I asked for Mike to come too.

I made it home around seven.

I put my sketchbook aside because I'd been staring at the pages for the last thirty minutes and no inspiration had come. "Ugh," I groaned into my pillow, hoping these thoughts would go away.

I wanted what my parents had never had.

My phone rang. I answered without checking who it was.

"Hello?" My voice sounded muffled since my face was still against the pillow.

"Do you miss me yet?" Leo's voice filled my ear, and my heart skipped a beat. I sat up and hugged the pillow to my chest.

"Um, who is this?" I said, trying not to laugh. I put my phone on speaker, and his laughter filled my room.

"A man who can't wait to see your beautiful eyes again."

I bit my lip and blushed like a damn virgin. *You are a virgin.* Shush, brain. I was so happy he couldn't see how flustered I was. "How was your flight?" I tried to make my voice sound soft and sexy, but it sounded more like a strangled whisper.

"It was good. I just landed. We're driving to my apartment now." He sounded tired.

"What do you do in Florida?" I asked.

"I do security for some of the major banks. That's the company I started on my own since I need a break sometimes from my family's company. I didn't expect it to grow so much that I now have to travel back and forth constantly, but I plan to have someone take over soon."

Tech guy. Interesting. This was the first time we had talked about what he did. I was happy he wasn't involved in investments. We had plenty of enemies on that side.

"You don't look like a tech guy." He looked more like a sexy fireman. Or maybe a professional dom.

My phone rang again—Leo was requesting a video chat. I glanced in the mirror and ran my hand through my hair before answering. He was in his apartment already.

"I wanted to see you before I went to bed. I have an early morning, so I showered on the jet." He paused and then continued, "Wait, let me take my clothes off. Check your texts."

I wished I was there so I could see him get naked. Checking my messages, I saw he'd sent me a link to the website of a medical lab with an email and password. He got in bed and left the bedside light on. I laughed as soon as I saw the document, but my heart beat a little faster. "You didn't have to. I believed you." He could have just sent me a screenshot of the document showing he was STI-free, but instead he'd sent me the login information so I could see it was real. The result of the test was dated today.

"I know, but I wanted to," he said. I already knew his previous STI test was negative since Milton had pulled his complete medical evaluation from three weeks ago. The fact that he'd gone and taken another test to give me peace of mind was incredibly sweet. "Make sure to have fun tomorrow. I'll text you when I have some free time."

We should give each other space. I didn't verbalize my thought because I wanted him to text me and tell me about his day. I wanted to know everything there was to know about him.

"I will. My assistant, makeup artist, and hairstylist will arrive tomorrow so I can prepare for Friday and Saturday. They're also bringing my dresses. I can't wait to try the one for Friday. I had my last fitting for it, but since it's such a unique dress, I want to ensure that the look I have in mind ties together." He didn't stop me as I babbled about clothes. He just looked at me attentively with a smile on his face. "And I also got one from the same collection for Amber. I'm happy she loved her gift because she'll look . . . stunning!" I said the last word after an exaggerated pause.

"I chose an Iris Van Herpen mermaid gown from her Sensory Seas 2020 collection. The sheer black fabric makes my silhouette look amazing. The white curved lines down the dress create the perfect pattern. I finished the look with a white Oriana 110 Jimmy Choo sandal. Amber is wearing a cocktail dress with circular cutouts from the same collection. I'm not sure about the shoes. I wish I'd had the foresight to request a pair with a black chain instead of gold. I don't know if the gold will clash with the gown. Now there's no time to have them make a pair for me." Leo just nodded, like he knew exactly what I was talking about. "The dress is more conservative than I would typically go for at a party like this. But I couldn't miss the opportunity to wear it because it fits perfectly with the upscale beach theme Amber is going for. Plus, no one does it better than Iris when it comes to revolutionary clothing ideas in this day and age." Well, I went a little crazy there. I bit my lip in embarrassment, hoping my mouth would stay shut now.

"This is the first time you've talked about something with so much passion. I love it," he said, with those beautiful white teeth on display, making me respond the same way.

"I love fashion. It's what keeps me sane." His eyes closed briefly and I could tell he was barely awake. "I'm going to let you sleep now. Goodnight, Leo," I whispered.

"Goodnight, Fee. We will talk tomorrow."

Coming to Whitlock might've been the best decision I'd made in a long time.

13

DANCING IN THE KITCHEN

Felicity

"What do you think about this one?" Jane asked, showing me the designs that had come in this week.

The blouse she was holding up was dark red with black accents. "I think there might have been some miscommunication. I'm looking for a collection of hope and openness. What do you get from this?" I asked, pointing at the pictures she had displayed on the bed before me. They were all dark tones, and while I understood this was a winter release, it didn't go with the vision I had in mind. I had finished the sketches last month. Now it was up to my team to do market research and figure out the color scheme.

This new generation of teenagers was more straightforward. Dark colors, no matter the season, were not in style. As designers, we needed to evolve with our audience.

"It looks on brand to me, but not in line with the theme," Jane answered.

"We're already a month behind. This needs to be decided by

the end of this month so we can release it in December," I told her. Our customers knew the release dates for every season's collection, so we didn't spend much on marketing. "We need to stay away from red and black, especially if it looks like we're dressing someone for *A Nightmare on Elm Street*. Ask them to send more ideas for review."

Jane sighed, making me smile.

"Did you do anything during your vacation?" I asked.

She took her shoes off and lay on the couch delicately, like a fairy princess. "I slept."

"You could have taken the plane anywhere you wanted, and you chose to sleep . . . at home?" I rolled my eyes at her.

"I already go all over the world with you. Vacations are for relaxing," she said as she closed her eyes and covered them with her arm. "Ana complained about you not calling her and how she won't make you anything you like as punishment for being ungrateful."

I laughed at the ridiculous thought of my nanny staying mad. The moment she saw me, her anger would be gone and forgotten.

My father used to be like that.

One time I'd accidentally spilled ink on top of important documents, and he hadn't yelled or gotten angry. He'd grabbed napkins and showed me how to clean the ink, then he'd showed me how to start writing a contract. I was only four years old, but I'd never forget how I thought he was the best dad in the world.

"Come on, let's go to the beach." Jane's hand was stretched right in front of me. I hadn't noticed her getting up.

I took her hand and let her guide me where my memories wouldn't follow.

Friday finally arrived. Leo and I had been texting, but with our busy schedules, we hadn't talked much. I didn't know what time he slept because this morning he'd texted me at 4 a.m. his time. I wished he didn't have to work and could spend this last night with me. I didn't care if it was wrong. No one had ever made me feel as safe as he did. When I was with him, I forgot all about my family; it was a version of me that I hadn't known existed. He made me feel like I was enough. Like he could love me no matter what I had done in the past.

Sean, my hairstylist, was curling my hair so he could do a cute, loose, messy updo. We'd leave strands of hair out to frame my face. We went heavy on the makeup. Amy, my makeup artist, went for a black smoky eye with my signature red lips.

My phone rang, and my heart deflated a little when I saw it wasn't Leo.

"Ayden." Ayden Black was currently the number one pop-rock artist and heartthrob. He'd just released his fifth album, so the public was going nuts for him. I'd met Ayden the same way I'd met Leo. Running from a party. He was new to the business and thrust into stardom when his album came out. He hated parties, but his agent kept pushing him to stay with the "it" crowd. We found the same hiding spot and had been acquaintances ever since. He reminded me of Benjamin, so part of me felt protective of him.

"I'm in town for the party. I'll be picking you up at half past eight," Ayden said. He had a low, raspy voice that drove all of his fans crazy.

"Are you trying to use me to shield you from your fans?" I asked. Paparazzi went crazy around him, and today was not a day that I wanted to be shoved around. They followed him everywhere.

"When have I ever used you? I just like your company. Send me your address; I'll see you in a bit." With that, he hung up.

I sent him my address and packed a bag to take with me since

Milton and I were both staying with Amber tonight. That way, we didn't have to drive home late.

Before leaving the house, I texted Leo goodnight and reminded him to eat.

We arrived at Amber's mansion, and as soon as I got out of the car, cameras flashed. Ayden rushed to my side and put a hand on my back to guide me inside. The music was loud, and there were people everywhere. Ayden and I made our way through the crowd while saying hi to everyone. He stayed close to me so people wouldn't try to pull him into conversation or ask about his music. Being from Southeast Asia, he was too polite to deny them, so that was why he had me.

"Let me get you a drink," he said close to my ear. Amber had hired multiple DJs for tonight. Dancers, performers, and the entire staff were dressed in killer mermaid costumes.

"Thank you!" I yelled at him. He gave me a toothy smile and walked away. I looked around and finally saw Amber talking to a guy. His back was to me, so I didn't know who it was. I rushed to her side, and that dress looked even better than I thought.

"Happy birthday." I opened my arms, and Amber hugged me with all she had. I could barely breathe.

"Yay, you're here. It's amazing!" She waved at the party. She had decorated her house with different shades of blue flowers and drapes to simulate the ocean.

"It looks incredible." I finally looked at the guy next to Amber. "Ryan!" I exclaimed. "How are you doing? Are you enjoying the party?"

"This is quite different. I always thought the Whitlock parties were extravagant, but this is a whole new level." Ayden came back, handed me a shot, and then put his left arm around my shoulder.

"Holy shit, you're Ayden Black!" Ryan exclaimed. Ayden gave him a smile he reserved just for his fans, and I rolled my eyes at him.

"Unfortunately, he decided to grace us with his presence today." I patted him on the chest and pointed to Ryan. "Ayden, Ryan. Ryan, Ayden."

"Nice to meet you, man," said Ayden, offering his hand to Ryan. I downed my shot. Kamikaze, yum.

"Let's get more shots," Amber said while waving at the waitress. We got two more rounds of shots, for everyone except Ayden, who didn't drink, and Cassandra joined us for the last one.

"Okay, guys, I can't keep drinking unless I get some food in my system," I said. Everyone shouted their agreement and followed me to the Nobu stand on the patio. Ayden stayed close to me, and I saw Ryan eyeing us curiously. I supposed explaining that I was his best friend and he wasn't interested in any kind of relationship might make Ryan less curious, but I'd never felt the need to explain my actions to anyone, so I wasn't about to start now. We found a six-chair table away from the noise and sat down to eat our food.

People kept coming to us to talk with Amber and me about the party, my engagement, and other planned events. I didn't want to ignore anyone, so I tried to include Ryan and Cassandra in the conversation. It didn't always work, so I was grateful when Ayden made conversation with them.

"Mike is here," Ryan announced. Just then, Mike walked out to the patio with a frown. He was wearing a black T-shirt that said "Nobody Likes a Shady Beach" and red swim trunks. Ryan and I waved at him, and he made a beeline toward us. He quickly took a seat and motioned us to get closer to him.

We leaned in as he whispered, "What the fuck, man? I thought this was a beach party. What is everyone wearing? I feel like I landed on a weird alien planet."

Amber and I laughed at him, but the rest just muttered their agreement.

"Mike, this is Amber, the birthday girl," I said while laughing. His eyes went wide, and his lips formed an O.

"I'm sorry. I didn't mean to offend you. It's just that there's weird shit going on. Scary mermaids are handing out drinks. Not the *Little Mermaid* type either, more like pointy teeth and blood around their lips," he explained as if she wasn't the one who'd planned the party. Amber burst out laughing and just waved her hand at him.

"Let's go dancing." Cassandra motioned us to get up and follow her to the dance floor. Ryan and Mike declined, but the rest of us followed her.

I loved dancing.

"Die Young" by Kesha was playing in the background, and I moved my hips to the music. Ayden followed my lead, and we kept dancing for almost an hour. Four shots later, my feet needed to rest. We headed back to the table and ordered some water. Cassandra and I laughed about how uncomfortable Mike had looked when he'd arrived. She'd had a crush on him since they were kids.

"You need to seduce him today," I told her in a serious voice. I was between the lines of tipsy and drunk. I elbowed Ayden, making him groan. "Right?" I asked him.

"Ah, I know little about this, but sure, he's good-looking," Ayden said.

I gave Cassandra a pointed look. "See?"

"Okay, I'll try, but it's hard with my brother there." She looked around like Ryan was about to pop out right next to us.

This was going to be my mission for tonight. "Don't worry, we'll find you guys some alone time." I leaned on Ayden because my wobbly legs didn't want to support me. We made it to the table, and Ryan ordered another round of shots.

One of Ayden's songs played, and I sang it with my imaginary microphone. The girls followed my lead. I motioned for Ayden to share the mic with me. We laughed more than we sang. Ayden's eyes suddenly shifted to something behind me, and soft lips landed on my neck.

I turned around so fast that I almost got whiplash. Leo was there with a shit-eating grin and a gorgeously tailored dark gray three-piece suit. It was most definitely a Hugo Boss. I screamed at the top of my lungs and jumped into his arms. He chuckled and held me close to his body.

"You look beautiful," he whispered, placing another kiss on my neck. I took a step back to look at him. He had a hungry look in his eyes. His thumb brushed my nipple, making me shiver.

"Find a room," Mike said in the background.

Everyone laughed, but I was too busy trying to kiss Leo. I leaned in and mentally thanked Amy for using liquid lipstick.

Leo pulled me to his body by my ass and squeezed it. I broke the kiss when the server brought our shots. He sat down, and I automatically made my way to his lap. I brought my arms around his shoulders as he pulled me tight to his chest. I breathed him in, feeling my body relax into him. Every time I was near him, he reminded me of the world around me. He made me vulnerable in a way that, even though my walls were down, I felt entirely safe. I was free to live while he battled my monsters.

"I thought you weren't coming. Also, full disclosure, I'm a little drunk." I was so happy he was here.

"I overworked my team so I could make it." He gave me another kiss.

There were dark circles under his eyes. He looked like he hadn't slept. Wow, he'd done that for me? My heart skipped several beats. Tears welled up in my eyes, but I blinked them away. Father would have never done that for Mom.

"Here." I passed him the shot. "You need to catch up."

Everyone was chatting, but I was focused on Leo and how his hair felt against my fingers. His eyes looked at me like he saw my soul.

Ayden cleared his throat, and I turned to look at him. "Leo, this is my friend Ayden." Leo outstretched his hand, and Ayden took it. "Ayden, this is Polo—my man?" I said the last part as a question. Apparently, alcohol also gave me a *no fucks given* attitude, because I'd admitted out loud how much he was starting to mean to me.

Everyone fell into a simple conversation, but I just leaned on Leo, enjoying the peace he brought me. Amber left to spend time with the friends she introduced me to last Friday, but she told us she'd return later.

"Your man? Are you claiming me?" Leo whispered in my ear.

"I'm claiming you," I confirmed. "Do you have a problem with that?"

"None. I'm yours." He kissed me without reservation, just out of the primal need to claim each other.

"Are you hungry?" I asked. When we'd talked yesterday, he had only had breakfast and promised he would be better today.

He looked at me like he'd just been caught doing something wrong. "A little. I didn't have time to eat anything before leaving."

"I'll get you some food, then. Wait here." I jumped out of his lap and swung my hips, knowing he'd look at me. Once I ordered his food, I looked back at the table. His eyes were on me, although he was responding to someone. I blew him a kiss that he pretended to catch and put against his heart. I giggled like an idiot.

Giggling was totally contagious.

When I headed back with his food and water, I started to sit in Amber's unoccupied chair so he could eat comfortably, but he grabbed my hand and deposited me back on his lap.

"Thank you, love." I was rewarded with my favorite kiss.

"Dude, isn't this party something else? I can never go to one of our parties without being bored now," Ryan joked. "It's like all my senses are engaged."

"I agree. It threw me off a little when I first came in, but Fee explained everything to me last night, so I was prepared." I couldn't believe he was paying me so much attention, even though he was clearly exhausted. I shifted in his lap and felt his erection on my ass. He shrugged as I looked at him. I was learning that Leo was insatiable. Last night we'd somehow ended up in a steamy video chat where I'd lost all shame. I envied everyone who got to experience life like this, who could make mistakes and go through the process of a relationship.

I wanted more time.

As crazy as it sounded, I wanted to know what heartbreak felt like.

"Are you still hungry?" I asked.

He nuzzled my neck before responding. "Yes." I tried to get up, but he held me in place. "I want a peach."

"I'm sure I can find peaches. Let me go to the kitchen." He let me stand up this time but got up with me.

"We'll be right back," he told everyone. Ryan laughed and yelled back to have fun.

There were sections of the house that were closed to keep the party contained. The second kitchen was one of them.

"Do you have a thing with Ayden?" he asked as soon as we entered the kitchen.

I wished I could say the hint of jealousy in his voice was upsetting, but it just made me feel warm and fuzzy. "We're just friends." He nodded, satisfied with my answer. I searched the fruit bowls and finally found some peaches in the fridge.

"Aha! Found it." Leo was leaning on the kitchen island, looking at me with hungry eyes. I waved the peach at him and moved to the sink to wash it before giving it to him. He took a bite, but instead of chewing it, he leaned in and passed it to me.

"Eat it," he commanded.

I did as I was told.

Grabbing me by the hips, he sat me on the kitchen island, making my body heat up with his touch. He took the pins out of my hair while kissing my neck. I moaned loudly as my head fell back.

"Is it sweet?" he murmured.

"Yes," I breathed out.

When my hair was loose, he grabbed the hem of my dress and lifted it to my waist. He passed a finger against my pussy, making me moan at his touch. Our lips met in a sweet kiss before he leaned down, and his tongue was inside my pussy. He hummed against me, and my entire body shivered.

I knew I should try to be quiet, but the music was so loud that I hoped no one heard me. Besides, the staff shouldn't come in here since they were using the chef's kitchen.

"Not as sweet as you," he said before grabbing my hips and forcing my legs onto his shoulders while he attacked my most sensitive area with his tongue. His finger was suddenly inside of me, and it felt unbelievable.

"Leo," I moaned.

He pulled his finger out of me and put it on my lips. "Taste it," he demanded. I sucked on his finger and tasted myself. He put his finger in his mouth and did the same. Heat flared in his eyes. "You taste like peaches."

His mouth was on mine, and his finger returned to its relentless assault inside of me. He slowly added a second finger, and a little pain washed over me, but I was so wet that it had no problem making its way inside me. His fingers moved inside me while his thumb came to my clit, massaging gently. His lips moved away from me when he put his forehead against mine and looked into my eyes as my body pushed against his hand. I struggled to keep my eyelids from closing. We were both breathing hard, drunk on each other. I was holding his arm in a death grip as I tried to steady myself and not fall from the counter when his fingers shifted to a spot that had my entire body vibrating. A scream left my throat as he stayed in that perfect spot. He grinned, knowing exactly what he was doing.

"Who do you belong to?" he asked while his eyes held me captive.

"You," I said. I didn't understand how, but I knew in this moment that I couldn't keep denying that I was falling in love with this man. Leo's fingers started moving faster. I moaned his name and moved my hips to ride his hand.

"Say it."

I knew what he wanted to hear, but I was so lost in the sensation that it took me a couple of seconds to answer. "I, Felicity, belong to Leo." He kissed me before sucking on my clit and making me come so hard that I saw stars. I yelled out his name before collapsing on the kitchen island.

"Will you stay the night with me?" I looked at him expectantly, hoping he wouldn't reject me.

"I wasn't planning on leaving you, love." His smile was everything.

Tonight, I would take the last thing I needed from him.

Tomorrow, I would figure out a way to keep him.

14

YOU

Felicity

I pulled Leo toward my room and quickly grabbed my bag so I could get ready for bed. "You can wait here. If you need a bathroom, you can use the one next door." I hurried to the bathroom in my room. I took my makeup off, brushed my teeth, took a quick shower, and put on some silk pajamas. When I finally emerged from the bathroom, he was lying in bed shirtless. His hair was wet from a shower. I crawled into bed next to him and laid my head on his chest. His arm immediately came around me. We lay there in silence for a couple of minutes while I mustered up the courage to do what I really wanted.

"Leo . . . ," I said tentatively.

"Fee . . ."

I looked up at him and got up so I could straddle him. My shorts and his boxer briefs were the only things separating us. His hands came to my ass, and I wiggled it on top of his dick.

He let me tease him as I brushed my lips against his. I kissed along his jawline before returning to his mouth and claiming his lips. His hands tightened on my ass, and I deepened the kiss. I moved my hips to create friction, becoming lost in the pleasure.

"I've never been with anyone, but I want you," I whispered against his lips. His body stiffened, understanding what I was asking of him. "Please." He still didn't move. "Are you going to make me beg?"

"Fee, we've been drinking. I don't want to take advantage of you." His fingers caressed along my spine, causing me to shiver.

"I'm not drunk, I promise. I want this. I want you," I repeated. "I choose you to take all of my firsts. This week has been amazing, and I can't deny our connection. This is not a rash decision. I can't stop thinking about doing this with you." I kissed him until I felt him relax against me.

"You're possessive, but you hold back—maybe because you know how much I need to feel in control." Swallowing nervously, I looked at the warmth in his eyes, and I knew I was right. "You don't seem to like parties, but you stayed with me all night and never complained. I grew up around businessmen. The job always comes first, and I get it, trust me." I looked down, a little embarrassed by my rambling. "You'll never understand how much it means to me that you're here," I said, barely above a whisper.

He grabbed my chin and forced me to look up at him. There wasn't even a hint of a smile. His lips were parted as he slowly let out every breath he was taking. Everything in his body was tense. I hadn't noticed while talking, but now I could feel how his fingers were digging into my waist. Leo was fighting to stay in control, but I wanted all of him.

Slowly, I brought my hand to the back of his neck and let my fingers soothe him.

"I don't want to stay away from you," he admitted softly. There was a vulnerability in his eyes, like he was scared I'd deny him.

"I don't want you to stay away from me."

I kissed him again, relieved when he didn't pull back. As soon as I took off my shirt, his mouth landed on my nipple. I fisted his hair in my hands, needing to hold on to something. He gently bit down, making me whimper.

"Leo." I wanted him so badly. "More." I ground my ass faster against his erection. His thumb found my clit and started doing torturously slow circles against it. I moved my hips fast, desperate to get off on his hand. He continued sucking on my nipples but gave me what I wanted when two fingers slid inside me. He used the palm of his hand to create friction on my clit. I ignored the pain and rode his hand until my orgasm washed over me in delicious waves. I threw my head back and yelled in ecstasy.

Leo placed a soft kiss on my forehead, but I held his shoulders before he relaxed.

"I want more," I begged, satisfied but still desiring to experience him inside me.

He held the back of my head so I couldn't escape. "If we do this, you have to promise me something."

I nodded, feeling my heart beat faster in anticipation.

"Promise me we'll talk to your father about us," he said, and I tried to kiss him, but he pulled back. "And you won't be smitten with your fiancé as soon as you see him."

I laughed at the last part because I didn't see that happening. Before Leo, I'd looked at guys, but everything with him was intense and different.

"I promise," I finally told him. I feared my family, but I knew I would never forgive myself if I didn't give us a chance.

"Good, because I don't think I can let you go." Leo grabbed me and laid me on the bed. He pulled my shorts off slowly while his eyes roamed my body hungrily before licking his lips and looking back at me. "I dreamed about having you underneath me like this since I saw your hair blowing in the wind."

I wasn't the only one who felt a pull toward him. Leo's mouth came to my clit, and I hooked my legs behind his head. He licked and sucked until another orgasm had me pulling his hair. "I could eat your delicious pussy all day," he said while licking his lips. I felt the heat of the blush go from my toes to my cheeks.

"Inside, now," I demanded. He smiled at my order while taking his underwear off. He ran his fingers along my pussy, and I opened my legs wider.

His erection fell free.

I swallowed, feeling my mouth dry. That was not two fingers thick—not even close.

"This will hurt, but I'll go slow, 'kay?"

I nodded. I loved it when he said *'kay*.

I expected it to hurt, but I still wanted him to be my first.

Flipping me over like I weighed nothing, his hands slowly made their way from my ankles to my thighs. I shivered as his lips followed the same path all the way to my glutes. His fingers dug into my ass while his teeth sank into my skin, leaving no pain behind. His soft, warm lips left tender kisses along my back and then towards my shoulders. Everywhere he touched, goose bumps formed. The wetness between my legs was embarrassing.

I felt his chest slowly making its way up my back, and his fingers descended from my shoulders to my hands, interlacing with mine. Warm lips, barely touching my neck, prevented me from pulling air in slowly.

"I've never wanted anything more than I want you," he said. As soon as those words left his mouth, his body was off me. Panicked, I turned around to find him smiling at me. He lay on his back and grabbed my hips, forcing me on top of him. "It will hurt less like this."

I placed my hands on his shoulders, aware that his erection was millimeters away from my entrance. I bit my lip, not knowing if I should say anything. Leo's thumb tugged on my bottom lip, releasing it from my teeth before pulling my head down to meet his lips. He kissed me slowly, one hand on my neck and the other caressing the side of my breast.

Lifting my hips and pushing them back, I rubbed his erection against my clit, making him hiss as I whimpered. My eyes were on his as I leaned back, grabbed his length, and slowly lowered myself onto it. Leo held my hips, letting me guide him inside of me. He smiled at me reassuringly, but his entire body was tense. I felt him hit the first resistance, making me grind my teeth to avoid crying out in pain. His length was perfect, but his thickness scared me. It felt like he was ripping me in half.

Bringing his thumb to my clit, Leo slowly circled it, helping me relax. Without thinking much, I pushed my hips down harder, fisting my hands in the covers as pain slashed through me.

Leo sat up, pulling me into his arms without disconnecting himself from me. "I got you, love." Bringing my arms around his neck, I finished pushing him inside me. I felt his tongue move up my cheek, licking my tears away.

"You feel so good." His voice came out strained.

God, I hoped he was enjoying this as much as I was. Well, way more than I was. I relaxed into him, letting the feel of his hands caressing my back and his warm lips on my clavicle erase the pain.

"Mine," he said as he continued to kiss and lick my skin, murmuring words of encouragement.

He leaned back, taking me with him. I found his lips, letting him take the lead when he delivered tender kisses while smiling at me. I moved my hips forward, making him groan, and mother-fucker, that hurt. Ignoring the pain, I pushed back down, enjoying how his palm came to the top of my ass and his fingers dug into my skin. While he continued to kiss me, I started an extremely slow rhythm that he didn't seem to mind.

He pushed my hair out of the way, his lips landing on my neck, where he whispered, "How do you feel?"

"Full." His chuckle sent a shiver down my spine. At that moment, I didn't think I'd ever felt more satisfied in my life. Yes, I was in pain, but no pain had ever felt this good. "How do you feel?" I asked nervously.

He sat up and turned us to the side, so I landed on my back. "Like I just touched the gates of heaven."

I sucked my bottom lip into my mouth as I felt my cheeks heat. The way he looked at me melted my insides. I'd never thought something could feel like this. I stretched out my legs when his hands pushed my thighs further apart as he pulled out of me. "My enchanting siren. Do you even know how you call out to me?"

His finger traced my face as his eyes stayed on mine, like he couldn't look away. "You're breathtaking." I could barely breathe with how he was talking to me, like I was precious. Pushing inside me again, he closed his eyes and his head fell back. I ran a hand down his hard chest and abs while looking at my beautiful angel of redemption. Leaning in, he captured my lips while his hips moved slowly. I pushed his chest away to see him coming in and out of me.

I loved how we looked together.

Leo had a pained expression, but his smile could light up the world. "Fuck, Fee. Tell me if you need me to stop," he whispered.

"No, don't stop." *Never stop.*

He kissed my neck, and although it was so painful that I wanted to cry, the way he looked at me and touched me made it all worth it. "You're so tight. So beautiful."

I moved my hips to meet his thrusts, needing more of him. I wanted to make him come.

"Lips," he demanded. I turned my head to meet his mouth. Our lips separated every time he pulled out, but we continued to kiss each other. Leo's muscles tensed, and he tried to pull out, but I locked my legs behind his back. He smiled and shook his head before grabbing my hips and slamming into me.

I felt the exact moment he came inside me. I tightened my legs, lost in the feeling of being filled by him. As Leo collapsed on top of me, my arms went around him, needing every inch of him against me.

We stayed connected, neither wanting to let go. "We didn't use a condom," he whispered into my neck. His hand came to my stomach as if I was already pregnant.

Mom had put me on the pill when I was sixteen, so there was nothing to worry about. I didn't know why she'd done it since it wasn't like I was allowed to have a boyfriend. "I'm on the pill." I laughed at him and tried to move his hand away, but he spread his fingers, almost covering my stomach with his hand. His thumb caressed me, and his eyebrows were pulled together. There was a thoughtful expression on his face, but he talked before I could ask what he was thinking.

"How are you feeling?" he asked, pulling away from me and getting up.

I felt the loss immediately. I wasn't ready to let go. "I'm really sore," I responded, disappointed that he was far from me.

"Wait here. Don't move." He disappeared into the bathroom, and I heard the bathtub turn on. After a couple of minutes, he reemerged and carried me to the tub. I wrapped my arms around his shoulders and relaxed in the comfort he brought me.

He put me in the bubble bath and grabbed a small towel. The water was warm and smelled like lavender. He gently washed between my legs, and his expression almost made me laugh.

His face had such a look of concentration on it—like he was trying not to harm me—that there were lines on his forehead. I leaned in and kissed them.

His eyes captured mine, making my heart beat faster. The way he looked at me was always so fierce, but my body reacted to it every time like it was the first time. "Thank you for letting me be your first. You were perfect, Fee." *You are perfect for me.*

"I thought you didn't believe in perfection," I joked.

Gorgeous eyes met mine as he steadily said, "I hadn't met you."

"Get in," I managed to say as my throat closed. His stunning muscles flexed as he entered the tub. I pulled his lips to mine, and we kissed until the water turned cold. We returned to the bed, and I opened my arms so he could settle in them. He gave me an amused expression but didn't complain.

"What time should I set the alarm for?" he asked.

"Noon's fine. Unless you have somewhere you need to be."

He shook his head and came back to me. The weight of his head and arms pressing against my chest and stomach made me feel completely safe.

"What do you plan to do when you move here permanently?"

I thought about his question for a bit. My father hadn't told me what he wanted me to do here, but there was something that I'd always wanted to do. I ran my fingers through his soft hair, saying, "I want a karaoke club. Do you guys have one of those here?"

Leo leaned into my touch, making me smile. "No. Tell me about it." He placed a kiss on my throat.

"I was thinking of opening a dance club with private event rooms. You can have private karaoke parties in the rooms. Many people want to go out and dance, but nightclubs can be rowdy. It's almost impossible to have a conversation. This way, they can have both things in the same place. What do you think?"

"Where do I sign?"

If we're business partners, we can have an excuse to see each other, even if my father says no. I smiled at the idea.

I pulled his hair softly so he looked at me. "On one condition. You have to sing for me."

A smile broke out on his face. "Love, I'm the best at many things, but singing isn't one of them."

"I found a flaw," I said jokingly.

Pulling himself up, he brought his lips so close to my cheek that it almost felt like he was touching me. My breath hitched as his lips traveled to the corner of my mouth, leaving a trail of goose bumps. "Let me show you what my lips are best at," he whispered before finally letting his lips touch mine. *And the best kisser award goes to . . . Leo.*

15

CANDLELIGHT

Felicity

I left Leo and went home to get ready. He wanted to come with me, but I told him that no distractions were allowed, especially since I only had five hours to get prepared. He told me he would pick me up after dinner so I could stay at his house. I was excited to go there since I hadn't seen it yet. Now that his mom knew about us, we didn't have to hide at the apartment.

"Your father is here," Milton told me as we turned into the street. There were four black SUVs parked outside. I promptly hung up on Benjamin, who I had called to see how he was doing. Milton opened the gate for us to enter, and the other SUVs followed us inside. A personal visit from my father was never a good thing. He was here either to tell me how he expected me to behave that day or because he wanted to threaten me. I sent Jane a quick message to let her know my father was here and that they should go to their rooms.

Okay, Felicity, bliss week is over. Bring your walls back up and add some extra layers for good measure. I gave myself an internal pep talk before getting out of the car. My father was already on his way to the door and completely ignored me as he passed by.

Not good.

I nodded at Jerry, my father's oldest bodyguard, before straightening my shoulders and putting on a brave mask. Levi, Daniel, David, and Omar were also here. I already knew they would arrive today; they might be my bodyguards, but unlike Milton, my father was their real boss.

Father entered the house and looked around, disgusted, like he disapproved of the rented house. It was probably too colorful for him. He passed the lobby, and I silently followed him. He stopped in the dining room and threw something on the table. He motioned for me to get closer, and I saw the picture from the first night I'd met Leo. There was a scowl on my face. You could clearly see I was straddling a guy. Because of the angle, my hair was covering Leo's face, and I breathed a sigh of relief. He didn't need to know who Leo was yet.

Why was he upset? It wasn't like this was the first boyfriend scandal I'd had, and he'd never cared before. I stayed quiet. I knew better than to mess with him when he was already mad.

"Did you take a good look at it?" he said in a quiet voice. "Because Simon did. You're lucky the one who took the picture was trying to sell it to the highest bidder and our team found it before the press could buy it."

At least the picture wasn't as bad as it could have been. It wasn't like I'd been doing a good job of staying hidden that week. I knew it was a possibility for the Whitlocks to find out I was dating Leo, I just wasn't worried about their reaction since the engagement meant nothing to me. If they wanted to cancel the engagement because of a picture, they would be doing me a huge favor.

"Do I need to remind you how to conduct yourself in public?" I felt goose bumps forming on my skin at his cold tone.

"No, Father. It won't happen again." I kept my voice firm.

He finally turned to me. "I expect you've stopped seeing that boy. After all, you will meet your fiancé today, and nothing can overshadow that news. Do you understand me? Or do I have to repeat myself?"

I didn't dare look into his eyes. My gaze remained fixed on his neckline.

"Father, I thought maybe you could meet hi—" He slapped me so hard that I lost my balance and knocked down a crystal vase. I tried to grab the chair for support, but it was too late. I used my hand to break the fall and it landed right on top of the broken glass. Pain shot through my right hand, but I kept quiet. He hated it when I cried.

"Go get ready." He took a step out of the room but stopped before he left. "I expect you will look your best tonight."

I didn't move a muscle as I heard him walk out. Rage filled me, and I forgot about the pain.

"Get up, princess. He's gone." Milton rushed to my side and cursed when he saw my right hand. He made me sit down and brought a first aid kit. I didn't make a sound while he cleaned my hand. When he was done patching it, I walked towards my room to shower and start getting ready.

Levi was standing at the bottom of the stairs, and I could see the pity in his eyes. Not bothering to mask my scowl, I stared at him until he looked away.

I got a text from Leo, and I wanted to text him back and tell him to take me out of here because I needed him and I wanted to be in his arms, where nothing could touch me, but instead, I ignored his message.

Amy came to my room to do my makeup and squeezed my hand when she looked at my cheek. I stayed still, patiently waiting for her to finish. When she covered the bruises that were forming, she called Sean so he could start with my hair. They could see I was in no mood for talking, so they both worked silently. Jane came into the room to review my schedule, but I waved her off and told her to get ready. She would typically force me to talk about it, but today she just nodded and hurried off. I was thankful because I didn't want to lose control.

My father hadn't hit me in months. I should have stayed quiet. Today wasn't the day to talk about Leo.

I put on my haute couture Valentino gown. It was an ankle-length turquoise-green dress with a cape that started at the front of my neck and fell behind my arms. I paired it with a Jimmy Choo rose-gold Avril crystal pump. I looked at myself in the mirror, and for the first time that week, I looked plain again. The natural makeup hid the bruising well, but I could still see that my left side was swollen. My hair was in a modern chignon with a Dutch braid accent.

A knock came at the door. Jane stuck her head in and told me it was time to go. I gave her one of my signature smiles, but she didn't seem happy with it.

I looked at my hands and saw tiny cuts still on my palms where the blood had dried. I sighed. This would have to do. We made our way to the Whitlock mansion in silence. I arrived with three SUVs and six bodyguards, which I considered excessive, but I wouldn't voice my opinion on that. Their main job was to report back to my father and help me do whatever job I assigned them, not actually take care of me.

As I walked towards the front of the house, I plastered on a carefree smile. The Whitlock mansion was on the outskirts of the city. Its modern architecture fit well with the location. The house was nice—around thirty thousand square feet—on acres of land. The butler opened the door for us, and I gave him a warm smile. I didn't bother looking around. All I wanted was to get out of there. He guided us to a guest room I requested so Amy and Sean would be comfortable.

When I arrived at the ballroom, my parents were already there. They were talking to who I assumed were Elias's parents. The butler announced my arrival, making everyone look at me.

Jane and the bodyguards stood against the wall, leaving me completely alone. Elias's mother happily rushed to my side and threw her arms around me.

"You look phenomenal, dear. My name is Ellen. It's such a pleasure to meet you." She had a familiar high-pitched voice.

"I love your dress," I told her. Ellen was in her midfifties. She had green eyes and short light brown hair styled with soft curls. She was wearing a midi-length black dress with short sleeves that went well with her curvy figure. "I've been looking forward to meeting you all week, Mrs. Whitlock. I'm Felicity."

"*Querida*, call me Ellen. We'll soon be family." She reached for my hand, and I let her guide me. She reminded me of my nanny, Ana.

"Ellen," I repeated with a smile.

"Let's go find Elias. He's probably messing around somewhere with his brother." I followed her but nodded hello to my parents and Mr. Whitlock. "You know how these boys can get if you don't whip them into shape. You must have a firm hand with my Elias."

Why couldn't I just get a mature man who wouldn't cheat on me with his secretary? I smiled at Ellen, like I agreed with everything she was saying. We walked into a game room, and two men were on the couch playing video games.

"Elias," Ellen called. "Felicity is here. Come say hi." Elias couldn't hide the lust in his eyes. I internally rolled my eyes at him, but externally I gave him a shy smile. His eyes traveled slowly down my body. If I didn't know any better, I would think I was naked. Ellen gave me a gentle push towards him.

"Felicity, this is Elias," she said, pointing to her son.

Elias was around six feet and lean, but a lean where you could tell he was ripped underneath his clothes.

"Hi, Elias," I said shyly and gave him my hand so he could greet me. The jackass barely grabbed my fingertips and gave them a rough shake. He acted like I was the one who was less than him, but I wasn't the one wearing a basic and uninteresting black suit with a plain white shirt.

"And this is my baby boy, Nicholas." Nicholas had similar features to his brother, but with light brown hair and green eyes. His jaw was a little more rounded, making him seem friendlier. Nicholas got up to greet me, but instead of taking my hand, he grabbed an imaginary skirt and did a curtsy.

"Nice to meet you, princess," he said with a mischievous glare in his eyes. Elias snorted behind me. So boring and unoriginal.

Nicholas also wore a simple black suit, but at least he had a black tie. And, no, I wasn't being a bitch. It was disrespectful to my family and me that they didn't at least try to look presentable. It was an obvious message that they weren't happy with the arrangement.

I bit the inside of my cheek to avoid grinning. If Elias wasn't happy with the engagement and he saw that we weren't compatible, maybe I could convince him to talk to his father and break the agreement on their end.

"Let's go to dinner, everyone. Come, come." Ellen grabbed Nicholas and forced Elias to take my hand. They walked in front of us, and I could see how much Ellen loved her children. Nicholas was nuzzling his mom's neck and hugging her while they walked and laughed.

"How long will it take for you to give me a divorce? A year? Maybe two?" I could feel his eyes, but I didn't turn around. I should have been playing him, faking sweetness, and finding his weaknesses, but I couldn't seem to find my usual cold heart.

"Who says you'll survive that long?" I looked at him with a sweet smile.

He burst out laughing. "Maybe you're not that bad after all, little princess." I tried to pull my hand away, but he didn't let go. After a couple of failed attempts, he leaned in.

"Give it up, kitty. I'm not getting scowled at by my mom because you don't want to play nice."

Well, would you look at that? The douchebag was a momma's boy.

When we reached the ballroom door, Ellen hurried towards it with her arms up in the air. "My boy's home!" she yelled.

"Great, another asshole," I sighed.

"What did you say, kitty?"

Oops, I didn't notice I'd said that out loud. Plastering on my best sweet smile, I responded, "I said, 'Great. I'm dying to eat.'"

Elias laughed and held my hand tighter. I ignored Ellen's cries of joy as I made my way to the dining table. I hadn't introduced myself to Mr. Whitlock, so that must be done first. I made my way toward him and pulled Elias with me.

When Mr. Whitlock turned to look at me, my eyebrows wanted to pull together, but I managed to hide my shock. He looked so much like Leo, same hazel eyes. Elias's arm fell to my waist, and I really wanted to punch it off me. "Mr. Whitlock, it's nice to meet you. I'm Felicity." I extended my hand towards him so he could shake it.

"I've heard so many great things about you, Felicity. Your dad tells me you just graduated top of your class at Tuck." He gave me a gentle smile, and I wished my father could someday look at me like that again.

"It helps when you have someone like my father to ask for assistance." A lie, but it made him laugh, and my dad gave me a slight nod of approval. It shouldn't affect me, but that nod made my heart jump at his validation. Mom didn't even look at me, so I repaid her with the same courtesy.

Elias pulled me to our seat, holding me tightly around the waist. I elbowed him, forcing him to soften his hold. We sat to the right of his father, who was at the head of the table. My father was at the other end, with my mom to his left. Nicholas was sitting across from me.

"You are feisty, aren't you, kitty?" Elias whispered to me.

I didn't have the patience for this. With my left hand, I

pinched the skin right above his hip. He'd made the mistake of not buttoning up his suit, so I had great access to his body. Elias released a strangled yelp, which he covered up with a chuckle. He grabbed my hand, but I wasn't letting go. Mr. Whitlock glanced at him but continued to talk with my father.

I leaned into his ear so no one could overhear.

"Why don't we start fresh?" I said sweetly in his ear. "You will drop the 'kitty,' or whenever you say it, I'll pinch you somewhere it hurts. Same thing if you don't keep your hands off me. Do you understand me?" I leaned back to look at his face.

"Yes," he whispered, clearly in pain. Before I let go of him, a voice came from behind me.

"Brother, why don't you introduce me to this lovely lady?"

Brother?

I knew that voice, but it couldn't be. I quickly let Elias go and turned around to meet the eyes of the only man who had ever made me feel something, and relief followed by dread washed over me.

Leo!

16

FOR TONIGHT

Leo

I left Amber's house excited about tonight. Fee was going to be in my bed all night while we made the plan to tell her father. If all he cared about was money and status, I could provide all that for her. I'd promised Mom I would go to the family dinner, but as soon as Fee was done with her dinner, I was out of there. I decided to send her a text to remind her that she was staying with me tonight.

I pulled out my best Brioni suit in royal blue—Fee would love it. Now for a shirt. She wouldn't settle for plain white. Sky blue with a micro design, bingo. Dark blue tie, and I was done.

There were five black SUVs parked at my parents' house. Wasn't this supposed to be just a family dinner? I walked into the house, and our butler welcomed me. I gave him a warm hug. It had been weeks since I'd seen him. Mom kept calling, but work had been busy, and Fee had stormed into my life this week, so I'd had no time. This was the first time I'd pushed work aside in years, but she was worth it. I'd meant what I said when I told her she reminded me of my grandma. She had the same determination in her eyes. Like the world was hers, and we were all just simple bystanders.

I made it to the ballroom door and saw a man everyone in the business world knew. Alexander Price was talking to Dad. I immediately stopped. He was the last person I expected to see today.

No, this couldn't be happening.

If Alexander was here, *she* was here. I searched around for her, but I didn't see her.

Mom came walking through the other corridor with my baby brother. As soon as she saw me, she yelled for me. I didn't respond to her because my mind was too occupied seeing Fee and Elias walking behind her and smiling at each other. Mom's arms landed on me, and I hugged her back since my body was on autopilot. She was talking, but I couldn't hear anything she was saying.

"What is Felicity doing here?" I asked even though I already knew the answer.

"Did your father not tell you?" Mom looked at me, confused.

"Tell me what? That I'm marrying Felicity Price?" That better be what he hadn't told me because my eyes were trained on my girlfriend and my brother. Elias's arm came around Fee's waist, pulling her closer to him. Elias, my brother, who was wearing a suit that didn't look like it had been shoved in the back of a drawer for the past ten years. He'd actually taken it to the dry cleaner. Fee shifted a little, and I could tell she was uncomfortable with his touch, but my asshole brother didn't let her go.

Mom chuckled, unaware that my heart was being painfully squeezed in my chest by an invisible force. "Of course not, she's marrying Elias. Don't they look great together?" She turned around and looked at them like they were a dream couple.

"No," I growled. I took a step forward, ready to claim my girl-friend—until Mom grabbed my arm.

"I know you have a thing against the Prices, but please try to put that aside for tonight. I think Elias likes her. She looks like a good girl. She will be good for him. She's exactly what he needs." I slowly turned to look at her. Could she not see that she was killing me with her words?

She had a stern look on her face, the one that told me that even though I was a grown man, I would pay if I messed this dinner up.

"Don't worry, I don't plan to make a scene." Fee was already nervous about today. I wasn't going to make it worse for her. I didn't know how Alexander would react if I just announced our relationship, but by the way Fee talked about him, I didn't think it would be good for her.

I walked towards the table, and Mom followed. Elias? Really. Why had no one told me? And why the heck was he the chosen one? He didn't even want to get married as far as I knew. I hadn't either, but that was beside the point. How could Dad keep this from me? Was this why he'd been acting weird?

"Sit next to Mr. Price," Mom told me, but I acted like I didn't hear her and walked toward the chair next to Fee.

Fee leaned into my brother's ear and started whispering, a sweet smile on her face. She had never given me that smile. Had I been reading the situation wrong? Did she actually like him? I finally got behind them, and Elias practically moaned, "Yes," to her. Oh, hell no. He needed to stay away from her.

She was mine.

"Brother, why don't you introduce me to this lovely lady?" I asked through gritted teeth. It took everything in me to act like I didn't know Fee. Why was he all over her? He had just met her. I wasn't being a hypocrite.

It wasn't the same.

Fee dropped the hand that she had on Elias's hip and turned around to look at me with wide eyes.

"It's not what it looks like," she blurted out. "He keeps calling me kitty, and I hate it, so I pinched him." Nick was the only one paying any attention to us. Her big brown eyes begged me for forgiveness. She looked frantically between Elias and me.

"And here I thought I was just receiving love from my future wife," Elias said.

I was about to take a step closer to Elias when Fee stopped me.

"My name is Felicity. And yours?"

She extended her hand to me and looked at me with pleading eyes. I took her hand and kissed her knuckles. She trembled at my touch, and I tried to hide my grin. She caught it because her eyes narrowed at me. The tabloids were right. She was the most beautiful woman of this era. An angel sent just for me.

The uneasiness I'd felt when I'd first seen her next to my brother slowly disappeared. It didn't matter who it was, I would fight for her.

"Leopold," I finally answered. "But you can call me Leo." I loved that she called me Leo. I wanted her to be different. Everything about her invited you in. It implored me to please, protect, and care for her.

"Leo," she repeated. Her full lips begged me to kiss them. I was about to let her hand go, but it felt weird. I turned it and saw several cuts along the palm. She tried to pull it away, but I held it in mine, not letting her.

"What happened?" I demanded a little too loudly, catching Dad's attention.

His eyes reprimanded me. You could never tell from his joyful voice. "Leopold, you're finally here. Say hi to Mr. Price."

I reluctantly let go of Fee's hand. My goal now was to win over her father.

I had been prepared to fight with Rothschild for Fee, but I hadn't been prepared for the fight to be against my brother. Maybe this would be easier. If I told Dad about us, we could just cancel their engagement.

"I've heard a lot about you, sir. Leopold Whitlock, at your service." I extended my hand, and he gave it a firm shake.

"I have a few Florida associates who spoke highly about you." His words were pleasant, but his cold blue eyes analyzed me. Fee looked nothing like him.

The food arrived before we could continue our conversation. I introduced myself to Mrs. Price, who barely acknowledged my existence.

Mom pointed at the seat next to Alexander, but I ignored her again and took the seat between Fee and her mother. I needed to speak with Dad and figure out why he would make deals with a Price, and not just any Price—the devil. He took advantage of people who needed help and forced them to give him most of their equity. He was a loan shark, not an investor. The only good thing about this was that Fee was closer to me, but did that mean Dad was in trouble?

Dinner was uneventful. I actively engaged in the conversation, knowing Felicity's father would notice me. I wanted him to see that I knew what I was doing and could take care of his daughter. Meanwhile, Elias focused on his phone, so there was no competition. I loved my brother, but he was lazy. I kept my hand on Fee's lap, only moving it when the servers passed.

Dad took Mr. Price outside for cigars. Mom motioned for us to go to the living room but only grabbed Mrs. Price and didn't pay us any attention. They wouldn't come out until Alexander announced it was time to leave, so I leaned closer to Fee. "Walk straight towards that corridor and wait for me at the bottom of the stairs," I said. She nodded and got up.

"I have to go get something in my room. I'll be back," I said as Elias pulled me to him and hugged me.

Elias replied, "You need to come more often, Polo. Hurry back so we can play some COD."

I placed a hand on his shoulder and took the main ballroom corridor. It was a longer walk, but there was less chance of us getting caught. Fee was waiting for me at the stairs. I motioned for her to go up, and I followed a couple of seconds later. I grabbed her hand, guiding her to my room.

As soon as I closed the door, she grabbed my hair and guided me to her lips. I picked her up and put her on the table next to the door. I tasted her until I was drowning in her sweetness.

"What happened to your hand?" I asked.

"I fell on top of some glass shards. I'm okay," she replied, pulling me back to her, but I resisted, trying to find the truth in her eyes. "Are you mad at me?" Her sweet voice was full of regret. I had nothing to be mad about.

"Why would I be mad, love?" I licked the spot below her ear that I knew she liked. Her soft tremble brought a smile to my lips.

"We could have avoided this awkwardness if I had let people tell me your full name." Those eyes of hers were going to be the death of me.

"If you had known, would you have gone out with me?" She shook her head. "Exactly. So, no, I'm not upset. If it had been any other way, I wouldn't have been able to spend time with you. We never would have gotten to know each other."

"Do you think you can convince your father?" Her eyes were full of hope. "I don't want to marry your brother. That would be disgusting."

"We can do this. I'll speak with my dad." I'd never let her marry my brother. They had nothing in common. She was my equal. Her eyes roamed my body, and I felt damn proud of myself.

"You look handsome." Fuck yeah. "James Bond could be standing right next to you, and he couldn't hold a candle." I knew she would know the suit brand.

She held my face in her delicate hands and closed her eyes. "Leo . . ."

"Yes, my love?" My fingers itched to unpin her hair, but that would have been hard to explain when she returned.

"Can you make me feel good? I've had a hard day."

The vulnerability in her voice upset me. Her eyes were still closed, and I was sure she was trying not to show me her sadness. If she didn't want to acknowledge it, I'd wait until she was ready, but right then, I'd help her forget.

I kissed her like my life depended on it, because it genuinely did. I never thought I would have been the corny, cheesy guy, but it was hard not to be when I found someone who connected with me on every level.

Her dress didn't allow me to do more than rub her nipples, and it was frustrating. Fee moaned in my mouth as her nipples tightened, and it was music to my ears. I could tell she was trying to be quiet, so I picked her up and took her to the bathroom. My girl was loud, and I loved it. Her legs instantly went to my waist.

There was no reason why she needed to hold back when I had a bathroom across the room. Although I doubted anyone would have been able to hear us since our parents were at the other end of the house.

I placed her on the counter and reached out to unzip her dress. I took it off and hurried to my bed to lay it neatly there. Fee was waiting for me, completely naked on the counter, her legs wide open for me to see her glistening pussy. My mouth went dry.

She was fucking gorgeous.

I took off my shoes, jacket, and tie as I walked toward her and started unbuttoning my shirt. Fee wrapped her legs around me as soon as I was within reach. Her hands reached for my belt and pants. She pushed them down, and I kicked them off. She tried to finish unbuttoning the shirt but got frustrated when it wasn't fast enough and ripped it open. I chuckled while closing the door.

"I'll buy you a new one," she panted.

Fuck the shirt. It had served its purpose. I took off my underwear, and she reached for my erection. She licked her lips hungrily. I kissed her again, needing to feel how much she wanted this. I wanted her to enjoy it as much as I did. She didn't understand how long I had waited for her or how hard it was to stay in control around her. All those years of yearning for a connection that I couldn't find was my soul waiting for her to show up.

Fee tried to guide me inside her, but I used my finger first to ensure she was ready for me. She was soaking wet. I let her take control and almost lost it when my dick slid inside her. She was so hot and tight that I had to grab the counter to regain my composure. I had never had sex without a condom before her. Her warmth was addicting, and I didn't want anything between us. I grabbed her ass and put it on the edge while placing her legs on my chest, forcing them to fall on my shoulders. I looked at us in the mirror—two pieces that fit perfectly. She still had her shoes on, which made it even better. I brought my arms around her and hugged her tight to my chest. I moved inside her, thanking every star that had sent her to me.

She felt so good. So perfect.

I didn't notice when I started pounding into her, but as the pain sliced through her face, I stopped.

She's sore, dickhead.

Pulling out of her, I put her on the floor and turned her around to face the mirror. I brought my finger to her lips, and she sucked it into her mouth. It took everything in me not to moan like an idiot. Moving my finger to her clit, I rubbed it slowly. Her head fell to my chest, and she closed her eyes, moaning loudly.

She was so sexy. So mine.

"Look," I commanded. *Look at us together. Don't tell me you can't see it.* She opened her eyes again, and they were full of lust as she looked at our reflection. "Grab the counter. Do not close your eyes." She bent down, leaving her ass at my mercy. There was so much I wanted to do to that ass, but we'd have more time for that later.

I entered her again. "Does that feel better, love?"

"Yes . . . Leo . . . yes."

I smiled at her. She gave me the most fucking radiant smile ever. The sun couldn't compare.

"Tell me if it hurts, so I can kiss it better." She moaned and reached back for me. I grabbed her hand and hip and started guiding her to an orgasm. She blinked rapidly but didn't close her eyes.

Good girl.

Her hips moved with mine, perfectly synchronized. I moved my hips around, trying to find her sweet spot. I knew I'd found it when her knees buckled and she pushed forward. Holding her in place, I quickened the pace, letting her moans fuel me. Her walls tightened around my cock, and I enjoyed how my name went higher in pitch as she got close. I grabbed her harder.

Letting her hand go, I bent over to get better access to her clit. "Who do I belong to, Fee?" Her big brown eyes stared right into me before she answered. She needed to know I was just as invested in this relationship as she was. I didn't plan on going anywhere.

"You belong to me, Leo." She screamed her orgasm, and I followed right behind her. Emptying every drop inside her, not caring about the consequences.

It was hot in there, so I opened the door before hugging her tight.

I'd never let them separate us.

Picking her up, I placed her on the counter and grabbed a towel so I could clean between her legs.

I lifted my eyes to hers before saying, "Tell me a secret."

There was a hurricane behind her eyes. She opened her mouth but quickly closed it. After what felt like forever, she finally responded, "Will you sing for me?"

The way she was looking at me let me know she didn't want me to sing. One day she'd trust me enough to help her carry the weight on her shoulders. One day, she'd let me close those open wounds. Her pain was written clearly in her eyes, and I wanted to take that pain from her.

Seeing movement out of the corner of my eye, I turned around to find my brother staring right at us. I moved in front of Fee, who yelped and grabbed my shoulders, trying to shield her body.

Fuck!

17

AFTER YOU

Leo

"What the fuck, Nicholas?" I yelled. "Turn around." Nick turned around, and I quickly left the bathroom to get Fee's dress. When I returned to the bathroom, I handed her the dress. She was pale, and her eyes were wide.

Pulling her into my arms, I kissed her forehead until I felt her relax. "It's okay. He won't say anything." My brothers and I were very close. Nick might disagree with our relationship, but he wouldn't tell anyone.

"You can go. I'm okay," she said. I leaned back to look at her, noticing how her eyes told a different story. She was worried. She kissed my chest and gave me a reassuring smile before taking a step back.

Reluctantly, I let her go. I grabbed my boxers and closed the bathroom door. "What are you doing in my room?" I asked my shocked brother while I put my underwear on.

"I came to talk to you about—" He paused and turned around to look at me and then at the closed door.

He wanted to talk about Fee.

"Why are you fucking Elias's fiancée? What's wrong with you, man? I saw how you looked at her, but I never thought you would do anything about it."

"I prefer 'making love to my girlfriend.'" I passed a hand across my face and sighed. This was getting complicated. I didn't want to hurt Elias. It was evident that he was interested in her, but there was no way I was letting her go.

I was starting to love things about her. Like the way she fell asleep at any moment or how she always tapped the table with two fingers when she wasn't paying attention.

"Your girl . . . friend?"

"Yes, Nick. We just discovered that she's engaged to Elias."

Nick's eyes widened as Fee left the bathroom fully clothed and rushed to my side. I was annoyed that our moment was ruined. I wanted to talk about us.

Wrapping my arm around her waist, I pulled her to me. She wrapped her arms around me, one hand behind my back and another on my chest. She was showing that she was with me, and we were a united front.

Nick was looking at me like I was an idiot. "What do you mean just found out? Dad told us. This is why I don't talk to you unless your eyes are on me," Nick muttered.

"Dad never ran this by me! We're talking about a Price, for God's sake. I would remember!" I exclaimed.

Fee pulled away from me, tears forming in her eyes. "What is that supposed to mean?" Her voice broke. I tried to pull her back into my arms, where she belonged, but she didn't let me. She took more steps away from me. "Are you lying? Did you know?"

"Love." I stepped toward her cautiously, not wanting to upset her more. "I'm sorry that came out wrong. This is about your family, not you."

"I don't care about that. Have you been lying to me?" Her eyes scoured my face, and I took advantage of the fact that she was distracted to close the distance between us. She struggled against my hold for a couple of seconds before doing something I wasn't expecting. She grabbed my forearms, leaned back, and kicked me right in the stomach with her knee, effectively pushing me back.

The bed broke my fall, and I quickly pulled myself up. She was scowling at me with eyes full of fire.

"You're ravishing," I extolled.

Her face softened a little before I grinned at her. Uncertainty crept into her expression, but I gave her no time to flee. I ran to her and lifted her in my arms, throwing her on the bed, and caged her in with my body. I had been gentle with her earlier, not expecting she would put up a fight, but that was no longer the case. She wasn't going anywhere.

"Nick, wait in your room. Lock the door as you leave."

I waited until I heard the click on the door before focusing on the woman beneath me. Her defiant expression made me want to fuck her into submission. "I would never lie to you. I knew who you were when you said your father's name. I Googled you when I was in Florida."

"Get . . . off . . . me." She said each word slowly, making me smile.

We weren't leaving this room until we fixed this. No matter how long it took. I didn't care if our parents found out. They'd find out soon anyway. "Not until you listen to what I'm saying."

"Nick says you knew! How do you expect me to believe you when nothing ever escapes you? That's written under one of your qualities." When I was with her, she was my focus. That was why I had my assistant cancel my meetings.

"You keep a list of my qualities?" Her response was a glare. "Dad and I never had a conversation about this, and if he told Nick while I was in the room, I was probably working. The past year has been crazy for me at the company. Anyone can tell you that paying attention is not my forte. With you, I'm different. I pay attention to you because you're important to me. You and work. Those are my priorities, in that order."

I shifted so I could pull her hands out, which could have earned me a punch. Grabbing them, I put them on either side of my face. After a couple of seconds, she brought one hand to my heart.

"Do you treat anyone else how you treat me?" I asked. She shook her head immediately. "Neither do I."

I kissed the palm of her hand, and her body relaxed. I knew she would no longer run, so I lay beside her, pulling her into my body.

"I'm sorry I reacted that way. It's been a rough day. It's like I knew I was being crazy, but at the same time, I couldn't stop myself," she whispered, hiding her face in my neck.

I grabbed her neck and leaned back, not letting her hide. "Don't apologize, you don't need an explanation in a stressful situation."

"I know. I just hate fights. I don't want to fight with you, ever." I wouldn't consider this a fight. Nick might think that my father had told me, but I knew he hadn't. I'd been making all the deals in the company for the past six months. Dad had purposely hidden this from me, knowing my reservations about the Price family.

"Fee, fighting is normal in a relationship. If you still have doubts, I need you to tell me now. Don't hide it." I kissed her forehead gently and whispered against her skin, "Don't hide things from me. I'm not scared of your darkness. I think it's beautiful, just like every part of you." I leaned back so I could meet her gaze.

She swallowed as her eyes watered, and I knew this had to do with her family. "I know it's normal, but why fight over dumb stuff, right?"

"It wasn't dumb. You had a valid reason to be upset," I said, trying again.

She sighed before saying, "Can we move on from this conversation? Forget I apologized, okay?"

"Okay," I responded, but I didn't like it. I didn't want her to think she needed to hide her feelings from me. For the past week, I'd caught hints of when she went into hiding and tried to give me a fake version of herself. It didn't last long, but I hated it every time she did it. I hadn't pushed her because I knew we'd only known each other for a couple of days. I was hoping she'd stop once she was more comfortable with me.

"Did I hurt you?" The worry in her voice was cute.

"Just my ego." I kissed her fingers, enjoying every second of being next to her.

The next words that came out of her mouth shocked me. "Are you going to punish me?" The way she bit her lip told me that was exactly what she wanted. I was relieved, knowing she didn't care if I was rough with her.

"When you're not sore." Her laugh filled my room like it would one day fill our house. I kissed her until I was on the verge of slipping inside her again. I wasn't ready to let her go, so I asked her to sing for me. She obliged by singing "After You" by Meg Myers. My hand went around her face and neck. I caressed her cheek as she sang about being after me.

She already had all of me.

When she was done, we made our way to Nick's room. He was playing on his Xbox but quickly paused the game when he saw us.

"What are you gonna do?" he asked, not beating around the bush.

Good question.

"We're trying to figure it out," Fee said shyly. I pulled her closer to me.

"You both have been gone for a while. People will notice."

He was right, but I didn't want this to end. Fee said I couldn't say anything right now.

"Can you take her downstairs while I get ready?" I asked. My brother nodded before offering her his arm.

"I can't sleep over today," she said.

This day kept getting better and better. "Why not, love?" I kissed her soft, full lips, relishing the taste of her. She tasted like what I imagined heaven to be.

"My father's increased security. There's no way I can get out."

I really disliked that man.

"Are you guys cheating?" Nick asked.

I turned to look at Nick with a dumbfounded expression. Fee stiffened in my arms. Rather than answering my idiot brother, I guided her to the bed and kneeled in front of her.

"We are not cheating, Fee." I tilted her chin so I could look into her eyes.

"It technically is," she admitted. Her eyes filled with tears, and now I wondered if I fucked up. I should have waited. Yes, I wanted her, and being inside her was glorious, but I could've waited as long as she needed me to.

"We didn't know, plus it's only cheating if you're in a relationship, and you guys didn't even know each other," I whispered.

A lonely tear fell from her eye, but she quickly wiped it away. "We didn't know it was your brother, but we knew my father had arranged a marriage for me."

"Yeah, and I also knew it didn't matter who it was because there's no way I'm letting you marry anyone else. We can just run away." I nuzzled her neck, meaning every word coming out of my mouth. Asking Dad was only a courtesy. There was nothing he could do to stop me. "Do you remember what you told me less than an hour ago?"

"That you belong to me." Her lip quivered, and it did something to my heart.

"And what did you promise me last night?" *Please stay with me.*

"That we'll fight this," she said.

I grabbed her hands in mine. "Together. We'll fight this together," I assured her. She hugged me, and I tried to soothe her as best I could.

"I can't leave my father," she sobbed. "He needs me. None of this is his fault."

I rubbed her back, pulling her closer. "Okay, love." Her father was a topic for another day.

"I promise not to touch you until we sort this mess out, 'kay?" I grabbed a lock of hair that fell out of the bun and put it behind her ear. I didn't want her to feel like she was cheating. "What we have is not about the physical. The sex is fucking phenomenal, but it can wait." She hugged me before nodding against my neck. "Now go with Nick. I'll be down there soon."

She got up and took the arm that Nick offered her. "Can you please take me to the guest room where my friends are? I need to fix my hair and makeup."

"Of course, sis," Nick told her with a big smile.

I needed to talk to Dad today.

18

WE'RE IN THIS TOGETHER NOW

Leo

The last Price SUV left, and I looked at Dad. "Mind if I speak with you?"

He looked at me warily but nodded. "Sure, son. Let's go to the study." He turned around and went inside the house.

"You look great today," Mom said, wrapping her arm around me as we walked inside.

I put my arm around her shoulders and pulled her closer to me. "So do you."

"Why didn't you tell us that we looked good?" Elias asked, pulling Mom away from me.

"Yeah, Mom, why didn't you tell us?" Nick chimed in.

"Maybe because you both look like you got your suits from the dollar store," I told them.

Mom laughed, and my brothers faked indignation. "You all look perfect in my eyes," she said.

"What do you mean 'your eyes'? That sounds like no one else will think we look good. Have you seen how handsome we are?" I grinned at Nick's words; they were clueless.

I left them behind and made my way to Dad's study. His study resembled a small cabin in the woods, fireplace included. He was already sitting on the leather couch and had poured two glasses of scotch. I grabbed my glass and took the seat in front of him. "Is there something I should know? Are we in some sort of trouble that you're doing business with Alexander Price?" I asked.

He kept his face blank as he answered. "No, the company is fine. We aren't doing business with them. Elias needs to learn some responsibility, and I think Felicity will be good for him. I did consult with your brother before accepting the marriage proposal."

"So you're okay with forcing Felicity to get married to someone she doesn't know? Does she get no say in this?" This wasn't the nineteenth century. Elias's opinion wasn't the only one that mattered.

"I'm sure that was discussed with her father. In any case, that doesn't concern us. I thought you would be upset because I invited a Price to the house, but it seems like you're more concerned about the marriage." I stared at Dad, trying to figure out what was wrong with him. He was never cold. Sure, sometimes we might disagree, but it was never something that we couldn't fix easily, and he never talked about a person like they didn't matter.

"Is this why you've been acting weird?" I asked, focusing on his expression and trying to see what I was missing.

"Yes," he said dryly. "I knew you wouldn't have a positive reaction to this."

"I'm in charge of the company. Don't you think I should have been made aware of this? You know what I think about the Price family, and you still didn't bother to tell me. If Mom hadn't invited me to dinner today, were you even going to tell me before the wedding?" I downed the scotch and left the glass on the table next to me. I ran the numbers in my head, and I couldn't find anything out of place. We weren't losing money. There had been no weird transactions coming in or out, so why would he accept something from Alexander? Was this really only about Elias? He might be immature, but he was a good man. Having him get married just to show him responsibility made no sense. That had never been the way our parents taught us to do things.

"No, I didn't know your mom was going to invite you until it was too late. This doesn't concern you, and it doesn't concern the company." His tone was harsh, and his arms were crossed against his chest. Dad never gave vague answers, not even when I was a child. If he corrected me on something, he always explained the why and proposed new options for me to choose from; he was never closed off.

I pushed the uneasy feeling away before I muttered, "It does concern me."

"How so?" Dad looked at me expectantly as he waited for my response.

"You're marrying my girlfriend to my brother." He stared at me, blinking as if his brain was trying to process what I just said. When realization kicked in, his brows pulled together for a second before he lost it.

"Your what?" he shouted as he jumped out of his seat. "Have you lost your mind?" What the heck was happening? Why was he upset now? It wasn't like Elias and Fee knew each other.

I stayed calm as I told him, "Cancel whatever contract you have with Alexander. Fee is not marrying Elias."

"Fee? Fee!" The vein on the side of his forehead was popping out as he turned red. "Do you even know who she is? She's the one they call the devil's daughter. Did you know that? How could you date someone like her?" For a second, I felt guilty and worried about how upset he was, but the moment he decided to say *someone like her*, I felt my body go cold.

"Do not go there." Dad's eyes widened at my low, menacing

tone. I didn't care what Fee had done. No one was going to insult her in my presence. That just wasn't going to fly. "If you get to know her, you will find out she's nothing like her family." My fingers tightened around the arm of the sofa as I tried to keep my breathing steady.

"I know *exactly* who she is," he declared, but he didn't. I was willing to bet no one really knew how many layers she was protected under. I'd barely scratched the surface, and I knew whoever was hiding under those petals was worth fighting a million wars over, and I didn't care how long it took. I was going to protect her like I told her I would.

"Two seconds ago, you were saying how she was good for Elias, and now all of a sudden she's not good enough? What kind of logic is that?" A messed-up kind of logic, that was what it was.

In twenty-five years, I'd never doubted Dad, but right now, looking at how inconsistent he was, I had to wonder if he was doing this for money. After all these years of preaching honor, was he really allowing himself to be corrupted over profit?

"Leopold, stay away from that girl. If her family finds out that you're opposed to the marriage, you will make it worse for her." He closed his eyes and massaged his temple before taking a seat.

"Why? Why are you okay with her marrying Elias but not me? I plan to talk to her father, so don't worry about that. I can protect her from him." At this point, I felt like I also had to protect her from my family. He only needed to give her one chance, and he'd see what I saw.

"She doesn't need protection from her father!" he exclaimed, raising his hands and waving them next to his face. "I will not have a Price controlling you. Step back and forget about her."

If Fee wanted to control me, she would have shown her cards by now. All she was trying to do was live her life. "I'm not stepping away from her." Not unless she truly didn't want me there.

"Please, son. You can find someone else, but you can't be with her." His eyes pleaded with me to listen, but I couldn't. Dad rarely asked me for anything, so when he did, I always conceded because I believed in him, but I couldn't do it this time. I wasn't taking Fee's happiness away from her. Even if her future didn't include me, which I really hoped it did, I wasn't going to let my family be part of the problem. I wouldn't let them decide her future for her.

I shook my head as I responded, "It doesn't work like that, and you know it. I'm not letting her go."

His eyes softened, and his shoulders slumped. "Leopold, whatever you think you feel for her is just a figment of your imagination. How long could you have possibly known her? Two weeks? Take a vacation. Go and clear your head. We'll talk about this when you sound more like yourself. This is not something to be stubborn over."

"Give her a chance. When have I ever not thought things through? Do you really think I would be here if I didn't know who she truly was? You don't know what she's been through, and that has taken nothing away from her beauty." He shook his head as I spoke, not even trying to give her a chance.

Someone knocked on the door before it opened slowly. Mom stuck her head in and looked at us with her lips pursed. "Please calm down. Whatever is going on, it's not worth losing your temper over. Why don't we all rest and talk more tomorrow?"

Dad walked toward me and put a hand on my shoulder before whispering, "Think about what I said—don't be stubborn or you'll just complicate things."

That was it? He was just going to walk away?

"Why? Why Elias and not me?" I wasn't ready to give up.

"Son, we can't keep going in circles." When he saw I wasn't leaving, his shoulders fell in defeat, knowing we weren't done.

"I know what you're worried about, but Fee is not playing me. She's not the type to take advantage of the company. She understands better than anyone how hard it is to build a company. She would never hurt us. Which isn't possible anyway, because she won't have access to anything." I had heard the stories about the Price family and believed many of them myself, but most were just rumors.

He closed his eyes and took a deep breath. I waited patiently for his answer. "Even if I asked Alexander to void the contract, which I won't, he would deny the request. There's nothing you can do," he whispered.

"He would void it for me. I'm better suited for his daughter. All they want is power. Make him believe I'll give him that." I had no tangible proof, but I knew Fee wasn't deceiving me.

"Son, he never asked for you. He was clear from the beginning that he would only marry her to Elias. I would have never agreed to it if I thought he would gain anything from this."

I shook my head, not wanting to believe what he was telling me. "That makes no sense. The Price family always has a reason to do something. There's always money involved. I want to talk to Alexander. What if Elias talks to him?"

"Alexander is a businessman. The contract has been signed. Nothing you tell him will make him change his mind. If it were possible to change his mind, don't you think Felicity would have already convinced him? He's giving Elias half of his fortune to marry her."

It was me who fell back in defeat then. "That's impossible," I said, barely above a whisper.

Why Elias?

Half of his fortune had to be around sixty billion dollars.

"He gave me all his stipulations and let me write the contract. There are no loopholes." Dad was looking at me with pity.

My hands balled into fists. So this was it? He was doing this for money? I didn't want to believe it, but there it was. This wasn't the dad who'd raised me. Of course he didn't care about Fee and me when he was going to have his hands on all that money. I hadn't lost, and I wasn't giving up. I got up from the chair and pointed at Dad. "There must be a way. She won't marry him, and I won't allow it."

Fuck the money. I'd find a way.

Dad closed his eyes and shook his head.

"Stop being so stubborn, you will end up hurting someone one day! He didn't tell me why it can't be you, but isn't it obvious?" Dad asked. "The Price family has always left everything to their firstborn. No matter if it's a man or a woman, as long as the Price blood flows through their veins, they're trained to take over the family business. In Alexander's eyes, you're just my bastard child. You're not even my firstborn. He would never marry his only daughter to someone he doesn't consider a legitimate heir."

I took a step back as I lost my balance and gripped the chair next to me. *How? How did he find that out? No one was supposed to know that.*

"Dad, what are you saying?"

When Dad opened his eyes, there was a storm behind them. "Alexander knows you're not Ellen's son."

"How does he know that? How's that possible? Not even Elias and Nick know. Is he threatening you?" Rage filled me at the thought of Alexander threatening him. I knew Mom wasn't my biological mother; my parents had told me when I was young, since they thought I deserved to know.

Mom and Dad had been taking a break after Elias was born. They'd lived in separate houses for a couple of months and Dad had made a drunken mistake that resulted in me being born nine months later. My biological mother died from an overdose the same year I was born. My parents hid what Dad had done to protect his reputation and for Mom's sake. People talked, and Mom would be humiliated. I'd never understood how he could cheat on Mom, no matter how stressed he was. I wasn't one to believe a break gave you a free pass, but she'd forgiven him, and he'd tried to be the man she deserved ever since.

"I don't know how he found out, but when he came to me, he had hospital records and bank statements showing me giving money to your mother."

I took a deep breath. The last thing I wanted was for my voice to break. "Why didn't you tell me before? Did he threaten you or not?"

"I told you what I thought you needed to know. Alexander didn't threaten me. He just wanted to show his power. I promised him I wouldn't talk to anyone about this. I can't tell you the reason and I can't give you the details or stipulations of the contract; not even Ellen knows. But I need you to trust me and stay away from Felicity. She will marry Elias." He finished the scotch in his glass and poured himself some more.

The air rushed out of my lungs as I lost my ability to breathe.

I could never be with Fee.

I tried to pull air in, but as I breathed in as much as I could, it still wasn't enough. If Felicity knew I was a bastard, would she also see me as a nobody?

What was I going to do now? If I pushed Alexander, would he release that information to the press? The Whitlock elites would drag Mom through the mud, and if there was one person that never deserved to be put through the wringer, it was her. There wasn't a day where she'd treated me differently than my brothers. Was Fee serious about us? Would she choose me if I fought for her? I couldn't continue to play this game with her if Mom would be caught in the crossfire.

"I need to process this," I murmured.

"You know I don't think that way," Dad said as I passed him by.

I nodded, unable to speak.

I walked out of the room and toward my car. I couldn't stay there any longer. There was a lump in my throat, and I wasn't sure what I was feeling, but it was a mixture of confusion, anger, and sadness.

I hit the gas and started driving to my house, but there was nothing there—there was no one there. There was only one person I wanted to see right now, and it was the only person I shouldn't want to see.

I needed her.

I needed Fee.

19

MISSING YOU

Felicity

I felt the bed dip beside me and turned around, panicked. The room was dark, so I couldn't see anything other than someone's outline. Strong arms came around me and pulled me to a hard chest. "Leo?" There was no one else who smelled this good. My arms went around him as his lips found my neck. My body instantly reacted to his touch. I hugged him tighter. "How did you get in? Do you have any thieving skills I don't know about?" His body vibrated with laughter, making me smile.

"Milton snuck me in," he said.

I loved Milton. He deserved a vacation. When he'd started working with us, he'd tried to stop my father from hitting me. That had almost gotten him fired. He could have left and taken any other job, but he'd stayed, protecting me as best he could.

"Go back to sleep," he whispered against my neck.

I didn't want him to go. "Will you still be here when I wake up?" I had to go back to New York next week for work, and I wasn't sure when I would be back in Whitlock, so I wanted to steal every moment we could.

"Do you want me to?" he asked.

More than anything. "Yes, only Jane would walk into my room, but she wouldn't say anything. Security doesn't come up here, so I can keep you all to myself."

"Happy you want me to stay because I brought clothes and my laptop for work. It would have been awkward if you wanted me gone."

He was holding me so tight it was getting hard to breathe. "What's wrong?" I asked. I tried to reach for the lamp on his side, but he flipped me over and spooned me from behind.

"I'm just tired, it's been a long day," he mumbled against my neck.

"If you want to talk, I'm here. You can trust me." I put my hand on top of his and interlaced our fingers.

I could feel him nodding. That was the only response I got. What happened after we'd left? Had he talked to his dad?

I pulled on the hem of his shirt, and he tensed.

"Fee . . . ," he said with a shaky breath.

I turned around in his arm and pulled up his shirt. "I just want to feel you and for you to be comfortable. Take your shirt and pants off." He let me take his shirt off and pulled his pants off, leaving him in his underwear. I found the crook of his arm and wrapped myself around him. "See? much better."

What was he not telling me?

His whisper interrupted the silence. "If one day something happened and I lost everything, would you still be with me?"

"Why are you asking me this? What do you mean?" I asked. I lifted my head, trying to read his face, but the room was too dark.

"If I wasn't a Whitlock or didn't belong to a powerful family, would you still be with me?" His fingers tightened against my waist as he waited for my answer.

"I've never cared about your last name or money. I only care about you, my Leo. The man that takes time to be with me no matter how busy he is and is always happy whenever he's with me. No matter what happens in the future, you are the only man I want to be with."

He grabbed my hand and placed it against his heart. "That's all I needed to know," he whispered. I wanted to ask what had happened. Had his dad threatened to take the company away from him because of me? Before I could ask, he whispered, "Goodnight," so I closed my eyes and didn't bother him with my questions. If there was one thing I appreciated that people did for me, it was when they gave me space, so I would give him space.

I slowly opened my eyes as I felt the light pouring in. I turned around, but Leo wasn't in bed. I heard the shower running on and headed to the bathroom. Thank you, glass, for making a girl's dream come true. Leo was completely naked. His eyes were closed. His head was leaning back as water fell over his perfectly sculpted body. My eyes trailed down from his chest to his eight-pack, to that delicious V that I wanted to run my tongue over, and finally stopped on his dick. A dick that was getting bigger by the second. I licked my lips as I looked up, and his eyes were burning into mine. I walked towards him, but he quickly left the shower and wrapped a towel around his midsection without drying himself off.

"Your siren eyes will be the death of me," Leo mumbled as I reached him. I smiled at him, but when he looked at me, his eyes darkened, and the smile that was forming died. "We need to go to the hospital. Get ready."

Dammit.

I'd forgotten about my cheek. I also hadn't expected him to show up in the middle of the night or I would have worn makeup to cover it up.

"It's just a bruise," I told him and placed my hand on his jaw, hoping it would soften under my touch, but it didn't.

His voice came out a little colder than I expected. "That's not a bruise. Those are multiple bruises, and we need to get some medicine for them."

"One, we can't go to the hospital for a bruise. Two, I can't have people see me walk into a hospital, or they'll know something is wrong. Next thing we know, there's a scandal on our hands. Boyfriend beats Felicity Price." I put my hands in the air, pointing out every word on an imaginary banner. "Three, we can't go out now because security will see you, and my father will not be happy. I'll never be able to see you again. Is that what you want?"

"Fine," he agreed reluctantly. I quickly took a shower and put on makeup.

I wasn't sure if I should bring up last night, because he didn't want to talk about it, but it had been obvious all day that his focus was elsewhere. While he ate, he just stared at the space in front of him. If I talked, he responded and smiled accordingly, like nothing was wrong, but I could tell his mind wasn't there.

I sat on the bed, and he was on the couch watching a baseball game. I was sure he wasn't paying attention because he didn't react to anything. His entire body looked tense. He was frowning, his lips were pursed, his shoulders were tight, and his hands were clenched. I made my way to him and sat on his lap. His arms immediately pulled me closer as if he was just going through the motions.

"Whatever it is you're going through, just know that I'm here for you." I placed a kiss on his jaw and caressed the back of his neck.

Leo's eyebrows slowly relaxed, and his eyes went warm. Before I realized what he was doing, his hand was wrapped around my neck, and his lips were on mine. His kiss was rough, and his tongue invaded my mouth without warning. His lips left mine just as fast as they came, and we were both panting with our foreheads against each other.

"No one is able to read me, but you can. That's one of the

things I love about you." He loved something about me? My heart liked that. It liked it a lot.

"What did your dad say?"

His fingers tensed briefly, but his face was completely blank. "Give me more time. There are a couple of things I need to discuss with my parents first."

I didn't like the sound of that, but instead of pushing, I just nodded. The only way for me to get out of this agreement was if Richard Whitlock agreed. If I were being honest with myself, I could admit that I was scared of going against my father's orders. There was nothing I could offer Father in return for letting me be with Leo. Aside from Mom and being head of the family, he didn't care about anything. I was also terrified of not being respected by my family. I had feelings for Leo, but I still craved power more than anything; that was why leaving my family had never been an option for me.

"Are you not going to work?" I asked, leaning my head on his shoulder.

"Why do they call you the devil's daughter?" My body became rigid. I tried to get up, but his hand was firmly around my waist. "I'm not attacking you, love. I want to—" I didn't let him finish.

"Make sure you're not a target," I whispered as a lump formed in my throat. He had every right to think I was there to manipulate his family and force them into an unbreakable contract. I didn't know if he would believe me if I told him the truth. Father still hadn't been clear about what he wanted. Of course, it must be about the money, but some things still didn't make sense. If I moved to California, I'd be out of my family's reach. They'd still own me, but I wouldn't be as useful.

"No. Siren, look at me." He lifted my chin until I met his gaze. His eyes were gentle, and his shoulders were relaxed. "I trust you. All I want is to understand what you do."

I searched his eyes, trying to see if there was something he wasn't telling me. When I couldn't find anything but calmness, I felt the pressure settle in my chest. I grabbed the hand holding my waist so I could get up, and he didn't stop me this time.

Walking towards the bedroom window, I opened the curtain so I could see the ocean. The waves were falling harder than I had seen since I arrived. I heard Leo get up and make his way toward me.

Pulling my hair away from my shoulder, he rested his chin there while pulling me into his arms. "Tell me a secret."

I took my shoes off and walked to the bathroom without answering him. I turned around and saw that he was watching me. I took my clothes off slowly, making his eyes flare. Once I was completely naked, I reached for him, silently asking him to come closer. He seemed hesitant, but after a couple of seconds, he closed the distance between us. I took his tie off and unbuttoned his shirt. I let him take the rest off as I closed the bathroom door. He kept his pants on, but after I turned on the shower, he got the hint and got fully undressed. I waited until he was done to get in.

I pushed him against the shower wall and let the water fall on us. I wrapped myself around him and hugged him tightly while he held on to me. "My name is Felicity Amira Price. I'm the daughter of Alexander Price. I belong to Simon Price. My life and death are bound to my family. I'm whatever and whoever they need me to be, but . . . I would never let them hurt you. Do you believe me?" I wasn't sure when I started crying, but I was thankful that the water was washing away the tears.

"Yes." He brought his forehead to mine. Our lips were less than an inch apart. Neither of us closed the distance. I met his soft eyes, and there was no judgment yet.

"I collect the debts of those who owe my family money. Outsiders with big dreams always approach my aunts and uncles. Most lose all the money we give them. They have no option but to sign whatever contract I give them because they're already going to lose everything." I didn't tell him about what I did for the family internally. "I didn't get any instructions about your family other than to marry your brother, but I don't know what they'll ask of me next. They only tell me what I need to know to do my job."

He nodded and pulled me closer to his body. "You're not marrying Elias."

I opened my mouth, but I realized I had nothing to say. I couldn't promise that. I wanted to promise it, and I wanted to believe it was true, but what if the order came directly from Simon? If my father wanted me to marry and I disobeyed him, it would probably be a little torture, maybe a remote prison where he would leave me to reflect on my sins, but with Simon that might as well be my death sentence. Simon took any kind of disobedience as a sign of rebellion.

"Fee, you're not marrying Elias," he said again with more conviction. He looked at me intensely, and I was unable to look away.

"Leo, I . . ." A phone went off.

"Fuck!" Leo turned off the water before quickly getting out and drying his hair and body. He handed me a towel and put on his clothes. I followed him to the couch, where he was already opening his laptop. A couple of seconds later, the room was filled with loud voices. "Good morning," Leo said.

"Thanks for joining, Mr. Whitlock. Cynthia, you can start the meeting," someone responded. A feminine voice spoke, which I assumed was Cynthia's.

As I was about to turn around, Leo got up and turned me to face him. "Say it," he demanded.

I swallowed back the tears and told him the words that I wanted to be true more than anything. "I am not marrying Elias." I could tell he didn't believe me, but he still crushed me into his body and placed his lips on my temple.

"I'll be on camera for ten minutes. After that, I'll turn it off so you can sit with me. If the voices bother you, I can put on headphones."

I placed a light kiss on his jaw and shook my head. "They don't bother me." He smiled at me, and I wanted to capture that moment forever.

When ten minutes had passed, Leo patted the spot next to him. I grabbed my sketchbook, but instead of drawing anything, I stared at a blank page.

The days went by, and we were secluded in my room. We worked perfectly together, and it didn't feel crowded or like we were bothering each other, but something still felt off. Leo was already in his head, and after our conversation, I was in mine. If I made the relationship between Leo and me public, that would force our families to accept our relationship, but if that ruined whatever my father or Simon was planning, I would have to face the consequences, and Leo would probably be dragged in with me.

Although I trusted Levi and his team, they were still under my father's supervision and should have been reporting everything to him. I knew there were things Levi didn't tell him, but after the conversation with my father about the picture, I knew he would have threatened Levi to make sure he was getting a full report on everything I did. So, I kept Leo hidden in my room, and the only interactions we had were with Jane, Amy, and Sean, who ate dinner with us.

Leo had calls, Zoom meetings, and a gazillion emails to get through. His schedule was crazy. Waking up at five a.m. without an alarm was already impressive to me. I had only caught him once because he got up so quietly. My gym was downstairs, making it inaccessible to Leo, who was apparently addicted to exercising every morning. The light from the bathroom filled the room with only a touch of light. I watched as his body glistened with sweat while he did repetitions of push-ups, sit-ups, squats, and other exercises I didn't know the names of. Every so often, he let out a soft grunt that traveled all the way to my core. He was striking. I should have told him I was watching so I didn't feel like a creepy stalker, but I fell asleep as soon as he hit the shower.

Sometimes I wondered if he didn't give himself a moment off all day just because he didn't want to be thinking about whatever was bothering him.

While he worked, I checked on how my design team was doing with the next collection and reviewed my stylist's suggestions for upcoming events.

Leo and I talked for hours about our childhood, favorite things, and dreams. He told me things about his family, and I told him about Benjamin. Sometimes we just talked about random things, or he told me about business changes he was trying to make.

On other nights, we watched one of my favorite rom-coms. Even if he wouldn't admit it, he enjoyed *The Princess Bride* as much as I did. I didn't think he enjoyed the part where I pressed watch again when the movie had finished a couple of seconds before. I knew this because he grumbled in my ear and said, "Love." I smiled at him and bit my lip, making him mutter something about sirens and heads being bitten off. He then pulled me tighter to his chest as we watched the movie again.

We watched every Cubs game that week, and I must admit, they weren't that bad. Leo got very vocal during the games. Watching him try not to act annoyed when a play went wrong while he was in a video meeting was fun.

No matter what we did, the night always ended the same way. With us wrapped in each other's arms until we fell asleep.

20

FAREWELL, LOVE

Felicity

*T*oday was my last day in Whitlock. It was also the day I had a date with Elias. I wasn't thrilled, but I'd do anything to appease Father. I put little to no effort into getting ready. He was taking me to a friend's birthday party. *Which was an excellent place for a first date.* Even a ride around the block would have been a better first date. I put on my pink viscose dress from Fendi. If he wanted to be basic, then I could be basic too. I walked out of the closet, and Leo's jaw went slack.

"You're wearing that to see my brother?" he asked.

I looked at myself, wondering if it was too ugly. I frowned at him because I thought he would be happy. "Yeah, you don't like it?"

"It's a skintight dress that hugs every curve. My brothers' wild friends will try to get their hands on you. I can't say it's my favorite."

I smiled because he was too adorable. "Should I take it off then?" I teased, reaching for the zipper.

He shook his head.

I walked into his arms and placed a lingering kiss on his lips. He didn't move away.

"Do you really have to go?" he whispered against my lips.

"Father arranged this personally, I can't disobey him." I started to move away, but he held my hand.

He played with my fingers absently, and his gaze was fixed on them. "If there was no future for us here, would you . . ." He ran his hand over his face, and his watery eyes met mine. "Would you run away with me?" *What did he just say?* "We could move to Florida, have a life there, and not have to worry about our families. I can take care of you. Maybe help you start your own fashion label if you want. I know how much you love designing and sketching."

I scoffed in disbelief. Was he insane? "Did Milton put you up to this?"

His brow furrowed, and he shook his head. "No, you're about to go out with my brother, Fee. When will you stop worrying about disobeying your father? Either you're all in with us or you're not. I can't afford to do this halfway. You can't even promise me that you won't marry Elias, and I'm supposed to just sit here and wait for everything to be okay?"

"Yes," I snapped. "That is what I expect you to do."

"Oh, it's what you expect me to do?" he snarked. "I'm sorry that I'm not meeting your expectations. Not everyone can be as perfect and obedient as you." His chest rose and fell rapidly, and his hands were fisted next to him.

"Why would we ever come to Miss Perfect?" April's words repeated in my head.

The doorbell rang, and I turned around, heading toward my bedroom door. If there was one thing I was good at, it was ignoring my feelings, and right now, I wasn't ready to face whatever was going on between Leo and me. Would he leave me? Would he not like me anymore? Could I not make him happy? As

I turned the doorknob, Leo's hand smashed against the door before I could fully open it. The door closed with a loud bang, and his body pressed against mine. His warm breath fell against my neck, and I could immediately feel the goose bumps forming.

"I'm sorry for being an asshole. None of this is your fault," he said.

I turned around to face him and leaned against the door. This wasn't either of our faults; it was all my family's doing. "I'm sorry too." I let my fingers run through his hair, trying to get him to relax. "I shouldn't have said that. I'm so used to my family's expectations that I put that on you without even realizing. It's not fair to you."

"It's not fair to you either, Fee. We can't stay in this limbo of not knowing if we're going to make this work or if we'll continue to just be puppets. If you don't want to disobey your family and you don't want to leave, then what are our options?"

"Kiss me," I whispered. I didn't have an answer to his question, so the only thing I could do was show him that this was real for me, that he was important to me. I didn't know where he fit into my life, but I was desperately trying to find a place for him.

He hesitated as his eyes searched my face.

"Kiss me, or I leave." That was all I needed to say. His hand grabbed my hair as he pulled me to his lips.

Sparks.

Fireworks.

Explosions.

Everything happened at once when his lips met mine and his taste invaded my mouth. There had been a week of tension between us, and everything felt like it had been multiplied to the max. Leo's hungry kisses left me breathless and panting. His leg separated mine, lifting my dress and rubbing right against my most sensitive area. I moved my hips, creating friction, and pleasure invaded my body. My moans and his grunts echoed across the room as we pulled at each other, trying to get closer.

There was a loud knock against my door that made me jump. Leo rested his hand firmly against the door before motioning for me to speak.

"What is it?" I called out.

"We heard a loud noise. Are you okay?" Levi asked.

Leo and I looked at each other and grinned. "I'm fine."

"Mr. Whitlock is waiting for you downstairs."

The smile on Leo's face died.

"Ask Elias to leave. Apologize and let him know I'm sick—I can't see him today. I don't want anyone to bother me again tonight." I think Leo forgot he was holding the door in case Levi tried to open it, because he cupped my face and looked at me like I'd just made him the happiest man in the world. I quickly turned the lock on the knob just in case.

"Miss Price, your father's orders are for you to go out with Elias." My father's orders would have to wait. My man needed me right now.

"Levi, I won't repeat myself."

I pushed Leo toward the bed, and he obediently lay down. I crawled on top of him and pushed his hands away when he tried to hold me.

"Miss Price, please reconsider," Levi begged.

I unzipped my dress and threw it on the floor with my thong.

"Leave," I ordered. I'd just call Elias tomorrow and set up another date. Father wouldn't like my explanation, but at that point, there wasn't much he could do about it.

"Okay, Miss Price."

Leo fucked me until we were both exhausted. When we were done, we lay in each other's arms without saying a word. The moment was perfect, and nothing more needed to be said. Leo put my hand on top of his heart, and I brought his to mine. Our hearts beat to the same tune as they always did.

I woke up as my body was lifted from the bed and thrown on the floor. The light suddenly turned on, blinding me for a second.

The room was filled with men dressed in black shirts and cargo pants. I recognized all of them.

Jerry, my father's bodyguard, threw me a robe and I wrapped it around my naked body. Leo was on the bed motionless. I tried to crawl toward the bed, desperate to check his pulse, but Jerry pushed against my shoulder, holding me in place.

"He'll be okay," he said, "he's just sedated."

I tried to stand up, but Jerry was at least three times bigger than me, and I wasn't in a position where I could easily gain the upper hand. "Let him go now," I ordered.

My father's men just stared at me as if I hadn't spoken. Milton must have been dismissed by my father as well as the rest of the staff. Even if they wanted to help, there was nothing they could do. Their job wasn't to protect me from my father. My father's laugh echoed across the room as he came inside. He was wearing a light gray suit with a white shirt and a sapphire tie. "It's funny that you think you're in a position to give any orders."

"This is between you and me, just let him go," I begged.

"I have failed as a father. I have been too lenient with you." He shook his head and looked at me remorsefully. "I saw the way you two were looking at each other during dinner, so I decided to stay behind. After all the lessons I taught you, you still dared to disobey me? Was he worth it?"

I stayed quiet.

Whatever I said would only make things worse.

Father waved at Jerry. Next thing I knew, I was grabbed under my arms and dragged until I was in front of my father. I fell on my knees and instinctively bit the inside of my cheek to not yell out in pain. I kept my eyes on the floor, refusing to look at him.

"Do you remember this?" Father said.

The familiar sound of a revolver cylinder made me look up. A wave of nausea hit me, and I forced myself to swallow the feelings and the memories. Father smirked at me as he closed the cylinder and pointed the revolver directly at me. "I don't think you remember the lesson from that night. Maybe if we try again you won't forget this time."

He opened the cylinder again and put six bullets in the chamber. I stayed as still as I could, knowing my father was testing the control I had over my emotions. He wouldn't shoot Leo—that was too messy—but I wasn't going to test him. I fisted my hands, trying to force the emotions down, but my tears betrayed me. "Father, please," I choked out.

He started to point the gun toward Leo. I kicked Jerry as hard as I could and launched myself at my father. I was barely able to touch his suit jacket when two guards pulled me back, holding my arms so painfully it felt like they were about to be pulled out of their sockets. I screamed at my father, who had stepped out of my reach, and struggled against the guards. "If something happens to him, I will kill you. I will kill you!"

"Detach, Felicity. He's not worth it."

I growled as I continued to struggle, but a third guard was now in the mix. They forced me facedown to the floor and tied my hands and arms behind my back. I sobbed, knowing there was nothing I could do. It was useless to keep fighting.

I laid my cheek against the cold tile floor and tasted the saltiness of my tears. "He's worth it to me. I can't let him go."

Father stared at me with cold blue eyes. I could feel his disappointment. "Why can't you do it? I'm not asking for much, just forget him," he snapped.

"For the same reason you're still with Mom," I spat back. His eyes flared, but he didn't respond. He was a hypocrite, and he knew it. He loved Mom even if she'd never loved him. He was the one who'd begged Grandfather to arrange their marriage.

Father pointed the gun in Leo's direction again. "Whether he lives or dies tonight is up to you."

"I'll do anything, anything you ask of me, just let us be together. I won't let my feelings for him interfere with my work."

I could barely talk as my throat closed and my tears refused to stop.

"Be honest with yourself, Felicity. Do you think you can keep your job a secret from him? That he'll never find out how far you're willing to go to get the job done? Do you really think he's never going to wonder, never going to look further into your affairs? You are the keeper of all the family secrets, and he's too stubborn. I can either give him an easy death now, or he will die by your hands later. You choose."

I wanted to argue with him, but I knew he was right. How long until Leo decided to stop turning a blind eye to my late-night disappearances or the rumors about me? "What about Elias?" I asked.

"Elias is focused on his own issues. He won't care about what you do or hire a private investigator to follow you around. You've met them, you know how different they are. We can use the Whitlock name while you still work for the family. Do you still not see how this will keep you safe? Simon will think twice before he touches you. You will have more value to him alive."

"I can't accept it, I don't want to," I hissed. "I can keep Leo safe from Simon as long as I don't break any family rules or disobey him."

"That's enough!" Father put a knee on the floor and pushed my hair away from my face. "I will never allow you to be with him. You can have everything in this world, but not love. Do you understand?"

I shook my head because, no, I didn't understand.

I could feel everyone's eyes on me, but I wasn't embarrassed. I had seen many people in this position before, and I never understood why they cried or begged, why they would willingly be weak in front of me. But here I was, at my father's feet, crying in front of his bodyguards, with only a silk robe for cover.

I understood it now.

Who cared about their self-worth when the life of the person they loved was on the line?

I couldn't keep doing this.

I couldn't keep holding on to Leo. I wouldn't forgive myself if I hurt him.

"Since I can't reason with you, I will make the choice for you," Father said, nodding at one of his guards, who took out a syringe with a yellowish liquid inside. Shooting Leo would make his murder hard to hide—there would be an investigation. But that drug would make it look like a natural death. I knew because I'd used it before.

"No, no, no!" I yelled, struggling to get up. "Wait, I'll do it. I'll leave him. I promise, please, stop!"

The guard grabbed Leo's foot, ready to insert the syringe. My body was shaking and sobbing so much that I could barely get the words out as I kept begging. "Please, Father, please. I'll do anything."

"Show me," he said.

I closed my eyes tightly and started building the walls around my heart that I had let down. Brick by brick, the pain of losing him intensified. I tried to get up so I could see Leo, but the knee on my back just pushed down harder. I sobbed until I had no more tears left and my body stopped shaking.

Even if Father didn't hurt Leo today, if I didn't let him go, it would eventually happen—or worse, Simon would come for him. I closed my eyes so I could focus on my breathing and lowering my heart rate. I opened them once I knew every memory with Leo had been safely locked in the void. Father searched my eyes, and when he found no emotions, just the empty shell I used to be, he smiled at me like I had achieved something incredible.

He got up and put the gun away. "You will stay away from him forever."

"I promise, I'll stay away from him." The words hurt to say, but if this was the only way to keep Leo safe, then I would never be with him again.

"Good, very good," he said. "Untie her."

The guards untied me and helped me to my feet. Leo hadn't moved a muscle since the last time I saw him. I wanted to go to him and run my fingers through his hair one last time, but instead, I followed my father downstairs and out of the house.

Goodbye, Leo.

2 1

NOTHING FEELS BETTER

Leo

I placed her on the floor and pressed her against my body while I adjusted the shower temperature. Pulling us inside, I turned my back to the water so she had time to prepare. Her hands roamed my chest, making my fingers tighten around her waist.

Grabbing my neck, she gently tugged me toward her, letting our lips brush. We both smiled as our lips caressed each other softly. "I love your kisses," she said while her tongue darted out and touched my lip. A tongue that did exactly what she'd said it would do, then she let me do the same to her. I couldn't believe she'd canceled the date with my brother. I knew she didn't like going against her father's orders, but that gave me hope that she was willing to fight for us too.

"If I start listing things I love about you, we might never leave." She smiled at me incredulously, but I wasn't exaggerating.

Nibbling on my lip, she pumped my erection, making me jerk in her hand. "We have time." The teasing was stopped when she pressed her lips firmly against mine, finding the perfect harmony.

"I love your hair," I said, breaking the kiss and passing my hand over her silky-smooth locks.

"I love your eyes." I kissed both while running my finger between her pussy lips, ensuring she was ready for me.

"I love your ass." I lifted her abruptly and pressed her against the wall. My member immediately found its home, making her head fall against the shower as she arched her back, welcoming me in. I went slowly, giving her time to adjust to my thickness.

Pressing my nose to her neck, I breathed her in. "I love your scent."

My tongue licked from her throat to her luscious lips.

"I love your taste."

Her moans were drowned out as I kissed her, thrusting deeper into her warmth. "I love your lips."

Releasing her mouth, I found her rosy tips and sucked on them. "I love the way your nipples pucker at my touch."

Her hands came to my neck as she held onto me while I quickened the pace. "I love how your pussy squeezes around my cock."

My balls tingled the more she kept moaning my name. Her eyes were glassy, and I took her harder. "I love that every moment with you is incomparable." I let our gazes lock, and I knew she felt the same way. It couldn't get better than this.

"I love falling asleep with you in my arms and waking up with you in them." Pure bliss washed over me when her nails dug into my neck and her walls squeezed me inside of her. She came on my cock while milking every drop of my release.

As her screams filled the room and I buried my face in her neck, I told her what I loved most, even though she couldn't hear me.

"I love you."

I smiled at the memory of being with Fee last night. I was surprised that the sun was pouring in as I opened my eyes. I typically was awake way before the sun rose. "Shit!" Fee was leaving early. I rushed to the bathroom, and when I couldn't find her there, I opened the bedroom door, but there was no sound coming from the house.

She was gone.

Why didn't she wake me up?

I sent Fee a good morning message and took some Tylenol; my head was killing me.

It had been a week since I'd seen my parents. Mom kept calling and texting to make sure I was okay, since I'd left abruptly last time, so I promised that I would meet with her this week. I wanted to tell Fee, but I wasn't sure where to start. She was counting on Dad to break off the engagement, but if Alexander decided to retaliate by revealing Dad's secret, how could I forgive myself? Even if he had never said anything before, I didn't trust Alexander. Whatever I decided to do, I had to be careful. I wouldn't let her down. I would find a way to break off the engagement myself.

I quickly got ready, packed my stuff, and headed to Ryan's house. Most of Fee's stuff was still there, so it looked like she hadn't packed anything. Did that mean she planned on coming back soon?

It wasn't even eight in the morning when I was banging on the door of Ryan's condo. He was in his boxers when he opened the door, rubbing his eyes. "I know you like waking up before the sun, Polo, but normal people like to sleep," he grumbled.

"I need your help," I said, walking past him and into his office.

"What's so urgent?" he asked, sounding more alert.

If Fee and I were going to fight against her family, we needed leverage. It didn't matter if her father cared that I was a bastard as long as she didn't care. I could take a page from their book and find information I could threaten them with. "I need to hire the best private investigator money can buy."

2 2

BETTER OFF WITHOUT ME

Felicity

I threw a punch, but I only hit the air. Milton grabbed my left arm and forced it behind my back. "You're dead," he said.

Pushing my foot back, I tried to get his knee, but he was faster than me. He released my arm and took a step to the side. As my foot hit the ground, I lost my balance and fell on the mat.

"I didn't think it was possible to get worse over the years. Your nine-year-old self could beat you right now."

I groaned at Milton's words. "I'm tired. It's not even seven yet. You could have let me sleep more." We both knew that wasn't the reason I couldn't concentrate. Ever since I'd left Whitlock, I couldn't focus on anything.

Leo had been texting and calling all week, but I'd ignored him. I focused on all my appearances and tried to forget the man who'd stolen my heart. I understood why some people jumped from relationship to relationship. It was hard to breathe when you had a giant hole in your stomach. I'd never been a hugger, but now I wanted to throw my arms around every person I passed to see if they could heal me. Nick called me daily to check on me and tell me about his day. I think Leo told him I wasn't responding to his calls because he never mentioned his brother's name.

Jane pushed me to eat and kept me organized. I was so thankful that I had my team. Otherwise, I would have done nothing that week. If it was up to me, I would have canceled everything, but I still had some sanity left in me.

Work came first.

I had several fashion show appearances scheduled, which I would typically be excited over since I got to see the models walk down the runway displaying pieces of art, but not even clothes were doing it for me. When the designers talked to me about the inspiration behind the pieces they created, I couldn't focus. My mind was on trying to keep everything I felt for Leo locked. It was as if, if I left the door to the void unattended for even a second, all my feelings for him would consume me.

I smiled at the cameras and waved at the fans, faking happiness. I never had to fake anything with Leo. I searched the crowd, wishing he was there but at the same time hoping he wasn't. I knew he was probably confused as to why I was ignoring him, but lying wouldn't work with him, and how could I tell him we couldn't be together because my father would hurt him?

This was karma for my sins.

"What if we ran away? Do you really think you could keep Leo and me hidden?" I sat up and met Milton's analyzing gaze. "If we did leave, how would that affect his family?" My grandfather would be so disappointed in me for even thinking about leaving the family. He'd trained me to be the heir, not a deserter. "Do you think my family has something on them and that's why they agreed to the engagement? Why else would they even let me marry their son? Leo doesn't have the best impression of my family, so it doesn't add up."

Milton started rolling the mats and took a couple of seconds to answer me. "Why are you thinking about this? I thought this was a subject we couldn't touch, so why did you change your mind?"

Because I fell in love and I can't imagine a life without him in it. "He asked me if I would run away with him. I was upset at first, but looking at the situation now, what other options do I have? I thought I could keep him safe, but I can't even keep myself safe. Since I became the cleaner, I understood that I'm walking the line between life and death, and I was okay with that. But now that I found Leo, I want to keep living. He gives me something to live for." I wiped my tears before they fell; I was tired of crying. I didn't know I was capable of producing this many tears.

Milton nodded before saying, "I can get you both out safely, but I don't know what would happen to his family. I investigated what your father said about wanting more political power. The Whitlocks are well connected, but your father hasn't made any contact with any candidates or other families on the West Coast, so the reason for the marriage makes no sense."

That didn't make sense to me either. What exactly was my father planning? "The night he brought me back from Whitlock, Father said being a Whitlock would keep me safe from Simon. Do you think he's doing this just to protect me?" Was it really that simple? Was it too ridiculous to believe that he was doing this because he cared about me?

"Could be," Milton said pensively, "but why is there a sudden need to keep you away from Simon?"

The ringing of my phone disturbed our conversation. Rolling towards the edge of the mat, I picked up the phone and sighed when I saw the name.

"Cochran," I answered and put my phone on speaker.

"You have sixty minutes to get to the airport. The jet is being prepared as we speak." Milton immediately left the gym, and I followed right behind.

"Good morning to you too, Cochran. Where am I going?" I

said sarcastically, already making my way to the closet so I could pack.

I heard a sharp intake of breath that clearly didn't work to calm him down because his voice was even more agitated than before. "Texas," he bit out. "Don't start with me, Price. If you can't fix this today, you and I will be in a world of trouble, so I suggest you move." He disconnected the call without another word.

Nathaniel Cochran had been my family's lawyer for decades. He and my father had known each other since college, and he could be considered his closest and only friend. He was also my godfather. I'd never understand why one of the most prestigious law firms in the country—that most would consider the best— did business with my family.

Uncle Cochran had even less patience than my father, which was saying something. Most days, he treated me like a severe case of herpes he'd never get rid of, but sometimes when he thought I'd done a good job, I got a squeeze on the shoulder with a sideways grin. The truth was, no matter how twisted it made me, I looked forward to that shoulder squeeze that told me that he was proud of me. God knew no matter what I did, Father showed no appreciation for all the hard work I put into cleaning up their mistakes.

Fifteen minutes later, I headed out to my private hangar. New York was already awake. Parents held their children tightly to their sides as they walked them to the bus stop. Others clutched their coffee cups in one hand and deli sandwiches in the other as they ran to the train. What they all had in common was the unsatisfied look plaguing their faces. There was always a what-if that tainted the happiness trying to get through. How could we ever be content if we never learned to be happy with what we had?

A little boy fell as he tried to run to another group of children. Tears streamed down his face as he looked at what I assumed were scraped hands. The other children laughed while he cried. A girl stretched her hand out to help him, but he just pushed it away, his face contorting in anger. She took a step back, a sad look plaguing her features.

Ignore it, I wanted to tell her.

Don't let the feelings consume you.

Don't give them power.

I turned to find Milton's eyes on me in the rearview mirror. I gave him a reassuring smile and turned my head back to the city. My phone vibrated, and I answered without looking at the caller ID.

"I'm on my way." I sighed, a defeated feeling settling in my chest.

"I would ask if you're on your way back to me, but somehow I know that's just wishful thinking."

I felt the air being pulled out of my lungs. I choked on absolutely nothing, a strangled noise leaving my mouth. I felt eyes on me as I tried to take a breath.

"Fee?" So much pain was reflected in three letters.

"It's four in the morning," I finally said. Was that even important? No, it wasn't, but I couldn't think of anything else.

David turned around from the front seat with a concerned look on his face. "Are you okay?" I nodded. His light brown eyes gave me another look before he turned back.

I shifted my attention back to Leo's annoyed voice. The calmness that usually surrounded him was gone. "Did you hear what I said?" He didn't understand how dangerous this was for both of us.

"No."

"Are you giving up on us?"

"Yes. It's over." I had no other choice.

"Fee, listen to me." I didn't.

"No, you need to listen to me. Forget about me. Forget everything that happened. None of it was real. I'm not who you think I am. If you knew, you wouldn't be calling me. Whatever you believe you feel is fake. There's a reason I never told you my secrets. I'm ugly, disgusting, evil. I'm nothing!" I hung up on him. Clutching the phone tightly in my hand, I pushed down my traitorous emotions.

Idiot.

I should have looked at my phone. I should have blocked his number. So many things I should have done, and I didn't want to do any of them. I'd always been a coward that hid behind a mask. Hiding my feelings for Leo was no different. It was easy to be brave in front of millions of people when you had money and influence, but when it came to my family, I stayed in the shadows. It was easy to love Leo when there was no one else watching, but now that my father knew, I was too scared to even think of him. There was a part of me that begged me to acknowledge his existence, even if it was just when I was alone in my room, but the other part of me reminded me that feelings were a weakness I needed to correct.

I could feel David's and Milton's eyes on me, but I ignored them. I ignored their words, the hand that landed on my knee, and the world surrounding me. The numbness took me, and I let it wrap itself around me; everything was just a blur of figures that didn't matter, just like me.

The moment we arrived at the tarmac, Cochran rushed us inside my jet. He looked older than I remembered. There wasn't much hair left, and the little there was at the back of his head was completely white. The wrinkles around his eyes and mouth had become more prominent. His short, slender figure and small features made him look like an adorable grandpa, but there was nothing adorable about him.

I took a seat across from him, not liking the guarded expression on his face. He threw a folder in front of me. I lifted an eyebrow at him, confused by how fazed he was by this. Opening the folder, I felt my stomach drop at the first picture I saw.

God, no.

The pictures got progressively worse. I flipped through the documents and reports, my mind already working on the best plan to get us out of this mess.

"How many?" I asked. My demeanor was calm and collected. This was not the moment to lose my head.

My entire life was on the line.

"Seven during, eight overnight." I closed the file as the stewardess approached. The petite brunette served us drinks as we got ready to take off. I tapped my middle finger on the champagne flute, thinking about him. What would he think of me?

Fifteen dead.

Seven people were burned to death.

Eight killed by carbon monoxide poisoning.

Six were kids.

Kids!

Because of me.

I had never taken a child's life. What was I becoming?

Cochran's displeased eyes roamed my face. "What is wrong with you? I've never seen you care before."

What did that say about me?

I wasn't expecting the gates of heaven to open for me when I died. I was okay with that. It had been years since I'd lost sleep over it. Sometimes I wondered if there was something seriously wrong with me. I wanted to feel something while I ruined someone's life. Pity, satisfaction, power—any emotion would work, but I felt nothing.

Maybe the emptiness that kept growing inside me was the emotion I was looking for. I kept getting sucked into a bottomless pit that I'd never be able to leave.

"If you're worried that this will affect my ability to do my job, don't." I was impressed by how steady my voice sounded. A memory I kept hidden rushed to my mind before I could force it down.

Blood gushed out of the cut above Mom's eye. "Please." My plea fell on deaf ears.

"None of this is your fault." This was new. I didn't like the way he was looking at me, like I was about to break.

"Are you getting sentimental on me, old man? It doesn't suit you. Besides, I barely care about people I know. Why would I care about someone I've never met? You're reading too much into it." As the words left my mouth, I knew they were all lies. Whether or not I wanted to admit it, I was starting to care. Maybe I always had. It was just easier not to acknowledge it. What would be the point? There was no redemption for me. I was stuck in this world by choice. I could have left with my grandfather's money, but I stayed. Whether it was for revenge or because I couldn't bear the thought of not being a Price, I still didn't know.

No number of righteous acts would ever erase an evil deed, and I had those in spades. I could only imagine all the fun things prepared for me when I got to hell.

Cochran shot me a look that told me he knew I was full of shit before closing his eyes and leaning his head back. No matter what he said, this was my fault. I was the one who'd signed the papers for the relief houses to be built. Not only had we used cheap materials, but the job was rushed and faulty wiring was suspected. Dad didn't want to spend more time and money fixing it, so I delivered the houses without reporting that there was something wrong with them. Hundreds of people lived in that community.

I pulled out my laptop and earphones, needing to work on a plan. I felt someone sit next to me, and I didn't need to turn around to know it was Levi. He always did the same thing. I didn't protest when he unplugged my earphones and connected the splitter cable. Once both earphones were connected, he leaned back and relaxed in his seat. It was hard to see him after what happened with Leo. I knew he was the one who'd reported to my father that I'd ditched Elias for Leo, but I also knew he was just following orders and I couldn't blame him for that.

Six townhouses were completely burned. The only good thing was that it hadn't spread to the next set of houses. The fire started in the one in the middle before making its way to the rest of them, leaving no survivors. They might have had a chance if we had built better houses, but the second floor had collapsed almost immediately.

The fire investigator assigned to the case was Noah Evans. Forty-three and married to his high school sweetheart with two kids. They'd moved from El Paso to Fort Worth three years ago. Their older son was six, and their daughter was four. The son was in school, but the daughter was in daycare. "I think I have a way in," I murmured to no one in particular. Levi leaned in, taking more of my personal space than I was comfortable with. His body tensed when he saw the screen. I turned to look at him. His eyes were already on me. There was disappointment mixed with something else that I couldn't read. Refusing to be judged by anyone, I closed the laptop and made my way to my room.

We still had another two hours left on the flight, so I took my time showering and getting dressed. I chose a vintage brown dress from the Prada Spring 1996 collection. I left my hair down, letting it fall in waves down my back. Just how Leo liked it.

Leo wouldn't like a thing about you if he knew the type of person you are.

Taking a deep breath, I made my way to the main cabin. As soon as I opened the door, all eyes were on me, except for Cochran's. Most of their faces were blank and unreadable. At the end of the day, they were soldiers. They'd get the job done, no matter what I asked of them. I grabbed the seat before me to steady myself as I told them my plan. I tried to shut down my emotions, but they fought me all the way through. Thankfully it wasn't long before we landed. The sooner we were done here, the better.

ONLY LOVE CAN HURT LIKE THIS

Felicity

I made my way to the ninth floor of Price Constructions. The receptionist's eyes went wide when she saw me exit the elevator. The sound of my pointy heels traveled through the floor as I walked to the back conference room. I ignored the welcoming calls like I always did and kept my chin held high.

I wasn't here to make friends or waste my time with chitchat.

The director's secretary stood up and opened the door for me. Five pairs of eyes landed on me while they stumbled, trying to get out of their chairs quickly. I took my sunglasses off slowly while making eye contact with each one of them.

They were scared.

They should be.

Making my way to the head of the table, I sat down and relaxed on the chair. I tapped my fingers once on the table, and they all sat down. Most of them hid it well, but it was clear in their faces how much they hated me. I represented all the power they'd worked their entire lives for but could never achieve.

I could be the daughter of any of them, but they still had to respect me without expecting the same in return because they knew they'd never earn it. What they didn't know was that I would respect them more if they had the balls to quit, but they were just like my family—corrupted by power.

The secretary placed a cup in front of me. I already knew it would be ginger tea with one sugar. I waited until she closed the door to speak.

"Who are you?" There was no friendliness in my tone. The time for emotions ended when the flight landed.

I was now the devil's daughter.

The handsome blond sitting behind the door in a dark green suit looked around the room, expecting someone to answer. I turned my head a little so my eyes landed directly on him, and as soon as he noticed me, his shoulders straightened up. There was an arrogance there that showed he thought that because I was young, his daddy or mommy would protect him from me.

I raised my eyebrow, waiting for a response, but the guy was determined.

"He's my son. I'm showing him the ropes," Marlene Price said. She was the director my father had left in charge and a distant cousin. I didn't turn to look at her. I focused my eyes solely on the guy, who now had a smirk on his face.

"Leave." I watched as his smirk faltered for a brief second. He looked at his mom, who had remained quiet. He scoffed before he got up and walked out. "This is a board meeting, not Bring Your Child to Work Day. If you haven't noticed, you're all about to change those expensive suits for jumpsuits."

"Isn't that why you're here? To make sure that doesn't happen?" Albert asked, or maybe it was James. Who really cared? None of them meant anything to me.

"Why did you call us in?"

"Don't forget, if you don't fix this, you're going down with us."

"You can't come in here and intimidate us."

I let them all speak while I sipped my tea. Ignoring all their questions and checking messages on my phone, I waited until they all shut up before looking back up. The shock and disbelief on their faces at my disrespect was priceless. I was enjoying this more than I should. There was a knock on the door, making me smile. "Come in."

Butch and David entered the room, giving me a nod, indicating that the building was clear. They closed the door as I addressed the room.

"Hand all of your electronic devices to us." Anger filled their faces, but they did as they were told. They knew better than to piss off my family. Board members had been rumored to disappear.

We turned all the devices off before they went into the bag. "You'll stay here until I get this sorted out. Stay out of my way. The faster I'm done, the quicker you can all return to your miserable and meaningless lives. I've sent everyone else home for the day."

"You can't keep us here. We have things to do."

I rolled my eyes at the lame excuse from Albert/James. I didn't trust any of them not to go directly to the cops and mess up everything I was working for. That would force me to stay longer than necessary to deal with the police and the rat.

"What do you think, Butch?" I asked, raising my eyebrows.

His smile lit up his entire face; there was no way they could get past Butch. Grabbing my tea, I left the room with David, hearing a string of curses behind me.

Forty minutes later, my office door opened. Levi pushed in a short gentleman with dark brown hair and a defiant expression. "Good morning, Mr. Evans. Please take a seat." I pointed toward the chair on the other side of the desk.

He stayed where he was, not making any indication that he'd sit down. I respected that, so I let him stand. Levi went to stand in the corner.

"Mr. Evans, you're here because you will do something for me." I opened the folder containing the photos of the fire. I waited for him to look at the pictures. "This fire needs to be caused by a worn-out refrigerator compressor. The appliance is old, so you should have no issues making this believable."

"No."

I ignored his response and opened the briefcase containing half a million dollars in cash toward him. His pupils dilated, but his body remained tense.

"You misunderstood. I wasn't asking."

His eyes met mine with rage, his lips pursed, and his hands turned into fists. It didn't matter how he felt. No one was leaving this building until the job was done.

"And you misunderstood me, Miss Price. I won't lose my integrity for money." I let the revulsion in his voice fall off like it meant nothing to me. I'd already known he would refuse the money, but he'd soon find out that he had no other choice.

"This isn't about your integrity, Noah. Can I call you Noah? I feel like we'll become best friends." I watched as his eyes flared, but I didn't wait for a response. Taking out another picture from the folder, I placed it on top of all the burned corpses. Recognition dawned on his face as he saw a little girl with brown hair and dark eyes on a hospital bed. A picture that had been taken while his daughter was in treatment.

"You have some balls, bringing me here and trying to threaten my family. I have powerful friends just like you. I'll make sure you spend the rest of your days rotting in a prison cell."

A smile pulled at my lips as I watched his barely contained rage. He turned around and pulled the door open, but David was right outside the door. He was fit but lean. He had no chance of moving David out of the way.

"Close the door," I told my guard. David grabbed the doorknob and forced Noah to take a step back. "I'm trying to help you. This is a mutually beneficial agreement. You need the money for your daughter. I can only imagine how hard it is for you and your wife. I've seen how much both of you work. Working two jobs each and still not having the money to cover the medical bills must be hard." I felt pity for them, which was the only reason I was being nicer to him. They'd suffered enough, but I needed his help no matter what it cost.

He scoffed but finally took a seat. "What would you know about the struggles in life? You've had everything handed to you. Don't pretend like you care about anyone other than yourself."

I'd heard that my entire life. Having money invalidated my right to have feelings. "You'd be surprised how lonely it can be to sit in an ivory tower." Especially when everyone around you, even your friends, made it a point to make you feel worthless.

"Is this where you tell me that your mom and dad didn't tell you 'I love you' enough?" That burned more than he could ever imagine.

"No, this is the part where you take my deal," I responded calmly.

He lifted his shoulder and his chin before answering. "I already said no."

"I'm urging you to reconsider. This is your last chance before you force my hand." I took his silence as a refusal. Leaning my head back in my chair, trying to avoid using my last card, I gave him one last chance.

"There was a girl once. Just like you, she refused to bend. She thought she could take anything thrown her way. She believed the words her therapist had told her. That if she had a strong mind, she could survive. She could fight for what she believed in. That she could be different. Be good." I opened the desk drawer and pulled out a bottle of whiskey and two glasses. Pouring two fingers into each, I pushed a glass toward Noah. He eyed it but didn't take it. Swallowing all the contents of the glass, I served myself more before continuing.

"At nineteen, she stood her ground for the first time. It wasn't that she'd never tried it before. She had, many, many times, but she always broke within a couple of minutes. This time, it was different. She was asked to do something abhorrent. So, she stood her ground. She said no." That girl was naive. That girl was dead. "Every day, she endured pain like nothing she'd ever felt without a single complaint, and every night, she was held down while a doctor would come to clean her wounds. Food was forced down her throat. She was cuffed to the wall for a week, lying on the floor of a cold, dark room, wishing for death. One life, her life, to protect someone else's, to protect her soul. It was a deal she was willing to take, or so she thought." I raised my glass towards Noah, and he finally drank while I poured all the liquor down my throat and filled my glass once again.

"What was she asked to do, and by whom?"

I ignored Noah's questions, and for the first time since he'd come in, I remembered that Levi was still here. Grabbing the remaining chair, he moved it next to me and sat down. He grabbed my glass, downed the whiskey, and poured more. He wasn't supposed to drink on the job, but I decided not to point that out. He had been there the first time I'd given the order to take someone's life. The first time I'd tortured someone. All in the name of protecting my family.

"When the second week started, she thought, 'This is for sure the day I die.' After letting our arrogance get the best of us, we forget that there will always be something else that can break us. The door opened, and she watched as the drunk man dragged her mom down the stairs. Her face was like an act from a horror show, but there was a cut right above her left eye. The blood wouldn't stop. She thought her mom would bleed out from just that cut." Levi's hand landed on my knee, squeezing it softly.

I didn't move away.

"'I'll teach you this last lesson,' he said, pulling out a gun. With her mom kneeling in front of her, she didn't feel like a hero anymore. She watched as the barrel rested against her mother's temple. Shocked and in denial about the man's cruelty, she stood still while he pulled the trigger. Her ears rang from the deafening sound. She struggled against the cuffs, begging, but it was useless. After a couple of minutes, she noticed her mom's passive eyes were still open. The noise had come out of her mouth. There were no bullets in the revolver." Another glass of whiskey later, I continued. "The room was suddenly filled with the man's laughter. He pulled a single bullet from his pocket and put it in the revolver, spinning the cylinder as he locked it. 'Let's try this again,' he said with a smile. Letting her shoulders fall and with tears burning in her eyes, she whispered the words he wanted to hear. 'I'll do it.' The gleam in his eyes said that wasn't enough for him. She yelled for him to stop, but he still pulled the trigger." I closed my eyes tightly, trying to push away the feelings that threatened to consume me. So many emotions, so powerless. Although Mom wasn't in my life, and she hated me, she was still my mother. How could I let her die because of me?

I drank more whiskey.

Noah's trembling voice disrupted the silence. "What happened?" I heard a glass fall on the desk.

Why are you telling him this? Why are you wasting time trying to convince him instead of just using your last card? Because his daughter had leukemia. *Surely you can have a little bit of heart.*

"Nothing," I finally said, then added, "With a big smile on his face, he said, 'You're lucky.'"

Shaking my head, I licked my lips anxiously. "You see, to him, it didn't matter what happened to the two of them. They were expendable pawns in a game for dominance. Ultimately, she chose her mom and became the monster he needed. She did all the dirty work without question and never read a contract he gave her, she just signed." In the end, a part of her still wanted to make that man happy.

"Why are you telling me this, Miss Price?"

I didn't know. *Yes, you do. You want to be worthy of him.* "Sometimes, we must make hard choices. I'm giving you a chance to save your daughter and give her the best medical attention money can buy. All you have to do is help me. There's nothing we can do for those people, but your daughter is still here. Of course, you'll stay on my payroll in case there are more incidents."

Lowering my eyes to meet his, I could see the internal battle he was going through. His moral code wanted to say no, but he knew I was right.

"I need to take a walk. I have to think about it." Needing some space to calm my drunk self down, I let him go.

"David!" I called out. He opened the door right away. "Take Mr. Evans for a walk." Once they left, I took a deep breath before turning to the man who had been trying to comfort me.

"Levi . . ."

Strong hands grabbed my waist and lifted me up before crushing me to a hard chest. I wrapped my arms around him and squeezed until my arms were shaking. I wasn't going to cry. I couldn't cry. That time was over, and I was never going back into that room. "I love him," I choked out. "I love him so much that I can't breathe without him, and I don't know what to do because choosing Leo means everything I've endured up until this point will be in vain. All the horrible things I've done will have been for nothing, and Simon is going to win again. He was the one that forced Father to do those things to us. Even if I did give everything up for Leo, Simon will never let me go, and I can't keep him safe forever. Father is right."

Levi patted my head and stayed silent while I tried to compose myself. *Ignore it. Just ignore it.* I focused on repeating the words until my emotions didn't feel like they were controlling me. I couldn't do that again. I couldn't lose it like that. I was no match for Simon if I couldn't control myself. Pushing away from

Levi, I took a seat and leaned my head back as I stared at the ceiling.

The door opened, and I looked down to find Noah with David close behind him. I knew what the answer was before he spoke. "I told you not to force my hand, Noah." Dreading what I was about to do, I waited for him to respond. I had never taken this long to convince someone. I either gave them money or threatened them from the beginning. I couldn't be soft; I had already offered him more money than I had ever given anyone.

"I want to be a father that my kids are proud of. I can't do it."

How noble. "Suit yourself, Mr. Evans. Let's see if you're better than me." Grabbing my phone, I dialed Daniel's phone number. I left it on the desk, right in front of Noah. The call connected, and the camera was pointed at a small child lying in a bed with a superhero comforter.

Noah stood up fast, making his chair fall. He reached for me, but David held him back. "You fucking spineless bitch! Get them out of my house! I'll kill you. Do you hear me? I will kill you!" The veins in his neck and forehead popped out, and his teeth were bared as he growled at me.

I smirked at him, which made him launch forward, but David's hold on him was solid. "Hard choices, Mr. Evans." I wiped the smile off my face. He needed to understand that I wasn't playing with him. This was serious. "One life over fifteen or their lives for his."

"You wouldn't dare."

I envied his kids. His love was written in the way he was trying to hurt me with his eyes. Looking directly into those murderous eyes, I let him know. "You have sixty seconds to choose."

As the countdown started, Omar appeared in the frame with a gun in hand.

"Fifty seconds." Noah and I were staring at each other as I

kept counting. His eyes were hard. My heart was beating faster as time went by.

"Thirty seconds, Noah." I ground my teeth as he studied me closely. I grabbed the phone and put it close to his face. "Look at him."

There was sweat forming around his eyes. "Twenty seconds."

I couldn't take it anymore. Leaning over the desk and getting in his face, I watched as my saliva landed on his cheek as I screamed, "Choose, goddammit!"

His eyes met mine as his shoulders fell, and the fight left his body. "I'll do it."

Falling on the chair, I let out the breath I had been holding as Levi told Omar and Milton to stand down.

I grabbed the folder, took a stack of papers out, and threw them in front of Noah. Then I opened a drawer, grabbed a pen, threw it at him, and slammed the drawer. I wasn't made for this. I couldn't do it anymore, not since Leo. Trying to stay as collected as I could, I breathed as normally as possible so Noah couldn't see how flustered I was.

Watching Noah closely, I waited until he signed the last part of the contract before getting up and snatching the papers. I looked at David, who was calmly standing in the corner. "Bring Cochran, then you and Butch meet me downstairs. He can handle everything else. We're leaving now."

Noah's voice stopped me as I made my way out of the door. "My son was never in any danger, was he?" I turned to look at him. His hands were fisted in his lap.

"Take care of your family, Noah. If your daughter needs anything, contact Cochran."

I rushed to the SUV and collapsed on the seat.

I was done.

The flight took off, and I could feel everyone feeding off my emotions. They didn't know what to do with this new version of me—one who had lost control and cussed out loud.

I leaned towards Milton, who was sitting next to me. "Why didn't you tell me who Leo was? Don't say it was because I said so. I know you would have said something if you wanted."

"I don't understand business. All I knew was that I had never seen you smile like that. I thought that in the end, the brother you married wouldn't matter."

That was what I had hoped for, too.

IF TIME STOOD STILL

Felicity

J sighed and threw my pillow across the room, still frustrated about everything that had gone down yesterday. Cochran had called to let me know everything was going smoothly. The board was happy. My father was happy. Everyone was freaking happy.

Everyone but me.

"Whoa. Who hurt you, kitty?" I turned around and saw Elias at my bedroom door.

"What are you doing here?" This was the last thing I needed. My heart clenched as his familiar features brought back memories of Leo.

"I came to visit my fiancée." He shrugged. "We have the family dinner coming up, and your father thought it was a good idea for me to arrive early. Did you forget about that?"

Yes, I had forgotten about that stupid family dinner my father was hosting for the Whitlocks.

"Of course he did," I mumbled. He just wanted to ruin everything in my life.

"What's wrong?" Elias's concerned face would have been cute if he didn't remind me of his brother.

I had always been good at faking. What was wrong with me? "Nothing. You do know I'm not your fiancée, right?" Our parents had signed a contract, so it was official, but he hadn't proposed.

"Yet," he answered with a wink. I rolled my eyes at him.

"Get out. I'm going to shower and get dressed. You can wait outside."

I showered and threw on some shorts and a T-shirt. Should I have tried harder? Yes. But this was Elias, not Leo, so I wasn't trying to impress anyone. Elias was waiting for me in the game room.

"Who let you into my house?"

"Your assistant. But this guy has been following me around like I'm about to rob the place." He pointed at Milton, who was standing in the corner. "Which would be hard since you have like ten armed security guards up front." Fifteen, aside from Milton and Levi's team. I didn't bother to correct him. When you had as much money as my family, you could never be too careful. Plus, I had staff living in my house—I had to make sure no one hurt them because they couldn't get to me.

I sighed and threw myself on the couch. "It's okay, Milton. You can leave. He's harmless."

Elias scoffed in fake disbelief. "Why is your house so big? Did you buy it yourself? It's bigger than my parents' house. Do you live here alone?"

Jesus, any other questions?

I stared at the ceiling as I answered his questions. It was painful to look at him. "Yes, I bought it myself. I don't live alone. There are over forty of us."

"So your staff lives here?" he asked.

"Yes, some of them and their families." I had known most of my employees all my life.

"Does that mean you're my sugar momma?"

Grabbing the cushion where my head had been resting, I threw it at him with all the force I had, but he easily deflected it. We both laughed, and it felt good. That had been the first time I had genuinely laughed that week.

He winked at me before saying, "Okay, get up. Take me around New York. I've never been here with a local, plus you owe me a date." He hopped off the couch and started jumping like he was stretching.

"I don't think you'll like any of the places I go to." We were completely different. I liked quieter things. Things that helped me focus.

"Try me, kitty." He had a devilish grin on his face. *I could feed him to the crocodiles at the zoo.*

Zoo.

Why had I thought about the zoo? Memories of the way Leo had held me in his arms as I watched all the animals filled my brain. *He's so much better without you.*

But I wasn't.

"Would you stop with the kitty? I hate nicknames. Why do you call me that, anyway?" I noticed my words were too harsh when his face fell a little.

"Polo calls you Fee, and I didn't hear you complaining." Fee, sleeping beauty, siren, and my favorite, love. I missed hearing all of them.

"That's different," I muttered. I walked to my room, and Elias followed.

The house was designed so that my room faced the driveway. I had bought the land because I had fallen in love with the gorgeous peach blossoms. While the trees were in full bloom, I sat on my balcony and sketched all day.

"I thought you would be a lifeless Barbie doll, but then you showed the claws, and I liked it." Ignoring Elias, I texted Milton to let him know I wanted to go out.

"Where are you staying?" I lived in Great Neck, and it would be easier if we were close by.

Elias whistled as we entered my closet while he spun around. He stared at the enormous crystal chandelier that was in the middle of the two-story room. All the cabinets were made with glass doors, so I could use the clothes as decoration since they were already art. "The Landon," he responded, distracted.

Of course, my father had put him there to spy on us and probably had the paparazzi ready. The Landon was one of my family's hotels. My father had illegal cameras all around it to use as ammunition against his allies if he ever needed to.

"Next time, you can stay here."

"Are you saying you want me to come over often?" He wiggled his eyebrows suggestively, and I snapped at him.

"You know what? Forget it. I was trying to be nice." I was so tired of this week. I just wanted it to end. I turned around, but Elias grabbed my arm.

"Hey, I'm sorry. I just like to joke around."

Happy, Felicity? Now you're being a total bitch. God, I missed Leo. He was so easy to be around. "Is everything okay?"

His eyes softened, and at that moment, he looked so much like Leo that I threw my arms around him and let out all the tears I had been holding. Elias hugged me back and pulled me to the couch.

"What's wrong, kitty? You can trust me." He passed a hand up and down my arm, trying to comfort me. I tried to talk and tell him I was okay, but I couldn't stop sobbing, so I gave up. They were a good family. They didn't deserve this. Why did my father want to mess with them? How could I face Leo when I knew he was giving his heart to the wrong person?

I was a killer.

I hugged Elias harder until my arms were hurting. After what felt like hours, I finally calmed down enough to walk to the bathroom so I could wash my face.

Elias was waiting for me outside with a worried look on his face. "Thank you," I choked out.

Closing the distance between us, he hugged me tight against his chest. "We can stay in if you want." His voice was soft, and it made me want to cry again. I took a step back and shook my head.

"No, it's fine. I need the fresh air." We headed to the garage, where security was already waiting for us.

"Where are you taking me?" He looked so excited that he was practically jumping in his seat.

Thank you, I told him in my head. *Thank you for not making this awkward.*

"It's a surprise." My phone rang, and it was Nick. I hesitated before I answered.

"Hello?" I said tentatively. *Please don't let it be Leo, but please let it be Leo.*

"Hey, sis." I was disappointed and happy at the same time.

"What's up?" Elias eyed me curiously.

"It's Nick."

"I'm arriving tomorrow night for Sunday dinner. Do you have space for me? I'd rather be with you than at a hotel with nothing to do."

"Yeah, you can stay with me. What time do you land? We can pick you up." I was excited to see Nick. I could take the boys out for dinner and maybe he would tell me something about Leo without me having to ask.

"Great, I'll text you the details. Thanks, sis."

We disconnected the call, and Elias told me about his passion for music. He wanted to start his own record label and was trying to find new artists. He used to spend a lot of time at clubs and parties, networking so he could make connections. I respected that he hadn't used his family name to start his business. He hadn't told anyone yet because he wanted to wait until he released his first album. I understood what it felt like to start a business on your own. I also understood what it felt like to watch it thrive from the outside. I had never set foot in my store. Most of my designers believed Jane was the owner. Keeping it a secret was the only way to keep my family away from it.

Having Elias open up to me made me feel even worse about how I had judged him. He was just trying to create his own path.

We arrived at our destination. There were no telltale signs outside, so Elias didn't know where we were. He looked around and gave me an exasperated look. I laughed at him and grabbed my bag. "Come on. You said we would do things I like. No backing down now."

"Never. I'm not afraid," he said with a grin.

Unlike his brothers, Elias had dimples, which made him look more boyish.

We entered the building and walked toward the back door. I opened the door and looked at Elias, waiting for his reaction.

"An ice rink?" He had a massive smile on his face.

"Yeah." There were no classes right now, so the ice rink was empty. "Grab a pair of skates from that wall. I'm going to change. I'll be right back."

I changed into my skating dress. It was a sleeveless red turtleneck that fell next to my breasts and connected at the back. There were rhinestones around the neck and the front. Elias was ready by the time I got back. He gave me a once-over and smiled.

I opened the rink door and got inside. Elias grabbed the door and looked at the ice like it was the enemy.

"Is this your first time?" I skated back to the door and held my hand out to him. He took it and smiled shyly.

"It is. Don't let me fall," he said, taking my hand.

He stepped inside and squeezed my hand while trying not to fall. This was adorable. I wanted to laugh so badly, but I didn't want to embarrass him.

Elias finally got both feet in but had a death grip on the rink topper.

"Open your feet like this and move them slowly. One at a time." I pulled him along with me, and he wasn't that bad.

"I'm skating!" he yelled and then fell on his ass. I barely stayed up, but I couldn't contain my laughter anymore.

I showed him how to keep his balance, and he slowly got better. "Wait, I need to record this. Can we ask one of your henchmen?" he asked, stopping in the middle of the ice, which was an awful choice for him. He looked like Bambi trying to stay up. I shook my head at him but skated to the door and gave Milton his phone. Elias yelled the passcode to Milton: "It's 143831."

I skated back to him and held his hand again. "Like the title of Ayden's song?"

"Yeah, he's my favorite singer," he said. I could get him back-stage passes for Ayden's next concert.

"Ready?" I asked.

"Let's do this." Elias moved around the rink slowly. I tried to hold him as best I could so he didn't fall, but every time he tried to go a little faster, he fell on his ass. After a couple of laps, he could finally stay upright on his own for a few seconds. "Okay, I'm exhausted. I need to sit down."

"Low stamina," I joked, and he gave me a devilish smile.

"Not where it counts, kitty." He winked at me, and I punched him in the shoulder. "I want to see you do it."

"You've seen me skate for the past hour." I massaged my thigh muscles, feeling a little tight. It had been a couple of months since the last time I'd skated.

"No, you've been helping me stay off of my ass for the past hour. You did a poor job, by the way." He wiggled his eyebrows, and I wished I had let him fall more.

"Fine, I'll do one routine." I waved at Daniel and signaled a two. He immediately went to put on the music. "Prepare to be amazed." I winked at Elias and took my spot in the center of the rink.

The music blared from the speakers, and I did Gracie Gold's "And All That Jazz" routine. Elias filmed and cheered me on. I even picked up a hat from Milton to make the dance more exciting. Elias went crazy when I did the axels and my final spin. I skated back to him and bowed. The phone was still pointed at me, and his mouth was wide open.

"That was amazing, kitty." My pride liked the look of fascination he gave me.

"I know." I got out of the rink and started taking my skates off. Elias started furiously texting with a huge grin on his face.

"Are you hungry?" I asked.

"Hell yes, where are you taking me now?" he said, pulling his eyes away from his phone.

"Surprise," I said, winking at him.

Milton escorted us to the SUVs, and we hopped in. We were now headed to Midtown Manhattan.

"I know where this is. It's Times Square. We have a friend that lives close by," Elias said with his face plastered to the windows and waving at the yellow cabs. His phone rang. He answered and put it on speaker. "Did you see the video?"

"I did." Leo's gentle voice filled the car, and my heart beat a million miles per hour. He was here. Well, not here, but I could hear him.

"Dude, she was amazing. You should have seen her." Elias gave me a huge smile. I forced myself to smile back, but my body was in shock. "You're on speakerphone, by the way."

"She looked beautiful and happy. You're a lucky man." Was that for me? Or was he just talking to Elias? Was he the man?

I'm not happy without you. I'm miserable. I miss you, I wanted to yell.

"We're here," Milton announced. He turned around and looked at me. I knew he could see my pain. He gave me a sad smile before getting out of the car with David. I quickly got out to avoid listening to their conversation.

Levi parked next to us and tilted his head when he saw I was flustered. I turned around, ignoring his question while we waited for Elias to finish his call.

When he was done, Elias walked directly toward me and grabbed my hand. I tried to pull away, but he intertwined our fingers and pulled me along. I put on a fake smile and let him keep my hand for the time being.

"Ready to eat the best meal of your life?" My voice sounded as cheery as I could make it. Thoughts of Leo were still floating around in my mind. The way he kissed me and how he held me in his arms, protecting me from the world outside of the bubble we built.

"Yes! Which direction are we going in?"

I pointed to the hot dog cart and laughed at him. Times Square was always busy. Sometimes I came here just to get lost in the people, the noise, and the smell. The faint odor of exhaust and sewage was comforting.

"Come on, you can't come to New York and not eat a hot dog." Elias loved the hot dogs and made conversation with the owner of the cart. I bought hot dogs for everyone, and we all enjoyed them while looking at the bustling streets of New York. We walked around, entering different buildings and stores, because Elias wanted to see everything. I pulled him away so we could go to the Statue of Liberty, where we bought fake crowns and posed for so many pictures that I was exhausted. One thing I was learning about Elias was that he loved taking pictures. Once the statue was closed, we headed back home.

"Do you want to pick up your things from the hotel so you can stay with me?" I could see he wanted to joke, but he just gave me a small smile and agreed. This was for my benefit, not his.

We made our way through the parking lot without cameras. It was reserved for private use. I waited for Elias to come back, not risking getting out of the car in case someone saw me. Not even fifteen minutes later, Levi and Elias were making their way back.

"Do you have an issue with kids?" My question caught him off guard, and I could tell his mind was going places mine was not. His hand reached for mine and gently caressed it. I was frozen in place, unsure of what to do with that intimate touch. My body wanted to yank my hand away, but my brain knew to stay calm.

"I want as many as you want. Preferably a lot of them." Only one man could get me to share my body with another human for nine months, and he wasn't in this car.

"The staff gets together every Friday. They put bouncy castles for the kids in the backyard. I was wondering if you were okay with having dinner with everyone." The Whitlocks didn't seem like the type to look down on anyone, but I wouldn't let Elias be an asshole in my house.

Friday nights were always a lot of fun. I rarely joined them since I didn't want everyone to feel like they couldn't enjoy themselves with their boss around.

"Oh . . . yeah . . . no, of course. Sounds fun."

I averted my gaze to stop the awkwardness, although I didn't think it helped. We rode in silence the rest of the way.

Was Leo happy? Did he not care about us? Was that why he thought I looked happy? Was life supposed to be this complicated?

"Felicity?"

The car stopped in front of the house. Milton and David got out. I turned to Elias, who was already looking at me. "Yes?"

"I'll treat you right. I know there are a lot of things said about me, but they aren't true. Give me a chance. Let's get to know each other. I admit I was a bit of an ass when we first met, because I was so nervous, and I know that's not an excuse. I just want you to know that I really want to make this work, and not just because you are, without a doubt, the most beautiful woman walking this earth."

My eyebrows rose without my permission—I was surprised

he didn't mind that our parents had arranged our marriage without inviting us to the discussions.

"Sorry, everyone always says it. Don't get me wrong. You're a dream in pictures, but in person, I understand why they say you're achingly beautiful. Sometimes I feel like it's a sin to look at you, and I would have to go to hell just for doing it, but it's gotten to the point that I would rather go to the abyss than take my eyes off you."

"Elias, I . . ." *I love your brother.*

The Whitlock brothers made it so hard for you to break their hearts. Why did they all have to be so good?

"It's okay. Just think about it. Let's go inside." We'd been here before, but I let him walk us inside. What else was I supposed to do? Honesty had always been my policy, but it wasn't my place to tell him. I didn't want to start a fight between him and Leo, especially when I couldn't even be with Leo.

My phone rang, and Benjamin's name flashed on the caller ID. "I have to take this." I turned from Elias and headed toward my office. "What is it?" I answered.

"Cousin, help." Benjamin's sobs echoed across the silent room. I took a deep breath. This night was about to be long.

I pushed the worry aside and kept my voice calm. "Where are you?"

"Apart"—a sob—"ment."

"Doc or bag?" Please let it be a doctor. I'd had enough of the bags. It didn't help that I'd covered fifteen deaths and threatened a child.

His answer came with more cries. "Bag."

"Okay, don't touch anything. Sit down. Don't move, call, or text anyone. I'll be there in thirty." I quickly sent a message to my team, letting them know of the emergency.

Leaving the office, I went to find Elias, who was currently in the kitchen with Ana, my head of staff. They were both laughing, and he was helping her chop some vegetables. Everyone else was probably using the outside kitchen.

"Hey, I have to go out for about two hours, but I should be back for dinner," I told him.

He searched my face but gave me a soft smile.

"No problem. Ana will teach me how to make pico de gallo. We're having Mexican food tonight." He winked at her before going back to work.

Ana had white midlength hair that was always styled in a layered cut that framed her face beautifully. She was short with a medium build and soft, round features. The best part about her was that she gave the best hugs in the world. Ana had been my nanny since the day I was born, and I didn't know where I would be without her. She was like the mom I'd never had.

"That's great," I said and walked toward Ana, who hugged me. "*¿Vas a hacer flan?*" Typically, Mexican nights meant the smell of flan would be in the air.

"*Sí, mi corazón.*" She'd called me my heart since I was a little girl.

I kissed the top of her head and walked out.

YOUR HAND IS SAFE IN MINE

Felicity

"Come in," I said when a sharp knock came from my bedroom door.

Milton walked in with a tight expression and hard eyes. I finished putting my black hoodie on and prepared for whatever speech he was about to give me. "We're not going to save Benjamin again. You already covered fifteen murders this week, and you're acting like that didn't take a piece of your soul. I'm done watching you destroy yourself."

"Milton, step away. No one is asking you to come with us." I fisted my hands, dying to push him out of the way.

He took another step toward me, and I could feel his barely controlled rage. "How do you expect to catch Simon making a mistake when the only loose end he has, you so graciously help clean it every time? How do you expect to destroy Simon and be the heir when every time Benjamin is in trouble, you drop every-thing to go fix his problems? Do you think Simon doesn't know about his son's addiction and how you're covering it up for him? How stupid do you think he is?"

"I don't care if he knows or not. I'm not going to leave Benjamin on his own. I'm the only one he has! Do you think I don't want to take his place? Of course I do, but there must be another way. I'm not going to hurt Benjamin to get to Simon!" I shouted.

Milton kicked the door closed before responding. "Leave your family. Leopold is in love with you, whether you want to admit it to yourself or not. He'll come with you if you ask. I can take you away where no one will ever find you. I know you're scared that he will get hurt, but look at you. You've been a mess since we left Whitlock."

I wanted to go, but I couldn't risk his safety. Milton was amazing, but everyone we hired was just as good. "I'm not going anywhere. I've spent years of my life getting to the top. Running away means I'm letting down my father and grandfather. I promised him before he died that I would always do what was necessary for the family."

After I'd met Leo, I hadn't given any weight to that promise, but it was time to wake up. I knew what my family was capable of, and we would never be safe. "If it comes down to Benjamin and Leo, I'm going to choose Benjamin. I can't leave him to go play house with Leo. I already left him once when I went to that asylum, and he lost his way. If I hadn't left him, he wouldn't be using." Leo and I were over, there was nothing that could change that and I had to accept it. I couldn't lose Benjamin too. "If Simon fails, I'll take my chance, but if not, I'll follow my orders because that's the only way I can protect the people I love."

He shook his head and looked at me with pity. "Simon isn't going to fail. He's untouchable. If you stay, you'll be miserable for the rest of your life. Benjamin at least has people that care about him. He has his family. Leo is willing to fight for you and be in your corner. You can't give up just because you're scared. And don't think I don't know that you don't want to leave your father either."

I opened my mouth to deny it but I couldn't, so I closed it.

"Your father doesn't even deserve you. He was demoted for good reason. You still have a bargaining chip against him—use it!" Milton roared. I shook my head. I couldn't use it. I would lose what little I had of my father too. "You're going to have to choose one of them. A cousin you only see when you have to clean up his messes, a father who doesn't value you or a man that loves you. It should be an easy choice, princess. You can't have it all, and the longer you wait, the harder it will be."

This would all be so much easier if I could get rid of Simon. I hated being reminded that Simon was untouchable. I hated that stupid clause that protected the head of the family and the heir. If it was up to me, he would have disappeared, but it was impossible. Even if I managed to get rid of him, the investigation that would proceed would point the finger straight at me, and when that happened, I'd lose everything. An attempt on their lives was punishable by death.

"It wasn't his fault. It was my fault. He started drinking because of me. I'm the reason my grandfather took everything away from Father." My voice broke, and my eyes betrayed me as tears streamed down my face.

"No, princess." He pulled me into his arms, and I buried my face in his chest. "You were a child. He's a grown man who has made the wrong decision at every turn. Even now, you still love him when he doesn't deserve it. Your father doesn't deserve your love. He never has, and he never will."

"You don't understand," I mumbled.

"You know I do."

"If I hadn't been born, Mom could have loved him. I was in the way. He loved her so much; he still does. If I give him back the company, he'll see that I'm not worthless." I wasn't expecting my father to love me again, but at least I hoped to make him proud. To make him like me.

"If he hasn't realized how wonderful you are by now, he never will. You have a chance at happiness. Why are you not taking it? Your father isn't more important than you." I wiped my tears and pushed away from him. Milton had a way of making me feel like quitting. I wanted to be by Leo's side, but I also wanted to help my father. Starting a fight with my father over a man would undo everything I'd ever worked for to keep our relationship stable.

"I'm still not letting Benjamin get hurt. You can come with us or stay behind." He groaned but followed me down the stairs and out of the house.

We took the side entrance into Benjamin's building and made our way up through the private elevator that led to the penthouse. There were no cameras in this area. We all had separate entrances with no cameras. It was one of the unspoken rules that everyone followed. I'd left David behind because, even though Jane denied it, I could see her squirming at the idea. She could do whatever she wanted, and no one would ask or care. See? I could also be a good best friend from time to time. Also, I needed to ensure she stayed in place and had an alibi.

Benjamin's place was a mess, and it smelled awful. The acidic fumes of dried beer and sweat made me gag. I forced myself to swallow and ignore the urge to empty my stomach. The floor was brownish and sticky, which I was hoping was due to alcohol. There was a brunette lying on the floor, and her lifeless brown eyes stared directly at me.

She had me frozen in place.

For the first time since I'd been doing this, I felt a sting of fear run up my spine. Milton squeezed my shoulder, helping me break free. I quickly looked away and headed toward Benjamin. He was cuddled up on the sofa, completely naked. His chest was rising and falling, and I sighed, relieved. I tapped him lightly on the shoulder. He stirred awake, and those vulnerable brown eyes met mine. "Amira." His groggy voice softened my heart, but I reminded myself that wouldn't help him.

He needed to stop.

"Get up. Let's get you in the bath." He nodded and grabbed my hand. I held his head to make sure he didn't look at the pale girl on the floor. If he saw her, he'd start crying, making everything difficult. The guys needed to work fast.

I placed him on the chair and started a bath. He didn't seem to be high, but there was still a residue of white powder on his face. Which wasn't the only thing they'd done tonight. There were pills and empty liquor bottles on the table.

Once the bath was ready, I helped him get in the tub and shampooed his hair. "I'm sorry," he said, hiccuping through the tears. I kept shampooing his hair since I knew it calmed him down, and I let him talk. "We've been together several times. We were just having fun. I passed out after trying to have sex, which didn't work. When I woke up, she wasn't breathing."

"Close your eyes." I waited until he did what I asked, and then I rinsed his hair. "Here." I passed him a washcloth and turned around, giving him some privacy to clean himself before I got him out. I didn't trust his coordination at the moment.

Wrapping him in a towel, I guided him to his room and prepared the bed before tucking him in. He wouldn't like what I had to say, but a Price could never walk down this path.

As I leaned away, Benjamin grabbed my hand. "Cuddle me?"

I rolled my eyes at him while saying, "Scoot over." I got on top of the covers since he was still naked. We hugged each other while I let him relax for a bit before upsetting him. "Do you trust me?" I asked.

"You're the only one I trust." He squeezed me harder, the vulnerability in his voice already gone.

"I'm sending you someplace to get help." The words came out gently. I didn't want him to go, but this was the third body that had come from this apartment, and I didn't want him to be next. Girls joined him, not understanding that he was like a drug vacuum. They would never be able to keep up with him. I was tired of sending bodies home to devastated parents who never knew their daughters had died trying to get Benjamin Price in their pants. I'd tried getting them to leave but given up when none of them cared about the warnings. They were only after the money.

He pulled back and gave me an annoyed look. "Amira, I don't need a parent."

He did. We all did. Someone like Ellen, who showed love willingly and cared about her kids. This was also his fault. Even if he never forced them to do drugs, it was his responsibility to make sure they didn't do too much, but how could he do that when he was worse than they were?

"I'm not saying this as your cousin but as the cleaner. It's my job to keep this family afloat and guard its reputation. Rule number one. You're failing at rules number two and four. You will no longer be the heir if you continue on this path." If he wasn't careful, he would lose everything. I wasn't sure how this had happened. When I'd come back home at nineteen, he was already using. It was probably a form of rebellion against all the rules we had to follow, but he chose the worst one to break.

"I won't go," his stubborn highness said.

"If you don't go, I'll have to go to rule five, which means you will lose your position. We'll both be in trouble if anyone finds out what you've been doing. You can make a mistake, but I can't. I promise I've found someone you'll like in a nice place. You'll take a vacation there, and when you return, he'll move in with you to help with the transition. He'll inform me of your progress. No one else will know." It would be easy to rat him out and become the heir, but I wouldn't do that to him. I loved him.

Resignation entered his eyes, his shoulders slumped, and he sighed hard. "You have everything ready, don't you?"

I stayed ready. "Omar will take you after you get some rest. I already submitted your vacation hours and approved them."

"Why do I always feel like you have more power than me, even though I'm the heir?"

Valid question. The system was always set up the same way. The head of the family was Simon. My father was his right-hand man. As the heir, it was Benjamin's job to maintain the family's reputation, but somehow, I'd gotten stuck with the job. This must be the two head honchos making my life miserable on purpose, and Benjamin was a rare breed of Price. He was thoughtful and caring.

Soft.

"Because I'm the one that has to do the tough shit around here," I said, smiling at him.

He gasped in surprise. "Amira, language." We both laughed, and I hugged my brother from another mother tighter. Clara might be his sister, but we had always been closer. Not that anyone in the family knew, because we played rivals for the throne in public.

"How's Clara?" The last family meeting was in December, so I hadn't seen her in a while. She never attended dinners, but meetings were mandatory.

"Being a crying bitch, like always. She's currently in Korea, trying to fix her face. By the time she gets back, we probably won't even recognize her."

Clara was special. No one cared what she did, and she was spoiled to the bone. It would be funny to see what she would do if both Benjamin and I died. The rest of the family would eat her alive. Simon had never bothered with showing her how to run the family business. She acted tough just because she had the power of the family name, but underneath all that, she hadn't done one important thing. She had no idea how it felt to be manipulated to preserve the family legacy. "You should have been my sister instead of the spawn from hell."

"You're my brother."

His eyes softened, and he kissed my forehead. "I can't let you keep covering for me. As the older brother, I promise to get better. Scout's honor."

Watching him act like a fool with two fingers held up, I knew he could do it. He had to. I didn't know how much longer I could get away with covering for him, but any wrong move would be a death sentence, and I wasn't ready to die.

"You better," I mumbled with a smile.

He gave me an exaggerated eye roll. "Whatever, Fifi." He laughed at my annoyed face. Clara would always say that before she turned her back to me. "Anything new?" he asked.

I debated whether I should tell him about Leo. He wouldn't tell his father, but I didn't want to take any chances. Simon was not someone you wanted to give your weaknesses to. "I met someone," I finally said.

"Do arranged marriages actually work?" He scrunched his nose at me. I flicked it gently, like I had done hundreds of times before.

"I fell in love with the brother." I guessed they worked . . . in a way.

Smiling at me, he tapped my forehead lightly and shook his head. "Uncle must be over the moon."

"He threatened to kill him." This was our life. Doing the dirty things for them and then getting it thrown in our faces.

Milton entered the room to let us know they were done.

"Pack light. You're going to Arizona!" I told Benjamin.

WHAT'S LEFT OF YOU

Leo

I'd texted Milton yesterday, needing to know how Fee was. I'd had an uneasy feeling all day, and nothing was making it go away. He said it had been a hard day for her but that she was fine. After not getting any more details out of him, I wanted to smash my phone into a million pieces.

My last conversation with Fee was an absolute disaster. I didn't know if I was stupid or brave for fighting for a woman who had admitted to being evil. The fact was that I was past the point of caring. I didn't care about the rumors. I didn't care that everything that had to do with her father's immoral business deals connected right back to her. I didn't care that she was my brother's fiancée. The only thing I cared about was that I wanted her to wake up every day in my arms for the rest of our lives, where she was free to make her own mistakes and we would work through them together.

During the week we'd spent together, she'd shown me who she really was—a girl who wanted to sketch and design fashion pieces; it was obvious that it was her passion. She didn't even notice how I stared at her for the entirety of my meetings while she was sketching. With her pencil between her thumb and index finger, she would tap her middle and ring fingers against her leg and sometimes mine while she was lost in her brilliant mind. I asked her why she didn't start her own brand, which made her cheeks turn pink while she shook her head.

I missed those days. I missed her. I wanted to go back to that room with her, where she made me smile, laugh, and live, filling my body with a peace that only she gave me. Where she looked at me like I was all she needed, and I could prove to her that she was all I needed because I loved every part of her, the good and the bad; without them, she wouldn't be the woman I loved and admired.

Elias was with her, and I felt useless. Showing up unannounced would probably piss her off, and I didn't have the energy to keep acting like she meant nothing to me.

"I can't work with all your grunting and sighing," Ryan declared, pulling me from my thoughts and turning to look at me with squinted eyes. I was sitting on the sofa in his office. He had been working all week with a private investigator I'd hired to follow Alexander Price. It wasn't easy to find dirt on him. The problem was no one would talk about their contract, and everything seemed to lead back to Fee. Nothing was under Alexander's name.

I was waiting for the investigator to call. He was a former federal agent who seemed to know what he was doing. We had meetings with him every day at noon since he was currently in New York. The phone rang and Ryan immediately picked up and put it on speaker. "Alexander met with his lawyer yesterday late at night. I'll try to see if there's anything useful we can find at the firm. There must be a reason they met so late. I also noticed one of Simon's men was following Alexander all day today. I was able to get the company's private financial records. I'm sending those to you right now. I'll have an update tomorrow same time."

"Thank you, I'll cross-reference the private records with the public ones," Ryan said before they hung up.

That was the most we'd gotten in a day. Ryan got to work while I waited for Amber, whom I had asked for help. If there was anyone who knew something about the Price family, it was her. "Have you found anything?" I asked Ryan.

"Not yet," he responded. "And for the love of God, stop twitching and your bouncing legs; it's driving me insane."

My body was vibrating with how fast my legs were bouncing, and I hadn't noticed it until he mentioned it. I stretched my legs in front of me, letting them relax and giving Ryan an *Are you happy?* look while his face said *Yes.*

An hour later, I heard a car pull up and immediately jumped off the couch and ran to the door. Amber walked in with a manila envelope in hand. "Hey, how are you?" Her eyes met mine before she looked around the living room and headed toward the couch. There was no expression on her face and no words were said, and to that I wanted to say, *Why the fuck is everyone acting so weird lately?*

"Please, take a seat," I mumbled.

"Is your friend going to come out?" she asked while sitting on the love seat.

"No," I said, sitting on the couch in front of her.

"Good, because I'd like to talk to you alone." I motioned for her to continue with my hand. Her stoic expression disappeared as she played with the collar of her black shirt and pushed her lips to the side.

"I've known Felicity my entire life, and I love her like a sister, even though she doesn't believe me when I tell her. Everything in this envelope is what my father has as leverage on the Price family. It's not much since it doesn't have anything that would implicate my family either. Before I give it to you, I need to know you won't use this to hurt her."

"Amber, I would never—"

"Let me finish, please," she said in a soft voice. I nodded. "The moment I saw you with her at the beach, I knew who you were, but I also knew she had never looked at a man like that. It was always with longing and resignation, but with you . . ." She shook her head gently and closed her eyes. "She looked at you like she had just discovered a new world." When she opened her eyes again, tears were forming in them. "I've hurt her, just like almost everyone around her, and the ones that haven't and are still by her side are her employees. She doesn't have anyone. Do you understand what I'm saying?"

I nodded in response. I felt my chest constrict, and although I had already suspected she was alone, I wished it wasn't true. I wished she had someone else.

"How did you hurt her?"

Amber averted her gaze to the wooden table between us. I stayed quiet, giving her time to decide if she would tell me. When she spoke again, it was barely above a whisper.

"My mom would always drop me off for playdates when we were about a year old. Her father wanted her to have friends since he was always working and couldn't spend much time with her. When we were kids, Felicity was the apple of his eye. Anything she wanted was hers."

He certainly didn't treat her like that now. "What about her mother?" I interrupted, unable to stop myself.

Amber rolled her eyes just like Fee always did. "Aunt Juliette hates Felicity. She always has. I never understood why, and I never realized it until we were almost out of high school since she was always so good to me. Before her seventh birthday, Felicity always had the most extravagant parties that her father planned for her. I was always jealous since mine were never as big as hers, and at that age, I didn't know any better. When her seventh birthday came, she didn't get a party, and when I asked her why, her mother walked in and said she didn't deserve it. I expressed how that sucked because her birthdays were always the best. The next thing I knew, Juliette planned a party for my birthday at her house and did it every year after that, each one more extravagant than the last, and the gifts were outrageous. Felicity never got anything, and I was a naive child who couldn't see how fucked up that was. I even uninvited her from several of my parties. One time it was because I was jealous of a Barbie her nanny got her, and she wouldn't let me play with it. I uninvited her from a party at her own house! Now tell me that isn't fucked up."

Amber blinked, and the first tear fell. I wished I could tell her it wasn't fucked up because she was just a child, but I was already pissed at Juliette, and honestly, I couldn't understand how Amber hadn't noticed how messed up it was until they were in high school. "Please, continue," I said, grinding my teeth.

"For someone who was part of one of the richest families in the world, I never understood why she would always wear the same clothes, and some of them weren't even brand-name items. We all made fun of her in school because of it. But after it happened a couple of times, Benjamin, her cousin, beat several boys up and ignored the girls that bullied her, and since he was the hottest guy in school, most of them stopped. His sister, Clara, didn't care. She and her group attacked Felicity every chance they got. But you know, Felicity being Felicity, it was hard to tell if she was bothered or not."

Was I living in another universe? "What is this teenage bullshit?" I said, annoyed with the turn the conversation had taken. "Why does it matter if she isn't wearing rich kid clothes?" It wasn't even important at that age, especially not for school.

Amber wiped away the tears that hadn't stopped falling and looked at me sheepishly. "My point is that Juliette purposely didn't buy her anything, and all that Felicity had were gifts from family members. Her nanny and Milton practically raised her and would buy what they could, but when you're in a school where everyone cares about showing off, it's noticeable. I'm sure

Juliette only did it because she knew Felicity would be treated poorly. Clara and Juliette have always been close, to the point where they would go on vacations, and I did join them for a few before I realized that Juliette was only using me to hurt Felicity. I excluded her in her own house and let her mom treat me as if I was her daughter, while Felicity just watched us and we wouldn't let her join. I was a total bitch to her and didn't wake up until Benjamin pretty much chewed my ass out and told me I didn't deserve Felicity because while she always had my back, I was a useless plastic doll that was going to die alone with no one to give a shit about me, and my husband would leave me for my daughter's best friend."

I couldn't help but smile at Benjamin's words. Out of everyone in the family, he seemed to be the only decent one. Her mom needed to be out of her life ASAP—no question about that.

Amber laughed softly when she noticed my smile, oblivious to the fact that my thoughts had already taken another turn. "Yeah, I definitely needed to get my head out of my ass."

"Where was her father? Why would he allow Juliette to do all that?" Alexander was the most confusing character in her family because although Fee seemed to have reservations about him, she still talked about him with respect, and when I saw them together, she didn't seem scared of him. It was more as if she wanted his validation. From what Amber said, it was like Fee was holding on to an eighteen-year-old memory.

"I'm not sure. I don't think he was aware of anything going on," Amber said with a frown. "They were close when we were kids. She was always with him, but suddenly he just disappeared. He was rarely at the house, and when he was there, all his focus was always on Juliette. It wasn't a secret that he loved Juliette and did whatever he could to make his father agree to their marriage. Juliette came from humble beginnings, and there was nothing that she could contribute to the success of the family." I didn't know that about Fee's mom or Juliette. From what I'd heard, I didn't think calling her a mother was appropriate. While researching Alexander, I'd discovered that Juliette didn't come from a prominent family, but that was all I could find on her.

Amber wiped away the last of her tears before placing the envelope on the table. I believed in second chances. Hell, I believed in third, fourth, fifth, tenth, and hundredth chances, but I couldn't find it in me to sympathize with Amber. Maybe Fee had already forgiven her, but my emotions were running high with how poorly everyone around Fee treated her.

"What do you need from me, Amber? Why are we having this conversation, and what were you hoping to accomplish with it? Because, to be completely honest, you've made my shit list. Saying those words makes me feel like I'm back in high school, but this is all ridiculous, and I don't know where to classify all of you. Fee is the most resilient person I've ever met, and what you told me just proves that I've been right all along. I'm taking her away from anyone who can ever hurt her again. That includes you if you ever decide to do something that makes her close off her emotions, even if it's just for a second. You'll never be allowed to take a step in Whitlock or do business with anyone here."

I took a breath when I was done speaking. We were too old for this kind of petty drama, but there was no way I wouldn't let Amber know where I stood. What I believed was messed up was that Fee didn't even seem to care about what had happened in the past. She never gave Amber a jealous look when I saw them interact or made a snarky remark. It was as if she hadn't endured years of watching her best friend have the love she must have wanted from her mother.

Amber raised her hands in the air and shook her head. "Of course I'll never do anything to hurt her. I just needed to know where you stood," she said.

"By Felicity's side. Thank you for getting those documents for me. Please see yourself out." Her eyes widened in shock, and I didn't bother to give her a second look while I grabbed the envelope and went back to Ryan's office.

"Don't you dare pull out that weed!" Grandma yelled at me from the kitchen window. I was cleaning the backyard and noticed a single weed growing through a tiny crack in the steps.

"It makes the steps look dirty," I yelled back, but she was already out the door and in front of me.

"Do you know why weeds are the prettiest of plants?" I shook my head. What could be pretty about them? They just invaded spaces they shouldn't. "They don't care how many times you break them down; they will rise again and again. No matter how small the crack is, they will always find their way to the light, and they will be greener and stronger than ever." She patted my head as her green eyes smiled at me. "There's beauty in resilience. Never forget that, my sweet boy."

Resilience had never been in a more beautiful form.

LOVE IS JUST A WORD

Felicity

The house smelled amazing. I rushed to my room and changed into something more comfortable before making my way outside; the party had already started, but hopefully, dinner hadn't been served.

I wasn't surprised to find Elias in the bouncy castle with the kids. They were yelling and laughing as they bounced around and fell. "Aunt Felicity!" the children screamed when they saw me. "Come in!" They couldn't control the volume of their voices. I was right there. I took my shoes off and joined them. Elias and I were the monsters they needed to get away from. They ran around screaming at the top of their lungs as if they were really in danger. I wished I had a child's imagination. It was wild.

Leo would be the best dad in the world. Watching the kids run around reminded me of how important it was for them to have a happy childhood. I wanted them to have everything I didn't. My kids would have the best role model and unconditional love. I'd always tell them I loved them, just like I'd tell Leo.

I took a deep breath and tried to clear my head. I had to stop thinking about that, about him. Elias was my future now.

We ran to the tables as Chloe, our chef, announced that dinner was ready. The tables were set up buffet style, but Chloe brought me a separate plate. She served me deconstructed steak fajitas. That had my stomach grumbling. The smell was divine; only she could make a delicious meal with minimal seasoning.

On Fridays, everyone helped Chloe prepare the food. I'd never done it, but I'd watched them. Cooking wasn't something I was interested in. I had to learn how to play the piano, violin, and cello. I did ballet, ice skating, and swimming. I learned Spanish, French, Italian, and Mandarin. So as a child and now as an adult, the kitchen looked exhausting.

When the plates were cleared, the best part of the night came. Ana pulled Elias onto the dance floor. The ladies got excited when they discovered his mom was of Puerto Rican descent. Now they were trying to show him how to dance while I played a game of Lotería. I chose lucky number four for my board, which turned out not to be so lucky tonight. Four games and several tequila shots later, the commotion started. I made my way to the dance floor as a full-time loser. Elias looked confused and panicked as we all ran toward them.

I grabbed him and pulled him to the corner, making sure everyone was safe from his feet. This would be fun to watch, but no one needed to get injured. "Just follow my lead. It'll go slow at the beginning. You're not allowed to leave." Of course he was allowed to leave, but what fun would that be? We stomped with a hand waved in the air as "No Rompas Mi Corazón" by Caballo Dorado played.

I could barely keep the steps right as Elias bumped into me and the person in front of him. I laughed uncontrollably at him, but he ignored me. He bit his lip and looked at his feet, concentrating hard on getting all the steps right. By the time the song ended, he had the steps down. He gave me a look of pride and winked. But the song had just ended. He didn't know the worst part was coming. He was about to leave and look for a seat when I stopped him.

"Where are you going? I thought you weren't scared of anything," I taunted. Understanding dawned on him as he saw everyone stomping faster. "Payaso de Rodeo," the fast version of the song, started playing. I didn't even wait for him to be ready. Everyone knew that if you couldn't keep up with this dance, you got pushed out of the way, and that was exactly what I did to him.

"Shit, kitty." He was out of breath as he tried to keep up with everyone, but we bumped into him when he was in the way. The crowd was laughing, but he had them chanting his name in encouragement. I'd give it to him. He wasn't giving up, even though he looked like he was about to collapse.

The song ended, and we all clapped for him. He gave a little bow and then fell to the floor, hyperventilating.

"Good job," I said. I was laughing, but I was proud. He pointed at me, trying to say something that never came out because he still couldn't breathe.

We danced around him until he got up and found a chair. I kept downing the tequila shots. One shot for every thought of Leo I had. I thought it would be a good idea since I never got drunk to the point where I couldn't walk. However, I should have expected that the drunker I got, the more I thought of him. *Didn't people drink to forget?* I must have been doing it wrong.

Butch was a great cumbia dancer. He twirled me around endlessly. I was so happy I had sneakers on, or else I would have struggled to keep up with the professional dancer that I didn't even know he was.

I was killing this dance floor.

I fell into someone's arms and then got hauled up. "Okay, that's enough for you." For me? I hiccuped.

"I wasss having ssso musht fun. Tell them, Busshy!" I yelled for Butch because he'd undoubtedly tell them what a great dance partner I was.

"I'm Bushy," the man carrying me said. I squinted my eyes because something was wrong.

"Oh, you look teeeeny tiny from up here." He had a pretty smile; he should smile more often.

Something soft was underneath me now. I felt around and saw my bed. Butch called out a goodnight and left me behind without the music.

Without Leo.

Reaching for the covers, I felt the tears burning in my eyes. I was lost and confused. My body was heavy with the weight of the alcohol, but my brain couldn't stop thinking of him. My life was no longer mine. I knew it when they gave me this job. I wasn't a rule breaker.

As I closed my eyes, the image of the girl from Benjamin's apartment flashed in my head. The fear I'd felt earlier ran through my bones, leaving me ice-cold. I hid underneath the covers, even though I knew that wouldn't do anything. I did the normal thing anyone would do in this situation. Relief washed over me when he answered the phone because he could vanquish all my monsters.

"Love? Is everything okay?" Leo's gentle voice made my body relax a little.

"Noooo! She's go . . . going to g . . . get me." I said the words as if they were being pulled from my mouth.

"Where's Milton?"

"I want youuu." Milton couldn't protect me. Only he could. "It'sss the girl. All are haunting me." Leo was talking, but my brain was trying to get the image out of my head and erase the last seventy-two hours. What was happening to me? The more I thought about forgetting her, the clearer I saw her. Her eyes were so empty, but I hadn't killed her. Not like I'd killed the children.

I'd done that.

I'd signed those contracts. I'd chosen to repay the debt I owed my mother over the lives of innocent people who needed help. I'd chosen the life of a woman who'd never cared about me over people who trusted my father's charity. People who had lost their houses when the tornadoes hit had been promised suitable homes where they could raise their children.

"Fee, my love, talk to me." How could his voice be so soft?

My door swung open, making me cry out. Getting tangled in the covers trying to escape, I fell to the floor. "I need you," I whispered, holding my throbbing elbow.

"Princess, it's me. Leopold texted," Milton said. He picked me up and put me back in bed. "Here, drink water."

"Nooo water." I swatted his hand away, trying to get rid of the offensive liquid. He leaned back, and I threw myself at him, squeezing as hard as I could. I didn't want to be alone. He held me until I released him and patted his shoulder, like I'd done numerous times.

"I'll leave the water right here. Call me if you need anything." He pulled the covers up to my chin and turned on my bathroom light before leaving.

I hid underneath the covers again, hugging my pillow for dear life. Benjamin's girl looked at me with dead eyes. The image changed to Leo kneeling in front of me with a revolver to his head. This was what I'd do to him if I didn't let him go. My sobs echoed across the room, leaving my face warm with my tears. Everything was happening too fast. I didn't have time to keep up. A sweet voice penetrated through my defenses.

The soft melody of his voice made me relax.

I fell asleep as he sang for me.

"WHY IS THERE SO MUCH LIGHT?" I groaned loudly and searched blindly for a pillow to put above my pounding head.

"Morning, sleeping beauty." His voice felt good, even when my head was about to explode.

"I'm hungover," I mumbled.

"What do you want for breakfast? I'll have someone prepare it." This was why I loved him, among other things, of course.

"Toast with butter and fresh orange juice." I searched for his warmth, but it wasn't there. "Why aren't you hugging me?"

His next words woke me up. "I'm still in Cali. You never disconnected the call." Say what? The taste of fear returned to the tip of my tongue, but it left as fast as it came.

"I don't remember calling. You stayed on all night?" My voice was making my headache worse, but his voice was soothing me.

"You've slept almost all day, and I would never leave you." The conviction in his voice was clear. I didn't need to see him.

"I should hang up," I said, but I made absolutely no move to get the simple task done.

"Should or want to? Because I want you to stay."

What was more important: what he wanted or what my father wanted? It didn't take more neurons than my hungover brain could currently provide to figure out that I would always want what he wanted.

"Tell me about your week, and once you're done, I'll disconnect without a word." Truth be told, I couldn't carry on a conversation, and I was tired of missing him. I shouldn't be doing this. Jane was right. No matter what I came up with, it didn't end well. I needed more time. I was scared of being without him forever. Scared of losing a chance at happiness. Scared of losing a man who would see me and respect me. Scared of feeling my heart break, but most of all, I was scared of losing my last name.

"One moment, love. Grant, please push back my next meeting," Leo said. I heard a voice before he came back to the phone. "'Kay, I'm back. I woke up without you in my arms for the first time in a week. It took all of Monday to stop feeling empty. Nick and I worked on training him to take over my company. That should give us more time to see each other more often. I'll fly more to New York, and when you can, you can come home to Whitlock."

How did someone like him even exist? He thought of everything. Also, he hadn't said "my home." He'd just said "home." My heart woke up from its week of slumber.

"Tuesday was more of the same, but I missed you more than I did on Monday because I also went to bed without you. Wednesday . . . you guessed it, I missed you to the point that I have no clue what happened that day other than a charity ball at night. I walked to my car without pants and didn't notice until I got there. All the cameras were on me. I'm internet famous now."

It was hard to control the laugh at his exaggerated story, so I went on mute for a bit. I chuckled and held my aching head, which didn't appreciate me at the moment.

"Thursday was harder. I felt like I needed to be with you. I wanted to go to you, but you seemed adamant about the space you needed, so I stayed. I texted Milton to make sure you were okay, and he said you were tired and had a long day at work."

What a traitor. I would have a word with Milton. No, I wouldn't. Part of me wanted him to know how I was.

"Yesterday, my eyes looked a little greener. It was hard to think he was with you and I wasn't. Then they were bright green when you called, and I knew you partied with him, but in the next second, they went back to normal. I realized that at the end of the day, it was me you called. I wished I had you in my arms as you fell asleep, so I could watch your adorable pout. I could finally sleep last night knowing that you were right next to me, even if it was thousands of miles away. I woke up with you still with me, and that brought a smile to my face. Today was one of the days that I wasn't looking forward to working, but you've been here with me." I was about to disconnect, thinking he was done, but he kept talking.

"I understand your family is different, but don't push me

away. This week has been torture, and I can't let you go." I knew how he felt. I didn't want to let him go, either. "I did this all wrong. I should have divided the days by what I did each hour. I have nothing left. Will you stay if I start over and tell you everything by the hour?" His hopeful tone had me reconsidering.

"Yes," I said softly. My breakfast arrived, and I quickly muted my phone. Jane left as soon as she placed the tray on my lap. There was Tylenol, toast with butter, orange juice, and a peach. Only Leo could find a sweet way of telling me he missed my taste. At that moment, I knew I had fallen for him all over again.

He told me everything that happened, even when he went to the bathroom—exactly what he did and how long it took. I loved every second. I should hang up since he had stopped talking, but I couldn't. "You can't hang up, can you?" Leo asked. "Why did you leave me, Fee? I'm still here waiting for you."

I took a shaky breath before I could answer. "We just won't work out. I'm not the person you met."

"So you think you'll be better with my brother?" Really? Was that what he was worried about? He was jealous of his brother. A brother I could barely look at without wanting to cry remembering all the happy memories Leo and I had.

"That's not the point. It's already arranged."

"Are they hurting you?" he asked. His words came out soft and I could hear the worry in his voice.

"No." At least not in the way he was thinking. I shouldn't have told him my father hurt me.

"Don't lie to me, love. Come home, I can protect you." *Leo, if you could I would already be in your arms!* I wanted to yell. *I would be waking up every day next to you for the rest of my life. I would know what it's like to finally be happy.*

I rubbed my temples. "There's nothing to protect me from. I don't want to be with you."

"Then why did you call me last night? Why did you fall asleep when I sang for you? And don't tell me it was my amazing voice."

He'd sung for me? How could I forget that? Why was that distracting me? It wasn't important. I'd called him because I loved him, and I was weak and stupid. I was trying to give him some closure to end it the right way this time, instead of running away without a word, but it wasn't going how I'd planned.

"Because that's just who I am—I use people when I need them. It didn't mean anything," I lied.

"I'm fine with being used," he countered.

I sighed, feeling my headache grow. "Why are you so stubborn? Just why?"

"Why does everyone keep asking that? How am I stubborn? I just want my girlfriend back. You can't just up and leave without saying anything and expect me to forget about you. That's not how it works."

"Isn't it? That's what Riley did, and you let her go." Yes, I was being a bitch, but he wasn't getting it while I was trying to be nice.

"Big fucking difference being you're not her. I can't let you go, Fee. You promised me we would try to make it work."

"I wanted to give you closure. I wanted us to be on the same page, but you're making this so difficult. Just let me go."

"I'm never letting you go, because I don't believe that you want me to. I think you're also trying to find your way back to me," he said. *Lord Almighty, give me the strength to deal with this man.*

I groaned in frustration. Why was he so damn obstinate? "I said everything I needed to say. I'm sorry I couldn't keep my promise, but I did try." I hung up without another word. Talking to Leo was like talking to a reinforced wall. Nothing was getting through. He would eventually forget me. He would realize like everyone else that I wasn't worth it.

By the time I left my room showered and ready for the day, it was already two p.m. Elias was in the television room, and he looked way better than me. "Don't say a word," I mumbled. I was already feeling miles better than that morning, but I didn't want to talk about whatever I'd done that I couldn't remember.

We watched a game show while we waited for the time to pick up Nick. Elias told me he'd won two rounds of Lotería after I was carried out.

My phone rang, and I debated not picking it up until I saw it was Father. "Hello."

"Come to my house. Now." He hung up without another word.

I passed a hand over my face and sighed. *What happened now?*

FIGHTING FOR ME

Felicity

"Sign." Father barked as soon as I entered his office. I walked to his desk with fear tickling my spine. I did something I hadn't done in a long time. I quickly read the document before signing and looked back at him. There was nothing wrong with it from what I could see.

Kyle walked in the room with a smirk on his face. Kyle was Simon's guard and loyal dog. He was the same height as me, had tan skin, brown eyes and short hair. "What is he doing here?" I asked, looking back at my father.

"I came to take you for a ride," Kyle said. My eyes cut to him. His body was blocking the door. Was he here for me? Was this the day it all came to an end? Even with all the training I had, I could never take on Kyle. Sure, I could defend myself from most people, but not the highly trained mercenaries my family hired. "Don't worry, I'm not here to kill you, *yet*. We discovered a PI broke into the company and has been following Mr. Price. I'm just taking you to interrogate him."

Okay, so I just had to go do my job. I could feel my body

relaxing although I didn't show it. "Be careful with how you speak to me, Kyle. I'm still a Price and you're just Simon's dog. We can get another one of those like this," I said, snapping my fingers in his face.

His smirk never disappeared as he licked his lips while staring at me. Father interrupted our stare-down by saying, "Jerry is going with you." How much supervision did I need for one job? It wasn't like I hadn't dealt with private investigators before. We typically let them do their thing while we monitored them. We were very careful, so it was hard for them to even get close to finding anything. I pushed past Kyle and out the door, but I still heard my father say, "Next time you disrespect my daughter I'll terminate you on the spot."

Father might be cruel, but in his eyes, only he was allowed to hurt me.

Kyle took us to a familiar warehouse that we used only for interrogations. Jerry and five men from his team as well as my team came with us. "You can leave now," I told him. "I know how to do my job."

"Boss is very interested in this one. No one has been able to get inside the company. I was ordered to stay." He looked at me defiantly, and as we both knew I had no other choice but to concede.

I'd changed to a black disposable outfit before leaving the house. I liked to keep things clean, but sometimes it got messy. The room where the naked man was being held was already prepared. Everything was covered in plastic, and he was tied to a chair. There was a table to his left with different knives and other devices. His face was covered in blood, which meant Kyle had already worked on him. The man looked to be physically fit, around fifty years old. His brown eyes were alert. "What, you couldn't get anything out of him?" I smirked at Kyle.

"Let's see if you can do better, *princess*," Kyle mocked.

"Wait outside," I ordered.

Kyle closed the door behind him. I looked at the mirror to my left. Kyle would be in that room, watching us from the other side of that glass. I grabbed a long, thin knife and pulled a chair in front of the man and sat down. "It's been a tiring week for me. Why don't you save me the work and I save you the pain, okay?"

"Why has it been a tiring week for you?" the man asked, making me grin.

"I see you're still working. I like hard workers. How about this?" I asked, crossing my legs and leaning back. "You tell me who you work for, and I give you a new job. Huh? That sounds like a great deal to me. What do you think?"

"Thanks for the offer, but I prefer to stay on the right side of the law."

I nodded, pursing my lips cynically. "Understandable." I slammed the knife into his leg. His scream echoed across the room. His eyes and body hardened as his attitude changed and he focused on my soft smile. They always underestimated me, but sooner or later everyone talked.

For the next hour I worked the man, but I had to give it to him—he was resilient.

The door opened and Kyle stuck his head in. "Want a break? I can continue."

I rolled my eyes. "I'm fine." I waved him out. He was just distracting me.

"You don't seem to like each other," the bloodied man noted. His voice was barely above a whisper.

"You spent time with him. Which one of us did you prefer? I think I'm the clear winner."

He chuckled, surprising me. Was he ex-military? He was calmer than I would expect anyone to be at this point considering I was slowly slicing up his body. "He was less painful, but you're sweeter. I can see why he loves you." His voice was so low that I wasn't sure if I'd heard him correctly. I leaned forward and looked into his eyes.

"What did you say?" I whispered.

"Do you know who I work for now?"

My father's words rang in my head. *Do you think you can keep your job a secret from him? That he will never find out how far you're willing to go to get the job done? Do you really think he's never going to wonder, never going to look further into your affairs?*

I leaned back and smirked as if the news of Leo's involvement meant nothing to me. "So that's your big secret?" The PI leaned his head slightly and the corner of his eyes tightened. "You're doing all this for money?"

There was a shift in his eyes when he understood what I was trying to do. Kyle was still watching and we needed to sell this for him. "Do you know how much I could sell your information to your competitors for? Millions. Who doesn't want to see the Price family fall?"

"And what information did you get?" I asked.

"You're going to have to torture me more for that, sweetheart." There had been a slight shift in his body as the tension slowly left it. He thought he was leaving this place alive.

I placed my hand against his chest, feeling his ribs. Before he could process what was happening, I dug my knife straight into his heart. I twisted it before pulling it out and watching the light drain from his eyes. Kyle busted into the room while I calmly cleaned the knife with a cloth.

"Why did you do that? He didn't tell you what he had or who he was working for," he screamed, pointing at the body.

I gave him a bored look. "He was clearly working alone since he wanted to sell the information to the highest bidder."

"There has to be more," Kyle growled.

"Why don't you ask him?" I asked, pointing at the dead man.

His eyes narrowed at me, but instead of saying anything, he stormed out of the room.

I let out the breath I was holding. My heart was thundering in my chest, no longer under control. The man had to die. What if

Kyle hadn't released him until he'd fully broken him? He would have talked—it was inevitable. I couldn't let Leo's name leave his lips. I washed the blood away, trying but failing to control my trembling body. I had never killed anyone before, not with my own hands. I knew I shouldn't be focusing on that when there were loose ends we had to tie up for Leo, so I pushed all those feelings away. I took a couple deep breaths and changed my clothes before going to Milton. I pulled him outside and told him what had happened. Now we had to trace all the steps the private investigator had taken and clean everything. Kyle found nothing on the PI's phone, not even a number, so that was a dead end, which made our job easier. Everything that connected the PI to Leo had to be erased.

I stopped talking when Jerry started walking toward us. I hid my hands behind my back, afraid that they would reveal something. "I'll be heading out unless you need me and my team," Jerry said.

"We can handle the cleanup."

Jerry nodded and left. I didn't blame him for what he'd done to me last time. He was just following orders.

I turned back to Milton. "Send Levi. Plant evidence that makes it look like he's done this to other families and is just looking for a paycheck. Nothing should lead back to Leo."

"I'll handle it. You have a dinner reservation with the Whitlock boys. David is taking you. Butch and I will be there when we're done here."

I plastered my best fake smile to meet Nick and Elias. As soon as Nick saw me, he came running to the car and gave me a big hug. "Have you missed me?" he asked.

"So much that I saved the best spot for you," I told him. "Let's go. It's difficult to get in, but I got us on the waiting list. Well, Milton did."

We arrived at Lucali in Brooklyn, and the boys went crazy for the pizza. Elias served the wine we brought, and Nick talked about his upcoming graduation from college. He was twenty-two, and Elias was twenty-six.

Ellen wasted no time.

We finished three bottles of wine by the time Milton and Butch arrived. I did my best to pay attention to them although my drunken mind was preoccupied with Leo. What information had he gotten from the PI? What else was he doing? Did he know about the things I'd done? I was careful—they probably had nothing. What had Kyle told Simon? If the proof planted by my team wasn't enough to convince him, I'd have to make sure he looked at someone else, even if that person was me. I just had to keep him from suspecting Leo. Father wouldn't be easily fooled because he knew how I worked, but he wouldn't go after Leo just because of a hunch that I was lying to him.

I jumped when I felt a tap on my shoulder. Milton was staring at me with his eyebrows pulled together. "Your father says he's been calling you and wants to see you."

I nodded still in a daze. I hadn't paid attention to my phone. "Let's go." I didn't know why I'd let Elias and Nick ride with me. I wasn't thinking, and I was still pretending to laugh at whatever they were saying.

"Can I use the bathroom?" Nick asked as we got to my father's house.

"I need to go too," Elias said.

"Sure, come wait in the car after you're done," I said.

The boys followed me inside the house. My father's butler stopped us and gave me a look. "Your father wants to see you alone in his office."

"They're just going to use the bathroom." I brushed past him and left the boys at the bathroom before making my way to Father's office on the same floor. Did he want a report on the PI, or had Simon called him?

"Hello, Father," I said, walking into his office for the second time that day.

"What did the PI tell you?" Father looked at me with so much hatred in his eyes that I flinched. I noticed the bottle of whiskey on his desk before looking back at him. That should have been my sign that something was wrong, since he'd been sober for the past year. He was sitting at his desk but stood up and started walking toward me. "Don't think about lying to me."

"That he was just doing this for money." The first punch landed straight in my stomach and knocked the wind out of me. I fell backward on the second one.

His foot connected with my ribs, and pain sliced through me. I cried out and tried to roll away from him, but he kicked me hard in the back. "Shut up!" he yelled as I whimpered. He kicked me again and again. I stayed silent, enduring the pain.

"Did Leopold hire him?" I shook my head, too scared to talk. "I told you not to lie to me. I know you better than anyone. You've never killed someone yourself. And you would never, ever terminate someone before you have every single detail—you don't leave loose ends. What will you do if Simon notices?" My father grabbed my hair and dragged me across the floor to the room.

No.

"No! Stop, please." I tried to use my nails against his hand in my hair, but he just stopped and kicked me again. I screamed in pain and fear. My father opened the door and threw me down the stairs.

I hit the floor hard, tears welling in my eyes.

Father slowly came down the steps. The pain was excruciating, making my vision blurry. "I'm going to give you time to tell me the truth. Love is a weakness, Felicity. Have you learned nothing? Look around and tell me if you think marrying for love is worth it." He shook me violently, and I couldn't hold back my whimper. "I'm doing this for you!" he screamed.

My head was forcefully pulled back as he yanked my hair. "Please," I begged. "This has nothing to do with Leo."

"One day, you'll understand, and you'll be happy I forced you to marry Elias." He didn't care what I said. He had made up his mind. I heard the first click of the cuff around my wrist, and my body froze as it felt the metal touch the skin. It took me a second to react, but when my body realized that it needed to fight, I tried to claw my way out of my father's grasp, yelling at him to let me go. There was once a time that I could bear the handcuffs, but not anymore.

"I am not marrying Elias!" I screeched, feeling my throat close up from the strain. "I am not marrying Elias!"

My hand fell on the floor when my father was pulled back by Elias, who punched him in the face. He roared in pain and took a step back. Nick came to my side, looking frantic, asking if I was okay, but as Elias took another step towards my father and grabbed him by the throat, fear for him washed over me.

"Elias, no, don't hurt him." Elias looked at me but didn't let go until I repeated it. He pushed my father away and knelt by my side. "It's okay," I told them, not knowing what else to say. I'd never expected anyone to see me in this vulnerable position. This was my fault. I knew my father was trying to protect me in his own twisted way.

Elias's face was red with anger, and his hands hovered over me, not knowing where to touch. "Nick, call the police."

"No!" I shrieked, grabbing Nick's phone. They would be taken into custody, not my father. "Please, just take me out of here." I felt my lungs closing. It was getting harder to breathe.

Elias pulled me into his arms and carried me.

Crying out in pain, I moved his hands away from my abdomen. I pointed to the key on the corner table. Nick took the cuff off and threw it on the floor.

"Don't you dare take my daughter out of this house," my father warned. Blood was spilling from his nose, and he looked dizzy. "Who do you think you are, coming into my house and putting your hands on me, boy?" he spat.

I held Elias's shirt in my hand and shook my head. Nick came up to my father and punched him. My father fell to the floor unconscious. I looked at him, waiting for him to move, but he didn't.

Pushing Elias's chest and using all the strength I had left to get away from him, I knelt next to my father. "Daddy?" I could see that he was breathing, but he wasn't moving. "Jerry! Jerry! Jerry!" I kept yelling Jerry's name until my father's guards showed up. He moved me out of the way while he called our doctor. I stood there frozen, with my father's blood on my hands.

Jerry looked back at me and then at someone behind me. "Take her away."

Elias carried me in his arms again. Every step he took made me whimper in pain. My ribs didn't feel broken. I'd had enough of those to know the difference.

Milton and David rushed to our side when they saw us exit. I gave one of them Nick's phone. "Elias, give me your phone." Elias looked at me. His jaw was locked, and his eyes were hard. "Trust me." Elias put me in the car before giving the phone to Milton. He got in next to me, and Nick was on the other side.

Elias put his arm around me, and I leaned on him, needing support since my body didn't want to listen to my commands. I heard him yelling something at Milton, but I fell asleep. I woke up when Elias was carrying me out of the car. He laid me on the bed, but I didn't let go of him, so he crawled in with me. I tried to kick my shoes off, but when it didn't work, Elias did it for me. I winced as the pain on my left side was unbearable.

"Are you okay?" Nick asked softly. I patted the spot beside me, and he got in too.

Butch walked in with a backpack and a bottle of water. His eyebrows were pulled together. Omar was the medic of our group, but he had already left with Benjamin. Nick got out of bed to give Butch more space while he checked my injuries. "You're not going to like what I have to say, boss, but I think we should take you to the hospital and get some x-rays done," he said.

"No hospital." I sighed. "Give me some medication, and I'm sure I'll be fine by tomorrow." Nick opened his mouth as if to say something but quickly closed it.

Butch looked for something in his bag as he spoke. "I'm just worried that there might be something else going on if you're in this much pain, but nothing is broken."

Not only was I getting older, but Father hadn't hit me like this in over a year, so of course my body wasn't expecting it. "I had just forgotten what it felt like, that's all. Thank you. You can go now." Butch gave me some pills and instructions for how often he wanted me to take them. When he was gone, Nick returned to my side, and I lay back, exhausted.

Elias shook with anger, and I put my head on his chest, passing my hand against his arm. "It's okay. We'll talk tomorrow." I couldn't keep my eyes open after that.

BROKEN GIRL

Leo

"That's it for today, good job, everyone," I said, ending the meeting. I checked my phone—I was waiting for a message from Ryan, but I had nothing. The PI had missed his meeting time. That could mean a couple of things. He'd found something important, he'd betrayed us, or he'd been discovered by the family and was now in prison. At least those were the things I thought were most likely to have happened. Ryan was investigating, but it looked like he had found nothing. There was no way for us to contact him—we didn't even have a number. I could only go by the worst possible scenario and that was that the Price family had discovered us and knew we were onto them. If that was the case, there wasn't much I could do other than spin it as if I was investigating them due to the marriage.

Dad walked into the conference room and closed the door behind him. Aside from a slight tension in his shoulders, he looked calm. He unbuttoned his suit jacket before sitting on the chair next to me. "Are you leaving for Florida soon?" he asked casually.

"Why the question?" I was leaving for Florida tonight since I had a meeting with a major bank tomorrow. We were starting negotiations with them so we could become their security provider. It was a big deal that should have me excited, but the timing was an inconvenience for me.

"What, am I not allowed to know where my son is anymore?"

"If you want to know if I'm going to the Price dinner, you can just ask," I said.

"I was just trying to start a conversation with my son, who's barely looked at me this week. You've never been upset with me before. I don't know how to approach you."

"You signed my life away, Dad. How am I supposed to feel about that? Fee isn't talking to me, and I don't know where we stand, but it looks like she's already accepted her fate and I'm the only one still fighting for us." Part of me wanted to forget Fee and erase her like she was erasing us, but I couldn't do it. I knew she still wanted me because when she was drunk and afraid yesterday, it was me she'd called, me she'd wanted by her side.

Dad shook his head and asked, "Are you really not going to let her go?"

"I'm not having this conversation with you," I said, closing my laptop and getting up. I had to go meet Mom for lunch and then I had another meeting, so being here was just wasting my time.

He sighed and passed a hand over his face. "Have you thought about the consequences of having the Price family as enemies?"

"You should have thought about that when you made a deal with them." Of course I had, or I wouldn't be trying to find dirt that could help me threaten them if they tried something against us or Fee. I shouldn't blame him for what he'd done. I would have probably done the same if I was in his position and there was the slightest threat against Mom. Alexander didn't need to verbalize his threat—the fact that he knew about my parents was enough.

I sent Ryan a message asking him for an update before making my way to my parents' house. Mom was in the kitchen dancing salsa while making what looked like eggs Benedict. There were four older ladies sitting at the kitchen island, watching Mom cook while they sipped mimosas. Mindy, Claire, Kim and Luisa all looked like they'd gone to the same plastic surgeon and gotten a four-for-one special.

Mom's face lit up as soon as she saw me. "You came!"

"Good morning." I nodded to Mom's friends, if you could call them that. They were more like the city's elite gossip committee. Their gleaming eyes scanned my body as they greeted me back. They had been looking at me that way since I was a teenager, so I was used to their creepy eyes.

Mom grabbed my arm and pulled me out of the kitchen. "Sorry about them," she whispered. "They showed up unannounced and I wasn't able to kick them out. Do you want to reschedule for another day, or should we make up a crazy story and ditch them?"

"You already cooked. I'll just eat here."

When we went back to the kitchen, I sat at the table behind the ladies and close to the window. Mom served me food and sat next to me, hinting at the women that they should leave, but they were too worried about whatever nonsense was going on in their lives to realize they weren't wanted. Ryan texted me back, letting me know he hadn't heard back from PI. Wonderful. I would give him until tomorrow before I considered that he was no longer working with us.

I pulled my laptop out and responded to my emails while I ate. What was Fee doing right now? Did she miss me too? Fingers caressed my hand, and I immediately pulled it away. "Hands off my boy, Mindy," Mom said sweetly, but I could still hear the warning in her voice. I hadn't noticed it when Mindy sat next to me, but she was staring at me expectantly.

"Did you ask me something?" I asked.

She nodded. "I heard you rejected Riley. My daughter is available."

I guess I missed the question the second time around too, and why had that even been a topic of conversation? "I have a girl-friend, but thank you."

"That's what I said," Mom mocked in a singsong voice. The whole point of me being here was because she wanted to bombard me with questions about my relationship.

"Do we know her?" Claire asked.

Of course they knew her. "I don't know," I said, looking back at my laptop and hoping they would take the hint and stop talking to me.

"If we don't know her, that means she's a nobody," Mindy said nonchalantly. My eyes went to hers faster than humanly possible. Had she just called Fee a nobody? "I didn't mean it in a bad way," she laughed. She placed her hand on my shoulder, which I quickly shrugged off, causing her to frown slightly. "We just know all the important people here, and if we don't know her, that means she doesn't run in our circles."

"I think you've got it backwards. You're not important enough to run in her circles. To her you're the nobody," I said with a smirk.

The ladies gasped and Mom laughed so hard she snorted. "I think it's time for you ladies to leave. My son has a lot of work, as you can all see. We'll be in touch." Mom rushed them out, but I could hear them complaining about my attitude all the way out. I didn't know how she put up with them. "I'm going to get complaints about you for the next couple of months and everyone in the city will hear a distorted version of what happened." Mom laughed, sitting back down.

"I know it's better to get along with them, but they're insuffer-able. How can you tolerate them?" I grumbled.

"Your dad does business with all their husbands and most of them are Whitlock natives. You're either on their side or shunned and sucked into their drama. I just ignore them and keep my opinions to myself," Mom said.

This was why I couldn't let them find out that Dad had cheated.

"Now that we're finally alone, tell me all about her." Mom's smile was so wide that I couldn't help but smile with her, and she was practically bouncing with excitement. "What's her name? Where did you guys meet? When do I get to meet her? Don't leave out any details!"

I felt like a woman as I answered Mom's questions until she was satisfied. I didn't tell her everything, just enough for her to stop calling and texting me, wanting to know more about Fee. It felt good to talk about Fee. It reminded me why I couldn't let her go.

If I wanted to protect the two women I loved, I couldn't make a mistake. I would exploit every dirty secret the Price family was hiding.

LOCKSMITH

Felicity

The light shining through the window woke me up, and I groaned. My body felt battered and bruised. My head was in the crook of Elias's arm, and Nick had an arm around me.

"How are you feeling?" Elias asked, his eyes filled with worry, though a trace of anger lingered.

"I can breathe, so I'm going to say I'm fantastic," I said with a smile, hiding the raging headache that pulsed behind my eyes.

"Don't smile like nothing happened," he said loudly, waking up Nick, who frowned and rubbed his eyes.

"Thank you for helping me," I whispered, looking down, embarrassed to meet their eyes. Elias grabbed my chin and forced me to look at him.

"Why didn't you let us call the police? He needs to pay for what he did. It seems like it's a regular occurrence."

"It isn't. At least not since my father stopped drinking, but it's not something I can't deal with. Nothing will ever change, and the police won't help. I was trying to protect you. He'll discredit your family and ruin you if you get involved."

"We can protect ourselves," Nick added, looking so convinced that I pitied him.

"No." I shook my head. "No, you can't. Not from my father. My family hasn't survived this long by playing nice." There was nothing my family wouldn't do to keep their reputation. The Whitlocks would face the best lawyers in the country, with no chance of winning. I wouldn't testify or press charges.

"You can press charges, and we'll be your witnesses," sweet Nick said.

"That won't work." This was deeper than they'd ever understand. My family was different. There were no consequences for the actions of the powerful. The more powerful you were, the more control you had over the people below you, and I was below my father.

"Why not? We can at least try." Nick's pleading eyes made me wish I could do more just so he would stop looking at me like that. I hated the sadness in his eyes.

"That's the thing. I have." My tongue felt heavier as I said things out loud that I'd only told one other person. A time when I was becoming someone I never wanted to be again.

"He was hitting my mother, and I called the cops. She didn't press charges, but I showed them my bruises. I tried." Tears wanted to fall, but I held them back. "I told them what he did to us. How he would cuff me in the room and leave me there for two to three days without food or water." I shook my head, trying to get the memories of that deserted and cold room out of my head. "They locked me up in an asylum for a year. They said I was imagining things and was a danger to the people around me. My father kept everything out of the press. All my friends thought I was in a boarding school." They were looking at me with pity in their eyes, and I hated it. I couldn't tell them everything that had happened, but this was close to the truth. "He could have gotten me out, but he said I needed to learn a lesson."

Nick looked at his brother with so much anger in his eyes.

"Let's destroy that son of a bitch," he said. Elias's fingers dug into my shoulder, and his eyes were unfocused.

"No," I said, panicked. "You guys need to forget this happened and not tell anyone. Promise me you won't say anything. This isn't just about you. It's your entire family."

Elias placed a kiss on my forehead. "But what about you?"

"I'll be fine. I know how to handle my father." They didn't look convinced, but my father had improved over the last couple of years. Sometimes I thought he might even remember who he was.

"How do you handle a psychopath?" Nick murmured. "Why did he do that yesterday?"

"Because I want to be with your brother." Elias grabbed my hand and linked our fingers.

Nick took my other hand and started rubbing his thumb absently. "How did he find out about you and Polo?"

"He saw us at the dinner." The fact that Leo was still trying filled me with dread. If he didn't stop, he would get himself killed. I needed to talk to him and make him see that I felt nothing for him. Leo would never see my family coming because there was no honor or respect. We took what we wanted, no matter who we hurt. Which was all I saw in Elias's eyes right now.

"Wait, you're in love with Polo?" he asked, clearly confused.

"They're together," Nick announced.

His pain made me feel like the lowest of scum. "Why did no one tell me?"

His words were directed at Nick, but his eyes were on me. I decided it was better to just lead with the truth. "I didn't know he was your brother until the day of the dinner. Leo was planning on meeting my father to convince him to cancel the marriage arrangement." If Leo found out about what had happened last night, he would lose it. I couldn't let him see that part of my life or any part involving my family. I needed to protect him.

Elias turned to Nick for his next question. "And how did you find out?" Nick blushed and turned his gaze away.

"He found us being intimate in Leo's bathroom," I confessed. Elias looked at Nick with betrayal in his eyes. This wasn't his fault. It was mine, even if I didn't regret a single moment of everything I'd lived. "We told him to keep quiet until we could figure out what to do. Leo thought maybe your father could break the arrangement. I should have known better, but we were so hopeful."

"No wonder Polo disappeared for so long," Elias said absently.

"When we go to dinner tonight," I began, but Nick interrupted me.

"Wait, we're still going to that?" He looked at me like I was crazy.

"Yes, if we don't go, it'll be worse. We must act like nothing happened." There was no way we could miss that dinner.

"I don't think I can do that, kitty." Elias's thumb came to my lips. He rubbed it against them, and I moved my head away, making his hand drop. "We never got a chance," he whispered. I cleared my throat, uncomfortable with the situation.

A knock came on the door, and Jane stuck her head in. "Your father sent the doctor." I motioned for her to bring him in. Dr. Smith entered the room with his permanent scowl in place. He'd been my father's doctor for as long as I could remember.

Elias and Nick stayed by my side while the doctor checked my bruises.

"It's not bad," he said, making Nick and Elias tense beside me. "I'm going to give you the usual. You should come to my office and get x-rays." He left without another word, while Elias cursed under his breath. The x-rays would have to wait until tomorrow.

There wasn't much bruising yet, but my left side killed me every time I moved. I called Ana to get Nick situated so we could all get ready for the day. Once we'd all showered, I tried to act like everything was normal and rushed them to eat breakfast.

"Hurry. Canali has agreed to see us today, and we don't have much time."

"What's that?" Nick asked over a mouthful.

"Suit. You guys need a suit for tonight," I responded.

"I brought one," Elias added.

I tried to give them my best puppy-dog eyes. "Let me style you, please." They looked at each other, having no faith in me. "I can't wear the dress I had planned for today, so I'm kinda bummed and want to at least have you guys styled to perfection."

Elias's eyes softened. "Okay, kitty, we'll go."

I threw my arms around him, excited. "Ow." Pain invaded my body when I collided with Elias. Two pairs of eyes reprimanded me. Somehow their look made me feel worse than if they'd actually said something. "I'm sorry." I bit my lip and let go of Elias.

He took my hand and kissed my knuckles. "Don't apologize for being hurt. I already feel like shit for letting you go back to that house."

I quickly took my hand back, upset that he felt responsible for my father's rage. An overwhelming need to leave the house came over me. When I noticed that Nick's plate was empty, I exclaimed, "To the car!"

My head and muscles were killing me, so I took more Advil. I was feeling nauseous and nervous about tonight. I didn't know how my father would react to what had happened last night. He hadn't canceled the dinner, so maybe he was willing to see how this played out. I had to protect the Whitlocks from him.

"Knock, knock." Elias was at the bedroom door with a shy look on his face.

"Hey," I said, going back to applying eye shadow. "What's up?"

He hesitated before speaking, but when he finally did, he

enunciated every word. "Do you think we can be happy together?"

I was happy he had been here and thankful for all he had done for me, but I only saw him as family. "I haven't thought about that."

"Why don't you try?" he insisted. "I heard what you told your father last night, but I think we could make it work. I promise I'll protect you from your family, and you won't ever need to see them again."

"I don't want to hurt you." I put the brush down and looked at him. "It's only him. I can't imagine a hypothetical scenario because I'll always love him."

"I love my brother, but everything always comes easy for him."

It might seem that way, but he worked so hard for all he had. I stayed quiet because I knew Elias wasn't trying to attack Leo.

"You were the first thing I thought was going to be mine, but you were already his before I even had the chance to try."

"I'm not a thing to own," I responded softly. "I never had the luxury to choose or live in a happy family where my parents respected each other. Every choice has always been made for me." I let out a shaky breath. "Leo lets me take control without being obvious about it. He takes care of me with small gestures that others might not notice, but I do. I'm his partner, not a possession. When we're together, we're like magnets. It's impossible to deny the connection we have."

"I'm happy for you guys. I'm just being a jealous asshole." He chuckled, but it sounded sad and forced. "So . . . are we still getting married?"

I knew Elias didn't love me, but I still felt guilty. I'd disregarded his feelings before I'd even met him. It wasn't fair to him. "I wish I could say I can't marry you, no matter the consequences, because it's killing me to hurt Leo, but I can't. The contract has been signed. We have to get married. I'm sorry."

"I understand you have to do it, but I don't want to hurt my brother. Is there anything we can do to figure this out? Polo is smart—whatever it is, I'm sure he can solve it."

"This is my way of keeping him safe," I murmured. "If I don't marry you, I don't know what my father will do to him." Elias's eyes went widened. He understood the threat to his brother. "I know I'm asking for a lot, but I need you to trust me."

"I can talk to Dad—"

"I'm sure Leo already tried that. This is our only option." I knew that I was ruining his life too. His chance to find someone he loved. "If at some point we can get a divorce, I promise I'll give it to you right away. I'll try to give you your life back."

Elias looked like he was a million miles away when he nodded before walking out.

I put on a short black embroidered Balmain dress with long sleeves and a zipper in the front. It wasn't my first choice, but this would do. I paired it with black Skye ankle boots. *Please let this night not be a disaster.*

The guys were waiting for me downstairs. They looked fantastic. Nick was smiling from ear to ear.

"What do you think?" he asked, turning around. "I look good, huh?"

"You clean up nicely. Maybe you'll let me give you a wardrobe change?" There was nothing more fun than shopping for a wardrobe. It would let me relax and forget about my stress for the moment.

Nick shrugged. "Sure, why not?"

I jumped but grimaced when the pain hit me. I tried to act like nothing had happened so the guys wouldn't feel bad.

"We're going to have so much fun," I assured him. Milton walked in and told us we should head out. I looked up at the boys I had just met but had somehow sucked into my world. I always had people surrounding me, but I never let them care for me. I barely knew these boys, but they'd stood by me when they saw me in danger. I feared letting people in because I didn't want them to hurt me, but now I was scared of hurting them.

We drove in silence toward my father's house. I couldn't shake the bad feeling in the pit of my stomach. Ignoring it, I slid my mask back on and forgot the fear. It was just one dinner. How much harm could he do in one dinner?

As soon as we got out of the car, Elias stood on my left side and loosely put his hand on my right hip. I knew he was trying to protect me from anyone who touched me on the left side. Ellen and Richard were already in the backyard with my parents. As soon as Ellen saw us, she rushed to our side, pulling Nick into a hug. Since Elias didn't let me go, she hugged us at the same time.

"You two look so cute together," she said while grinning at us. "Richard, look at them. Are they not the cutest couple?" Mr. Whitlock's eyes found mine. He looked just as torn as I felt. I was in the arms of the wrong son.

"They certainly are, sweetheart," he said before kissing his wife on the cheek and walking away.

Lies.

What was I doing to their family? Ellen went back to my mother's side after giving us another hug. My father took the opportunity to greet us. His features gave nothing away. He had a butterfly bandage on his nose and was clearly using makeup.

He gave us a disgusted look when he was in front of us. "I suppose you understand that my family's business should never be discussed." Elias and Nick stayed quiet, but I could feel the anger radiating from their bodies. "I'll let your disrespect from yesterday slide, but there will not be a second time."

Ellen's excited voice interrupted our stares. "Leopold is running late, but he'll be here any second now."

My breath caught, and my father noticed. His eyes promised me a world of pain if I didn't behave. Why was Leo in New York? He was supposed to be in Miami. I needed fresh air. I couldn't breathe. *You're outside, Felicity.* I felt Elias's fingers tighten on my hip, and I used that to come back.

I was going to be sick.

It was easy to ignore Leo when he was hundreds of miles away. I couldn't do this. "Excuse me, I need to go to the bathroom," I muttered, rushing inside without giving my father a chance to reply. My feet weren't carrying me fast enough. I turned another corner and crashed into our butler, falling on my ass. My lungs felt like they were burning, and I blinked the tears away. I heard my name being called, and warm arms picked me up.

"Fee, look at me." Leo's hands were firmly on my waist, and I tried to mask the pain. Suddenly, I was pulled away from Leo and into the arms of Elias. Relief washed over me as the pain dimmed. I closed my eyes and leaned into Elias without thinking. Our butler excused himself while I tried to pull myself together. The pain slowly disappeared, but not before a powerful wave of nausea hit me. I pushed it down, taking deep breaths, confused about why it still hurt so much. When I finally opened my eyes, I wished I hadn't. Leo's eyes were trained on me, hurt flashing in them. He looked at Elias, and his jaw tightened. I wanted to go to him. Elias must have sensed this because his hand tightened on my hip.

"Here you are. Come. We're only waiting for you to serve dinner." My father's crisp voice brought me back to reality. Elias turned us around, and we quietly followed my father to the table.

Ellen seemed to be the only one who didn't notice the tension. She continued talking happily while Leo stared at Elias across the table. I could feel Leo's eyes on me sometimes, but I avoided meeting his gaze. Mr. Whitlock's eyes shifted between his sons, and my father had a smug look on his face. I wanted to yell at him for dragging them into this mess.

The courses passed, and I barely touched the food. I was so nauseous that just looking at it made me sick. I felt Elias get close to me, but I didn't move. I knew Leo was watching. "Kitty, you need to eat." I shook my head and continued to smile at whatever Ellen was saying. The sickness was beginning to feel unbearable, so I excused myself by acting like I had a call to make.

I barely made it to the toilet before throwing up. Pain spread through my abdomen as I bent over. Falling to the floor, I took deep breaths to control everything I felt. After a couple of minutes, I brushed my teeth and made my way back. Leo was the first to notice me. As soon as I saw the concern pulling on his face, I straightened my back and widened my smile.

When dinner was over, my father directed us to the pit area. The pit had a fire in the middle and four couches around it. Nick and Leo sat across from Elias and me.

"Since we're all here, I think it's time to discuss Elias and Felicity's union." Father smiled our way before continuing. "I was with them yesterday, and they seem to be getting acquainted very well." Before I could stop myself, I turned to look at Leo. He was glowering at my father.

"We can all agree that they look good together. Perfect match." Ellen gave me a warm smile, but I didn't return it.

I could feel Leo's eyes, and I let our gazes lock for the first time tonight. There was a question in his eyes. I wanted to run to him and tell him the answer was yes—that he had my whole heart. Instead, I turned to Elias and kissed his cheek. Elias gave me a curious look and turned to Leo. Leo looked like I'd just shattered his world.

I could taste his resentment.

It was bitter and cold.

Our parents were talking about the wedding, but my father had a wicked smile. I knew he had witnessed what I'd just done.

Leo let out a slow breath and got up. "It was nice seeing you all, but I must go. I have a flight to catch." He was smiling, but it didn't reach his eyes. His calm demeanor was gone. His shoulders were tense, and his hands were fisted at his sides. Ellen got up to hug him, then wished him a safe trip.

I watched Leo walk away from me, and the selfish person I was couldn't take it. I got up without saying a word and calmly walked inside. I told myself I just needed to talk to him so he'd stop investigating my family. That was it. Nothing else. When I knew they could no longer see me, I ran. My ribs protested in pain, but I didn't stop. Leo was almost at his SUV, and I ran faster. He closed the door as I turned towards the car. As soon as I was at the door, I yanked it open. His shocked eyes met mine. I hopped into the car and straddled him. I closed the door, and all the noise from the outside world went silent.

There was so much hurt in his eyes, and I couldn't bear it. I couldn't lose him. I completely forgot about my plan of just talking to him when I leaned in and kissed him hard. He didn't respond and kept his lips closed. I didn't blame him. I hurt him and he still came to fight for me. I knew without a doubt that if I had answered yes to him, he would have announced our relationship to everyone.

"Leo, *amor*, open up for me." I leaned in to kiss him again, and he responded this time. His hands came to my hair, and I trembled at his touch. I ended the kiss and took off his silver suit jacket and tossed it in the back. The pain was barely manageable, but I didn't care. I needed to feel him.

I touched his erection and quickly worked on getting it free. Without saying a word, he pulled the seat back so we had more space. I moved my thong to the side and guided him inside.

Holy shit, he felt incredible.

Leo hissed and held my waist. I flinched at his touch, and he immediately removed his hands. Grabbing his right hand, I intertwined our fingers and brought his left one back to my waist. We were both panting and moving frantically. My orgasm hit me first. I buried my face in his neck, trying to muffle my moans. Leo kissed my favorite spot, and I moaned while I felt him come inside me. We were still connected, catching our breath, when his harsh words brought me back to reality.

"If that's all you wanted, you can get off now." His icy and detached voice hit me like a bucket of ice-cold water.

"Leo." What should I tell him? That I loved him? "You need to let me go. Stop investigating my family."

"What happened to my PI? Did you pay him off?" he fumed.

There were so many secrets I kept hidden. If he knew the truth, he would hate me. After a couple of seconds of me not saying anything, he opened the door and motioned for me to get out. I suddenly felt dizzy and almost fell while getting out, but Leo caught me. When I was safely on the ground, he closed the door without looking at me and drove off.

With tears burning in my eyes, I walked to the house, but my body felt weak. I took another step, feeling the floor getting closer. I collapsed right as my world went black.

31

NIGHTINGALE

Felicity

"Tell me a secret."

I called out for Leo, but he just kept walking away from me. I shouldn't have said anything. I should've kept the memories to myself. The more I ran, the farther away he seemed to be. I yelled his name again, desperate to be close to him.

Leo, please don't leave me.

I fell to my knees, begging him to look at me. He turned around, his eyes devoid of emotion, like I wasn't there. I crawled toward him, but there was so much blood. Where was it coming from? Everything turned red, and I lost him again.

I BLINKED RAPIDLY as I felt someone lift me in the air. I must have fallen asleep as I watched Daddy work. We were in his office, but I could tell he was walking toward my room. I closed my eyes so he didn't realize I was awake and make me walk.

"I know you're awake, pumpkin." I could hear the smile in his voice.

"No, I'm not." I held him tighter, which made him laugh.

He carried me to my room and tucked me in. "Goodnight," he said, kissing me on the forehead.

I grabbed his arm before he had a chance to leave. "Can you please read me a bedtime story?"

He looked at the clock, and I could tell by his expression that it was way past my bedtime.

"We'll read a short one today, and tomorrow I'll come home earlier so I can read you a longer one. Deal?"

I jumped out of bed in excitement and grabbed his favorite story. I fell asleep before he finished the fourth page of *The Three Little Pigs*. The next day, he came home early, just like he'd promised.

IT WAS SO COLD. I wrapped my six-year-old arms around myself, but it did nothing for the shivers running through my body. I turned around, looking at the metal racks filled with food. My stomach growled, confirming that I'd been there for hours. I looked around the walk-in refrigerator, trying to find something I could eat. There were racks and racks of frozen meats. I finally found a bag of peas and quickly opened it. I turned the temperature as high as the control would let me, but it was still freezing. The cold peas felt weird in my stomach, but I kept eating them.

Mom had said she would be back for me, but it had been hours, and I didn't know how much more I could take. I pushed the door again, but it didn't budge. I knew I shouldn't leave the safe spaces she'd left me in, but I really needed to go to the bathroom. Looking up, I saw a plastic container I could use to pee.

I put my foot on the metal shelf and made my way up. Making it to the container, I noticed how heavy it was and tried to hold on with one hand. My hand slipped, and I fell to the floor, taking several bags and containers with me. I cried out in pain as my shoulder hit the ground hard. Sitting up, I tried to move my arm, but it hurt so much. I felt the salty tears land on my mouth as the pain grew stronger. I pushed myself against the freezing wall with my good arm, hoping my mom would come soon.

"Felicity!" I opened my eyes as our chef yelled my name. "Felicity! Are you okay? Have you been here all night?"

"My arm hurts. I can't move it," I cried.

She helped me up and yelled for someone to assist her.

Milton took me to the hospital to get my arm fixed. Mom didn't come. The doctors said I was sick because I was cold for too long. The nurse was sweet. She made me laugh, but her eyes were sad when she looked at me. Everyone was always sad when they looked at me. I really wanted to make someone happy.

Daddy rushed in the door, and the worried look he had on his face immediately disappeared after he saw me. The coldness in his eyes returned. It was much colder than that freezer. I smiled at him, but he didn't smile back. There was no warmth anymore. He used to be happy when he saw me, but now he wasn't. I just wanted to make someone happy.

"You need to hurry." My mom was pulling me along with her, but I could barely keep up.

"Mom, I'm not staying there. Why do I always have to hide?" I was tired of having to run from my father. They treated me like I was naive and didn't know what was happening. He was violent, and he was always hurting her. Something had changed in him within the last seven years. He was no longer the man I looked up to. Some days, she knew he'd be angry. I didn't know who told her, but she'd get a message and then put me somewhere she thought I'd be safe. Some days she'd come back bruised; others, she was fine. By the time I was allowed to wander freely in the house, my father was already gone.

"Felicity, why do you always have to make things harder? Just do what you're told, like you're supposed to." I always did what I was supposed to, or at least I tried. That was what my family expected from me, and as long as they were happy, I'd do it.

"Stay with me," I begged, holding her hand tighter. "He'll calm down when he can't find us." Her eyes were shining with joy, and I didn't get it. Why was she always excited to see him?

"Shut up and stay here. I'll come back later." She closed the door to the greenhouse, leaving me with scary sounds. I stared at the night sky, hoping she'd return soon, but she didn't.

I STOOD COMPLETELY STILL with my head held high. He hated when I showed any weakness. Passing my sweaty hands over my skirt, I kept my breathing even. I was dressed impeccably, like he wanted me. The cream pencil skirt with the peach blouse made me look older than seventeen, but I knew how important it was to dress appropriately for my father.

"I saw Simon today at the ball. He was overjoyed with Benjamin ending up at the top of your class this semester," my father said sarcastically. "Of course he said this in front of everyone at my table, who were reminded that you finished second." His eyes were burning with anger. I could feel the room closing in on me, but I had nowhere to go.

"My grades were better than his all year. I don't know how he did it," I said through gritted teeth. Benjamin was upset that I'd beaten him freshman year. He'd either slept with the teachers or bribed them. Maybe both, with the way Mrs. Gallagher was looking at him. He only did it to annoy me. I knew Simon didn't care about his grades. Simon didn't care about anything other than making everyone around him miserable. He enjoyed causing pain more than he cared about the power he had.

Even though Benjamin was older than me, I had skipped a grade and gotten into college the same year he did. Like any cousin, he used this opportunity to mess with me any chance he had. I didn't hate him. We were family. He didn't know that his antics would cost me.

"More excuses. You need to always be one move ahead of your opponent. Who cares how he got the grades? The point is, he won. You lost. You made me look like a fool." I highly doubted anybody cared that I got an A– in one class, but I didn't point that out because it didn't matter. He was the only one that mattered. For someone who hated weaknesses, he didn't realize that he was his own worst enemy. No one liked him anymore.

Rage filled my body as his fist connected. He was pathetic and weak. I'd be free of him one day.

When he was done taking his anger out on me, he cuffed me to the wall. This was all a game to him. He enjoyed inflicting pain and stripping us of our control, but he'd always be nothing. He would never be the man he used to be, the one that people used to look up to.

The father I loved.

The room was dark, but my eyes were still open. Needing to go to the bathroom, I peed on myself, ignoring the uncomfortable wet spot beneath me. I'd probably be there for a day or two, so I better just settle in.

I WATCHED my father closely from my hiding spot at the end of the hallway. Jerry wasn't here today, so she wouldn't have anyone to help her. He was yelling at my mother over a jealous seed I'd planted, and it wouldn't be long before he snapped. I had been in the shadows for two weeks as I watched him hit her every day, but it was never enough. I wanted the police to see what he was capable of. I patiently waited until he beat her to make the call. "911, what's your emergency?"

"Please help me," I begged, pretending to cry. "My father is hitting my mom. I think he's going to kill her. Send help! She's not moving." The girl was frantic at the other end of the line. It sounded like she was new. I smiled as she stammered her words. She reassured me that the police and an ambulance would be here shortly. I stayed on the line with her like she asked me, annoyed by her questions and having to pretend I cared. Sirens sounded in the distance. I had broken the gates earlier, ensuring they wouldn't be stopped on their way in. I smiled as I watched the woman who'd birthed me still on the floor, bleeding. She was as weak and pathetic as he was.

I hated them both, but I hated her more.

Grabbing the door frame, I smashed my head against the wall. This was just for shock value; the real proof was on my body. Warm blood trickled down my face, making me smile. I checked the wall to make sure it was clean before making my way to my mother. She groaned softly as she moved to her side. Annoyed that she was still awake, I kicked her hard until she stopped moving. I heard the officers enter the house and fell to my knees as I pulled her to my chest, crying against her hair. My father came down to check on the commotion and tried to get the officers out of the house, but it was too late.

They had already heard me yelling for help.

I held my mother's hand all the way to the hospital. The paramedics watched my tearful face with sympathy. They didn't know these tears weren't for her. They were freedom tears. I was finally going to be free of both of them.

Her mistakes and his pridefulness.

My grandfather had left me enough money to start a life on my own. I wouldn't get the rest until I was twenty-one, but two million was enough to live in a nice apartment for the next three years.

I gave my statement to the officer. My father hadn't been detained, but the bruises on my body should be enough to ruin his reputation. I could almost taste my victory. It was just as sweet as I imagined.

My mother woke up and refused to press charges. She wouldn't even look at me. Whatever. I wouldn't see her again after this. If she wanted to stay under his thumb forever, that was up to her. It was all her fault anyway.

She'd created two monsters.

"Felicity Price." A short man with salt-and-pepper hair stopped in front of me. I nodded when I saw the badge. "I'll be taking you to the precinct. We need to record your statement. Do you mind following me?"

I wanted to jump out of my chair and do a victory dance. Instead, I calmly got up while responding, "Of course."

I bit my lip the entire way to make sure my smile didn't break free. We stopped at a tall building. It was quiet inside. The detective waved at the receptionist before leading me through several hallways. He finally stopped in front of a door and motioned me inside before leaving.

Opening the door slowly, I saw an older lady behind a desk. In the chair in front of her was a slender man in a tailored suit. I could only see his back, but I knew who he was immediately.

"Take a seat, Felicity," Father said.

I was such an idiot. I should have called the press too.

❧

"I'M HERE," a soft voice told me.

Where? Everything was black. I couldn't see where I was going. I called out for Leo because I knew he'd find me. A small white dot appeared in the distance, and I ran to it. It got bigger the closer I got to it.

"Leo, where are you?"

Everything was so bright. It hurt my eyes. I kept walking toward the light, but something told me to go back. Leo was still back there. I turned around and headed toward the dark.

Loralei Mental Asylum. That was where I was sent after my father's lady friend, who was a judge, got rid of all the evidence against him. They used my run-in with the wall to make it seem like I was a danger to myself. Since it was apparent that my father didn't cause my head injury, they said the rest of my bruises were also self-inflicted. My mother never spoke up.

One move ahead of your opponents.

I looked at the light blue robe that I was given. It was formless and ugly. The slippers weren't even comfortable.

I growled in frustration. *But you're free. Isn't this what you wanted?* Not like this. This wasn't freedom. I wanted to win.

The room that they gave me was small. My father used his connection to get me a computer I could use only for school. It was funny to see the things he believed were priorities. I immersed myself in my studies, not for him but for myself.

"Hi, Felicity. I'm Dr. Lewis. I want to speak with you for a few minutes." I didn't look at the doctor. I wasn't an actual patient here. I didn't need to do anything they told me.

"I don't have to do any sessions. Leave." I continued to study the chapter for my test.

She talked again, like I hadn't just told her to leave. "I read your file. I'm sorry about what happened to you, but I can help. You'll be here for another eight months, so let me help you." Finally, looking at the petite brown-haired girl in my room, I noticed she was young. Her shoulders were pushed back, and her chin was lifted a little too high. Her obstinate expression intrigued me.

"How old are you?" I asked.

"Does that matter?" she said while lifting her eyebrows at me.

"If you think I'm going to listen to someone who doesn't look much older than me, you're the crazy one." I turned to my book, hoping she got the memo and left me alone.

"It's normal to be angry when someone has experienced the things you have." Her assumption had me holding the book a little tighter. What kind of doctor spoke to their patients like that? Wait, I wasn't her patient.

"As I said, I don't have to do this. All I need to do is stay in this room for eight more months," I hissed.

"It's not your fault!" she exclaimed.

That had me looking at her again. "Of course it's not my fault. It's my pathetic mother's fault." She closed the door and sat on the chair at my desk. I closed the book and put it next to me on the bed. She clearly wasn't going anywhere.

"So, you blame your mother?"

What a dumb question. I thought they were supposed to be educated. "Who else?" I snapped. She was infuriating.

Her expression softened, but she still looked kind of scary. "She's also a victim. It's hard to understand what the people around us are going through. Everyone processes things differently."

I was strong. My mother was weak. It was as simple as that. "She could have said something, and I wouldn't be here," I said with as much conviction as I could muster because I knew it was a lie. If she had said anything, we would have both ended up here. But wasn't that what a mom was supposed to do? Protect her child?

"Do you truly believe that?" *Yes. No. Where did this voice come from?*

"It doesn't matter what I believe."

"Victims of abuse can feel trapped and scared. They don't know who to go to. Most of them don't trust the system, especially those from backgrounds like yours. It's rare to find someone who speaks up. It's not just about the physical pain. There's also the emotional and psychological abuse."

I let Dr. Lewis's words penetrate. I stayed there, processing what she said, for about ten minutes. She stayed silent while I thought. I was still angry, but there was something else coming to the surface.

Sadness?

Remorse?

Looking at my hands, I finally spoke. "I waited for him to beat her before I called the police. I could have called sooner. I was so angry at her. I could've helped her." Tears burned in my eyes, but I didn't let them fall. I hadn't cried in a while. Crying was for weak people. I wasn't weak. "I don't want to be bad like them."

"Sometimes we have to find our strength first before we can help others," she said.

But I was strong, wasn't I?

"You don't need to be like him. You're good."

Everything she was saying was confusing me. "Will you help me not be angry anymore?"

"I GOT MY INHERITANCE TODAY," I told the woman who'd helped me find inner peace. I'd called the asylum earlier to see what time she left. Then I'd waited like a stalker.

"Congratulations," she said with a warm smile.

"Come work for me. I'll pay you seventy-five thousand a month. You'll live with me and won't need to pay for housing or food." My words came out fast. I was scared she'd reject me.

I offered her my business card, and she took it.

She lifted her eyebrows at me, something she always used to

do. I found myself doing it sometimes too. "Was that a question or a demand?"

"It was me begging," I answered truthfully.

She shook her head at me but still grinned. "You have a weird way of begging."

"Please?" I tried again with a softer voice.

"Fine, but I still need vacation days, sick days, and medical insurance."

Easy. "All my employees will get that," I said with a smirk.

"I'll start in two weeks." She turned her back to me and walked to her car without waiting for my response.

"Thank you, Dr. Lewis!" I screamed before she got in the car.

"Call me Jane."

❧

I WAS SO THIRSTY. I needed water. I opened my eyes to a dimly lit room. I was groggy, and my vision was blurry. "Leo." Hands were holding mine.

"It's me, Nick."

"Nick," I repeated.

"Shh, it's okay. You're at the hospital. Everything will be fine," he said.

Hospital? This wasn't good. If my father found out, he'd kill me. I felt the dark trying to take me again. I wanted to fight it. Loud beeping noises were blaring through the room. "Leo."

"You can't tell Leo," I kept saying. The room filled with people I didn't recognize. I yelled for Nick, but they were holding me down. Nick wasn't there anymore. I felt sleepy now. A warm hand touched my arm. It was a boy with hazel eyes and gold specks all around. "You can't tell Leo," I told him. The boy smiled and nodded. I watched tears stream down his face as my eyes closed.

The dark took me back to a memory that had been sealed for eleven years.

A memory I didn't want to relive.

I COVERED MY EARS, trying to drown the sounds of the storm. The rain sounded like rocks as it fell against the glass roof of the greenhouse. Mom said she would be back, but it felt like I'd been there for hours. My body was shaking from the cold and the sounds coming from the dark. When the thunder roared, I couldn't take it anymore. I grabbed one of my mom's pots and used it to reach the window. I was barely able to fit through it, but I made it, falling to the ground hard.

I ran into the house, expecting to find the usual staff, but I didn't see anyone. Maybe that meant Mom was gone too. I tiptoed to my room just in case she was still around. I felt relief when I made it to my door, but before I could enter, I heard a cry coming from my parents' room. Their door was ajar, which wasn't normal—it was typically closed. The pained sound came again. Was Father hitting her? I should have ignored the sound and gone to my room, but instead I tiptoed closer. The sounds intensified, the screams getting louder. I grabbed the door handle and peeked through the crack. I couldn't see anything other than furniture. I opened the door a little further until I could see the reflection in the bureau's mirror.

My hand covered my mouth before a scream escaped. I stumbled back, losing my step. I was ready to crash to the floor, but a hand caught me. My body was shaking as I slowly looked up and met my father's eyes.

"What did you see, Felicity?" he asked.

"N . . . noth . . . nothing," I stammered. I swallowed back the confusion and focused on getting him out of here. He couldn't stay or his heart would be broken. He loved Mom too much.

"Have you eaten? We should go to the kitchen for some ice cream."

His eyes squinted and he leaned his head to the side. When Mom let out another scream of ecstasy, he smiled. Why was he smiling? Did he already know? How could he allow it? "Do you want to say hi?" He didn't wait for an answer. He grabbed my wrist and threw me inside the room where Mom was with another man.

I should have never left the greenhouse. I should have never learned Mom's secret. Maybe my life would have been better, and Father wouldn't take his anger out on me.

32

LIE TO ME

Leo

I saw Fee in the rearview mirror as I sped out of the driveway. The image of her lips on my brother kept flashing in my head. I tightened my grip on the steering wheel as I refrained from turning the car around and demanding an explanation. She wasn't ready to talk, and I was mad at her. I'd find her tomorrow, and we could discuss what the fuck was going on. She was shutting me out, and I didn't understand why. We were supposed to be a team. I'd given her a week, but I was done waiting. The longer I waited, the farther away I felt from her. It was like she was slipping from my fingers.

I lied about the flight. I canceled everything to come to her. I wasn't willing to let Fee go. I'd keep fighting until she told me she didn't want me. If Dad didn't want to stop that sham of an engagement, then I could do it on my own. Fuck whatever contract they'd signed. They couldn't decide our lives with one piece of fucking paper.

My chest tightened as I remembered how I talked to her while still inside her. My words were harsh and came from a place of anger, but now I wanted to take it all back and hold her in my arms. If I could figure out why she'd given up on us so easily and help her understand that I wouldn't be like her family, we could find peace again. I thought angry sex was supposed to feel good, but I guessed it wasn't the same when something was missing.

Once I arrived at the hotel, I headed straight for the bar. "Whiskey, keep 'em comin'." Dad kept telling me to forget about her, like that was so easy to do or even an option. She was all I thought about and all I wanted.

A hand landed on my arm and squeezed. I looked at the perfectly manicured red nails that were offending me. "You're in my space," I grumbled and shook the hand off. Everything had become foggy.

"I thought you might want some company since you've been drinking alone."

I looked up and found a petite woman with nice features. Another time, I might have taken her up to her room, but that was before Felicity had taken up permanent residency in my heart.

I scowled at her. I must have looked scary because she took a step back and quickly left. I kept drinking until the bartender cut me off and had someone help me back to my room. This wasn't how I thought tonight would go. I thought I would come here to declare my love and get the girl. Fee would sleep in my arms, and we would live happily ever after.

I fell asleep, imagining that my plan had worked and that she was safely tucked away in my arms.

I woke up with a massive headache. My chest felt tight, and I knew I needed to fix things with Fee now. My phone was dead, so I left it charging while I got ready. Thankfully, I found some Tylenol in my bag. I showered and threw on some jeans and a shirt. I grabbed the phone and noticed fifteen missed calls from Nick. I'd call him back when I fixed things with Fee.

With the amount of alcohol I'd consumed last night and how I was feeling, I thought it was safer to take a taxi. I'd memorized her address yesterday when Nick gave it to me. I'd seen her everywhere in the past week—magazines, TV, and phone notifications. She looked beautiful everywhere she went, but it wasn't my Fee. Her smile never reached her eyes. She needed me as much as I needed her. She just didn't want to admit it.

The taxi stopped at the gated community. The guard jumped out of his seat and opened the booth window. "Good afternoon. Who are you here to visit?"

"Hello, I came to see Felicity Price. I don't have an appointment, but if you can call her house, I'm sure someone can let me in." The guard eyed me one last time. I knew I looked exactly how I felt—like shit.

"What's your name? And would you mind giving me your ID?"

"Leopold Whitlock," I said while pulling out my ID and handing it to him.

"Oh, I see. I saw two gentlemen who looked like you yesterday. I was supposed to let them in, but they never came back, so I thought maybe you were one of them. I'm guessing you're related." He gave me a quick smile while taking a step back and picking up the phone.

"They're my brothers." If they weren't here, where were they? The guard turned around and spoke in a low voice. After a couple of minutes, he returned and handed me my ID.

"Go straight. It's the last house," he said.

"Thank you."

The taxi pulled up at the highest wall on the street, and the gates opened as soon as we got close. The driveway was long and full of peach blossoms. Two guards were waiting for us at the entrance. They both had their jackets pulled back, showing me their weapons. I'd expected a friendlier welcome, but I wasn't going back now. If she wanted to shoot me, so be it. Well, shoot at me, but hopefully not shoot me.

Ignoring the guards, I walked up the steps as Jane opened the door for me. There was a worried expression on her face. She took a step back without saying a word and let me in.

"Jane, how are you?" Fee's house was just like her. Elegant and imposing. The foyer had marble flooring and Greek-style columns with cream-colored walls. I already knew she had a story behind every detail of this house, and I wanted to know them all. I looked back at Jane, who still hadn't answered me.

"Where is she?" When she was about to answer, a man with a broad chest entered the room, his angry eyes directly on me.

"You have some nerve showing up here. Get the fuck out and never contact her again." He had a T-shirt and cargo pants on. He must have been one of her guards because he dressed exactly like the others.

"Levi—" Jane started to say, but I interrupted her, itching for a fight.

"No, Jane, let him finish." I smirked at the man, waiting for him to attack me.

"Out!" he barked at me like I was a fucking dog.

"I'm not going anywhere until I see my woman, so I suggest you take a step back before I make you." I stepped toward him, forcing him to look up at me. Rolling my shoulders back, ready for a fight, I saw the life being drained from the man in front of me.

"Then you better hurry the fuck up because the last thing I heard, she doesn't have much time left." With that, he pushed past me and slammed the door.

"Jane. Talk. What is going on? Where's Fee?" My heart started frantically beating.

Fuck.

"I'm sorry, she's at the hospital. She's been in and out of surgery all night. They don't know if she's going to make it." I felt my body go cold as a shiver ran through me. The back of my nose burned.

The floor felt like it was sinking beneath me.

I should have called Nick back. I'd left her alone when she needed me. "Leopold!" Jane snapped. I couldn't lose her.

I turned toward Jane for a brief second before yanking the door open and running outside. Fuck! I didn't have a goddamn car.

"We're on our way back to the hospital. You can come with us," Jane called out. She pointed towards an SUV as she ran down the stairs.

Pulling the back door of the SUV open, I found Levi in the driver's seat, but that didn't stop me from getting in. I'd take whatever got me to her faster.

"Man, do you have a hearing problem?" he growled.

Jane hopped in and answered for me. I couldn't process anything right now. *They don't know if she's going to make it.* The words kept playing over and over in my head. "Please," I whispered. I needed to be with her.

"Levi, you know this is what she would have wanted," Jane said.

Grunting, he finally put the car in drive and sped to the hospital. My heart was beating painfully in my chest, my stomach felt hollow, and no matter how much I squeezed the door handle, I felt like I had no strength left.

We arrived at the hospital, and both of our families were already in the waiting room. Our parents, my brothers, and Milton. Nick got up when he saw me and raised his hands as if trying to calm me down. I didn't care where I was. I needed to see her. I was tired of this fiancé bullshit; it ended now. "Where is she?" I demanded.

"You need to calm down." I took two steps toward my baby brother, and he held his ground. "Not here," he whispered.

"My girlfriend is in a hospital bed fighting for her life. I'm done playing this game. Now tell me where the fuck she is." I was done letting our parents control our lives. I was done letting her

deal with it on her own. I'd protect her from all of them if necessary. I had the power to do it, and I wouldn't let her down. Nick
opened his mouth, but Alexander interrupted him.

He was exasperated, like this was all just a big inconvenience
when he had better things to do.

"Why don't we all calm down? We're waiting for the doctor to
tell us when we can see her."

Mom looked at me with wide eyes while Dad whispered in
her ear.

"I know you didn't just talk to me. I know you didn't just act
like it means nothing that your daughter is in a fucking hospital
bed. Don't tell me to calm down. This is all your fault. Both of
you." I pointed to my father, who was looking at me with pure
disbelief. "If I lose her . . ." I shook my head, trying to get rid of
that dark thought. She'd be fine. She was stronger than anyone I
knew.

Alexander had a bored expression and went back to looking
at his phone. What kind of father was he? I'd seen articles online
that said Fee was his pride and joy, but he had been nothing but
cold every time I'd seen them interact. I looked at Nick, pushing
away the hatred I felt for Fee's father.

"What happened? She was fine last night when I left her." Was
she fine? Or had I blocked everything out so thoroughly that I
hadn't noticed she was sick? Nick and Elias exchanged a look.
"What?" I barked.

I just wanted to see her and make sure she was okay. Maybe
everything would have been different if I hadn't left last night.

"The doctor says there was internal bleeding due to severe
trauma to the abdomen." The butler? Fee had bumped hard into
him, but I didn't expect that to cause an injury. That couldn't be
it. I remembered her flinching when I touched her yesterday. I
should have asked, but I was so caught up in my self-pity that I
neglected her.

Elias cleared his throat.

He looked torn as he met my gaze. "It was my fault." I could feel the blood flowing through my veins as my brother kept talking. "I wanted to try a move while we were ice skating, and I dropped her."

My heart stopped. I had a reputation for being the calm one, not letting things directed at me bother me, but this was different. This wasn't about me. It was about her. It was easy to ignore ignorant comments, but how did I ignore my need to protect her? For the past three weeks, everything had been getting under my skin easily, and I didn't know what to make of it because she needed me to be her anchor and not a man who was losing his shit over everything, but the man I was would have to return another day because today I didn't think I could find him in me.

Elias had never skated a day in his life, and this was when he decided he wanted to risk Fee's life? "Why didn't you take her to the hospital?" I asked.

I should have let him speak, but all I saw was red. I swung at him before I could think it through. Milton's arms were suddenly around me as he tried to hold me back. Mom was yelling my name, begging me to calm down. Elias was staring at the floor as his lip bled.

Nurses rushed toward us, but I ignored them as I fell to the ground and buried my face in my hands. Nick sat down next to me and grabbed my shoulder.

"I can't lose her," I rasped. "I can't." There was so much more to discover about each other. We needed more time. Why had I given her space? I should have been on a plane the first time she'd ignored my call.

Nick squeezed my arm, trying to reassure me, but it did nothing to calm me. "I know."

I could feel someone sitting next to me. I knew it was Elias. "She'll be okay," he whispered. "She's a fighter." I hugged him and hid my face in his chest.

"I'm sorry I busted your lip." I barely got the words out. There was a knot in my throat. I couldn't breathe.

"But you're not sorry you punched me?" he said jokingly.

"You deserved that." Nick joined the hug, and we stayed like that until we heard Fee's name being called.

A short middle-aged doctor walked toward us with a tall blond nurse. "You're her fiancé, right?" he asked while looking at Elias, who nodded in response. "The surgery was successful, but she lost a lot of blood, so we'll keep her under observation."

I felt like I could finally breathe. "When can I see her?"

The doctor and nurse both turned to look at me, but the nurse spoke first. "Who are you?" She looked at me like she was assessing if I was good enough.

"I'm her boyfriend," I said, taking a step forward, leaving the fiancé behind.

The nurse looked between my brother and me before asking, "Which one of you is Leo?"

"I am." I tried to stay calm as she dragged out the answer. I just wanted to see Fee. I wanted her to know she wasn't alone.

The nurse finally answered my question. "She's been asking for you since she got here. You can see her now if you would like, but only for ten minutes. But . . ." She looked at Elias.

"It's fine. She loves him, not me." I was relieved that he understood, and I quickly followed the nurse as she turned around without another word. She gave me protective equipment to wear, and I almost fell as I rushed to put it all on.

The room was cold. Fee was in the middle of the room, hooked up to too many tubes. My chest tightened as I saw how fragile she looked. There were dark circles under her eyes, and her skin looked lifeless. I slowly grabbed her hand, scared it would disturb her. I kissed her forehead, careful not to touch anything else. She had a cut on the top of her left eyebrow from when she fell. A tear fell from my eye as I watched the girl who owned my heart lie unconscious in bed.

"Tell me a secret," I whispered, knowing she couldn't respond but still needing to ask. My legs could no longer support me. I fell to my knees next to her bed. Her delicate hand was cold. I inhaled, but the peach scent wasn't there.

"You can't leave me, love. They can't have you. Not until we grow old together, and even then, you'll still be mine because I'll follow you wherever you go. I'll never let you go. I love you, Fee, with every piece of my heart and soul. I can't live without you. Please come back to me. Don't let go." Her hand was wet from my tears. I cleaned them away as I was forced to let go. The nurse looked at me with pity when she guided me outside.

There was a ball in my throat, but I forced myself to speak. "Has her room been arranged yet?" My voice came out hoarse and thick.

"I can ask the front desk, and they'll help you with the arrangements." She gave me a sympathetic smile, and I nodded, unable to talk. She opened her mouth like she wanted to tell me something, but then she shook her head and turned around. I followed her to the front desk. My family's eyes were trained on me. Felicity's parents were no longer there.

"Sir, what accommodations are you looking for?" Her name tag said Stacy. "Sir?"

"The best VIP suite you have." I took out my Amex black card and handed it to her. "Charge it here, and please keep it on file to make sure anything she needs is available immediately." The nurse who'd let me see Fee waved me goodbye, and I mouthed a thank-you to her.

"Of course, sir. I'll need you to fill this out." Stacy handed me a form, and I turned around to see Nick and Elias beside me.

"I need to add her bodyguard to the list of visitors." I motioned for Milton to come over.

"We would like to visit her, too," Nick said sheepishly.

Stacy pointed at Milton, stating, "Actually, Mr. Carter is the person the patient identified, so we need his signature." We started the paperwork to get Fee transferred. I was pissed that her parents had left their daughter as if she hadn't just had major surgery.

"Can we decorate the room for her?" I asked Stacy.

"Yes, as long as you don't damage the property or put holes in the wall." I needed to talk to Jane about this. I wanted to make sure everything was perfect. Fee wouldn't want to be in a lifeless room or in boring clothes.

"We have nurses dedicated to the floor, but some families prefer to hire a private nurse at night to stay with the patient. Would you like to do that?" The thought of leaving Fee alone brought a sense of dread to my stomach. I could have lost her when I was passed out drunk.

"No, thank you. I'll stay with her every day until I can take her home." And by home, I meant my house, where she could be far away from that coldhearted man she called a father.

My parents waited for us to return before letting us know they were leaving. My mom hugged me tightly. I returned the hug, enjoying the comfort she brought. Mom had always been there for us. She showed us how to be kind and love each other. Dad was stricter because he wanted us to be the best men we could be, but he always led by example.

"Sorry, Ma. I should have stayed calm." Her warm smile made me feel a little better. While Elias and Nick always kept my parents on their toes, I always took it upon myself to make sure my parents' lives were easier.

"You love her," Mom said. My throat closed again as I remembered how fragile Fee looked. I nodded, not being able to speak. "I'm happy you both found each other. Take care of her. She needs you."

"I'm sorry, son," my father said as his hand landed on my shoulder.

I looked between my parents unsure of how to ask them for

their support. "Mom, could we go somewhere private? There's something I would like to ask."

She grabbed my hand and held it between her hands. "Your dad already told me. Don't worry about us."

"This isn't just about us," Dad interrupted. "This also concerns her safety."

"I'm going to keep her safe. I'll break the contract myself, don't worry." I didn't let him speak. I turned around and left.

Nick brought my things from the hotel as Jane and I decided on decorations. We chose what Jane described as delicate flower arrangements. Everything was colorful but not overwhelming. I only requested that there be lilacs since they were Fee's favorite color.

They moved Fee to her room the next day. I watched the nurses like a hawk and learned what they did and their routines. I set alarms for her medication in case they forgot. The doctor had come in a couple of times to check on her. They told me it was expected that she hadn't woken up yet. She needed time to heal.

"Hey, love. Ready for another chapter?" I kissed her cheek and fingers, wishing that she'd come back to me soon. I had been reading her *The Princess Bride* before I went to sleep. After I was done, I pushed my bed toward hers and interlaced our fingers. Every morning I prayed that she'd wake up with me, but my heart clenched when I still found her asleep.

"Leo." Fee's soft murmurs woke me up. "Leo."

"I'm here, love." I caressed her hair as she fidgeted. "I'm here." Fee kept calling my name in her sleep. I pressed the call button for the nurse and turned on the light. The nurse rushed in.

"She's talking again. Is she okay?" Concern laced my words as I prayed that Fee was finally waking up. I watched the nurse as she worked. When Fee stopped mumbling my name, the nurse assured me that she wasn't hurting and that she was fine. As the nurse left the room, I crawled back into bed, wishing I could pull Fee into my arms.

Nick came back for the weekend. My family returned to Whitlock once Fee was moved from observation.

Her family didn't come once.

Milton stayed with me during the day, but I sent him home at night. He brought me all my meals and clean clothes. Sometimes the other guards stayed for a couple of hours.

"She looks better. There's more color in her cheeks," Nick said.

I could see how Nick cared for Fee. In such a short time, she had us all wrapped around her little finger. There was just something about her that made me want to protect her. She was so strong and independent. Yet she hid behind so many walls, trying to mask the pain that the people who were supposed to love her inflicted.

I'd known who she was as soon as she'd told me her father's name. I had heard rumors about her and how she was just as ruthless as her father. But the more I talked to her, the more I knew those people had never met the real her. Her eyes shone fiercely with a light that couldn't be dimmed.

I'd make sure that no one ever took that away from her.

33

LOVE YOU ANYWAY

Leo

"You've told us six times already. We have all the notes you left us, and the nurses know what they're doing. We'll never need to use this." Nick waved the notebook at me before falling back on the couch.

I balled my hands into fists, annoyed at his casual demeanor. I needed to make sure they understood what to do. "Nick, just repeat the instructions."

"Just go. I'll stay here until you come back," Levi said. I nodded at him and grabbed my wallet.

It wasn't that I didn't trust Nick to take care of Fee, but Levi paid as much attention as I did. I'd seen him look at his watch repeatedly when it was almost time for her medicine.

The dark circles under Fee's eyes had disappeared. Her skin was going back to its natural peachy color. Grabbing her hand and interlacing our fingers, I brought them to my lips and placed a lingering kiss on them. I leaned next to her ear and placed my forehead on her temple. I wouldn't leave her side if I didn't have to go. I was scared of leaving her alone. I already had done that once. I'd never forgive myself for not being there when she needed me the most. "Love, I'll be back in five hours, max. I promise." Kissing her temple, I let her go and walked out of the room.

Milton was waiting for me in the car. I reluctantly climbed in, knowing this was something I must do. My PI had disappeared without any communication. I was sure it had to do with Alexander, but I had no way to prove it. I didn't know if he'd sold me out or if he was in hiding, but I had to find someone else to help me take down Alexander Price. What Amber had given me was not enough.

It had been the longest week of my life. The days had been never-ending. Every second that her eyes stayed closed was another second that I could barely keep my head above the crushing waves. "Do you believe in destiny? Does everything require balance? Is that why this is happening to her?"

We stopped at a red light, and Milton turned to look at me. I wouldn't say his eyes were judgmental, but he looked at me like I'd lost it. Maybe I had. I raised my eyebrows at him—something Fee did a lot, but she only lifted her right one. It was cute. When he saw that I was serious, he frowned and turned to face the traffic.

I watched the New York skyline pass by. There was something I used to love about this city, but now it felt almost empty. Entering a parking lot, I watched the cars try not to hit each other. Angry faces yelled inside their vehicles as they tried to find a spot before they were late for work.

Milton parked in a reserved space and turned the engine off. Opening the door, I stepped out, but Milton's voice had me turning back to look at him. "Destiny is just a construct. If the universe required balance, this wouldn't have happened. She never wanted anything enough to fight for it until she met you. No matter what happens, there are no regrets on her end." He got out, leaving me with more questions than answers.

I followed the brooding older man to the elevators, which we took to the top floor. Milton didn't like to talk. None of her bodyguards did. Not that I minded since I wasn't a talker, but everyone liked Nick, and he could barely get them to say two words at a time.

They talked to her, though, especially Levi. He liked to sit close to her and whisper in her ear. It drove me crazy that I didn't know who he was to her, and that he ran his knuckles against her cheek. He was more than just security. None of them even looked like regular security. Her entire detail could be confused with guerrilla soldiers. They guarded her room like they expected someone to enter the hospital and start a war. The only reason I hadn't kicked them out was because I felt better knowing she was protected.

Milton stopped at the desk of a middle-aged man. He didn't pay any attention to us as he typed. When he was done, he lifted his eyes briefly and said, "He'll be available in ten minutes. Take a seat."

Not bothering to sit down, I walked towards the window overlooking the city. My office had a beach view, but this Central Park view wasn't bad. When Fee woke up, I could show her my headquarters. We would make love on my desk and against the window. That way, when I was having a shitty day, I could think about what she looked like when she yelled my name. I wanted her to be in every space I owned. I wanted to build a life with her. We could be a great team. I just needed her to stop fighting me every step of the way.

Looking around to see if anyone was paying attention, I adjusted myself as memories of Fee taking me in her mouth invaded my thoughts. I had always been dominant in the bedroom. I liked to control everything, but I didn't mind holding back with her. Her eyes lit up every time she explored my body. She was tentative, sweet, adventurous, and hot as fuck. It would have been a turnoff with anyone else, but everything felt a million times better with her. Even holding her in my arms while she cried at the ending of *The Parent Trap* made for a perfect moment. Nothing had ever been dull with her.

She didn't push me to be social after an exhausting day. After all my meetings, all I wanted to do was sit back and relax. As long as she was in my arms and I didn't need to say much, I didn't give a fuck what she wanted to do.

My life wasn't as exciting as that of other people my age. I was okay with that because all I wanted was peace and quiet. The past two weeks without her had been hell. I didn't want a quiet house anymore. I wanted to hear her talk about a dress she loved. Although I didn't care about the clothes, they were important to her and made her happy. I wanted to hear her sing while she danced around the room.

She would always sing while she showered, and I would watch like the creep that I was from the bathroom door. Her sweet, sultry voice would carry across the room, and she was phenomenal. I had spent a week imagining how it would feel to have her legs wrapped around me as I fucked her against the shower wall. It had finally happened the day she'd left. It had been better than what I had imagined, and I had a wild imagination when it came to her. I should have whispered in her ear that I loved her. Unfortunately, there was no going back now.

I had my assistant look for places to put her karaoke club the moment she told me about it. He found a couple that were in a prime location. I had them on hold so she could pick the one she wanted.

God! I wanted her back.

Nothing had felt better than being loved by her.

She didn't have to say the words. Her eyes said it all.

"You can go in now," the secretary finally said.

Shit.

I counted down from sixty while I thought about why I was there. That effectively killed my erection.

"Mr. Whitlock."

Turning around, I nodded at him and walked towards the door that he was pointing at. It was a corner office with two walls of only windows. The wood decorating the office was black. A man with blond hair was staring out of the window. His back was towards me.

"Mr. Price, thank you for meeting with me today." I left the briefcase on the chair and walked towards him until I was next to him.

"Do you see that family down there?" He pointed at a family of four. The parents sat on the bench while the boys played some sort of jumping game. "Before you walked in, the older one pushed his brother, but they're still playing as if nothing happened. Family is complicated, isn't it?"

"Everyone is complicated. We all have our own agendas." Chocolate-brown eyes turned to look at me. He was guarded, but his body language suggested he was relaxed. It reminded me of how even when Fee's body was calm, there was always a storm behind her eyes.

"What can I do for you, Leopold?" The fake boredom in his tone didn't fool me. I knew all the Price tactics. They held all their cards closely.

I grabbed the briefcase I had left on his desk and headed towards the cream-colored couch in the corner. "I came to help you."

He pursed his lips when he saw that I took it upon myself to pick a seat. I wouldn't let him control this meeting. There was only one person I'd ever happily relinquish control to.

"Been doing this for a long time, son. You wouldn't be here if you didn't want something."

"Let's talk about what I can do for you first." I pointed towards the smaller couch in front of me. Not waiting to see if he would sit down, I took out all the papers I had collected the week that Fee ignored me. Pulling out the last paper, I saw Mr. Price finally take a seat and start reading the contracts. The first contract caused a slight pupil dilation. The next one had his fingers gripping the paper tighter. The more he read, the more he gave away his feelings. I wasn't happy with what I found. It closed all the legal ways I could get her out of her father's claws. That didn't mean I was going to give up.

"Where did you get this?" he said without looking at me. His body had relaxed on the couch. I smirked as I saw the telltale signs of someone pretending to read as he tried to control the uncertainty hiding behind his facade.

"That doesn't matter. What matters is what would happen if that information ended up in the wrong hands." His eyes finally met mine. I leaned back, placing my hand on the armrest, and my other arm stretched on top of the couch.

Mr. Price attempted his version of an intimidating pose by straightening his back and placing his hands on both armrests. "My family owns this city. We're the reason this city is as prominent as it is. You will get none of this to stick. My lawyers would destroy you before this even got to court."

"Arrogance is the camouflage of insecurity." His eyes flared as I used a Tim Fargo quote. An irrational feeling of fear crawled up my spine, but I ignored it. "Isn't the Price motto *Reputation Above All*? Your stocks would plummet with a family scandal like this. There's no way you and your brother would go back to playing together after this. Everyone knows he's been trying to best you for years." When I'd walked in, he'd made it clear he would stand by his brother, but everyone had a price. Their last name was fitting.

"We're done here." His voice came out sharper than he intended. I walked calmly towards the door, opened it, and motioned for a man to come in. "Take your things," he said. I continued to ignore him as I waited for the older man.

I didn't miss his surprised gasp when he saw the man walk in.

"Nathaniel," he said.

"Simon," the older man answered.

Unsuccessfully hiding his shocked face, Simon's voice trembled as he spoke again. "What are you doing here?"

The family lawyer sat on the couch before replying. "I'm here for my goddaughter." Nathaniel Cochran was known by all to be the most cutthroat lawyer in the country. It turned out he had a weakness for the only person he considered family outside of his wife and kids.

Closing the door, I leaned against it without bothering to hide my smile. "Are you sure we're done here?"

"Sit," Simon barked at me, and I fought the urge to take a step back. His eyes were filled with rage. He was still untouchable. We both knew it, but there was always room for negotiations when your lawyer was sitting in front of you and not beside you.

"I'll tell you what I want first." I looked directly into his eyes when I said my next words loud and clear. "I want Felicity Price. I want all illegal contracts tied to her to be amended. Actually, no, I want all those contracts to be terminated and the companies to stop operations."

Simon scoffed.

"Listen to what the boy has to say," Nathaniel told him. "He doesn't care about what you or Alexander are doing. He just wants Felicity."

"Are you here to threaten me?" Simon asked him. He was tapping the armrest with his middle and ring finger. Something Fee always did when she was stressed or in deep concentration.

Nathaniel shook his head. "I'm just here to advise you. Once everyone finds out about"—he looked at me, then back at Simon —"you know what, it will be better for you if Felicity is no longer involved with the family. That's one less person to worry about."

I didn't know what they were talking about, and I was certain they weren't going to share. All I cared about was that Simon gave me the chance to negotiate Fee's freedom.

The two men stared at each other for a couple more seconds

before Simon turned to me. "Do you know how much money you would be costing us?" he asked incredulously. "What about all the employees? Do you think they stay quiet because they're loyal to us? No, we pay them well. What's going to happen when they're all suddenly out of work?"

I already had a plan for how to relocate the employees. It would take time and money, but they didn't deserve to be unemployed. "I'll cover those losses, but first you're going to show me those contracts."

I knew that no matter how long I searched, it would be impossible to get all their internal records. If I wanted to make sure everything Fee ever did never became known, I had to erase everything I could that pointed to her involvement. I had to make sure that if anyone ever tried to accuse her of something, the evidence they had wouldn't be enough.

Simon's lips pursed, but his eyes seemed like they were smiling. "For a Price, anything can be negotiated."

After hours of negotiations, I arrived back at the hospital. Nick and Levi were watching one of the Jurassic Park movies. Going directly to Fee, I rested my face against her neck and kissed her there. "I'm back, love."

"You look like shit." Ignoring Levi's comment, I went to the bathroom and showered.

Pushing our beds together and interlacing our fingers, I got as close to her as possible. These might be our last days together. Once she woke up, she'd have a choice to make.

After the movie was done, Levi grabbed his things. "Thanks for staying," I told him.

"I didn't do it for you." There was no animosity. It was just a fact.

"I know, but I'm still thankful," he grunted and walked out.

Nick got up and stretched. "I'm dying for some coffee. Where can I get something good?" The good coffee was at a machine hidden on the third floor. The nurses told me about it after they heard me complain about the cafeteria.

"I'll go get us some." I grabbed my wallet and gave Fee a quick kiss before leaving. We'd been in this hospital for six days. The smell of chemicals and disinfectants had become familiar to me. I grabbed two coffees before heading back up to the room.

After everything that had happened today, I should have felt satisfied, but I couldn't stop thinking about what she'd do when she woke up. The elevator doors opened, and screams filled the hallway.

Fee.

I rushed to the room as the doctor gave her what seemed to be a sedative. Fee's eyes were wide open as she murmured something I couldn't understand. I quickly handed the coffee to Nick, who was standing in the corner. As the nurses moved back from her bed, I leaned down and held her hand. Her eyes found mine, and they were filled with tears. My chest tightened painfully. She was awake.

"You can't tell Leo," she told me softly. "You can't tell Leo," she said again. I nodded, and tears started falling down my face as she looked at me with a defeated look. I held her hand until she closed her eyes again and her breathing evened out. I knew she was trying to protect me, but I wished she would let me be there for her instead of pushing me away. I couldn't think about that now. All that mattered was that she'd finally woken up.

3 4

ARMS

Felicity

My body felt stiff, like I had just run an entire marathon. Or one of those races where you have to run, swim, and do a gazillion other things. I groaned as I opened my eyes. The room was dark, so I had to blink several times to let my eyes adjust. I didn't recognize the layout of the room. There was light coming from underneath a door.

I looked behind me, and machines were ringing softly. What had happened to me? I felt something heavy on my left hand. Someone was holding my hand. I didn't need to look to know it was Leo. My heart constricted in my chest. He had come for me. "Leo," I breathed. "Leo."

"Shh, love," he said as his thumb rubbed my hand. "I'm here. I'm not going anywhere."

A sob escaped me as I thought of what had happened the last time we'd seen each other. "I'm sorry, I hurt you, and I just expec —" He pulled his hand from mine, and I heard his feet land on the floor. Light filled the room, making me wince.

"You're awake." There were so many emotions on his face that

I wasn't sure what he was feeling. He rushed to my side and brought my hand to his lips, kissing my knuckles. His eyes were glassy as we looked at each other. He cleared his throat. "I'll call the nurse." He kissed my hand again before letting go. He moved to the other side of the bed and pushed a button. "Don't cry, love. We'll explain everything. All that matters is that you finally came back to me." He leaned in and kissed the tears away. I closed my eyes, relishing his touch, something I thought I wouldn't be able to feel again.

I heard someone walk into the room. "Is everything okay, Mr. Whitlock?" Leo kissed my hand again before responding.

"She's awake!"

I opened my eyes and saw an older lady smiling warmly at me. "It's great to finally meet you. My name is Julia, and I'll take care of you tonight. Let me call the doctor, and we'll be right back."

Leo's smile was so big, I knew it must hurt.

I reached out, trying to feel him. He brought his face to my hand, and I caressed his jaw. "You're real." He closed his eyes for a second, and when he opened them, I saw his soul bared to me. I knew what had happened was serious from how he had reacted, and I couldn't keep making the same mistakes.

"I love you," I whispered. His eyes lit up, and I smiled at him, knowing that no matter the consequences, I would choose him. I just hoped he would choose me too.

"Felicity Price!" A short doctor with graying hair walked into the room. "I was just about to leave. I'm happy I was running late. I'm Dr. David Rivera. Is it okay if we perform a checkup?" A stunning blond nurse with piercing eyes entered the room with Julia.

I turned to look at Leo, and he nodded at me. His beautiful smile was still in place. I turned back to the doctor. "Of course." Leo let my hand go to give the doctors some space, and I panicked. "Wait!"

Everyone in the room laughed at my reaction. I blushed and bit my lip, embarrassed at how desperate I sounded. Leo came back to my side, and I relaxed at his touch.

The doctor finished the checkup and eyed Leo nervously. Leo was solely looking at me, so he didn't notice. "Leo."

The way he looked at me when I called him made my insides burn. With how much everything was always burning when I was around him, I wasn't sure how I was still alive. "Yes, love." He hadn't stopped kissing me everywhere he could—hands, neck, shoulders, face . . . my body was too aware of him.

"Would you mind getting me a cup of coffee?"

Leo looked at the doctor for confirmation.

"She can drink a little coffee," Dr. Rivera said, confirming my suspicion that he wanted Leo out of the room.

"I'll be right back." He kissed my forehead before rushing out the door.

Julia followed behind. "I'll wait outside," she said before closing the door.

I looked at the doctor nervously. The blond nurse, Mary, was still in the room with us. She was looking at me with pity.

Dr. Rivera cleared his throat before speaking. "Miss Price, you were admitted to the hospital due to internal bleeding caused by abdominal trauma." I didn't show any emotion on my face. The doctor continued, "Mr. Whitlock's brothers insisted on keeping the cause of your injuries from him at your request."

"That's correct." The last thing Leo needed was a head-to-head battle with my father.

"I read your medical record, and this isn't the first time you have been admitted due to injuries like these. We know this can be hard, but if you want to take legal action—"

I interrupted him. We needed to end this conversation before Leo returned. "That won't be necessary. It was an accident." Dr. Rivera pursed his lips. "Please don't mention this to Leo. You've seen how protective he is."

"We're required to detail everything we found, so it'll be kept in your record. Regarding your care, we'll keep you here for another week or two. Everything should heal in two to three months. During that time, please make sure you're resting and avoid putting any pressure on your abdomen. Also, don't drink the coffee."

"Thank you," I told him.

Leo walked in with the coffee, smiling at me. Dr. Rivera and the nurse excused themselves, leaving us alone. I took the tiniest sip of the coffee since he had already taken the time to get it, and I handed it back to him.

"How are you feeling?" he asked.

Nervous. Where was Milton? Why was only Leo here? "I feel a little stiff, but there's no pain." I tried to study his expression, but he gave nothing away. "It's late. You should probably go back to bed. I'm sorry for waking you up." Leo looked at me for a beat before he dimmed the lights and got on his bed.

He was lying on his back, his hands on his stomach, not reaching for me. "Before I can respond to what you told me earlier, I have to say something."

I was expecting him to address my *I love you*, but I was also hoping he had forgotten. "Go on," I whispered.

"The day we discovered you were to marry my brother, I was hopeful. Hopeful because if your dad was trying to find someone for you in my family, I could prove I was worthy of you. In the back of my mind, a voice told me I didn't want to be married, so why was I rushing to marry someone I had just met? I spoke with my father that night about us. He told me to forget about you— that he wouldn't allow so much power to go to your father. Everyone knew that your father might be considered the devil, but you were his enforcer. I snuck into bed with you, trying to prove that this was real. That he couldn't understand because maybe we were meant to find each other, and I wasn't delusional."

I wished he would look at me, but his gaze stayed fixed on the ceiling. *Look at me! Show me what you're feeling.*

"When you stopped answering my calls and texts, I knew something was wrong. I was upset that you shut me out like we meant nothing, but I wanted to give you space to realize what I already had."

My fingers itched to touch him. "What did you realize?" He ignored my question and continued.

"I took that week to do some digging on your father. I wanted to have something I could use as leverage against him."

He finally turned around to look at me. He was angry. His eyes looked downright menacing.

"Do you know what I discovered?" I did.

Bile rose in my throat. I knew this conversation was coming. I just wasn't expecting it to happen while I was lying in a hospital bed.

"That the signature of the woman I loved was all over those papers. I couldn't use a single piece of that evidence against him without hurting you in the process."

He loved me? I didn't have time to process that because he didn't stop talking.

"But as I said, I had already realized you were mine, no matter the consequences or other people's unwanted opinions." His thumb came to my quivering lip. "You belong to me as much as I belong to you."

"Leo, what did you do?" His calm demeanor gave me chills.

"I made a deal with the devil." My heart stopped. He grinned. "I'm buying anything that's tied to you. I even got the charitable organization. We'll clean it up, and you can run it. I saw how much time you dedicated to it, and you used your own money to fund a lot of things, so I know you care for it."

"But—" His thumb brushed my lips, pushing lightly against them.

"We'll get everything within the year. We clean up what we

can and cut our losses on what we can't. We'll find everyone a new job. Your uncle Simon will take in half of the employees. We get the other half." The next time I spoke, he didn't interrupt me.

Wait, what? Had I heard him correctly? "Simon? How did you convince him? They only play under the table. They would never go against each other like that."

"Nathaniel Cochran."

"Cochran? The old man helped?" Pure disbelief filled my brain.

"He came to visit you, and we talked. He didn't want to say much, but what he said was that you had changed. He seemed conflicted before he left, so I told him what I felt for you. When I assured him I didn't want to harm the company and that I only wanted you, he agreed to help us. We met with Simon. Alexander had no other choice but to concede. Nathaniel had much more information on him than he was willing to give me. I didn't care what it was if I could get you out."

He didn't know what he had just done. Simon had never had a heart. My father might have been violent, but that was his way of hiding his true feelings. Simon would kill his own child if it benefited him, and Leo had just walked up to him, putting himself on a silver platter.

"Cleaning those companies will take millions. You need to break this deal. You should have never gotten involved. Why would you do this?" This was precisely what I wanted to avoid. It would take millions of dollars just to relocate the workers. Cleaning up both construction companies would mean making updates to the hundreds of homes already built. Not only in Texas, but also Florida and New Orleans. Homes that could collapse at any moment if the wind blew the wrong way. Homes that had already caused the deaths of fifteen people. I was prepared to take the fall for that. Not even I could front the cost of what it would take.

"As long as you don't mind being with a poor man. I can't give you the life you're used to now, but I can give you your freedom. It'll take me a couple of years to build our wealth again, but as long as I can protect you, I don't care."

"But what about your family?" My voice was shaky, but my tears didn't want to stop. He wiped the silent tears from my cheeks.

"My sleeping beauty doesn't always need to save herself. You have me now, and I'll never let anyone hurt you. Besides, I'm only using my money, love. My family's business won't be involved in anything."

That wouldn't be enough. He was giving up everything for me. I did what I desperately wanted to avoid. I ruined him.

"Remember what my grandfather told my nana?"

I nodded.

"What do you say? Would you choose me?"

Was there any other choice for me? No. He was it.

I didn't need anything else if I had him.

"I don't need to marry your brother?" I sobbed.

He grinned, closing his eyes, and shook his head slowly.

I took a deep breath, trying to get my breathing under control. "With my money . . . we can cover most of it . . . and I can also sell my house." I hiccuped. If he was going to use all his money on me, then I wanted to do my part too.

"You don't need—" It was my turn to interrupt him. I put my hand over his lips.

"I want to. We'll do this as a team." I looked away from him, embarrassed that he knew some of the horrible things I'd done. He wouldn't know everything, but he had a clearer image of who I was. I'd endangered so many people's lives to save my mom and me from my father. I was willing to do anything not to go back into that room. I'd given my soul to the devil and stopped feeling remorse. Now it was coming back to me in painful waves.

"Do you still want to be with me after everything?" My voice was thick with emotion. I didn't need to elaborate. He'd seen it.

Although, he didn't know about all the bodies I'd buried. I'd stopped looking at the papers I signed long ago, as if it would make my sins less evil if I didn't know what I was signing.

"Fee, look at me." His voice was soft, but I kept my eyes closed, trying to fight the sobs that wanted to escape. "You're not your father!"

"How do you know? I'm just as selfish as he is. I know you want to believe the best in me, Leo, but I'm a monster just like him." My blood was boiling.

Angry at what I had become.

Angry that my family had won again.

Angry that he didn't know the whole truth of what I'd done.

"I stopped asking questions because it was easier not to know. Then I forgot about the pain I was causing others just because it was convenient for me." My heart was beating fast. My anger burned out the tears that were pouring down my face.

"Maybe we should talk about this after you rest," he said.

I ignored him.

"I was okay with marrying someone else to manipulate them and use them how my father wanted. There's a reason I'm the devil's daughter." I turned to face him. I was expecting to find disgust, but there was only concern. "I would have married your brother and manipulated him to go against you without a thought. Trust me. You would have hated me if you had met me under different circumstances." I felt like I was running out of air. I couldn't stop now. He needed to know who I really was. "Then you came into my life, and I forgot the real me. I became someone different—someone I liked. For once, there was something I wanted, and I tried to take it for myself. You made me feel like I was beautiful and not just some plain girl with nice clothes." I took a deep breath. "It's not the real me. You won't like the real me. You're wasting your money on someone who doesn't deserve it." His lips landed on mine so fast that I barely had a chance to react.

His mouth was demanding. I let him take whatever he wanted from me because he already owned everything. He slowed down once we both needed air.

"There's nothing you can say that will make me love you less. We all make mistakes. What matters is how we redeem ourselves." I wanted to argue that I'd done nothing. He was the one who had made the leap for me. "You're wrong about us. It doesn't matter when I met you." His lips traced my jaw and made their way down my neck. A soft whimper escaped my lips. "You were always meant to be mine, and I always take what's mine." A sting of pain hit me when he sucked the flesh on my neck for a couple of seconds before leaning back and looking at his mark with pride. "And never let go. I love you, Felicity. No matter where you were, I would have found you because we're meant to be together. Two pieces of the same soul."

I choked as the lump in my throat got bigger, not letting me breathe. Fresh tears cascaded down my face. I tried to use my hands to cover myself up. I'd truly lost it this time. I heard Leo asking me what was wrong, but I couldn't answer him. How did I tell him he was the first person who'd made me feel like I was worth it? Like I wasn't nothing?

A soft knock came from the door, interrupting us. Leo spoke first. "Give us a minute." After pulling me into his arms and giving me time to calm down, he said, "Come in."

The door opened, and my mother stood there. There were emotions in her blue eyes instead of the usual stoic face she gave me. "I asked a nurse to call me when you woke up." She blushed as if she'd done a bad thing by asking the nurse to inform her about her own daughter. She looked at Leo shyly, keeping up the pretense of the loving mother, but I could see through her act. I looked up at Leo as I felt his arms tighten around me. His eyes were slightly squinted, and his jaw was tight as he stared at her. I squeezed his thigh, and he immediately turned toward me.

"It's okay. I'll be fine. Can you please give us a minute?" I asked. He hesitated for a brief moment before giving me a slight nod.

Placing a kiss on my forehead, he murmured against my skin, "I'll be right outside." He turned the lights on as he walked out. Once he left, my mother sat on the couch next to me, and I pushed the button that made my bed lift to a sitting position.

"How are you feeling?" she asked.

"Good." The awkwardness extended as we were both silent. I didn't know what to tell her.

"That's a nice robe."

I looked at the soft lilac gown, which I hadn't noticed until now. Leo must have done this. I looked around the room and took in the beautiful flower arrangements. Soft pinks, oranges, purples, and greens decorated the space. The room was big. It had a kitchen, dining area, and living space on the left side. There were two closed doors. I guessed one was a bathroom.

"I know about the deal," she said, making her way next to me.

I reached for her hand, but she didn't give it to me. "You can come with me." I thought about when I'd left that greenhouse and how I'd hated her and blamed her for all of our suffering. I'd tried to build our relationship, but it was clear I wasn't the daughter she'd wanted.

She couldn't hide the revulsion in her eyes. I wasn't expecting her to approve of Leo, but at least I would have liked her to be happy for me. Her hand connected with my face before I even realized what she was doing. I held my cheek, feeling the sting of her slap, and looked up at her. Gone was the woman who had come in through the door pretending she cared about me.

"Alexander has always been weak with you." She clasped my hair in her fist and yanked it back painfully. "You are nothing. How many times do I have to tell you before that doltish brain of yours can comprehend it? I knew that before you were even born, and you think that someone like him will ever love you?" Her laugh echoed across the room as I swallowed back tears.

"Alexander gave you a way out, and you're so vacuous you didn't even see it. You're so blinded by love that you threw it all away. I'm going to enjoy watching your father break you."

She shoved me back as she let me go. Picking up her purse, she strolled out of the room. I closed my eyes, trying to block her words. I knew now they weren't true. I wasn't nothing.

"Are you okay?" Leo asked as he entered the room.

I let out a shaky breath before nodding. I didn't want to talk about it. I didn't want to voice my insecurities because I already knew what he was going to say. I believed him when he said he loved me. He opened his mouth but closed it before saying anything. I knew this wouldn't last forever and that eventually I'd have to answer his questions and share some of my secrets, but tonight wasn't the right time.

Leo turned the lights off before getting in bed and interlacing our fingers.

"Leo?"

"Yes, love?"

"Thanks for the room. I love the flowers."

"Anything for you."

"Leo?"

"I'm here."

"I love you."

"I love you too."

35

BREATHING

Felicity

"Am I interrupting something?" Ayden's voice was typically music to my ears, but today, not so much. I had just finished showering, and Leo and I had been lost in each other, and it was clear neither of us was happy with the interruption when Leo's growl broke us out of our soul-devouring kiss.

It had been that passionate.

"No," I murmured.

"Yes," Leo whispered softly against my cheek.

Jane also walked in and looked between Leo and me before rolling her eyes and making her way to the couch.

"It's good to see you too, Jane," I told her.

Ayden came to my side and hugged me. "I can't believe you got in an accident just to get out of going to my concert next week," he joked.

"It's a shitty concert." I teased, squeezing him tighter before letting go.

I had taken all the people around me for granted. Never really letting them in. I had kept them at arm's length and pushed them away, blaming them for the reason I was lonely, but it was all me. People had wanted to be around me. I just hadn't let them because I was ashamed of the person I was.

I could be good. Just because I had been lost once didn't mean I had to stop trying. I understood that now. There was always something to fight for, even if it was just for myself. Staying down was easy. Getting back up was the hard part.

I turned to the man who had taught me so much in so little time just by showing me the world around me. He had no idea what he had done for me. The impact he had had on my life. I smiled so big that it hurt. He looked at me, frowning, but his jaw loosened up slowly, his eyes melted, and his lips twitched.

"I love you," I said out loud.

"I know," he said, finally giving me that heavenly smile.

"I never thought you guys could be more disgusting than before, but here you are, making me want to throw up," Nick said while entering the room with bags full of food, Milton right behind him.

By the time I had woken up that morning, Milton had already been there with breakfast and clean clothes for Leo. I could tell he liked him, but Milton was never one to express his feelings. When I told him we needed to switch rooms, he had looked at me like I was the stupidest person he had ever met. "I'll cover it," was his response.

"This is an expensive room, Milton. It's a waste of money." I didn't know how much it was exactly, but it had to be a couple thousand.

"Do you like it?" he asked while drinking his coffee.

"Yeah, it's nice," I said with a shrug.

"Then you're staying." He had let me know the subject was closed by turning away from me and looking at the TV.

I watched as my friends and family took the food out of the bags and started opening container after container of Chinese food. The nurse brought me food, and we all ate while they caught me up to speed with everything that had happened for the past week, which wasn't much. Jane had canceled the only event I had scheduled. They had promised to keep it a secret when she told them about the skating accident.

Daniel, David, and Butch took turns bringing employees and their kids so they could see me. It was nice to see everyone. They had always been more than just my employees. Most of them had been with me since I was a child. After I had bought my house, I had offered them the choice of working for me instead of my father. It had been a simple transition for all of us.

Ana cried as soon as she saw me. I hugged her close. Her graying hair was neatly tucked into a bun. She smelled like cookies. "*Me asustaste*," she said between sobs. I couldn't imagine how she felt. This was different from the other times.

"Don't be scared. I'm right here. Everything will be fine now," I told my old nanny, kissing the top of her head. She had tried to protect me when I was a teenager, but I had been too rebellious then and hadn't appreciated her. It had taken going to an asylum for me to realize what type of person I was becoming.

A hand landed on my shoulder, squeezing gently. Jane was staring at me with unshed tears shining in her eyes. I was surprised by the contact because if I hated people touching me, she despised it. Jane certainly wasn't emotional, even though she had forced me to express my feelings. She walked away quickly and grabbed her purse.

"Ana, let's go. She'll be back at the house by the end of the week," Jane said. Ana stayed in my arms for a couple of seconds before kissing my temple and leaving with everyone.

Leo excused himself sometime during the afternoon because he had a couple of meetings he needed to attend. It was already nine, and I had only seen him a couple of times. He would stick his head in the room, look at me, and then leave again without saying a word. I grabbed my phone to text him, but I stopped when I saw the man that walked in.

"Father," I said, lifting my chin. "I wasn't expecting you yet. I thought you would plot for longer."

Although my father had never been handsome, he still looked like he was in his mid-fifties. His short white hair was neatly styled back. His tailored suit looked impeccable, with not even a single crease.

"Watch how you talk to me. I'm still your father."

There was nothing to read on his face, but he was here, and that said all I needed to know. "Are you?" I taunted, knowing he wouldn't touch me right then. "Leave him out of this."

His eyes narrowed at my warning. "I didn't raise you to be naive."

Which was why I wasn't falling for the contract they had signed with Leo. "He already did what Simon asked. We are done with the family." My heart beat a little faster, at my authoritative tone, but he needed to see that I wasn't scared. I could keep Leo safe from them.

"He reminds me of the man I used to be, but he's still young. It'll be interesting to see what he can do when he's more experienced."

He will never be like you. I didn't vocalize my thoughts, not wanting to poke the bear more than I already had.

"I heard your mother came. Stay away from her, or you'll lose this newfound freedom." The warning in his voice was unmistakable.

I nodded.

I shouldn't have said more, but I just needed to know.

"He told me he loved me." There was no change in his features as the words left my mouth. "Did you ever love me?" My nails dug painfully into my palm while I analyzed the man in front of me.

One.

Two.

Three.

The seconds passed, but the mask he had on never faltered.

"Stay away," he finally said before he turned around and left.

This wasn't over. I still had a card to play to make sure they honored their agreement with Leo. Leo was now a challenge for my family, and they wouldn't stop until there was a winner. So, I had to use the leverage I had against my father even if I hated it.

> Everyone's gone. You can work here if you want.

LEO

> I'll be right there.

Not even five minutes later, he was walking in. He looked exhausted. There was stress that hadn't been there that morning. I stretched my arms out to him, and the corners of his lips tipped up. He brought the guardrails from my bed down and pushed his bed against mine. As soon as he got in, he laid his head on my chest and hugged me tightly. I put my arms around him and caressed his hair, trying to ease his tension. I knew he liked it when I did that. We stayed there, silently enjoying each other's company, for about an hour. Then he broke the silence.

"How are you doing?" he asked.

"Good, it was nice to see everyone. I missed you." I placed a kiss on the top of his head. We still had several hurdles to pass, but having him in my arms made me feel like we could overcome anything thrown at us.

"Me too," he said while kissing my arm.

"Do you want to talk about it?" I asked.

"The marketing team released the wrong specs for the new chip. We still don't understand where they got those numbers from. The files they presented for approval had the correct information. There's no way to meet those expectations, and correcting that mistake will cost a couple of million in another campaign. The board isn't happy."

I could only imagine how badly the board took it. Most of

them did nothing and only had something to say when things went south. I would know. That was what I did.

"I'm sorry, *amor*. I'm here if you need me."

He pushed himself up by his elbows and brought his face to mine. "I always need you," he said before giving me a sweet kiss. "I love you, my siren."

"I love you," I said and closed the distance between us.

THE DOORS to my house opened at the exact moment everyone yelled, "Surprise!" I had only been at the hospital for a week, which was great because I was ready to leave. Lying in bed all day was getting boring, even though watching Leo work was amazing.

The foyer was filled with people and balloons. The kids ran to me, and Leo held my stomach protectively, but they all stopped before they collided with us. I hugged the little rascals and accepted their drawings and gifts before they ran off to the back-yard while their parents greeted me.

I was surprised to see that Amber, Elias, and Ellen also came. They stayed in the back until everyone had said hi and left. Ellen walked slowly toward me, looking a little shy, something I didn't think she could do since she was always so energetic.

She pushed Leo to the side and pulled me into a hug. "I'm sorry I made things awkward. I did notice Leopold was acting weird, but I never expected you to be the girlfriend he kept telling me about. He's always wary about people."

"Not many people knew since we were keeping it a secret. I'm sorry for lying." Ellen let me go and gave me a huge smile.

"I'm not surprised you stole his heart," Ellen said with a genuine smile. "He's always been the smart one, never letting rare things pass him by." I could feel the blush spread across my face; I nodded, not knowing what to say.

Leo pulled me back into his arms and kissed my temple. "Let's go eat before she gets even more red," he said. I smacked him in the arm, feeling even more embarrassed now that he brought it up, but everyone else laughed.

I knew Benjamin wouldn't be here, but I still expected him to pop out and say, "Amira." Omar said he was doing better, but now that Simon had called him to his side and forced him to move back home, I didn't know anything about him. I worried that the pressure would get to him and he'd make a mistake. Benjamin was the only family I had left now, and he'd been taken from me. Yes, I had Leo, but leaving Benjamin behind made me feel like I was abandoning him. I hoped he could one day forgive me.

Amber pulled me to the side before we went out. "Does Leo know?" she asked.

I wasn't surprised that she didn't buy the skating accident; it wouldn't be the first lie she'd heard about how I got hurt. "No, he doesn't need to." There was no reason to tell him how I got injured. She pursed her lips and pulled me into a hug.

"You need to trust him. I know you don't like people getting close to you, but he's different. He won't hurt you," she said, pulling back and looking into my eyes.

I did trust him. There was only a slight doubt in my mind that he'd leave me if he knew the truth about everything, but my heart knew he wouldn't. Knowing would only make him an accessory, and I wouldn't do that to him.

"I know he won't, but Leo is stubborn. He won't let it go. I could force him to go against my family, but the only thing that's going to accomplish is feeding my ego. Why would I want to lose the peace we have? It's not fair to him." Before we stepped outside, I wrapped my arms around her. "I'm sorry for being a shitty friend all these years. I never check up on you."

"When you have a sister, you don't need to be with them all the time—just the moments that count, and you have been there for all of those." If I could have hugged her tighter without hurting myself, I would have. "Besides, I'll always be the shitty friend here." We both laughed before letting go.

We spent the rest of the day with my and Leo's families. Chloe created a Mediterranean feast for everyone. The backyard was filled with tables and laughter. Leo kept trying to get stories about me out of everyone. It was embarrassing. He learned about when I drew my makeup on with poop, and now they wouldn't stop laughing. "I was a baby!" I yelled, trying to defend myself.

"Oh my God, I'm crying," Nick said, bending over.

Leo's head was bent back as he tried to catch his breath. He turned to look at me, and his entire body shook as he failed to control himself. I pouted at him, but he just laughed harder and gave me a quick kiss.

"I had to put her in a warm bath to scrub it off and make sure she didn't do it again. I still don't know how she pulled her fingers out of the diaper without making a mess," Ana added, like we needed more information.

"Kill me now," I mumbled, crossing my arms and trying to hide my smile.

As the night fell and people dispersed, I leaned more on Leo, trying to fight the fatigue. "Let's get you to bed before you fall asleep here," he said. Of course he noticed.

I nodded against his chest.

We said goodnight to everyone before making our way up. I shamelessly threw my clothes all over the couch, not bothering to fold them. Leo chuckled and, being the saint he was, grabbed them and found a hamper, knowing I'd have an issue with the mess in the morning. Getting into bed, I relaxed, happy to finally be in my space. As soon as I felt the bed dip, I searched for his warmth.

"Does everyone live here? It's like a big happy family. I've never seen anything like it," he asked. I moaned when he massaged my scalp. He'd gotten extremely good at that since he'd been the one washing my hair. It's not that I couldn't do it. He just insisted on it.

"Most of them do. Some have rooms on the fourth floor, and the ones with kids live in the townhouses on the edge of the property. I wouldn't be where I am without them." Jane was already looking for other jobs for them and places to live. It was a hard decision, but I had to sell the property. I couldn't afford to maintain it anymore. My freedom started with this house and all the people in it. It was hard to imagine not being able to come home anymore, but I had a new one in Leo.

"Who are you, Felicity Price?"

I looked up at him. He was looking at me in awe. I didn't deserve it. Tracing his jaw with my finger, I said, "A woman that wants to make you happy."

"You already do that," he said with a grin.

"I do?" I scrunched my nose in surprise, which earned me a kiss.

"Just knowing that I get to wake up with you in my arms makes me want to speed up time so I can enjoy that beautiful smile you give me when your eyes are barely open," he responded. I saw my world—my everything—in his gaze. He looked at me how I always wanted someone to look at me. No sadness, just happiness. If I thought I was in love before, I was wrong, because what I felt at that moment was more than love. It was infinite.

Leo got up and grabbed his phone. He searched for something before looking at me lovingly. "Come here," he said.

He placed his phone on the nightstand and pulled me into his arms as "Heaven" by Calum Scott played. Butterflies swirled around my entire body, and I felt the warmth of his arms around me while we swayed to the music. Resting his forehead on mine, we looked at each other, living in the moment. His eyes spoke to me, letting me know there was no place he'd rather be. A soft smile played on his lips while I tried not to get emotional. As the song ended, he tilted his head to the side, caressing my lips with his. I brought my hand to his face. Our lips tenderly met each other, creating their own dance.

The following day, as we woke up, I gave him that smile and kissed his chest. My finger outlined his jaw, feeling the five o'clock shadow. We both laughed, which was weird because neither of us was talking, but it felt right. I felt whole with him by my side. "Just want to make sure you're still real," I said.

36

BLOOM IN THE DARK

Felicity

"Felicity," Father exclaimed, surprised. His eyebrows pulled together tightly. "What are you doing here?"

He was sitting on the sofa in his office. I took the seat right in front of him. I couldn't believe I was here, but I had to do this. I had lied to Leo and told him I just needed some alone time and fresh air so he would let me leave the house with Milton. "I would like to have a conversation with you. Is it too much to ask you to pretend like you don't hate me for just a couple of minutes?"

Father looked at me with a blank expression before pressing a button on his desk. His butler showed up almost immediately. "Bring my daughter ginger tea," he instructed, then to me he said, "Go ahead, what do you want to talk about?"

"I know things changed for you when you found out Mom was cheating on you. I know you wish I was never born. I also know you're not my real father." My throat closed, but I managed to choke the words out. After I'd found my mom with her lover, I'd made a guess as to why my father suddenly started to hate me, so I'd taken a DNA test when I turned eighteen. Father's eyes tightened but he didn't say anything, so I continued after doing my best to compose myself. "I never loved you less. Yes, there were times I hated you because of how you treated me, but I still loved you and respected you as my father. I'm sorry I couldn't give you the company back."

"I didn't expect you to give me the company back, Felicity." He sighed. He leaned his head to the right and stared out the window, looking at the sky. "I wanted you to have it." Me? "I haven't been able to stop hating you and I don't know if I ever can. Every time I look at you, it's just a reminder of him. I hate your face."

"Why did you want me to have the company?" The butler brought my ginger tea and left.

"Because if you have it, Simon doesn't. I can never be the head; Father was very clear in his will." Of course, this was just a competition between them. It wasn't because he thought I deserved it. "And because you deserved it," he continued. My eyes widened at his words. He thought I deserved it? "Have you ever wondered why Father left you so much money when he died yet no one else got anything? He also thought you deserved it. It was his way of giving you a head start."

"How did that give me a head start?" I'd used that money to become independent and start my company. I hadn't used it for our family.

Father sighed as if this conversation was taking a toll on him. "There are stipulations to become the head. One of those is that you have to earn a certain amount of money before you're thirty from your own company. The amount changes every generation —it depends on the economy. You had already accomplished that, but you threw all that hard work away for a *boy*," he spat.

"I don't have my own company," I corrected, taking a sip of my tea.

Dad leaned his head slightly to look at me. He rolled his eyes and went back to staring out the window. Was that the only way he could speak with me? By not looking at my face. "Why do you think I left you in that asylum for so long? You thought I didn't know what you were doing? Working day and night on a business plan and designs. I've told you. You can't hide anything from me. I know you're already a billionaire. Although, I doubt Simon left you with any money with the deal he forced Leo to take, and I know you won't let Leo pay everything on his own. I didn't think he would accept such a high price for those companies, but he understood that it was your freedom he was paying for."

"What are the other stipulations?" I asked.

He shook his head slightly. "I can't say."

"Why?" How was someone supposed to become the head if they didn't even know how to do it? Father ignored me and I took it as a sign that he was done with the conversation. "Thank you for talking with me. I have to ruin the moment now." I placed my phone on the table between us and pressed play on the video. Father turned around at the sound of his own voice. He grabbed the phone with wide eyes. My cries and pleas filled the silence between us. He looked up at me with squinted eyes and threw the phone on the table.

"You had a camera in your room?" he asked in disbelief. The video had a clear view of him threatening to kill Leo. "What do you want?" He was shaking slightly, but I knew it had nothing to do with him being nervous. He was furious.

"You said it yourself—I don't like leaving loose ends. I want you and Simon to stay away from him. If anything happens to him, that video will be released, and trust me—no power on this earth will save you from jail. I have more videos and piles of evidence against both of you. So, I suggest you keep your brother under control. We will pay what you guys wanted. I will keep my mouth shut because I still believe in our family, but he's my family too and I will never let you hurt him." I didn't have anything big against Simon, but a threat to the family's reputation should be enough to keep them at bay for now.

"Is that it?" he asked through gritted teeth.

"I want to see my brother. Benjamin's number changed and I want it."

Father scoffed. "Forget about Benjamin. He's never been your brother. He only keeps you around so he can use you. Has he ever looked for you or cared about you unless he wants something from you? How many times do I have to tell you to stop being weak?"

"Love isn't a weakness."

He shook his head, letting out a heavy sigh. "I'll stay away from Leo, but Benjamin is out of my reach. Simon has him confined somewhere. Without you, who's going to keep Benjamin out of the press?"

"I don't believe that. You have men everywhere; I know you can reach him."

We stared at each other, neither wanting to concede, until he finally grabbed his phone and made a call. He spoke with someone on the line and after a couple of seconds he was handing me the phone.

"Hello?" I said tentatively.

"Amira?" Benjamin's voice sounded hoarse and tired. My father was staring intensely at me.

"How are you? Are you safe?" I asked my brother.

"Dad has me locked up in a house, I don't know where. It's so boring, I have nothing to do, and these guards don't even talk to me. Can you get me out?" I breathed a sigh of relief, knowing he was okay.

"I can't help you. I'm sorry. You need to take care of yourself from now on, okay? No more parties," I said.

"Are you getting married already? I should be out of here by the time you get married."

"It's not that, just promise me no more parties," I insisted.

"Scout's honor, remember? I said I would get better for you. I've been good, I promise." I could hear the smile in his voice.

"I want you to get better for yourself."

"Yeah, that too. Why are you acting so weird?" he asked.

"I'm leaving the fami—"

I was interrupted by a deep voice that said, "Your time's up," then he hung up. I stared at the phone for a couple of seconds before putting it on the table. At least Benjamin sounded okay.

I grabbed my phone and got up slowly. My abdomen still hurt a little. "Remember the video whenever you or your brother want to touch Leo," I told Father.

A slow smile crept on his face as if this was a challenge to him. "At least listen to one piece of advice from this old man. Don't marry him."

I rolled my eyes at him and walked out. He was no longer in control of my life. I was, and that brought a smile to my face. I opened my arms wide as I stepped out of the house. I was free. I could finally fly.

"LOVE, WHAT ARE YOU DOING?" Leo asked diplomatically, though his eyes clearly said, *Did I not tell you to sit down?* Which he had told me several times, but I didn't want to be useless.

"Helping," I responded, taking the last of my blouses from the rack in my second closet. I was separating everything into three piles: one to donate, another to sell, and the last were the ones I was keeping.

"What do you think we're here for?" Jane asked, clearly annoyed. She was only patient when she had to be, but other than that, she had no problem letting everyone know when she wasn't happy with something.

If it were up to Leo, he would tie me to the bed. He thought I moved around too much, even though all I did was walk around the house. My healing was going great. He had nothing to worry about.

"I thought I would help with these since you guys still have the basement." We only had a couple of days before we flew back to Whitlock. Leo needed to handle some things with the company, but he didn't want to leave me until I was settled. We would stay in his house until it sold, but we would move most of our stuff to the apartment to ensure everything was ready when the time came.

"Basement?" Leo asked, stunned. His mouth was slightly open, and he looked at me like I was some weird creature. I knew they had just finished the main closet, which was two levels, but I only had the clothes I would wear soon in there. I kept everything else in the basement. The entire basement was just one big room that was temperature-controlled to ensure my clothes were well maintained. "How many clothes can you possibly have?"

I bit my lip. "Well, I'll sell most of the clothes in the basement, so those aren't coming with us to Whitlock," I said reassuringly.

"How many?" his insistent ass asked again.

Jane and I exchanged a look before I finally answered, "A little over twenty thousand."

"Jesus, woman!" he exclaimed.

"I promise I'm only taking the essentials. But I thought maybe I could use the second room as a closet?" We hadn't really discussed boundaries, which we should since we were moving in together and neither of us had any experience with that. Also, we were both moving from mansions to a two-bedroom apartment, which meant we wouldn't have the space we were used to.

"You don't need to ask. It's your house too. I draw the line in the living room, though. No clothes are allowed there. I want to be able to walk through the door," he said, trying to hide his smile.

"Ha, ha. You're so funny." I rolled my eyes at him. He closed the distance between us and gave me a long, rough kiss that made my legs feel like noodles.

Packing was hard work. It took days to finish everything, but it was finally over—not that I did much. Jane, Ana, Amber, Nick, and Leo did everything while I gave orders about where I wanted things. After he saw me grimacing, he didn't let me bend down again. He was commanding, which I honestly wasn't surprised about. Now that he knew I wouldn't break, he was taking the reins, and I was okay with letting him take care of me. It was time for me to be free.

I watched out the window as the jet landed in Whitlock. Leo kissed my sweaty hand and smiled at me. I seemed to be the only one nervous about how fast we were moving. It had been an emotional day. Having to say goodbye to everyone didn't feel real until it happened. At the same time, I was excited about the future. Before Leo, I went through the motions. Now I wanted to enjoy everything.

"We're here," Leo said.

The contemporary house had an open-plan layout. There were windows everywhere. The best part was that you could see the beach as soon as you walked in. Too bad we wouldn't be here for long. His arms wrapped around me as I stared at the beach.

"I'm scared," I admitted quietly. "I'm new to this. I'll make mistakes, but I promise, if you're patient with me, I'll get the hang of things. I should have told you I've never cleaned anything, cooked, fixed something, or taken care of anyone. I know those are things women are supposed to know." The words rushed out of my mouth. It was embarrassing to admit that I'd never thought I would have no money. I had always appreciated what the people around me did for me, but how was I supposed to take care of Leo?

Turning me around in his arms, he pulled my chin up. "I never thought those were things you knew how to do," he said with a smirk.

"Oh." My stomach dropped. I was hoping he didn't think I was utterly useless.

"Love, you have so many employees. You have a head of staff. You have an employee that takes care of the rest of your employees, and that's just for your house. I'm not expecting you to cook me a three-course meal. In fact, I like to cook, so I've got us covered. And who says those are things you're supposed to do? It's a relationship. We do things together."

I knew he made most of the things he ate, which was crazy to me because I rarely traveled without my chef. I wasn't concerned about the things I was leaving behind. I was more upset that I never learned when I had the chance to.

"I'll do my part. I promise," I said firmly, so he knew I would do my best to learn. I had always been an excellent student. I could do this. Something else came to mind, making me feel uneasy. "Do you think we're moving too fast? I don't even know your favorite color."

"I don't have a favorite color," he said, shaking his head at me like that wasn't important.

"Who doesn't have a favorite color? That gives out serious serial killer vibes," I joked.

"You're right. I do have a favorite color," he said while running his eyes down my body and licking his lips. That heated look would have made me rub my thighs together if I weren't trying to stay calm. His eyes dipped to my lips, but when he leaned in, I put my hand on his chest, stopping his advances. My curiosity had been piqued.

"What's your favorite color?" I asked, lifting my eyebrow.

"The color of whatever you have on." He leaned in again, but I stopped him and smiled at his frustrated sigh.

"That's not an answer." I licked my lips, making his eyes flare. I loved the effect I had on him.

His hand came to my hair, successfully keeping me in place

while his lips slowly kissed their way up my shoulder. "It's the only one I have."

"You're infuriating," I said, wishing it came out annoyed and not in a breathy moan.

"You've told me." His chuckle made my entire body vibrate. I hated the effect he had on me.

"Good," I whimpered when he sucked on my clavicle.

"Kiss me now," he demanded, and I did. The kiss was shorter than I would have wanted, but as I tried to pull him back to me, he smiled while resting our foreheads together. "I know you think we're moving too fast, but I'm not scared. It's okay if you are. Love is about learning to do things together so we can grow as a couple. I'm ready to take the next step with you."

I didn't doubt what we felt for each other. In everything I did, I was prepared for the outcome, but since meeting Leo, I had been confused and emotional. What if I hurt him? What if I couldn't change?

"Why me?" I whispered. I knew I loved him, but if anyone asked me why, I couldn't explain it. I just knew that I did. I knew he was where I belonged.

"There are many things I love about you, but if you want to know why I love you, there is no answer. I love you without reason or logic. I love you because it feels right to love you. There is nothing that makes me happier than doing anything and nothing with you." I bit my lip, feeling the blush creep in. His fingers gently caressed my hair, and his voice became softer. "Are you regretting this?"

"No, no, of course not." I shook my head fervently, appalled by the idea of being without him. "I wanted to define our relationship like others I'd seen, but I'm realizing no one can do that. Everyone is different, and only the people in the relationship will ever understand what it feels like."

"You have your friends, and I have mine. It is normal to discuss things with them, but if anything is ever bothering us, I wanted us to come to each other. Never bottle it up, but talk about it and work through it. 'Kay?"

"'Kay." I gently pressed my lips to his. He was right. This was our relationship—our story. It might not be glamorous, perfect, or simple, but I'd never let it become like my parents'.

I gave him my heart that night. Ripped it right out of my chest and put it in his hands. As I did that, I finally accepted his. I was ready to take care of it.

37

BEFORE YOU

Felicity

Before I opened my eyes, I could tell he wasn't in bed. The nightmares only came when he wasn't with me. It was always the same one. A bloody Leo, looking at me while I screamed for him, and ashes fell around us. I hadn't told him. I was scared of what it all meant.

I had hoped we would have more time to be blissfully happy, but as I heard a loud voice, I knew that wasn't the case. The sun wasn't even fully out yet, and someone was already here. I put my robe on and made my way quietly toward the living room.

"This is an embarrassment for our family! What were you thinking? I don't care if she's the reincarnation of Aphrodite. Get your head straight!" Richard yelled.

"I won't ask again. Keep your voice down," Leo said calmly.

Richard completely ignored him and continued to yell. "How am I supposed to trust you if these are the choices you make? You spent all your money and everything your grandfather worked hard for on someone known to use people like they're her personal play toys!"

Pressure built on my chest. The fact that Richard thought so poorly of me made my heart hurt. Leo admired his father. They had always been close. Now they were fighting over me, and Richard was right.

"Leave," Leo commanded. "I told you to keep your voice down. We'll talk when you can have a civilized conversation." There was an edge to Leo's voice, but it still sounded calm.

"You're more worried about me waking her up than fixing your mistakes?" Richard scoffed in clear disbelief.

"I'll always choose her. Now leave." Leo used that voice that said there was no room for discussion.

After a couple of seconds, the front door slammed. I slid down the wall until my ass hit the floor. How selfish had I been for staying with him? I knew I could be better. I had to prove that to Richard. Leo believed in me, and I couldn't let him down. I couldn't let myself down. I was not my family's pawn.

I felt warm hands on my knees. Leo sat on the floor in front of me and pushed his way between my legs until he was close enough to lay his head on my shoulder. I caressed his hair, letting the tension leave my body while his warm breath fell on my skin.

"He hates me," I choked out, swallowing my emotions.

He pulled back to meet my eyes. "He just needs time to get to know you." His voice was soft as his eyes searched my face. "I'm sorry you had to hear all that."

"It's fine, I understand where he's coming from," I said.

"There's something I've been hiding from you," Leo whispered. He pulled back to meet my eyes. His body was rigid, and I could feel the tension.

I kept my voice soft as I asked, "What is it?" No matter what he was hiding, it couldn't be worse than everything I hid from him.

He closed his eyes and took a deep breath. "Ellen isn't my birth mother. Father cheated on her."

I sucked on my lip to hold back my laugh. He wouldn't understand and I couldn't explain what was so funny. A bastard for a bastard, we were a perfect match. "Is that why you asked me if I would still be with you if you weren't a Whitlock?"

He nodded.

I bit his earlobe gently before sucking it in my mouth. "Open your eyes, Leopold Phineas Whitlock." I used his full name, which made him groan. It was a mouthful of a name, but I liked it. I leaned my forehead against his staring into his worried eyes. "I'm sorry your mom went through that. You're still a Whitlock, and even if you weren't, I don't care. I don't like you because of your name."

"I know, but it's my fault your dad doesn't approve of us." That was why he was worried? He blamed himself for everything.

Placing a gentle kiss against his nose, I said, "That's not the reason he didn't approve of you. He just likes to do things how he wants and doesn't like to be contradicted." Father didn't approve of us because I loved Leo. It had nothing to do with his background. He knew I would never fall for Elias, so of course he would let me marry him. I had realized Father knew me better than I'd thought.

"That's it?" Leo asked. His eyebrows were pulled together, and I found it cute.

"That's it," I confirmed with a smile. He smiled back.

Letting my hands fall, I pushed him back so I could get up, but he held my legs down, preventing me from leaving. "Do you want breakfast?" he asked.

"Won't you be late for work?"

He bit my neck gently before licking up my throat. My body reacted to his touch as always. "I have time for breakfast." I knew exactly what kind of breakfast he was talking about, and it didn't involve cooking.

~

LEO HAD BEEN GONE a lot the past couple of weeks. He had pushed most of his responsibilities aside for three weeks, and now he was trying to catch up with everything. He left before I woke up and came home late at night. Although he smiled at me like everything was okay, I could see how tired he was. As soon as he got home, he carried me to the couch and sat me on his lap. He hugged me until he relaxed or fell asleep right there.

I had spent most of my days trying to organize the charitable organization's transfer from New York to California. The accountant had been working on the numbers and reviewing how much had ended up in my father's pockets that shouldn't have gone there. Leo wanted to return all the money in case anything came back to me.

Leo had done more than I'd initially thought. He had even taken care of the active contracts I had with my family's debtors.

Jane was still in New York, helping me make sure everyone at the company was doing what they were supposed to do. Many were upset with the relocation, but we were paying them for their troubles, and they were all getting similar jobs in one of my family's many businesses. The construction and electricity companies that had helped build the relief houses were being closed after all the houses were rebuilt correctly. We released a notice advising that there had been errors in the construction, so we moved everyone into an apartment building until all the houses were fixed. There was no way to get money back from that, but at least I could sleep better at night.

Every penny I had made was now being used for this. My only income came from my portfolio and the appearances I would schedule soon. Something I had done for extra money that I hadn't even needed was now my full-time job. Felicity Price had fallen from her ivory tower, which would probably be the headline if anyone ever found out. But I had learned that it was okay. I was happy, and that was something I would never give up.

I was excited to see my new office, which would be right next to Leo's. They had built a new building last year, expecting their business to grow and the space to be needed. He was giving me an entire floor from which I could run the charity. The only condition was that I needed to be right next to him. I had pointed out that it wasn't smart not to be close to my team, and his response had been that they didn't need me as much as he did. I had replied that he would tire of seeing me at work and home. He had smirked at me and replied that it was impossible to get tired of art. Then he had proceeded to tell me the wall between our offices was already being replaced by a glass wall so he could watch a masterpiece while dealing with dumbasses. I had had no say in the matter since construction had already started, so I had let it go. There were other battles to fight. It was a two-way street anyway. I could also watch his handsome face all day.

Grabbing the lunchbox, I hopped out of the taxi and headed towards the entrance of the building. I was excited for Leo to try the spaghetti I made for him. My phone rang, and an unknown caller ID popped up. "Hello?"

"Look at you being the dutiful wife. What's in the lunch box?"

"Simon," I breathed. I could hear the smile on his face.

I turned around, looking for whoever he had tailing me, but I didn't find anyone. He chuckled, making my blood run cold. "Felicity, Felicity," he mocked, letting out a long breath. "You made a mistake. Alexander prepared the perfect man for you, but of course you went and messed that up." I ground my teeth, hating his tone. "Did your Leo buy my little act? It was hard not to laugh at his smug face."

I let out a small laugh. "Leo is as naive as they come. His stubbornness gets the best of him, unlike Elias, who's too observant."

"So which one would you like me to kill first?"

I shrugged. "If I can choose, I would rather keep Leo for a little longer. I can't get enough of his pampering, but ultimately it's up to you." I kept a smile on my face, knowing he was watching me.

"I'll see what I can do," he taunted. "Do you remember April? The cousin whose brother you took?" I didn't answer his stupid question. "She has your old job, and she's just dying to see you again."

"I'm sure she is," I mused. There was nothing she could do to me since I'd legally left the family. Cochran had confirmed the contract was ironclad, so as long as I kept my mouth shut, I was safe. The rest of the family had nothing against me. Having a Whitlock disappear would raise too many questions, so they wouldn't go that route.

"Alexander told me about the evidence you collected against us, but I have a bet going that perfect Felicity wouldn't dare to release it. Let's see if I'm right. Wait for us."

I walked inside as calmly as I could, but my heart was beating fast. If Simon dared to try me, he would lose that bet.

I had been waiting for Simon to make an appearance, and of course he chose the worst moment to do it. Today was about fixing Leo's relationship with his father, not worrying about my family. By the time the security guard finished taking my information, I had managed to slow down my heart. A mature lady motioned for me, and we made our way up.

Richard was on the phone when I arrived, but he pointed to the chair in front of him. I waited patiently until he was done, trying not to think about Simon. He kept eyeing me warily, but I just smiled at him.

"Miss Price, to what do I owe the pleasure?" he said in a surprisingly pleasant tone.

"I heard what you said when you came to the house. I came to tell you that you were right and that whatever story you heard, it was probably a watered-down version because I was much worse than the rumors suggested." His eyebrows pulled back as his mouth fell open. I had never been one to beat around the bush, so

I continued. "You had no problem marrying me off to Elias because you thought you could use my image to boost your family's popularity. This was all about business, so I understood, but you underestimated me. No matter which brother I married, I could manipulate my way in."

"So, you admit that you're only trying to use my son," he said, a sad look briefly flashing across his face.

"I admit that I would have done it if I hadn't fallen totally and unconditionally in love with him, but I did. I'm not good with words like these. This is Leo's specialty, but I want you to know that nothing will stand in the way of your son and me. I do this as a courtesy because your son loves you, and I hate that he misses you because of me. I don't need to prove anything to you, but I will. In the meantime, fix things with your son. You're punishing him for my mistakes. That sounds nothing like the man he told me about and that I admired before we even met." Staring right into his eyes, I waited for him to respond.

"Are you done?" he asked as his lips twitched. His resemblance to Leo was uncanny.

"Yes." I smiled.

"You remind me of Mom. My wife wants to have both of you over for a family dinner. Let's do it this Saturday at six. Does that work for you?" I was about to respond when I felt uncomfortable with how fast his mood had shifted.

"Did you want to use me to boost your family's image?" I said, catching him off guard.

"Excuse me?"

"I said, did you want to use me?" The corners of his eyes tightened, his jaw locked, and his lips were pursed together as he looked at me with a blank expression. "See, I thought you did, but you didn't react the first time I said that, so I'm starting to think that my initial assumption was incorrect. So tell me, why did you agree to my marriage with Elias? What were you getting out of it?"

"What keeps the world running?" He looked at me as if waiting for me to respond. I didn't. "Money," he finally said.

I snorted, making his eyes narrow. "That's a lie. If you cared about money, you would be wealthier. Sure, you have money, but I've been doing research on your business. You make fair deals with your clients. You donate a lot of money to new businesses in Whitlock, you built an orphanage in Whitlock, so the kids didn't have to go through foster care, and you make sure the city is extremely well kept. So tell me, what exactly is my father giving you?"

I took his silence as a response.

"Did he threaten your family?" I stared at him, waiting for a reaction, but he didn't give me one. What was I missing? What had my father been hiding from me? Did he truly just want to give me a way out of the family? This hadn't been just him wanting to control me?

"I like you, Felicity. My wife thinks you're perfect for our son, and Leopold seems to share the same sentiment. Alexander did threaten me at the beginning"—now *that* I believed—"but I agreed to it in the end. Elias had been spiraling out of control, and I thought the responsibility would wake him up. From what your father told me, you—"

"You can stop with the lies." His eyes narrowed at my interruption. He was a terrible liar and even worse at hiding his emotions. "Elias isn't an alcoholic, an addict, or spiraling towards anything. I believe you might see him as lazy, but even if you were that uptight, which I know you're not, you wouldn't call that spiraling. So I'll ask one more time, and this time I would really appreciate it if you told me the truth. Why did you agree to my marriage with Elias?" He stared at me, giving no indication that he would talk. I saw where Leo got his stubbornness from. Mom said Father had given me a way out. I was sure that had slipped out in her moment of anger. "You don't need to speak; your face says it all. Is my father protecting me from someone?"

His left eye twitched. I would take that as a yes. "Is it Simon?" His eyes widened slightly. That was a yes.

I nodded, done with my questions. Father wouldn't have given him more information, but that proved that he cared about me and used Richard's good nature, knowing he would help him.

This had nothing to do with political ties. Father had said last time we'd spoken that there were stipulations to become the head. Was marriage one of them? And did that mean he was trying to prepare me to become the leader of our family? If the answer to those questions was yes, and I was sure it was, that meant Father had something big on Simon. Which meant whatever it was, when the time came and I needed to protect Leo, I could use it. I didn't care about being the head of the family anymore, but the more information I had against my enemy the better. If Father was willing to ask Richard for help, he would help me, I knew it. I smiled as my body filled with happiness, knowing that in his own twisted way Father still loved me. I had his love.

"I don't understand. Why would you help someone like me?" I asked Richard. People couldn't possibly be that good to put their families in danger to help an outsider. Looking at the way he'd raised Leo, I knew that was just who they were. They wouldn't kick you while you were down. They were the type who would give you a hand and leave without expecting a thank-you in return, no matter what you'd done.

Richard misinterpreted my question, and I didn't correct him when he answered. "Since he refuses to let you go, what other choice do I have? I don't want to get stuck in a war between your father and uncle, but here we are, in the eye of the storm, and you are the storm. Although your father asked for you to marry Elias, I know that would make all of you miserable. I'm a father who wants his sons to be happy. Leopold either thinks too much or jumps, but I trust his instincts. However, you and I both know that you've been marked for death, and I don't want him to suffer because you couldn't stay put and cherish your time together. I only ask that you distance yourself from your family." His voice sounded so defeated that a pang of guilt entered my chest.

"I'll never let them hurt him," I promised.

Richard studied my face before letting his body relax. "I will hold you to that promise."

38

INFINITY

Felicity
Two months later

"**O**ver here, Felicity!"

I kept posing for the flashing cameras. Leo's arm was securely around my waist. I looked at him, and his beautiful hazel eyes were already on me. He gave me a soft peck on the lips, and the cameras and fans went wild.

Leo and I had moved into his apartment two months ago. I had sold ninety percent of my closet, but I was happier than I had ever been. We both had steady incomes from our jobs, but we only bought the necessities while the rest of the money went to our debt. After we'd sold everything, we'd ended up just sixty million short, which was significantly better than I'd thought.

We had both been working hard to get everything on the right track. Leo still ran his family's business and his company. Nick helped him as much as he could, but he barely understood how everything worked. Elias showed up at the company once in a while, but he spent most of his days driving to colleges across California, looking for talented singers. He still hadn't told his family he wanted to be a producer, so they all thought he spent his days partying.

The money for the charity was finally going to the right place instead of my father's pockets. I had started taking every appearance opportunity that came my way. I was offered a spot as a judge on *USA Top Model*, and the pay was good. The problem was that I barely got to see Leo with all the traveling.

"Felicity, over here." We made our way to the next reporter. We were at the Venice Film Festival, so there were people everywhere.

"Hi," I said excitedly. Before, I would have found this kind of event tiresome and would most likely not bother coming, but now I was genuinely excited to be here. I couldn't make the mistake of taking things for granted. Not when I had the man of my dreams by my side. "How are you?" I asked the reporter.

"I'm doing great. What about you guys? You look stunning, by the way. I've been waiting to see you because we all know you deliver."

"Aww, thank you. I'm just so happy to be here." I put my hands on my hips to display the fabulous way the dress design accentuated my curves. "Marika did a great job, as usual. Such an honor to wear her designs." The good thing about being on a budget was that it helped me discover so many unique talents. Some up-and-coming designers were geniuses. Marika was one of my favorites.

"Leopold, I think this is the third time you've been on a carpet. How's everything going?" one reporter asked.

When news broke out that I had been in a skating accident, people tried to get inside the hospital. Leo was, of course, seen several times coming in and out of my room.

I released our relationship to the press a couple of weeks after I woke up. Although my father was out of the picture, I didn't want to take my chances. The media went crazy over Leo and how perfect we were for each other. They weren't wrong. We might not have the money for gifts, but he was attentive, kind, and respectful. He valued my opinion and treated me like an equal. Sometimes I wondered what our future held. The pedestal he had me on was too high. I was bound to fall.

"When you have the smartest and most beautiful woman in your arms, life couldn't be better." Leave it to Leo to make everyone swoon. I knew he didn't enjoy coming to these events and was only there for me, but people adored him.

I was suddenly lifted off the ground, and a little yelp escaped me. I realized who it was as I was being thrown over a shoulder and spun around. "Ayden," I said, laughing and hitting his back. "Put me down!"

Leo watched us with amusement in his eyes. Everyone turned to look at what was causing the disturbance, and I saw some annoyed eyes on us, while others were just laughing. The reporter tried to talk to Ayden as he put me down.

"Ayden! When will your new album come out?" He ignored the question in favor of talking to Leo. Ayden spent more time in Whitlock than in his own home in LA these days. Leo and Ayden acted like they were long-lost brothers. Ayden didn't like to be around people, but now he was all over Leo. He had yet to meet Elias, but I would get them together one day.

Ayden took my spot next to Leo, and they both hugged like they hadn't seen each other in years. Which I knew wasn't true, given they had flown in together last night. "Ayden, stop stealing my man," I joked as I pulled Leo between us.

All three of us posed for pictures as Ayden and I finished our interviews together. I was so happy Ayden had brought Leo with him. We hadn't seen each other in two weeks, so they'd given me the best surprise ever. I wasn't going home until next week, so I would enjoy this night as much as possible. Which meant I was dying to get Leo back to the hotel. Just three more hours.

A car door closing woke me up. I blinked rapidly, trying to get my foggy brain to function. Warm fingers caressed my cheek. No matter where he touched me, my body instantly wanted more. I closed the space between us and straddled him. I found his lips, but he felt different. I opened my eyes to see a pair of tormented ones.

"What's wrong?" I asked. He was hesitant. I guessed nothing good could last forever. I looked around, but we weren't at the hotel. We were at the beach.

"Nothing, love." He opened the car door and helped me get out of the back seat. He motioned something to the driver as he grabbed my hand and led me through a stone pathway. I held the bottom of my skirt carefully so I didn't ruin it with the sand. It was dark and a little chilly.

I could feel Leo's hand sweating in mine, but I stayed silent, waiting for us to stop so we could have the conversation. As we turned the corner, I saw a gazebo decorated with candles and an array of the most colorful and beautiful flowers. Roses, tulips, lilies, hydrangeas, and so much more. My breath caught in my throat. Now I was the one with the sweaty palms. When we were in the center of the gazebo, Leo released my hand and turned to look at me. My heart was beating so fast that I could hear it in my ears.

He cleared his throat. His beautiful eyes looked almost like liquid gold. "I used to think love was easy and required nothing in return, but you showed up in your Jimmy Choo stilettos and walked all over that idea." What sounded like a laugh mixed with a sob escaped my lips. I couldn't contain my emotions, and I didn't want to.

"Love is being thoughtful, compassionate, supportive, and loyal. It's choosing to love a person day by day, no matter their faults. It's caring about someone other than yourself and finding ways to communicate even if you want to shut everything out because, at the end of the day, there is no one better to lean on than the person who always wants the best for you." There was so much love shining in his eyes that my entire body felt warm. His hands came to my face as he used his thumbs to wipe away my tears.

"I love you with every beat of my heart. You fill every missing piece in my soul. I choose you again in this life, and I will follow you to the next because I'm never letting you go." My heart stopped as Leo fell to one knee and opened a ring box in front of me. A beautiful cushion-cut diamond framed by a row of pavé diamonds stared right at me. It was set on a rose-gold band.

"Felicity Amira Price, would you make me the luckiest man in the world and marry me?" As soon as the words were out of his mouth, I fell next to him, wrapping my arms around his neck.

"Yes, yes, yes, yes." I found his mouth and kissed him with every ounce of my being. Tears streamed down my face as I cherished the happiest moment of my life. Leo grabbed my hand and slid the ring onto my finger.

WE BARELY MADE it past the door of our hotel room before Leo ripped my dress off and knelt in front of me. With one leg over his shoulder and a hand in his hair, his tongue devoured me, making my knees weak. "Look at me while you eat me." I pulled his head back, forcing him to look at me. The warning in his eyes made me shiver. "You like how your fiancée tastes?" His tongue stroked my clit, making my head fall against the door.

"You're fucking delicious." He got up in a flash and turned me against the door. I felt the sting of a bite on my ass. He quickly licked and kissed the spot, soothing the pain. His tongue went up my ass, then my spine, and finally my neck. My body trembled as he kissed and licked my flesh. "Every part of you is sweeter than the next."

"*Amor*," I pleaded, needing more.

He slapped my ass hard while kissing the spot below my ear,

making me whimper. Leo nuzzled my neck as his fingers teased my pussy lips.

"Tell me what you want, and I'll give it to you," he said while his other hand pulled on my nipple.

"I want you to fuck me all night." I barely managed to say it since his hands were all over me, and I couldn't seem to catch my breath.

"As you wish." He turned me around before slamming his lips against mine. I wrapped my legs around his waist as he carried me to the bed.

Dropping me on the bed, he took off his clothes. There was a mischievous gleam in his eyes as he grabbed his tie. He covered my eyes with it, then wrapped his belt loosely around my wrist, lifting them above my head. It was more to keep them together than restrain them. I could pull them free at any time. I hadn't told him why I couldn't stand the feeling of my hands being tied down, but one day I would.

I felt the bed dip under his weight. I squirmed, trying to find some contact with him.

"Please . . . Leo . . ." His hot mouth landed on my nipple, circling it with his tongue before sucking it into his mouth and then doing the same to the other. His fingers teased the outside of my pussy. I lifted my hips, hoping to get more friction.

"My fiancée is so impatient."

I snarled at him, making him chuckle.

He used his fingers to separate my pussy lips and hummed in approval. I knew he could feel how wet I was.

"Is this for me?"

"Only you," I whispered.

"Let's not waste it, then." He was inside of me in one swift movement. I cried out as pleasure spread through my body. Holding my legs towards my chest, he pulled out completely before slamming back into me.

"I love you."

"I love you too," I breathed.

After being teased for so long, my orgasm built quickly. Leo pounded into me steadily, finding the perfect rhythm.

"Leo . . . ," I moaned as my body was ready to explode.

"I love when you moan my name," he groaned, digging his finger into my thighs hard enough to leave bruises.

"More, more!" I yelled as my orgasm ripped through me, making my legs shake and my toes curl.

"Yes, love. Squeeze my cock, just like that." I felt him pull out of me, but before I could complain, his head was between my legs.

"Oh, God," I said as Leo's tongue went deep inside my pussy.

Heat ran through my body as he ate me like I was his last meal. His fingers found the perfect spot as he licked my pussy and sucked on my clit until I felt like I was no longer in my body. Tension built up, and I couldn't take it anymore. When I was close to falling, he bit my clit hard before sucking it into his mouth.

"Yessss." My legs shook, and I squeezed his head between my thighs as I came again. "Ahhh, Leo."

He spread my legs and entered me again, slower this time. He untied my hands and took his tie from my eyes. I reached for him and hugged him to my chest.

"Are you going to be a good girl and come with me?" he said while leaving a trail of kisses from my neck to my jaw.

"I can't." I was pretty sure it was impossible since I couldn't even see clearly yet. Leo picked up the pace.

"Yes, you can. Feel how good we are together." He moved to the side a little, hitting that perfect spot again. It was like his dick had a map.

"Do you feel that, love?"

"Yes, fuck, Leo." I held his shoulders, digging my nails into his skin.

"Lips." He kissed me roughly as he worshipped my body, making me want more.

"You want me to come inside you?" He knew I did. There was nothing better than feeling him finish inside me.

His finger found my clit, gently making circles around it before flicking it. My poor sensitive clit was being tortured. I opened my legs wider for him.

"Yes . . . I need you inside me," I moaned.

He left another trail of kisses around my neck before sucking the top of my breast in his mouth. He sucked until he knew he'd left a mark. His eyes came to mine, and he gave me the most beautiful smile.

"Ready?" he asked before kneeling and lifting my hips off the bed, holding one leg towards his shoulder and driving deeper inside me. I reached for the top headboard and gripped it as my body was suspended in the air.

"Come with me, and I'll come inside you."

I was already there. "Yes."

"Fuck," he growled.

"Harder."

He gave me what I wanted. I wrapped my leg tighter around his hip, digging my heel into his back as I flew for the third time.

"I love you, Fee, so fucking much."

I was so high on him that I couldn't even answer how much I fucking loved him too.

It took us a couple of minutes before our pleasure slowly subsided.

"Tell me a secret," he whispered while still inside me.

I couldn't tell him anything that had to do with my family or my past because that would make him an accomplice, but I could tell him my biggest fear.

I looked deep into his eyes and let him have a piece of me. "When I woke up in the hospital, do you remember how I lost it before my mother interrupted us?" He nodded with a serious expression and a slight frown. I reached out and passed my finger along the crease that formed above his eyebrow. "You were the first person in eighteen years to tell me those three words, and I believed them." The hand touching my leg tightened. "I never thought someone could love me." My mother certainly never had.

Watching his stone-cold face made my chest tighten. I shouldn't have said anything. At least not tonight.

Not expecting the gentleness in his tone, it caught me by surprise when he asked, "Marry me?"

"You already asked me that. I said yes," I reminded him with a smile pulling on my face.

"I'll never be done loving you. I'm your family now. We're in this together through thick and thin. I could never live without your love," my beautiful angel of redemption stipulated.

"What if I stop loving you?" I asked jokingly. There was not even the slightest chance of that happening. He completed me.

"I'll win you back." Leo did nothing without giving it his all. There was a reason even his competitors respected him.

"What if you stop loving me?" I meant to continue joking, but as the words left my mouth, doubt settled in my gut.

"That would truly be the definition of the word *inconceivable*. If you could only feel how my heart beats just for you, how every cell in my body reacts just to you, you would know without a shadow of a doubt that no one has ever loved anything in this universe as much as I love you." The conviction in his voice left no room for uncertainty.

And just like that, he healed that piece of me.

"So, what you're saying is that I'm stuck with you, no matter what?" I moved my hips and clenched my pussy. His eyes narrowed at me, but his thumb came to my nipple, making the soft pebble harden underneath his touch.

"What I'm saying is that I will not make the same mistakes they did. I'll cherish every day I have with you. Let you give me that sweet Felicity that few get to see, and I won't ever do anything to lose that. So, yes, you are stuck with me no matter what, and that's exactly where you'll always want to be."

Two hours later, we finished together for the last time that night, watching the Venice sky from the balcony.

Streetlights illuminated the room. We left the balcony curtains open, and I watched Leo as he slept. It wasn't long ago that I'd felt worthless. Now I was surrounded by his warmth, feeling like I'd accomplished everything I'd ever wanted. I touched my ring, smiling at how perfect it was.

I owned several buildings in New York and other states. I'd had my fashion design label for young adults since I was nineteen. My father had started my portfolio when I was a baby. I was like one of those nightmare shareholders that he had to deal with. I'd inherited a lot of money from my grandmother and way more from my grandfather. And even with all that money, I could never stand up to my family. He gave me freedom, and I finally understood that it was worth more than trying to gain more money to play a game of power with my family. I'd lost a billion dollars in the last couple of months, and every penny had been well spent.

No matter how long it took, I would clean up all my mistakes. I was done being a bystander in my own life.

No matter what our future held, I would put Leo first because no one was above him.

FELICITY'S OUTFITS

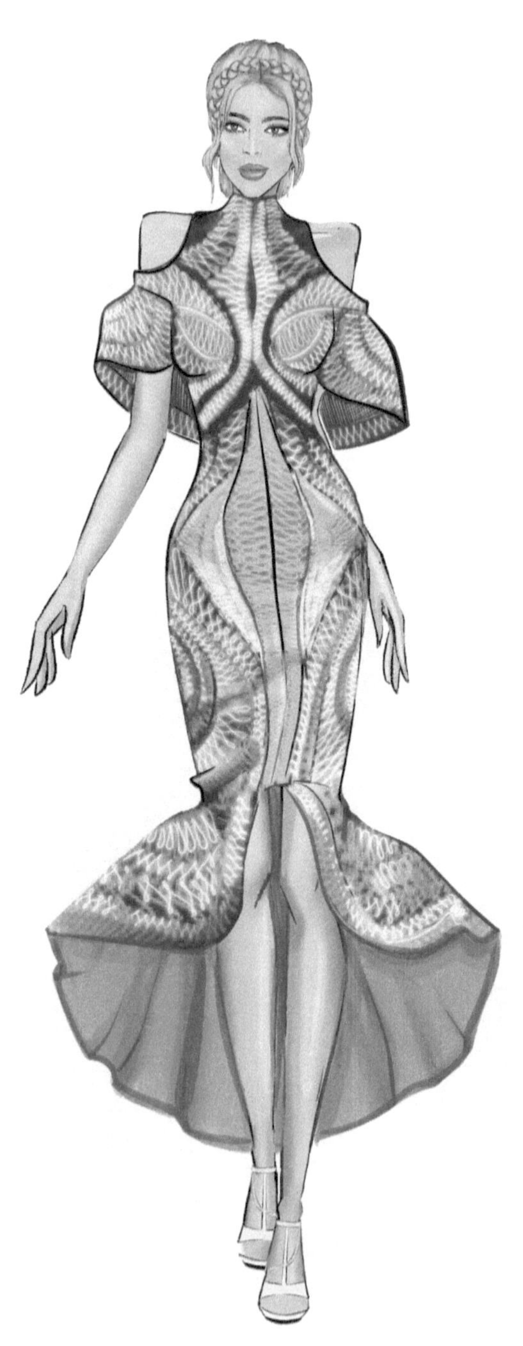

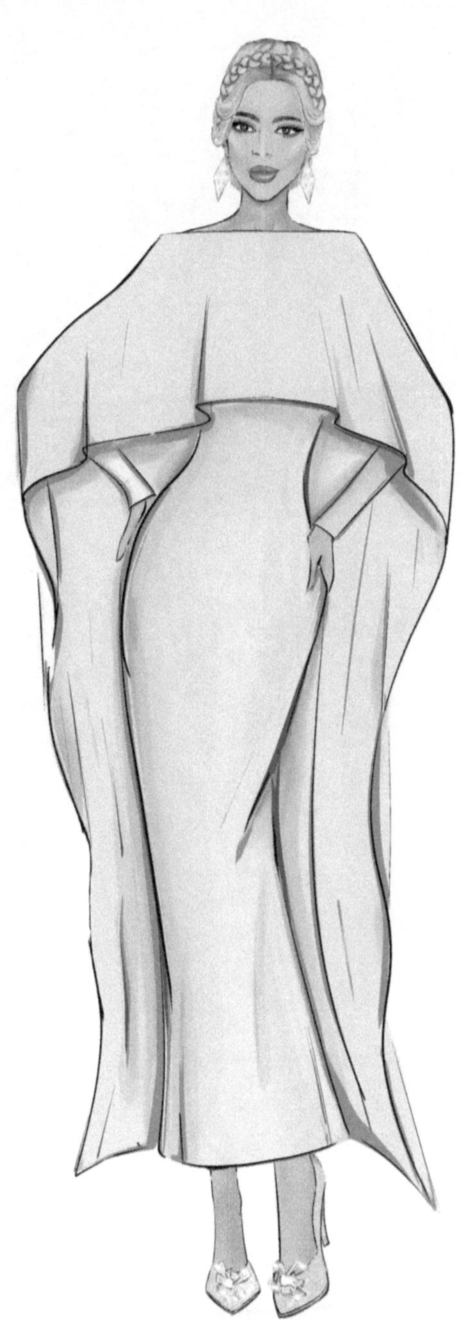

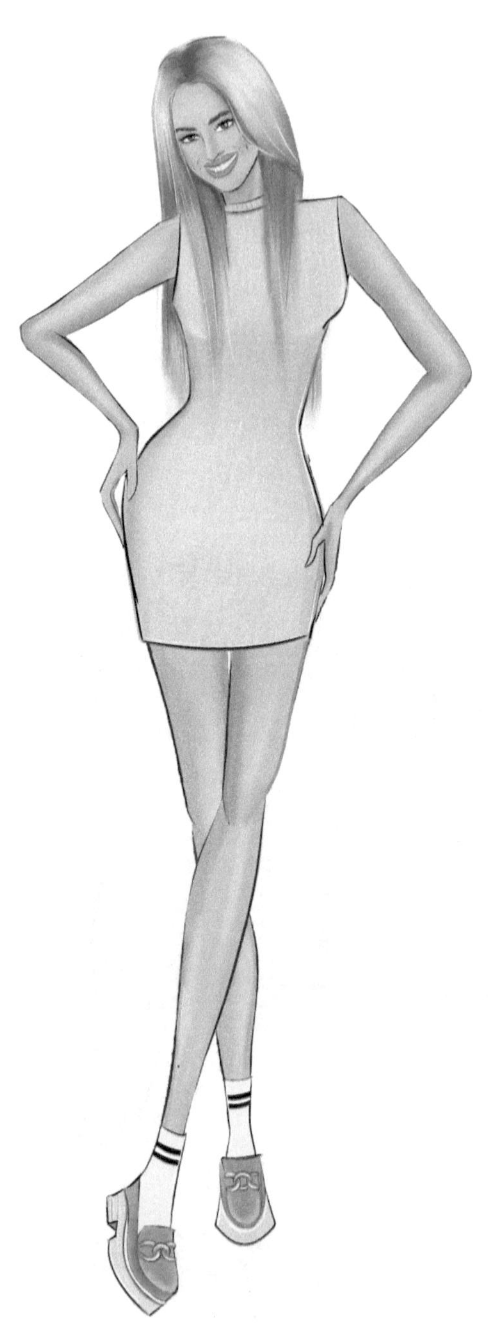

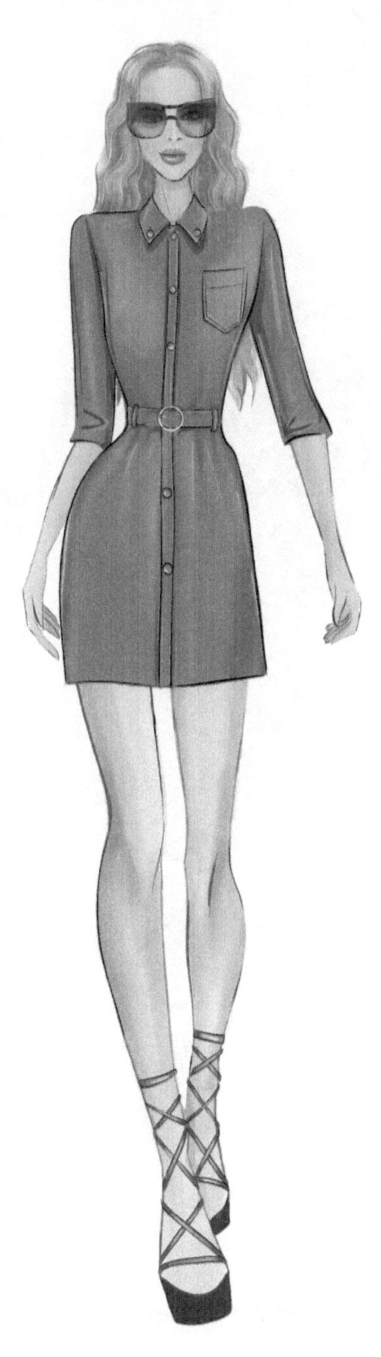

ACKNOWLEDGMENTS

When I first embarked on this journey, I was completely unprepared for the tremendous effort it would take. During the months of dedicated work, I was lucky enough to receive support from friends, old and new, without whom this dream would not have been possible.

Mom, I'm forever grateful to you. Throughout this past year, you quietly respected my need for solitude, understanding the importance of an undisturbed writing process. Your support has been nothing short of amazing, and I am immensely grateful for your presence in my life.

And to Ariaunna, my best friend and companion, thank you for always being by my side. Without you, a girl is incomplete. Your consistent cheerleading has been instrumental in my journey, and I am truly fortunate to have you in my corner.

To my incredible editors, I extend my deepest gratitude. Thank you for allowing me to maintain my voice while providing invaluable suggestions and feedback.

Miblart, thank you for your patience as we worked on the book covers. Your willingness to explore my suggestions and your dedication to bringing my vision to life were huge parts of this book's realization. You gave me the time and space I needed to fall in love with the covers, and I am forever grateful for your patience and artistry.

And to my readers, thank you for reading my words and for trusting me to share my stories with you. I hope you will join me for many more adventures to come!

*Felicity and Leopold's story will continue in
Sing For Me.*

~

*Subscribe to our newsletter for updates or a chance
to join the ARC team at www.anaisventura.com.*